All Roads Lead to Murder

Other Books by Albert Bell:

Mystery
Kill Her Again

Non-Fiction
Exploring the New Testament World

Historical Fiction
Daughter of Lazarus

For Children
The Case of the Lonely Grave

All Roads Lead to Murder

*A Case from the Notebooks
of Pliny the Younger*

Albert A. Bell, Jr

ILLUSTRATED WITH DRAWINGS BY
WILLIAM MARTIN JOHNSON
FROM THE FIRST EDITION OF
BEN HUR BY LEW WALLACE

High Country Publishers, Ltd

Boone, NC
2002

High Country Publishers, Ltd
197 New Market Center #135
Boone, NC 28607
(828) 964-0590
Fax: (828) 262-1973
www.highcountrypublishers.com

This is a work of fiction. Although loosely based on historical possibilities,
the characters and events are entirely a product of the author's imagination.

Illustrations by William Martin Johnson from the first edition of *Ben Hur* by Lew
Wallace, from the 1978 edition by Bonanza Books

Library of Congress Cataloging-in-Publication Data

Bell, Albert A., Jr 1945-
 All roads lead to murder : a case from the notebooks of Pliny
the Younger / Albert A. Bell, Jr
  p. cm.
 ISBN 0-9713045-3-X (alk. paper)
1. Pliny, the Younger—Fiction. 2. Tacitus,
Cornelius—Fiction. 3.
çIzmir (Turkey)—Fiction. 4. Historians—Fiction. 5.
Authors—Fiction. I. Title.
PS3552.E485 A78 2002

2002003153

Manufactured in the United States of America
First printing: October 2002
10 9 8 7 6 5 4 3 2 1

For the Writers' Group at the Urban Institute for the Contemporary Arts in Grand Rapids, Michigan:

Steve B., Pat, Flannery, Roger, Kathy, Charleen, Lisa, Daphne, Elaine, Amy, Steve P. (the more or less regulars), and others who've heard and commented on various portions.

They have made this a better book and me a better writer.

All Roads Lead to Murder

I

I saw the slave girl stumble and knew

the cup of wine she was carrying was going to land on her master.

We were eating a hurried lunch on the side of the road between Ephesus and Smyrna, finding what shade we could. This girl's owner, Lucius Cornutus, more than anyone else in our traveling party, had been making demands on his slaves. He insisted they stand while he ate, except for the one female that he seemed to treat as a kind of concubine or mistress. She sat at his feet. Cornutus and another of our company, Tiberius Saturninus, had been throwing dice while they ate.

When the cup hit him, on the left side of his back, Cornutus leaped up from his camp stool, twisted around, and grabbed the girl. "You stupid cow!" He drew back his arm and the girl steeled herself for the blows to come. His concubine tugged at his arm, but he jerked away.

"Stop! Do *not* hit her!" The voice of a woman, one of those who had joined our caravan in Ephesus, rang out in Greek from off to my left, sending a chill up and down me, like the blare of a battle trumpet.

Her imperious tone and her arm outstretched as if to cast a spell, more than the words themselves, I think, brought Cornutus up short. Without letting go of the girl, he glared at the woman, then dropped his eyes. I had flinched the same way every time I spoke with this priestess or witch, or whatever she was. She stood tall, with a square face, long, wild black hair streaked with gray, and burning eyes that could buckle the sturdiest knees.

In the background I also noticed that the German merchant, a big strapping man who had been with us since we left Antioch, had his hand under his cloak. On a dagger, I suspected.

"There's going to be bloodshed," my traveling companion Cornelius Tacitus said under his breath. "The pot is just about to boil."

I didn't want anything to delay our return to Rome, so I decided to intervene. I stood and stepped between Cornutus and the witch, facing him, not her.

"Listen, Cornutus," I said, "it was an accident. We're all tired. Why don't you show the girl some compassion?"

Cornutus let go of the girl, who slumped to the ground. The German withdrew his hand and the witch lowered her arm with a clanking of bracelets.

"Show compassion to a slave? Friend Pliny," Cornutus said sarcastically, for I was by no means his friend, "this little cow just doused me." He tugged at his wet tunic like an orator in court showing a blood-stain to a jury.

I glanced at the girl and wondered why he kept calling her a cow. She was actually quite lovely, a blonde with eyes as green as young acorns, a slender face and arms, skin as milky white as a statue of Galatea. About fifteen, I judged, six years or so younger than myself.

Cornutus took a step toward me, thrusting his broad face into mine. "If I don't punish her, what will the others think?" He jerked his head toward the eight other slaves traveling with him. "Will they decide it's all right to punch me, kick me, perhaps slip a knife between my ribs while I sleep?"

He was putting every Roman slave-owner's nightmare into words. As the old proverb says: "You have as many enemies as you have slaves." We can't live without our slaves, and yet they heavily out-number us. Fear of punishment is the only real control we have over them.

"Your own slaves might get ideas," Cornutus said, raising a hand toward my four male slaves, who were sitting apprehensively in the shade of our wagons, alongside the three slaves belonging to Tacitus.

"The girl meant you no harm, Cornutus," I said, determined to stand my ground against a man almost twice my age and infinitely more menacing. I felt like a hare, frozen in front of an angry dog. Any move-ment or sign of fear and he would pounce. "She was doing the task you assigned her. We all make mistakes. Things happen that we can't con-trol." The fear constricting my throat made it difficult to form the elo-quent, rhetorically balanced sentences in which I typically try to speak.

Cornutus put his big paw on my shoulder. His leathery face broke into a parody of a smile, like a wine-skin splitting open. "Friend Pliny, do you really consider a slave to be your fellow human being?" The sarcasm flowed over me like the heat gushing from the hot room of a bath house.

"No, I consider all human beings to be my fellow slaves," I replied, relieved to be able to turn the argument so neatly to a philosophical point, with a nice chiasmus thrown in to boot. "Recall what Seneca said: 'Fortune holds equal sway over us all.' It is this girl's bad fortune to be the slave, your good fortune to be the master. Things could as easily have been reversed."

Another member of our traveling party stood and took a step forward out of the shade. An older man, Jewish I suspected. He and his companion had kept largely to themselves since joining us at Ephesus. At the moment I couldn't recall his name. In a calm voice he said, "Young Pliny is right, Cornutus. In God's sight there is no slave, no free."

Cornutus laughed, a sharp snort. It was a chilling sound, even on a warm spring day. "So you worship a blind god, do you?" He swept his gaze over the entire group. "You're a pack of fools, all of you." To the girl he said, "I'll deal with you tonight." He shot a glance around the circle, daring anyone to contradict him again.

The girl's face went pale and she looked at me as though pleading for help. How had I not noticed that face before today? There had been dozens of people, perhaps a hundred in all, in and out of our caravan since we left Antioch, but none of them could have compared to the face of this woman-child. She was at that exquisite age when most Roman girls are getting married and yet haven't quite left behind their girlish innocence. She might hug her father or her husband with equal pleasure on her part, though their reactions would be quite different. And there was some quality lurking beneath the dirt on her face from where she had fallen. Just as you can go into a tavern and find a mural coated with soot, but you know that beneath the grime there is a masterpiece, even so I thought I perceived a special quality – a kind of hidden divinity – in her.

Cornutus jerked the girl to her feet and shoved her toward his wagon. His concubine put a protective arm around the girl's shoulders. The rest of us loaded back into our wagons to resume the journey.

"Thank you for intervening," a woman's voice said behind me. I spun around to find myself facing the witch. Her voice may have softened slightly, but not her countenance. "That monster has no right to beat an innocent child."

"She's his slave," I said. "He has the right to do whatever he pleases with her. I stepped in because I thought there was going to be a serious altercation, not to protect a slave girl."

She sneered. "By the goddess, you Romans are all alike. You arrogant bastards think you can run roughshod over the rest of the world. There will be a day of reckoning, and it will come when you least expect it." She stalked away to her wagon, bracelets and amulets jingling.

"Maybe you should have stayed out of it," Tacitus said.

"I think you're right. I've just made everybody a little bit angrier. And I don't believe we helped the girl at all. If I had kept quiet, Cornutus would probably have slapped her a few times. Nothing she hasn't endured before. Now, whatever punishment he inflicts on her tonight will be redoubled by his frustration at the delay and his resentment of our interference."

As his slaves packed up, Cornutus bent over to pick up his winnings from the dice game. Saturninus had slunk back to his own wagon during the turmoil over the girl. Cornutus shook the coins in his hand and turned toward him. "Tiberius Saturninus, you thieving scoundrel! There was at least another twenty sesterces in this pile. Cough it up."

Saturninus skulked forward and flung the coins at him.

* * * *

"That's the last milestone before Smyrna," Tacitus said. "It was erected during the eleventh year of Claudius' reign."

Since we set out from Antioch, twenty-three days earlier, he had read every inscription on every milestone we'd passed. At least twenty of the damn things every day. And he acted interested in what they said – who was consul and how many times the emperor had been granted tribunician power – and what they revealed about when a particular stretch of road was built or repaired. He sounded more like a historian than one of Rome's brightest young orators.

"At least we'll get to the city well before dark," I said. "We'll have a chance to find an inn while we can still see."

"Are you sure you don't know someone here that we could stay with?"

"Regrettably, no." And I truly did regret it. I wanted to be nowhere in earshot when Cornutus unleashed his fury on that poor slave girl. "My uncle didn't know anyone in Smyrna."

"So this time he's your uncle," Tacitus said.

"I should make up my mind, shouldn't I?" My uncle, Pliny, had adopted me in his will. When he died four years ago while trying to rescue people from the eruption of Mt. Vesuvius, I became his son and heir and took on his name in addition to my father's family name, Caecilius. I am now Gaius Plinius Caecilius Secundus, to give it in its ponderous fullness. Sometimes I wonder if I can stand up under the weight of it. My mother – Pliny's sister – and I lived in Pliny's home after my father died. Pliny had always carefully insisted that I call him 'uncle'. He was very generous to me, a father in every way. That was how I thought of him, but a deeply ingrained habit was hard to break, so sometimes now I call him 'uncle' and occasionally 'father'.

"I'm afraid my *father* had no connections here," I corrected myself.

"That's a shame," Tacitus said. "His friends in Ephesus certainly treated us royally. Well, staying in an inn won't be all bad. There's always the possibility of an accommodating serving girl." He rubbed his hands together in anticipation. "Or boy."

I glanced at him disdainfully. His sexual versatility was the one thing about him that made me uncomfortable. We had met in Antioch as this caravan was forming for the journey to Rome. Pooling our resources, we bought some better wagons than either of us could afford by himself. I found myself enjoying his company before I became aware of his sexual predilections. There was nothing about his manners or his public life to suggest such inclinations. He had a wife, the daughter of the illustrious Julius Agricola, waiting for him at home. He was several years older than I and in the area of relations with sexual partners resented my attempts to stand on the higher moral ground.

"Don't look at me like that," he said. "There's nothing wrong with finding a bit of pleasure anywhere you can. Socrates and Plato and all those other Greeks you profess to admire did it all the time. Beauty is everywhere. Male, female – what's the difference beyond an extra appendage or an extra orifice here and there?"

"But your wife . . ."

His waved his hand tiredly. "Aristocratic Roman women have had all the fun bred out of them, my wife being the perfect example. I appreciate the . . . earthiness of peasants and the servile class. They've watched animals couple. They've slept in the same room with their parents and siblings, so there's no false modesty about them."

On this point I suppose he's incorrigible. I had made it clear that I didn't share his inclination. We had enough other points of common interest that our friendship was blossoming rapidly. I decided to drop the issue and turned my attention to the scenery.

The highway which we were following, the Via Sebaste, runs

almost due north from Ephesus until it veers northwest to skirt the range
of hills at whose base Smyrna sits, at the head of a long, narrow bay.
The land is fertile and, in early spring, the fields had been recently
plowed and crops sown. With an early spate of warm weather a few of
them were already covered by a green mist of tender shoots. As we
neared the coast I smelled a hint of sea breeze, a bracing sensation
when you're safe on land. I enjoy watching the ocean. But, may it
please the gods, I hope never to look on it from the vantage point of a
ship again. I made the outbound trip to Syria by boat; with time I trust
the nightmares will fade.

Tacitus and I were returning from Syria, where I served as a
military tribune with the legions, and he had been on the governor's
staff. All Roman men hold such posts if they have any ambitions for a
career in public service in the city. It had been a tense year. The dust
from the Jewish revolt in the neighboring province of Judaea, which
ended ten years ago, had not yet entirely settled. Many refugees from
the destroyed city of Jerusalem had settled in Antioch and other cities
of Syria. Those people cherish their grudges like a peasant guarding the
last embers of his fire to fan them into flame another day. I wonder if
there will ever be true peace in that part of the empire.

We were traveling in a caravan, of course. Tacitus and I had a
wagon and driver for ourselves and another for our slaves and baggage. There were nine travelers, plus slaves, who had been together all
the way from Antioch. Others had joined us for a time, then dropped
out as they reached their destinations. Except for a few days of rain, it
had been an uneventful journey. But, even under the best of conditions,
travel is hard. Tempers can wear thin on these long journeys. Without
the civilizing force of a city and magistrates, people sometimes resort to
violence to settle disputes.

Most of our traveling companions were congenial enough, or at
least not dangerous. Two others, like ourselves, had been on government service in Syria: Tiberius Saturninus and Gaius Sempronius, a
couple of complete nonentities. The only thing that marked Saturninus
in a crowd was that he wouldn't admit he was bald and combed his hair
up from the edges to cover his glistening pate. Whenever the wind blew
he appeared to have a horse's mane billowing from his head.

One fellow, Lysimachus, the most tiresome of the lot, was a
philosopher/teacher of some sect, an offshoot of Platonism. He wore a
long white beard and gloried in the sound of his own voice. I guess
those are the two essential criteria for being a philosopher. He wasn't
an old man, just one whose hair turned white at an early age. He was

on his way to Athens, to bask in the glow of walking where Plato had walked. I didn't spoil his anticipation by telling him how much the city has declined since those halcyon days. It bears as much resemblance to Plato's Athens as a grandmother does to the girl you were in love with all those years ago.

The merchant, a huge German who had mastered Latin and learned some Greek, was our biggest encumbrance, with several wagons laden with merchandise. He had shipped most of his goods by boat, but these items – silks and spices from India – he said he couldn't trust to the whims of Neptune. I had to sympathize. This humorless fellow had Latinized his German name – which was Garl or Karl or some guttural growl impossible for a civilized tongue, and added a Roman *praenomen*, dubbing himself Marcus Carolus. To the Roman ear the effect was comic, but I doubt many people laughed about it to his face.

A pair of self-important toadies, named Rhascuporis and Orophernes, were representing their city, some backwater east of Antioch, on an embassy to Rome, to ask permission to build a temple to the emperor Domitian. They kept working on their speeches, practicing their delivery during our rest stops. Tacitus and I both have achieved some renown in Rome for our oratory, young as we are. It was all we could do not to laugh out loud as we listened to their rustic grandiloquence. They are sure to be mocked and parodied for days after their appearance before the senate.

Dominating the mood of our party was Lucius Cornutus, who had just finished a year on the staff of the governor of Syria. Tacitus had told me stories about the lavish dinners Cornutus was fond of hosting. When a man who handles the government's money entertains on that scale, suspicions do circulate. Rumors followed Cornutus like a pack of hungry dogs trailing after a butcher's cart.

Several parties who had left Antioch with us concluded their journey in Ephesus. There we were joined by three other groups setting out from that city. All three of those parties aroused my suspicions, though for different reasons.

The first consisted of two men traveling without slaves and driving their own wagon. They kept themselves apart from the rest of us. One was tall, with dark hair, and appeared to be about forty. The other – the one who had spoken up to Cornutus at lunch – was shorter and older, about sixty I guessed. They took the last position in our train, frequently deep in whispered conversations. I caught occasional references to some kind of assembly, *ekklesia* in Greek. From their prayers at meals and what appeared to be secret signs they were using, I thought they might be Jews, or at least Greeks attracted to Judaism. There are a lot of such folks. They profess to admire Jewish ways, but not enough to undergo circumcision. I was quite surprised that the older of these men injected himself into my confrontation with Cornutus. Jews typically keep to themselves.

More unsettling was the appearance of another group, comprised of six women, with no male escorts and led by the one I thought of as the wild-haired witch. She wore an amazing number of bracelets, necklaces, and amulets. Their lead wagon was painted black and carried occult markings in bright colors on its sides. Ephesus is a center of magic and superstitious practices. 'Ephesian books' is used all over the empire to denote compilations of spells, even when they're not from Ephesus. They conversed in passable Greek but among themselves resorted to some Eastern babble.

But the most troublesome party who joined us in Ephesus was one man, Quintus Marcellus Justus, whom I immediately recognized as a protégé of Marcus Aquilius Regulus. If protégé is the proper term for a scoundrel and rogue-in-training.

Marcellus' presence troubled me because Regulus is one of the most notorious figures in Rome. Anyone who doesn't know him knows *of* him. Everyone fears him; no one respects him. Regulus would describe himself as an advocate. Most of the aristocracy in Rome serve their friends and family dependents in that capacity. It's one of the obligations that weigh against the privileges of wealth and class. So, admittedly, Regulus does nothing out of the ordinary by speaking for friends and clients. But he oversteps the bounds with his flamboyant – I might even say outrageous – manner in court and his insistence on handling the most sensational cases.

More troublesome is Regulus' sideline. He employs a network of spies who feed him information which he turns into sometimes ruinous charges against wealthy people. An accusation of treason is his most profitable ploy. He has been doing this for over twenty years, since the days of the emperor Nero, and has built up a vast fortune in the process, due to our government's policy of rewarding an informer with a quarter of whatever is confiscated from a convicted person. He debases himself even further by engaging in what aristocratic Romans sneer at as legacy-hunting – courting wealthy childless people in order to get oneself written into their wills.

From what I had heard and observed in Rome, Marcellus was an unusually adept pupil. Regulus doted on him more like a son than a student, and Marcellus picked up Regulus' rapacious inclinations and thieving techniques as readily as I hope any future son of mine will someday follow my example to a better end.

"We're almost there," Tacitus said. I turned my attention back to the scenery.

The highway broadened and a pedestrian pathway appeared alongside it, sure signs that we were approaching a city. Then we rounded Mt. Mastusia and could see the acropolis, on the east side of Smyrna, crowned by its marble temple of Artemis, and the tallest buildings of the lower town, their white-washed stucco walls and red tile roofs glistening in the late afternoon sun. Soon we passed among the tombs of the necropolis, that depressing introduction to every Greek and Roman town. Workmen were putting the finishing touches on a new tomb.

"It's a lovely city," I observed. "What do you know about it?" Tacitus has an encyclopedic memory, not unlike my uncle.

"It was built by Alexander the Great," he said. "Actually, *re*-built would be more accurate. The original city sat on the north side of the bay. That site was destroyed by the Lydians some six hundred years ago. A couple of centuries later Alexander re-established Smyrna on the south side of the bay, right at its head. The range of mountains behind it is anchored by Mt. Mastusia. The genius of Alexander's relocation of the city is that it now blocks the passage of any military force. Anyone traveling north or south along this coast must go through Smyrna or over the mountains. The town itself is laid out on a grid pattern, like a Roman army camp."

I leaned out of the wagon for a better view. "I often wish we could level Rome and start over again on such a logical basis. It's ironic that our capital is a hopeless jumble of winding streets – like the channels that termites eat in a piece of wood – when so many of our provincial cities are so beautifully and symmetrically arranged."

"Of course," Tacitus reminded me, "most of 'our' provincial cities – at least in the East – were built by Alexander or his successors. Perhaps if he had rebuilt Rome . . . but he would have had to conquer it first. And we certainly couldn't have that."

* * * *

We found a decent inn on the south side of town, one which boasted a large stable and the luxury of individual rooms, not just sleeping space in a large common room. The two men whom I took to be Jews said they would be staying with someone in the city and asked the innkeeper for directions to the house of Apelles.

"Are you friends of his?" the innkeeper asked.

"We have mutual friends," the older of the two replied. "We bear letters of introduction."

"I'm sorry to inform you," the innkeeper said, "that the noble Apelles died yesterday. He was much loved in Smyrna. In fact, he was one of our boularchs for this month."

"Oh, my," the younger man said. "Under that circumstance we can hardly impose on the family for lodging. Is there room for us here?"

The innkeeper nodded. "By all means, if you don't mind sharing a room."

"That's all right," the younger man said.

The older man smiled. "Yes. It's certainly better than hearing that there's no room in the inn."

The younger man glared at him as though he were betraying some private joke.

The inn's rooms proved small but tolerable for overnight lodging. The walls were whitewashed, though devoid of decoration. The straw in the mattresses was clean, and so were the chamberpots – both good signs. The innkeeper, a short, stout ruddy-cheeked man with a fringe of red and gray hair around his bald head, seemed a decent sort. He was named Androcles, which means 'noble man' in Greek. And he had a young wife and young children.

Having settled us in our rooms, Androcles directed us to the nearest bath house, just a block away.

"Do men and women still bathe separately here?" Tacitus asked.

"Yes," Androcles replied. "I've heard that in Rome the emperor has introduced the innovation of both sexes bathing together." He grinned in anticipation.

"That's becoming the common practice," Tacitus said. "And it's being copied in larger cities around the empire."

"Smyrna isn't one of them," Androcles said, "for good or ill."

I was glad to hear that. It's not that I don't appreciate the sight of women's bodies. My problem is that I appreciate the sight too much and can't always control the manifestation of my enjoyment. Strutting around in that state in the baths – raising a tent under one's towel, as they say – makes a man the object of Priapus jokes and other low forms of humor.

Tacitus and I posted a couple of our slaves to guard our belongings at the inn. Taking two others with us, we stopped to buy some perfumed oil on our way to the bath house.

"Are you sure you've got your strigl?" Tacitus asked me mockingly as we left the shop and resumed our walk.

"Please stop teasing me about that."

"Well, I don't see why you can't just use the scrapers in the public baths. Everybody else does."

"That's precisely the point. Everybody else does. And they don't just bathe with them. People scratch themselves everywhere with them as well as scraping off the oil. I'll bring my own with me, thank you."

This bath house rated among the nicer ones we had seen on this trip. The wall mosaics, depicting sea creatures and nymphs, were standard fare but well done. The floor mosaics, mostly geometric patterns, were fresh and unchipped. We left my slave in the dressing room to watch our clothes. Tacitus' slave accompanied us into the bath itself. The man gives massages that beggar description. After a long day of bouncing around in a wagon, he is worth every sestertius that Tacitus paid for him. That he's deaf adds to his value, for it means he can't overhear our conversations. His previous owner punctured his ears for that very reason.

Because of our late arrival in town the bath was almost deserted. Only two men were soaking in the pool by the time we reached that stage. One was a bald fellow with a snowy white fringe of hair and a matching beard. The other was much younger and had classical Greek features, large eyes and pouty lips. Did they speak Latin? Although Latin is the official language of the empire, it is rarely spoken east of the Adriatic Sea. Educated Greeks sometimes learn Latin, but all educated Romans know Greek. We regard it not as a foreign language, but as our other language.

Tacitus and I didn't dare talk about anything meaningful, in whatever language. Every city in the empire has its own Regulus, some bloated maggot waiting to fatten himself even more on the carcass of another betrayal. We confined ourselves to small talk.

"It's remarkable," I said, "how a year's post in a province takes up a good portion of *two* years. You have to get your affairs in order before leaving, then travel for at least a month to get there by the assigned date. You can't leave until your term ends, and it's another month and more of travel to get home. Then it takes several months to unscramble the mess your affairs have fallen into."

"But you do get to see a large piece of the empire," Tacitus pointed out. "We'll be passing near the site of Troy in a few days. Just think, Homer, Achilles, doomed Hector!"

"That just means we'll be approaching the Hellespont," I said with a shudder. "And to cross that I have to get on another boat.

'Doomed' is the right word."

The younger bather spoke up from across the pool. "Perhaps you could lash some ships together and construct a bridge, the way Xerxes did when he invaded Greece. He even put trees and dirt on it to fool the horses, as I recall."

So the fellow did speak Latin. Before I could form a witty response, Marcellus and Cornutus strolled into the bath, each accompanied by several slaves. Both men exuded an aura of largeness that made me feel even smaller and slighter than I am. Cornutus, the older by a decade, was the more muscular. His chest reminded me of a wall. His light brown hair and green eyes suggested Gallic ancestry. Marcellus personified the best and worst of Rome. He bore the classic Roman features, with dark hair and eyes and an aquiline nose. But his waist was already acquiring a ring of flab, just as Rome was growing flabby, feeding off its provinces.

"Well, fellow-travelers and now fellow bathers," Marcellus said with too much joviality as he eased himself into the water. Cornutus sat on the edge of the pool and dangled his legs in the water before lowering himself into it with a weary sigh. The bald fellow and his younger friend nodded in greeting but said nothing. I wanted to warn Marcellus and Cornutus that the strangers could speak Latin, but I couldn't think of any way to do it without being obvious.

No one mentioned the incident during our lunch stop. I wondered if Cornutus had already 'dealt with' the girl.

"Let's have some wine," Marcellus said. He sounded like one of those people who try to conceal their over-fondness for drink by forcing everyone else to drink with them. He sent one of his servants to the front of the bath house to purchase wine. The man returned, followed by a servant girl carrying six goblets on a tray. She handed one to Cornutus, one to Marcellus, and then offered the tray to us to select one. Marcellus motioned for her to take the last two cups to the Greek men on the other side of the pool.

"The dust of travel is difficult to wash away," Cornutus said, accepting the cup which the slave offered him. "What puts you on the road?" he asked Marcellus.

"I'm checking into investments on behalf of my friend, Marcus Aquilius Regulus. If things are handled properly, Regulus stands to make a great deal of money."

"And your commission won't exactly be small," Tacitus said drily.

"Is it unjust to be paid for doing a valuable service?" Marcellus replied. "Especially in a delicate matter where timing is so essential."

He looked to Cornutus for support, which he received in the form of a raised wine goblet.

"And you're returning to Rome after service in Syria?" Marcellus asked Cornutus.

"I was due to serve another year," Cornutus said in a robust voice that would have had a kind of reverberation to it even without the effect of the high ceiling in the bath, "but I've been informed that my father's health is failing."

"May we find him alive and well upon our return," I said, meaning it sincerely as one who had already lost two fathers. Tacitus added a hearty second to my toast.

"May the gods grant it," Marcellus said solemnly, pouring out a bit of his wine as an offering. The rest of us followed his lead.

* * * *

By the time we returned to the inn, Androcles and his wife were serving dinner to our party, other guests, and a crowd of locals. A buxom servant girl immediately attracted Tacitus' attention. The tables and benches had been placed closer together than earlier in the afternoon, to clear a space in the center for entertainment.

I suppose I groaned too loudly when a plate of greasy meat was set in front of us, the sort of thing one usually gets in public establishments, smothered with sauces to disguise how long it had taken to get from the market to the table.

"Too much for your delicate palate?" Tacitus asked with a trace of mockery.

"I find this sort of thing indigestible," I said, pushing the plate away and reaching for bread. "I suppose my uncle spoiled me in that regard. Meals in his house were lighter, fresher. And I hate to eat sitting on a bench. Why can't we find room to recline? It's so much more healthful."

"Why can't you just relax and stop being such a prig? We have convivial company. We don't have to sleep in our wagon tonight. And it appears we're going to have some entertainment."

"Oh, that will be the perfect culmination to the day," I said. I detest the noisy entertainments that so often accompany Roman (and Greek) dinners. My uncle spoiled me in that regard, too, I suppose. Or perhaps he just encouraged a natural inclination. Dinner in his house was always a calm affair, almost Socratic, with a trained slave reading a book, followed by conversation on the topic of the reading. If music was played, it was always of the most soothing kind, an aid to digestion.

The servant girl slapped a pitcher of cheap wine on the table. Tacitus grabbed her hand and kissed it before she could get away. She gave him a broad smile and a wink. Two musicians settled themselves in a corner and struck up a seductive tune on a flute and a tambourine. I braced myself for some sort of lascivious dance. I did not expect the innkeeper's twelve-year-old daughter to perform it.

As the throbbing of the music grew more insistent she threw her head back and waggled her skinny hips suggestively. Her gauzy costume made no secret of her budding womanhood. Androcles watched with a gleam on his pasty face, circulating through the crowd and nudging one man, then winking at another. This 'noble man' was auctioning his child off for the night. I couldn't stand to watch any longer, so I grabbed some bread and cheese and a cup of wine and went upstairs to my room.

* * * *

I was awakened just after daybreak by a loud wailing outside my door. In my first moment of waking I thought I was back at Vesuvius, during the eruption, with people running around in panic, screaming uncontrollably. Rushing out of my room, I found Androcles, wringing his hands in despair and moving his feet as though willing them to run but unable to make them obey.

"What's the matter?" I asked, grabbing his arm.

"He's dead!" the innkeeper gasped and pointed to the open door of Cornutus' room, directly across from mine. "Lucius Cornutus is dead!"

"Dead? By the gods! What are you saying?"

"His heart!" He clutched his hands to his own heart.

I couldn't believe this fellow had the medical knowledge to recognize that Cornutus had some problem with his heart. I grabbed his shoulders and shook him. "What about his heart?"

After several false starts, he managed to sputter out, "He doesn't . . . have one any more."

II

"He doesn't have a heart?" Tacitus

said groggily when I rousted him out of bed. The servant girl with him didn't even bother to cover her breasts. Something to be said for earthiness, I suppose. I was just glad I didn't find him with a boy. "You mean somebody . . . ?"

"Yes, somebody cut his heart out, as if he were a sacrificial ram."

"You've seen the body?"

"Just a quick look. There's a great, gaping hole going up under his ribcage. All the stuff in his guts is exposed to view, sort of hanging out."

At this point the girl bolted from the room, one hand over her mouth and the other clutching her gown. Even Tacitus, a devotee of the bloody spectacles in the amphitheater, was starting to look a little green. How odd. No Roman town considers itself 'civilized' until it builds a structure to stage these horrible shows. The sight of the blood throws even normally rational people into a frenzy. And yet my straightforward description of Cornutus' slaughtered body – which he hadn't even seen – was upsetting Tacitus.

"I've posted two of my slaves to guard the door until we can get the authorities here. Get up! Get dressed!" I urged Tacitus. "I need help keeping this situation under control."

"Why are *you* trying to keep it under control?" he asked. "You're not a magistrate in this province."

"In all the confusion no one seems to know quite what to do, so

I just started giving orders."

"You have a tendency to do that," Tacitus muttered.

I ignored him. I had vast responsibilities thrust on me at age seventeen when my uncle died. By now, taking charge of situations had become a habit.

"I'm not allowing anyone to go into the room," I said. "Nothing is to be touched. No one is to leave the inn. Cornutus was a Roman citizen, so we need to see that his murder is investigated according to Roman law."

"What about the local magistrates?" Tacitus asked. "Shouldn't they handle it?"

"They're being notified."

"Didn't the innkeeper tell us yesterday that one of them just died?"

"Yes. But there's a committee of them. They rotate in and out of service, two per month. I'm sure the other one will be here shortly. I've sent a message to the governor. But it'll take at least two days for that to get to Pergamum and two more for the governor or someone on his staff to get back here."

"What are they going to do in the meanwhile?" Tacitus asked. "In this warm weather Cornutus will raise a mighty stink in four days."

"I don't think *they* are going to do much of anything. Everybody I've spoken to this morning is too frightened of what Rome might do to them."

"With good reason," Tacitus said. I nodded in agreement. Nothing could bring the full wrath of Rome down on a provincial city faster than the murder of a Roman citizen within its walls. We regard ourselves as sacrosanct when among foreigners. 'Arrogant bastards,' as the witch put it.

"I think it's up to us to conduct some kind of investigation," I said, "before we have to burn the body."

Tacitus laughed. "What do we know about that sort of thing?"

"I've had some experience in legal matters," I reminded him, sounding more defensive than I intended. "I was on the Board of Ten Judges last year."

"Only as the most junior member," Tacitus shot back. I think he's still jealous because he lost the year that he was a candidate for the same post. "You never dealt with anything as serious as a murder case. And this sounds like a particularly brutal and bizarre one."

"It's all a matter of observing closely and questioning everything," I said.

Observation and inquiry – those were the principles upon which my uncle had based my education. He believed that decisions in criminal cases should be based on evidence gathered by rational observation, not on a speaker's ability to sway a jury. That was how he educated me, and that was why I thought I could take charge of this situation.

Leaving Tacitus to get dressed, I was on my way back to Cornutus' room when I encountered the older of the two men whom I took to be Jews.

"I've heard talk that someone has died," the man said. His kind eyes inspired trust. Of course, I upbraided myself, I had been favorably impressed with our nobly named innkeeper, who turned out to be nothing but a pimp for his own pubescent daughter. What did I know about character? Better to be suspicious of everyone, like Tacitus.

"Actually, someone has been killed," I corrected him.

"Oh, my. Is there anything I can do? I'm a doctor."

"It's a little late for your services, sir," I said, meaning to dismiss him. Then inspiration hit. "But could you accompany me while I examine the body? It's in here."

"By all means. I'll do whatever I can."

"We didn't make introductions when you joined our party," I said. "My name is Gaius Pliny."

"So I heard yesterday. Are you related to the author of the *Natural History*?"

"He was my uncle and adoptive father." Modesty prevented me from adding that he was one of the most respected scientific minds of our day. His *Natural History* is the standard work on phenomena of nature.

He bowed slightly. "I'm honored to make your acquaintance, young Pliny. My name is Luke." Receiving such deference from a man old enough to be my grandfather made me slightly uncomfortable. I had done nothing on my own to earn it.

"Well, Doctor Luke, brace yourself for a horrible sight."

We entered Cornutus' room and stood together beside the bed. The room, typical of any public lodging, contained nothing but the bed and a chair, over which a slave had draped a clean tunic for his master to put on this morning. Cornutus lay on his back, his arms at his sides. A great gash, beginning below his navel, ran up his chest. His viscera had been pulled out of the lower chest cavity and lay, still attached, on his stomach, to the great delight of the flies. His eyes were closed, mercifully. The open eyes, staring but unseeing, bothered me most about the few dead bodies I've seen. What puzzled me about Cornutus' face was the serene expression, his mouth even turned up a bit at the corners, as though he had passed from a pleasant dream to oblivion.

"At the risk of stating the obvious," Luke said, "it wasn't an accident or suicide."

I failed to appreciate his attempt at humor, if that's what it was. The day was already promising to be hot, and the room had been closed up all night. The stench was so strong I felt as if someone was forcing it down my throat. And something was coming back up. I looked around for the chamberpot. Failing to find it, I dashed to the window just in time. It was small, but it served my immediate need.

"Death's corruption takes some getting used to," Luke said gently when I turned back around. "Shall we proceed with our examination?"

I nodded, wiping my mouth and wishing for something to drink. Something strong. The body would have to be burned very soon. Anything we might learn from it would be gone. I had to do this. I *could* do this. My uncle had taught me how.

Whenever my uncle's slaves or soldiers under his command were injured or killed, he made careful notes about the appearance of the wounds and the bodies. Given the several days required to complete the Roman funeral process, my uncle observed how bodies change over time after death. The congealing of the blood, the stiffening of the limbs, all happens at a fairly predictable rate, depending on factors such as the temperature, covering of the body, whether it's been in water, and so on. In cases involving an assault he also learned that he could determine what type of weapon had been used and from what direction and angle the wound had been inflicted.

I had done more than merely read about his investigations. A few months before he died, he allowed me to assist him while he determined that a slave had died from poisoning, not from drowning. Faint discolorations around the mouth suggested a particular type of poison. My uncle drove a thin-bladed knife into one of the man's lungs and inserted a hollow reed. He discovered that there was no water in the lung. That meant the man was already dead before his body was put into the water. I could still recall his summary of the situation: 'Simply because a body is found in water does not mean that the person drowned. Appearances should not always be believed. A murderer often tries to conceal his crime by staging things to create a scene, just like a playwright.' That slave's wife and her lover − another slave − had killed the husband and tried to make it look as though he drowned accidentally. The lover admitted everything, trying to shift the blame onto the wife. Both were executed. Less educated people regarded my uncle as some sort of sorcerer, but he insisted he was merely making rational observations.

I had seen him do it, and I could do it.

A knock sounded on the door and one of my slaves stuck his head in. "My lord, Cornelius Tacitus asks to speak with you."

"Yes," I said impatiently, "it's all right. Let him in."

"You said to admit no one, my lord." The fellow was mocking me, I realized, but what else could he do? Owners of slaves often act as though we expect them to read our minds. Do exactly as I tell you, but figure out when I intend for exceptions to be made. And if they do act on their own initiative, we usually punish them for it.

The slave stood aside and Tacitus entered the room. "By the gods!" he gasped, his hand clutching his nose and mouth.

I was determined now to ignore the stench and show myself a better man than Tacitus. "It would be useful if we had someone to take notes for us. Could you do that?"

Tacitus nodded, went out and returned momentarily with a pen, ink, and a few pieces of papyrus. He seated himself in the chair, which he scooted close to the window. Not that it helped. There was no movement of the air, inside or outside, just oppressive humidity and the stench of death. Breathing in here was like trying to breathe underwater.

"Doctor, why don't you begin?" I said, stepping back from the bed and wishing that the room was large enough to get away from the stench. But it would have to be as large as an amphitheater for that.

Cornutus' strigl lay on the floor. Luke picked it up. "It's convenient for us that he was fastidious enough not to use the strigls from the public baths. Anyone concerned about cleanliness and good health should follow his example."

I glanced at Tacitus, but he was too busy trying to keep from vomiting to notice.

Luke used the curved piece of metal to probe around in the hole in Cornutus' chest. "The initial blow was delivered with great force, striking upward," he said, thrusting in the air with the strigl. Something from it splattered on me. "It reminds me of wounds I've seen on victims from the arena. The blade of the instrument must have been rather fine and extremely sharp. The edges of the wound aren't ragged."

I was pleased to hear Luke making those kinds of observations. I felt as though he and my uncle would have been comfortable with one another.

"Does it appear to you, sir, that Cornutus made no effort to resist?" I asked. "The body seems to be in what I would call a position of repose."

Luke ran his eye over the body and nodded. "I agree. The

arms are down by his sides, his legs straight out. That does strike me as odd. Even if he was asleep and didn't hear his attacker come in, when the blow was struck, there should have been some reaction, some instinctive clutching at the point of the pain." He put his hands on his chest and bent double. "Like that."

"Well, he was quite drunk," Tacitus said from his chair under the window. "He and Marcellus drank steadily until well past dark."

"Did he argue with anyone?" I asked.

"No, he and Marcellus acted like the greatest of friends. They largely ignored everyone else."

"Did you notice anything the least bit unusual about his behavior?"

"One thing did strike me as a bit peculiar. When Gaius Sempronius left to take the innkeeper's daughter upstairs, Cornutus said to him, in Latin, 'If she were my daughter, Sempronius, I'd kill you. You know that, don't you?'"

That wasn't helpful. I didn't want to know whom Cornutus had threatened to kill, just who might have wanted to kill him. "How did Sempronius react?"

"He sneered and pulled the girl closer to him."

"How did Cornutus get up here?" Luke asked.

"Marcellus and a slave practically carried him up the stairs."

"Do you think he would have been capable of defending himself if he were attacked?" Luke said.

Tacitus shook his head. "I don't think so. He was dragging his feet, he was so drunk."

"But he was a large, vigorous man," I objected. "Even in a drunken stupor, I think he would have jerked his knees up and tried to resist."

"I agree," Luke said. "That would be the most likely reaction."

I turned to Tacitus. "You said that Marcellus and a slave carried Cornutus up here. Whose slave was it?"

"One of Cornutus'. The one with the ears."

I nodded. We had speculated during the journey about what keen hearing the fellow must have, with auditory appendages of that size. If he could flap them, he might fly.

"Did they both return to the dining room?" I asked.

Tacitus shook his head. "Only Marcellus did. He drank several of the locals under the table. He seemed quite jovial and was very generous about buying drinks." His sheepish expression told me he had benefitted from that largess himself.

"So, to the best of our knowledge, Marcellus and Big-Ears, the slave, were the last two people to see Cornutus alive," I summarized.

"We'll need to determine whether they left the room together and where the slave went."

Tacitus drew himself up in horror. "Surely you don't suspect that Marcellus might have had something to do with his death." For all his disdain for aristocratic women as bedmates, he could be very defensive about the honor of the upper class.

I tried to placate him. "I'm not suggesting that he brought Cornutus up here, shooed the slave out of the room, and cut this poor man's heart out on the spot. For now I'm just observing. You can't always tell what's important until you reflect on it and fit things together in various ways. It's like putting a mosaic together. When you look at all those pieces scattered on the floor, you wonder how the workman will ever make sense of it."

An idea must have hit Luke. His face lit up. "Was Marcellus wearing the same clothes when he came back downstairs?" he asked.

"Yes, of course," Tacitus replied. "He was only gone for a very short time."

Luke placed his index finger on his nose and his thumb under his chin. We all have our thinking positions; I presumed this was his.

"Part of the problem," he said slowly, "is that we don't know exactly when Cornutus was murdered. It seems highly unlikely it was early in the evening. This sort of vicious attack would best be made in the very late hours, between midnight and dawn."

"We'll have to talk to the people in the rooms on either side of this one," I said, "to see if they noticed any unusual noises during the night. My room is across the way. I didn't hear anything – aside from you and that servant girl." I glared at Tacitus. His room was next to mine.

Tacitus looked up from his note-taking and smiled. "What can I say? She was quite . . . earthy."

"And quite loud. But, as for the time of death, why rely on our assumptions of what *could* have happened? Cornutus himself might give us some clue."

Luke and Tacitus looked at me as though I had proposed to raise the man from the dead for a little chat.

"Let me check a couple of things," I said. Luke stepped away from the bed to make room for me. I steeled myself, clasped Cornutus' cheeks firmly, and tried to move his head from side to side. It wouldn't budge. Next I tugged at one of his arms. The cold limb bent but only with some difficulty. His legs reacted the same way. Then I lifted his shoulders and buttocks and examined the parts of his body that were in contact with the bed.

"I would estimate that he's been dead eight to ten hours," I finally announced.

Luke looked at me the way the slaves on my uncle's estate did when he proved that the man fished out of a pond had not been drowned. I felt almost like a sorcerer. Necromancer might have been more appropriate. The credit has to go to my uncle, though. He bequeathed to me some 160 scrolls, his notebooks. He wrote on the front and back of the scrolls, so it's the equivalent of twice as many volumes. I've learned a great deal of what would appear to be arcane science from reading those notebooks.

"How can you say that?" Luke asked, drawing back.

"In some of his unpublished notes my uncle recorded his observations about what happens to bodies after death. The stiffness of the neck and limbs increases for a time, then begins to relax. The neck stiffens faster than the arms and legs. This process is affected by the temperature of the place where the body is lying. The blood also settles on the side of the body that is lowest. It's not yet the second hour of the morning. His neck is stiff, but his limbs still have some flexibility. The blood has completely settled, as you can see from the discoloration on the lower side of the body. It looks like large bruises. For all those things to have happened in a very warm room, Cornutus must have died long before midnight, probably by . . . the second hour after sunset."

"But that's when he was brought up here," Tacitus objected. "People were milling around. No one could have sneaked in here at that hour and done this horrible thing without somebody seeing or hearing something." Luke nodded his agreement.

"I entirely concur," I said. "But that can't change what Cornutus' own body tells us. Rational observation may not be convenient because it doesn't always fit our theories. It's our theories that need to change. One other thing about the condition of the body also puzzles me – "

Before I could finish, we were interrupted by the din of several voices from in front of Cornutus' door. Marcellus' was the loudest, in the way that drunkards sometimes are, without realizing how loud they are. I could tell that my slaves were having difficulty keeping him out of the room. I opened the door and stepped out. Luke followed me, shutting the door before poor Tacitus could escape.

Other people, also awakened by the commotion, were gathering outside Cornutus' door. The crowd even trailed down the stairs. Gaius Sempronius had spent the night in the room to the right of Cornutus', as one faced the door. I was appalled to see the innkeeper's daughter coming out of his room. The child clutched her flimsy dancing costume around her and rubbed the back of her hand over her mouth as she scampered away down the stairs. Sempronius leaned against his door, scratching his belly.

I quickly noted that everyone else in our caravan was also present. The witch and her acolytes huddled together in front of me. She had not assumed the center position in the group. Wherever she stood became the center of a group. Behind them Tiberius Saturninus was combing his hair over his bald pate with his hands. Lysimachus and the two eastern emissaries were easy to spot on my right.

Had I been traveling for all these days with a murderer? Or had someone else in the inn last night nursed some resentment of Cornutus? What motive would a stranger have had?

"What's going on?" Marcellus demanded belligerently.

"Lucius Cornutus is dead," I said without emotion. There was no need to try to evade the truth. The innkeeper had already spread the news like a fire through a peasant's hay barn. "He's been murdered."

A gasp passed through the small crowd. Heads began shaking and people looked at one another in disbelief. Or suspicion.

Marcellus seemed to have difficulty comprehending what I had said. "My friend Cornutus has been murdered? Why wasn't I informed?"

"You're not a magistrate or a relative of his," I replied. "There was no reason to wake you up."

"But he was my friend," Marcellus insisted stupidly. "We ate and talked together just last night."

"And you drank together, I understand." The reek of alcohol oozing from his pores would have confirmed that even if I hadn't had an eyewitness account. The front of his tunic bore a large wine stain. I was surprised he hadn't sucked it dry.

"Of course we drank together," he said. "That's what friends do."

I wanted to ask him if he had ever had a real friend, if he even understood the concept of friendship, except as a tool for manipulating people. Romans have long used the term to express political and social obligations. A 'friend' is one who votes for you or whom you're expected to invite to dinner periodically.

"What sort of shape was your 'friend' in when you left him?" I asked Marcellus.

"He was asleep. His slave and I put him in the bed, and we left."

"Both of you left together?"

He thought for a moment, then realization seemed to flash through the alcoholic haze fogging his brain, like lightning through a heavy cloud. "Why are you questioning me? When a Roman citizen is

murdered, you immediately round up his slaves. If you want information, you torture them. Then you put them to death. The law requires it."

I couldn't dispute him on that point. Roman law does mandate
that, if a master was murdered and the culprit cannot be identified, all of
his slaves are to be put to death. The reasoning must have been that
one of them did it, or they should have tried harder to protect him. The
last such execution took place under Nero. Four hundred slaves were
put to death in that case. The people of the city – so many of whom are
ex-slaves – rioted in an effort to stop it, but the emperor and the senate
were resolved to teach a lesson. Primarily a lesson in their own intran-
sigence and inhumanity.

"We need not act too hastily," I said, determined not to let
Marcellus grab control of the situation. "We know where Cornutus'
slaves are. They will be kept under watch and interrogated. No one
who stayed in this inn last night is to leave Smyrna until this matter is
resolved."

I hoped they couldn't see through my bluff. At that moment I
didn't know where Cornutus' slaves were. And I had no authority to
keep anyone from leaving if they chose to do so, not the German merchant who was eying me from one side of the crowd or the Ephesian
witch who stood directly in front of me, burning a hole in me with those
coal-black eyes.

"I have urgent business in Rome," Marcellus protested immediately. "You can't detain me here against my will."

"You seem eager to get away, Quintus Marcellus," I said in
that mockingly polite tone all Roman advocates cultivate. "As eager as
. . . well, a criminal in a hurry to leave the scene of his crime." It was
the kind of tactic one sees in Roman courts every day. I hadn't accused
Marcellus of committing a crime. I had merely likened his haste to
depart to that of a criminal. But with that damning analogy I had suc-
ceeded in planting in the minds of my listeners the assumption that
Marcellus – or anyone, for that matter, who wanted to leave – might
be guilty of murder. Now no one dared to leave.

Marcellus saw me constructing the box around him and could
do nothing. "That's preposterous!" he bellowed. "If my honor is going
to be impugned behind my back, if that's your tactic, then I'll stay and
defend myself." Even as he spoke, he was shifting in his mind for a
point of attack, like an advocate in court whose opponent has sprung a
surprise on him. Then he stumbled over one.

"I can't help but wonder, friend Pliny, if you're looking for someone to accuse in order to shift attention from yourself. You obviously

have more than a passing interest in that little slave girl. You interfered yesterday when Cornutus was about to punish her, quite justifiably, I might add. Your room is directly across from this one, isn't it? Did you step over here during the night and – ?"

"No one is on trial here, Marcellus." I cut him off. "No one has been accused of anything. I'm simply trying to gather information so the governor can conduct a proper investigation when he gets here in a few days. Everyone must cooperate."

Marcellus turned and faced the crowd, which by now jammed the narrow passageway. He straightened up and put on his best court demeanor, undermined though it was by his appearance. "Friends, we need not wait several days to settle this business. All we have to do is round up Cornutus' slaves and make them tell us what they know." He threw his arm out, pointing with his first two fingers, as though directing the crowd to move in that direction. That trick I recognized as one learned from his mentor, the detestable Regulus. I've seen him jerk a whole crowd around, like a child pulling toys on a string. Marcellus managed to get only a few heads turned. It's more effective, I suppose, when a man's bare arm shoots out from his toga, not a wine-stained tunic. Or when he's standing on an elevated speaker's platform. Or when he doesn't look like a disheveled drunk.

Marcellus had made a mistake Regulus never would have. He had seriously misjudged his audience. This was not a throng of Roman citizens in the Forum. More than half of the people around him were slaves. The rest were aware that they were outnumbered by the slaves. The tension was building like the heat before a late afternoon thunderstorm.

I have no idea what might have happened if Luke had not stepped from behind me at that moment. His gray hair and his *dignitas* drew the crowd's focus away from Marcellus in a way that my most earnest pleading could not have.

"My friends," he said, "there is no need for us to turn on one another, to let ourselves be worked into a frenzy by irresponsible words." That made Marcellus fume. "A horrible crime has been committed. Whoever committed it must be found and brought to justice. The victim was a Roman citizen, but there are no Roman magistrates here at present. If we do anything amiss, even in a sincere effort to find the culprit, we can be held responsible when the governor arrives." Heads nodded in agreement. "Gaius Pliny has shown remarkable initiative and good judgment in the way he has handled things so far. I intend to follow his leadership in this matter, and I urge you to put your trust in him."

Marcellus wasn't ready to concede. "He has no authority here."

"Neither do you," a voice from my left said. I turned to see Tiberius Saturninus glowering at Marcellus.

"It's not a question of authority," Luke said. "It's confidence that is at issue. I am a Roman citizen and a doctor. I place my confidence in Pliny."

He placed his hand on my shoulder. The sight of a senior man demonstrating his trust in one so young broke the tension. A murmur ran through the crowd, and heads nodded. I felt as if I was in the midst of an election campaign. I sensed it was time for me to say something, to acknowledge the anointing that Luke had just laid on me.

"We are in a difficult position, my friends," I began, hating the meaningless use of that last word. But it's how crowds expect to be addressed. "As Luke has rightly said, we will be held accountable for whatever we do between now and the governor's arrival. If you'll co-operate with me, I will make every effort to see that things are in good order. I do need to insist that no one leave Smyrna. If you must leave the inn, leave word of where you're going and why. I will be talking to various ones of you, asking questions about your activities last night. My friend Tacitus will be keeping records of this investigation, to turn over to the governor.

"While I appreciate the kind words which Luke has spoken on my behalf, I also want to assure you that I have some experience in these matters. Last year I served on the Board of Ten Judges in Rome, and I have been an advocate before the courts. I'll apply what I've learned to my investigation of this foul crime. None of us is safe until we find the killer."

That last line popped out of my mouth at the same time it popped into my head. Hearing it, I wondered if it were true. Was this crime directed specifically against Cornutus? Or would his killer strike again? I had no way of knowing, but perhaps suggesting the latter possibility would serve to frighten everyone into cooperation. My statement was true, none the less. Even if the killer didn't attack anyone else, none of us would be safe from suspicion in this murder until he was caught.

"Everyone please go about your business now," I said. "Stay close to the inn and be ready to talk with me at some point during the day."

The crowd began to disperse. Marcellus waved disgustedly and stomped off to his room. Luke and I breathed simultaneous sighs of relief and turned back to Cornutus' room. I tried to take one last gulp of good air before entering the death chamber, but poor Cornutus' stench was beginning to penetrate the door.

We found Tacitus standing on the chair with his head out the window. The retching sounds spared us the necessity of asking what he was doing. We were going to have to finish our examination of Cornutus' body quickly and proceed with the funeral preparations.

"Are you going to be all right?" Luke asked as Tacitus resumed his seat.

"I think so," Tacitus replied. "I couldn't find the chamberpot."

"You're not the first today to have that problem," Luke assured him with a pat on the shoulder. "Now, where were we?"

"While you two were out there," Tacitus said, "I couldn't help but contemplate our mutilated friend there. And a question occurred to me. Considering how he was ripped open, wouldn't you expect a lot more blood to be splattered around the room? In the fights in the arena, when someone gets cut in the chest or stomach, the blood just spurts out."

"That's true," Luke said. "You're keen to notice."

I was more than a little miffed to have my thunder stolen. "That's the other thing that I was going to say before Marcellus started that ruckus. From the way the blood has settled in the body, from the degree of stiffness of the limbs, *and* from the lack of blood splattered around the room, I believe Cornutus died early in the night. He had already been dead for several hours when someone cut out his heart, sometime in the early morning."

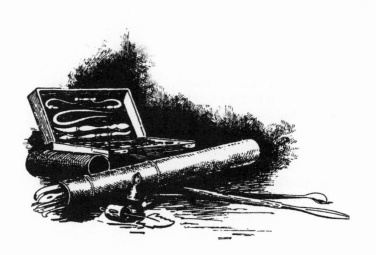

III

A stunned silence followed my pronouncement. No
one moved until Luke stood beside the bed again, running his eyes over
Cornutus' butchered body.

"You say he died. Do you mean of some natural cause? Or
perhaps from too much wine?"

"The only time I've known wine to kill someone," I replied,
"was when something was added to it."

Tacitus clutched at his throat. "You mean he was poisoned?"

"Are you afraid you drank from the same amphora?" I asked.

"Don't worry," Luke said. "If you had, you'd be dead by now.
I don't know any poison that acts *that* slowly." He turned to me. "Poison? Can you be serious?"

"It's the only logical explanation I can see. He didn't struggle
and he didn't bleed when his heart was cut out, so he must have already
been dead for several hours. Forgive me, doctor, for presuming to instruct you . . . "

"No, it's all right," Luke said. "Your powers of observation are
quite keen. You're causing me to look more closely. There are no marks
about his neck to indicate that he was strangled."

"What if somebody suffocated him?" Tacitus asked. "That
wouldn't leave any marks, would it?"

"No," Luke said, "it wouldn't. But it would be very difficult to
suffocate a man this large without leaving some sign of a struggle."

"With all other options eliminated," I said, "what else could it be but poison?"

Luke stepped closer to the body and ran his eyes over it slowly, like a man inspecting a potential slave for flaws. "I don't see any obvious signs of a poison," he finally said. "Many of them leave discolorations around the mouth or eyes, or mottled skin, or some such external marks. Others cause convulsions or loosen the bowels. There's no evidence of any of these things. Of course, it could be one I'm not familiar with."

I wished I had my uncle's notebooks with me. Medicinal and poisonous plants were a prime interest of his.

"One thing troubles me about your theory," Luke said. "If Cornutus was poisoned early in the evening and then cut open later, does that mean we have two killers to deal with?"

"It could. Or it could mean that someone wanted to cut out Cornutus' heart but wanted to disable him before doing it. I don't think somebody came in here intending to kill him, then decided, on impulse, to cut out his heart."

"Someone intent on murder would want to finish the deed quickly and be gone," Tacitus said.

"I think you're right. Whoever mutilated him had it in mind before he or she entered the room."

"'Or she'?" Luke shook his head vigorously. "Surely no woman would be capable of such a deed."

"Doctor, from even my limited experience," I said, thinking of the slave woman and her murdered husband on my uncle's estate, "I must conclude that women can conceive and carry out any crime a man is capable of, allowing for differences of physical strength. A woman might even be more likely in this case. Lacking physical strength, she might have wanted to disable Cornutus before the attack. Perhaps the dose of whatever drug he was given was too strong."

"But why, in the name of all the gods," Tacitus said, "would someone want to cut a man's heart out?"

"I don't think we can ask why until we know who, can we?" Luke said.

"No, Tacitus is right," I said. "Discovering *why* something was done is often an important key to learning who did it. Some kind of obscene ritual would be my first guess. People do all sorts of bizarre things under the mask of religion. Remember the Christians whom Nero condemned after the great fire in Rome twenty years ago?"

"Exactly," Tacitus said. "Stories I heard in Syria say that they eat flesh and drink blood."

"There is no basis in truth for such slanders," Luke said quietly but quickly.

Tacitus eyed him suspiciously. "How can you be so sure?"

"I am . . . acquainted with members of the group," Luke said. "There is no cannibalism involved in their mysteries, I assure you." He dismissed the subject by turning his attention back to Cornutus' body.

"That was just an example. Perhaps a bad one," I conceded. "I have no direct knowledge of them. My point is that people do strange things in the name of their gods. Priests of Cybele emasculate themselves. Those women from Ephesus may practice some kind of witchcraft which requires the use of a heart."

Luke scrunched up his face in disgust. "Necromancy. Blood for the spirits. It's revolting." He glanced nervously at Cornutus' body. "But this is a most peculiar way to kill someone, even for a witch."

"Oxen being led to a public sacrifice," I pointed out, "are sometimes fed drugs to calm them in front of the large crowds. Perhaps someone gave Cornutus a drug, planning to 'sacrifice' him later."

"Oxen are also whacked over the head with a big hammer," Tacitus reminded us. "Does Cornutus have any dents in that thick skull of his?"

Though intended as a morbid witticism, his comment prompted Luke and me to realize that we had not considered that question when we examined Cornutus' body. We went over the poor man again but found no injuries to his head or indications of blows elsewhere.

"I'm going to be sick again," Tacitus suddenly said as we turned Cornutus' corpse back over, forcing some rather noxious odors out of it. "Where's the damn chamberpot?"

He hung his head out the window again.

The question of that vanishing chamberpot perplexed me almost as much as the identity of Cornutus' killer. It must have been on Luke's mind, too.

"Are we certain it was in here last night?" he asked as Tacitus resumed his seat and hung his head between his knees.

"All the rooms had them when Androcles was showing us the place yesterday afternoon," I said. "They were sitting under the chairs, in plain view."

"Could Cornutus have used it earlier in the evening and sent a slave out to empty and clean it?"

I mulled that over for a moment. "That's certainly possible, but you've seen how harshly he treated his slaves. I think the slave would have gotten the chamberpot back immediately, or faced a beating. It certainly would have been returned before the master came up to bed."

A knock on the door interrupted any further deliberations. My slave opened the door a crack but didn't even stick his head in this time. The stench was getting that bad.

"My lord, Nicomedes, boularch of Smyrna, has arrived."

"All right. Have him wait downstairs. I'll be there in a moment." I realized I was beginning to sound like royalty receiving a visiting ambassador. Mustn't get too imperial – too arrogant – in my treatment of the local magistrate.

"Tacitus, make a note about that missing chamberpot. Then you and I should go talk with the boularch. Doctor, why don't you go over the body one more time, just to make sure we haven't missed anything?"

"All right. And I'll tuck him back together and sew him up while I'm at it."

Tacitus bolted for the door.

"Good idea. Then we can have his slaves begin the funeral preparations. Would you mind supervising them and watching how they react?"

Luke nodded. "And I'll ask about the chamberpot."

* * * *

Tacitus was leaning against the wall outside his own room, taking large gulps of fresh air, like a man who has emerged from the water after nearly drowning. My own stomach wasn't as settled as I was pretending, but I was enjoying a few minutes of being a better man than he.

"I think we'd better put on our togas before this interview," I said.

"Why be so formal? This isn't Rome."

"But we are Romans. And we need to remind these people of that fact."

"I'm not going to put mine on," he insisted. "The damn woolly things itch so in this warm weather."

"Well, give me a hand with mine. I guess the purple stripe on your tunic will have to suffice to impress the provincials."

I would have preferred to bathe before putting on the toga. Made of wool, it did feel particularly heavy on a day like this. No more awkward, ill-fitting garment could have been devised by the human mind, I think. What could have possessed our ancestors to envelop themselves in a large piece of wool, folding and draping it over and around themselves several times, the way a child dresses up a pet animal in play? Perhaps it's true that they designed the cumbersome thing to hinder hasty action on the part of the wearer. One must have assistance to don it properly, and once imprisoned in it, merely raising one's arm while keeping the rest in place takes practice. Still, there is something unspeakably grand about the sight of several hundred senators arrayed in their purple-striped togas, or candidates campaigning for office in their specially whitened ones. They become the embodiment of Rome's majesty.

But when trying to get into the garment, they look more like clowns. Normally I would have asked one of my slaves to assist me, but the only ones readily available were standing guard at Cornutus' door and that seemed the more important duty at the moment. Tacitus and I fumbled with the thing until I felt presentable.

"You certainly got stuck with a small room," Tacitus said as I stepped on his foot while turning myself and adjusting a fold. "I thought you were going to be in the room Cornutus is in."

"That was the original plan," I said. "But he prevailed on me after we got back from the baths to trade rooms with him. He said that the bed was bigger. And he is – was – a big man. He couldn't get comfortable in here."

"By the gods, Pliny! Have you thought about what that means?"

I looked at him blankly. "What are you talking about?"

"Somebody could have gone into *that* room intending to kill *you*."

"Don't be ridiculous. Why would anyone want to kill me?"

"Why would anyone want to kill Cornutus?"

* * * *

I tried to put Tacitus' troubling assertion out of my mind as we descended the dark narrow stairs to the main floor. At the proper time I might give it some consideration. For the moment I had to focus on our interview with Nicomedes.

I didn't expect much from the boularch. Such positions are largely ceremonial. Rome encourages the sharing of power in all political posts, to prevent any one individual from becoming too influential. All important decisions in any province are made by the governor sent out from Rome.

Nicomedes was pacing in a small private room off the main dining room when we entered and introduced ourselves. He was a swarthy, middle-aged man of what I judged to be mixed Greek and eastern ancestry, with beady eyes and a copious supply of sweat. I wondered whether he was reacting to the weather or to the predicament he was in. Murder of a Roman citizen in a province can bring harsh penalties on an entire town if the killer isn't caught.

"Sirs, this is terrible," he said. "Just terrible. I can't believe that any citizen of Smyrna would do such a thing."

"It's unclear at this point who the killer is," I said. "We've sent for the governor and are making preliminary inquiries until he arrives."

"What do you want me to do?"

I noticed he didn't challenge us, didn't ask on what authority we were acting. In most of these shared-power governing arrangements – and I include the consulship in Rome – you tend to get one man who actually has the gumption to do the job and a partner who wants it carved on his tombstone that he was boularch or duovir, or whatever the local title may be. In Rome the story still circulates of the year when Julius Caesar and a man named Bibulus shared the consulship. Bibulus was so terrified of Caesar that he spent the entire year holed up in his house. Wags referred to it as 'the year when Julius and Caesar were consuls.' From the way Nicomedes kept sweating and wringing his hands, it appeared we were dealing with Smyrna's version of cowardly old Bibulus.

That could have its advantages. He was likely to keep out of our way. On the other hand, we probably couldn't count on his support if any hard decisions had to be made. For that matter, the governor might not be much help. Asia is a senatorial province, with its governor chosen by the senate in Rome. The frontier provinces, such as Syria, where legionary troops and auxiliaries are stationed, have their governors appointed by the emperor. The more ambitious, decisive men end up there. The senatorial provinces are comfortable sinecures, where the governors spend most of their time sorting out disputes over property lines, deciding whether to build a new sewer, and finding a suitable mistress among the daughters of the local aristocracy. The only troops under their command are a small honor guard. Tacitus and I might find ourselves out on a limb if we pursued this matter too far.

"I'll be happy to help you in any way I can," Nicomedes added, "although the death of my fellow boularch, Apelles, has left a great void in our city's leadership."

I'll bet it has, I thought. A big void where the brains and courage used to be. At the reminder of Apelles being a boularch, Tacitus and I exchanged a glance. If Luke bore letters of introduction to a man of such prominence in the city, he was better connected than we could have guessed from his unassuming demeanor.

I raised my left hand to grasp the drapery of my toga over my chest, a position Roman men learn to assume when they want to assert their authority. "We have asked everyone in our traveling party to remain in Smyrna at least until the governor arrives," I said. "We would like to ask your city watchmen to apprehend any unfamiliar persons or anyone found engaging in suspicious activities."

Nicomedes raised a timorous hand to stop me. "What do you consider suspicious?"

"Gatherings at night. Any kind of unapproved religious cults, for example. You see, Lucius Cornutus' heart was cut out."

His gasp was predictable but apparently genuine. He steadied himself against a table.

"We don't know," I continued, "if there is a connection with the bizarre practices of some cult. Perhaps the Christians."

"I can assure you, sir," he said stoutly, "that Smyrna worships the gods and honors the emperor and Rome. Why, we built a temple to the guardian spirit of Rome in the days of your war with Hannibal, almost three hundred years ago. That was long before we were privileged to become a province of your glorious empire. This city was made a temple-warden of the imperial cult by Tiberius Caesar, son of the deified Augustus."

I stopped him before he fell to his knees and began reciting the oath of loyalty which emperors periodically require of provincials. "We have no doubt of Smyrna's loyalty. But even in the most loyal city there may be individuals who act disloyally. They threaten the safety of their own city as much as that of Rome."

His bulging eyes told me he had taken my point. If Cornutus' killer wasn't found, the entire city would be held accountable. That accountability would land squarely on the shoulders of its leading magistrates. And this murder had happened on Nicomedes' watch.

He swallowed hard. "You will have my utmost cooperation, sirs," he promised. "I will inquire about any recent suspicious visitors and keep a close eye on the town's nocturnal activities."

"Report anything you learn directly to me," I said, "or to my friend Tacitus, but to no one else."

* * * *

"That was impressive," Tacitus said as we had a bite of bread and olive oil. "He was 'sir-ing' you right and left, and you're not half his age."

We were sitting at one of the long tables in the main dining room, probably the most pleasant room in the inn. The frescoes had been redone recently. In fresh, vibrant colors they depicted famous banquet scenes from myths and literature, a common motif in dining room decoration. Anyone who wanted a morning meal had eaten by now, almost the third hour of the day. The servant girl who had shared Tacitus' bed was waiting on us. She seemed awkward around him, uncertain how to act. I guess my interruption and the nature of my news had shattered the romantic moment. Tacitus and I conversed in Latin, shifting to Greek only when necessary to talk to the girl.

I took a sip of the well-watered wine. "I watched my uncle dealing with soldiers the whole time I was growing up. He told me the secret of command is simply to take command. Never give the other person – whether a soldier, a slave, or any other subordinate – a moment to reflect on whether or not you're worthy to command. If you act worthy, that confidence will come across."

"And confidence is a quality you certainly don't lack," Tacitus said, "especially for someone your age."

"I don't see my youth as a disadvantage, as you apparently do. Remember, the deified Augustus was only nineteen when he was adopted by his uncle, Julius Caesar, in his will – as I was – and took command of Caesar's troops."

Tacitus leaned over the table and dropped his voice to a whisper. "If I were you, I would be very cautious about drawing analogies between myself and Augustus. That sort of comment, reported to the right people, could be interpreted to mean you have imperial ambitions."

I leaned over until our heads almost met and whispered back, "If you don't report it, I could report you for failing to do so. That could be taken by some people to mean you support me in my plot to place myself on the throne. Your head would roll in the dust right alongside mine."

We smiled at one another until Tacitus took a piece of bread and dipped it in the olive oil. As new as it was, our friendship had already reached a level where we trusted one another enough to make such jokes. Our teasing had a sharp edge of truth to it, though. Such comments had led to arrests and executions in the past, under emperors whose fear of plots against their lives had driven them to the doorstep of madness, or beyond. It was still too early in Domitian's reign to know whether he fell into that category.

"So what's our next step?" Tacitus asked.

"We need to round up Cornutus' slaves and question them, especially Big Ears and the blond girl."

"Her name is Chryseis."

"What a surprise." ('Chryseis' in Greek means 'Goldie.' I would wager that a third of the blond slave girls in the empire bear that name. My uncle, and now I, owned half a dozen.) "How did you learn this?"

"She was serving Cornutus at dinner last night. I heard him call her name."

"Did you see any sign that he had punished her?" I tried to hide my anxiety, without much success, I feared. "Did she appear to be injured?"

"Not that I could see. She was obviously afraid of him, but he gave no sign of being particularly angry at her. Unless she was serving him, he pretty much ignored her. He must have said something about her to Marcellus, though. At one point he gestured at the girl, and Marcellus looked at her and then at Cornutus in amazement."

"Probably describing some sexual antic he had engaged in with her," I said bitterly. Of all the things we inflict on our slaves, forced sexual relations seem to me the most reprehensible. Seduction of a free woman is one thing, a game of wits, as Ovid described it. The women play it as avidly as the men. But brutal domination of a woman by someone who holds the threat of physical punishment over her – I see no place for that in a civilized society.

"What difference does it make to you what Cornutus does with one of his slave girls?" Tacitus asked, taking a sip of wine. "Marcellus was right about one thing. You do seem to have an unhealthy interest in her."

I drew myself up. "I feel responsible for whatever he may have done to her after the incident at lunch yesterday. But there's something more to it. She has an aura about her, something dignified. Can't you see it? If I met her on the street, I would never suspect she was a slave."

Tacitus made a disgusted face. "Do you think this is one of those comic plays where the girl turns out to be the abandoned daughter of an aristocratic family so she can't be legally enslaved? Maybe you can free her and marry her." He laughed lightly.

"I am under no such delusions," I said stiffly. Sometimes Tacitus can really irritate me with his lack of seriousness. "I just recognize something that differentiates her from other slaves. I'm also concerned about what's going to happen to her now. Cornutus' slaves and his goods will be sent back to Rome. Assuming his father is still alive, all of Cornutus' property will revert to his father, unless he made other provisions in his will. It could be a legal mess that will take months to straighten out."

"So we'd better talk to them before anything else happens to them," Tacitus said.

* * * *

Upon inquiring of the innkeeper, we learned that Cornutus had ordered his slaves locked up for the night along with the slaves of several other travelers. The men had been kept in a storage room attached to the stable, the three women in a room on the third floor of the inn.

The other slaves had been released already, but Cornutus' were still confined while Androcles awaited orders about their disposition.

"I'll take responsibility for them," I said quickly. "The men and the older women need to see the doctor, Luke, and assist him with Cornutus' funeral preparations. Give them something to eat, if you haven't already. The blond girl I want brought to me immediately in that private room off the dining room."

"Right you are, sir," Androcles said, smiling broadly and winking at me.

It seemed to take a long time, but Chryseis eventually came into the private room and stood, waiting for a command. The sight of her almost overwhelmed my power of speech. They say that, in the legendary days of Rome's infancy, a goddess used to come to king Numa and advise him on laws for the city. Seeing Chryseis standing in that doorway, her hands clasped modestly in front of her, her long, golden hair and her gown being ruffled slightly by a breeze from somewhere, I could suddenly understand how stories of such divine apparitions arose. How could I not have noticed her before in all the days we'd been traveling together? Cornutus' wagons usually stayed farther back in our caravan, and there were over a hundred people in our group all together, but she should have stood out like the moon among the stars in the night sky.

"Please, Chryseis, come sit with us," I said, recovering as much of my composure and businesslike manner as I could.

She seemed surprised but did as I told her, taking a seat on the bench across the table from me. Tacitus was sitting in a chair at the end of the long table. I had put him there deliberately, to make the situation less intimidating for Chryseis. I put bread, cheese, and olive oil in front of her. She began to eat with little interest.

"Do you know what has happened?" I asked, folding my hands on the table in front of me.

"Yes, my lord," she said with quick, nervous nods. "My master's been murdered."

"Do you know what that could mean for you and his other slaves?"

She started to cry. "We could be put to death. But, my lord, we were locked up last night. How could we have killed him?"

I reached across the table and took her hand, ignoring the smile from Tacitus which I could see even without turning my head.

"I'm not going to let anything happen to you, Chryseis. Not to any of you. I promise. I just want to ask you some questions. You must answer them truthfully if I'm to be able to help. Do you understand?"

"Yes, my lord. Are you a magistrate, my lord?"

I was flummoxed that a slave had asked that question when Smyrna's surviving co-mayor had bowed to my assumed authority without a whimper. I withdrew my hand.

"Well . . . actually I'm not. But there aren't any Roman magistrates in Smyrna right now. We're waiting for the governor to arrive. Until then I'm making certain everything is done in proper order, since Cornutus was a Roman citizen and not subject to the laws of Smyrna."

That must have satisfied her, since she asked no further questions. She did seem a little disappointed about something, though.

"Now, Chryseis, did Cornutus punish you last night?"

"No, my lord."

That was two burdens off my shoulders at once. I had not caused her any hardship, and if Cornutus hadn't done anything to her, she wasn't likely to have killed him in revenge.

"Did he punish you often?"

"No, my lord. He threatened me sometimes but the worst he did was slap me once or twice . . . until four years ago." I hoped she might offer more of an explanation, but one of the first lessons a slave learns is not to give more of an answer than was called for.

"What happened then?"

She dropped her head, then looked up at me from under her eyelids. Women in Rome practice that gesture for hours, trying to look innocent and demure. To Chryseis it came as naturally as a baby's smile, and it had the same winning effect on me. "He . . . he branded me. On my . . . on my backside. The mark is a ram's horn, like his seal." She dropped her eyes again, as though unable to bear the shame of what she had just said.

The design of the brand made sense, since the name Cornutus was derived from the Latin word for horn. Its location and the man's motivation were another matter. "Do you know why he did that?"

"No, my lord, I don't."

"Had you done anything wrong?" I prodded.

She wiped tears off her cheeks with the back of her hand. "I wasn't aware of anything that I had done wrong."

"Can you tell me about it?"

She took a quivering breath. "Two of the other slave women brought me to him one night and tied me up. He branded me himself. It was horrible. I still have dreams about it. Horrible." Her reply was effusive by slave standards.

The story troubled me. Slave owners rarely brand their slaves unless they've tried to run away. The brand, usually placed on the forehead, makes it virtually impossible for them to hide. It also lowers the slave's value if he or she is to be sold. And yet Cornutus had branded this divinely beautiful girl. And had done it himself, not entrusting the task to another slave. I glanced at Tacitus to be certain he had noted that odd fact.

"Why don't we have a look at it, just for the record?" Tacitus suggested. Chryseis blushed violently.

"That won't be necessary." I shot Tacitus a glance intended to seal his lips. He gave me an innocent expression that seemed to say, What did I do? Why are you looking at me? Then I turned back to Chryseis. "Did Cornutus brand any of his other slaves?"

"None that I know of, my lord."

"Were you angry at him for branding you?"

"I was hurt, my lord, because I didn't know why he did it. But a master can do whatever he wants with his slaves, so there was nothing I could do about it." She shrugged, and endowed even that simple movement with grace.

"You could have nurtured a grudge and killed him," Tacitus said.

"You were locked up all night, weren't you?" I asked as a reminder to Tacitus.

"Yes, my lord. Melissa, Phoebe, and I, up on the third floor."

"And you're sure no one got out of the room at any time, even for a few minutes."

When she didn't respond immediately my heart sank. "You must answer the question, Chryseis."

By the way she twisted her hands she might as well have confessed her guilt. "Well, my lord, Melissa and Phoebe . . . it was so hot in there, you see."

"What did they do, Chryseis?"

"They squeezed out through the window and sat on the roof of the stable for a while. It connects to the inn right below our window. But they didn't go anywhere else."

Tacitus shifted noisily to a new piece of papyrus. "Did you go out the window?"

"No, my lord."

"We'll have to take a look at that roof," I told Tacitus. "It doesn't seem likely, though, that a woman could have climbed down from there, killed Cornutus, then climbed back up."

"Two women might have helped one another," he replied.

Chryseis' eyes got bigger as she realized the implications of what she'd told me. "My lord, I swear they didn't go anywhere. They just sat outside for a while. It was so hot."

"But you yourself did not leave the room at any time. Is that correct?"

"Yes, my lord. It looked too high. I was afraid."

So she couldn't have cut Cornutus' heart out. But she was serving him at dinner, according to Tacitus. Did she poison him?

I couldn't ask any questions about poisoning because Luke, Tacitus, and I had agreed not to make that public. But I wasn't ready to send Chryseis away. I wished I could think of enough questions to keep her sitting there all day. "All right, then. How did you come to be Cornutus' slave?"

"I was born in the household." She was obviously relieved to turn to another subject.

"How old are you?"

"Fifteen. I'll be sixteen in August."

"Tell me about your mother."

"I never knew her, my lord. She died during the birth. She was a German captive. She was very beautiful, my nurse used to tell me."

That was easy to believe as I contemplated the daughter. Sculptors often distort features ever so slightly – making the mouth minutely too large or placing the eyes just a fraction too far apart – so that they will appear to the viewer to be perfect. I could have sworn, though, that I was looking at a perfect face.

"Who is your father, Chryseis?"

"I don't know, my lord."

By the way Tacitus' head jerked up I could tell her response had raised the same possibility for him that it had for me. We had an entire conversation with just a couple of glances. If a male slave in the household were her father, he would have been given the responsibility of raising her, with the assistance of a female slave. Circumstances in this case suggested another possibility: Could Cornutus be her father? It's not uncommon for Roman aristocrats to father children by their female slaves. Legally such children are classed as slaves. Few aristocratic fathers acknowledge these children because they complicate the inheritance situation for their legitimate offspring. If the mother and Cornutus were both dead, how could we explore the question of Chryseis' parentage? And, if she was his child, why did Cornutus brand her?

"Did Cornutus ever sleep with you?" Tacitus asked from his end of the table.

"No, my lord." Chryseis barely turned her head toward him.

"Did he ever have any sort of sexual relations with you?" I asked. If he had sex with her in some other fashion, she could have answered 'no' to Tacitus' question, quite legitimately to a slave's way of thinking.

"No, my lord. He never did anything like that to me."

"Did he allow any of his male slaves to have relations with you?" Apparently I was going to have to pull the information out of her piece by piece. I hoped I didn't have to name each male slave in the household.

"No, my lord." She looked down, then caught my eye again. "One of the male slaves — a boy that I really liked — once told me Cornutus had ordered all of them to stay away from me. Any slave who slept with me, he said, would be castrated and sent to the mines."

That struck me as decidedly odd. It's not unusual for slaves to copulate with one another. Few slave owners attempt to regulate their behavior that closely, and sex certainly serves to relax tensions. Some owners welcome any children that result as a way of increasing their stock of slaves. It might be hard to find a slave, male or female, over the age of fifteen who wasn't already experienced in the ways of Venus. Was Cornutus saving Chryseis for some special reason? Or did he have other inclinations?

"Did Cornutus sleep with any of his other slave women?"

"Yes, my lord. But for several years Melissa has been his favorite."

So Cornutus was one of those masters who turns his house into his own private brothel. I heard Tacitus' pen scribbling busily in the silence as I pondered my next question.

Chryseis seemed to want to say something else. "You're *not* a magistrate, my lord? Is that what you said?"

"That's right. I'm not. I don't have any official standing here. I'm just trying to keep things under control until the governor arrives." I tried to exude a little extra confidence.

"I see," she said. "Is that all, my lord?"

"Yes, I think so. You've been very helpful, Chryseis. I hope it wasn't too difficult for you, talking about some of these things."

"No, my lord. You've been very kind." She stood and hesitated. "What should I do now?"

I realized she was in what a slave would find a very peculiar situation. Her master was dead. For the first time in her life, there was no one in authority over her, no one to tell her what her next move should be. And yet she wasn't free to decide for herself. For all she knew, she might stand there the rest of the day, waiting to be given a command.

"Why don't you go up to Cornutus' room?" I said, more as a suggestion than an order. "The other slaves are helping the doctor prepare the body for burial. He'll tell you what to do next. His name is Luke."

"Thank you, my lord," she said, with a shy smile. I was glad I was sitting down. I don't think I could have kept my knees under me if I had been standing in the path of that smile. I watched her turn and leave the room and couldn't take my eyes off the doorway even after she was gone.

"And you dare to criticize my taste in women as vulgarian," Tacitus said huffily. "At least I don't pant after somebody else's slave girls. I limit myself to the free ones."

"Can't you see there's something special about her?" I asked. "It's like that scene where Odysseus has difficulty disguising himself as a beggar because his natural nobility shines through the rags."

Tacitus shrugged, still not convinced. "She's pretty, I grant you, though I prefer a little more meat on the bones. I don't like being jabbed by elbows and knees when --"

His critique was interrupted by a woman's scream. We ran out into the main room and found Tacitus' bedmate standing over a crumpled body, lying at the foot of the stairs like a child's discarded doll. From the cascade of golden hair I knew at once that it was Chryseis.

IV

I rushed across the room and knelt over Chryseis. She lay on her side, her head cradled on her left arm, almost as though she were asleep. She was breathing very lightly.

"What happened?" I asked the serving girl. I didn't know her name. I wondered if Tacitus did.

"Androcles told me to clean upstairs," she said. "I just got to the stairs when this one come tumbling down. Like to scared me to death!"

Someone's heavy tread on the stairs caused me to look up as Marcellus turned on the landing and came trotting down the steps.

"Is she all right?" he asked, more out of curiosity than concern.

"I'm not sure. Do you know what happened?"

"She came charging into me on the stairs," Marcellus said. "Wasn't watching where she was going. She knocked me back and I couldn't catch her before she fell. Is she hurt?"

"We'll have to let the doctor determine that," I said. To the serving girl I snapped, "Go get the doctor, Luke. He should be in Cornutus' room. Tell him someone's been injured and we need him down here immediately."

As she scampered away up the stairs I looked Chryseis over superficially, afraid to move her yet. She wasn't bleeding, except for a couple of minor scrapes on her arms and legs. Touching her limbs reverently, I could find no evidence of broken bones. A large bruise, however, was already becoming evident on her forehead. That concerned me.

"Since she is in your capable hands, Gaius Pliny," Marcellus said unctuously, "I am going to attend to some things in town. I should return shortly. Is that the sort of notification you wanted?"

I wondered what kind of business he might have in a town where he'dp had just arrived the night before. More of Regulus' machinations? But I was too concerned about Chryseis to give Marcellus any more thought.

"What happened?" an anxious, unfamiliar voice asked. "Is she badly hurt?"

I looked up to find the German merchant, Marcus Carolus, peering down at us, his hands to his mouth in horror. From the smell of him I gathered that he was returning from tending to his horses. Tacitus retreated across the room to escape the reek of sweat and manure. I guess he'd had all his stomach could take for the morning.

"I don't know for certain," I said. "She's breathing. We've sent for the doctor."

"Can I do something?" he asked in his accented Latin.

"Find a cushion for her head, please." I didn't know if it would do any good, but I wanted him and his shitty smell away from me. He left but was back almost instantaneously with a cushion, still warm from whatever head he had yanked it from under. Given the set of his jaw, I doubt he got any argument.

"Will she be all right?" he asked, placing the cushion under her head and stroking her hair tenderly.

"The doctor will be here in a moment. I'll have to let him answer that."

I hoped Luke could answer the question. My uncle had observed slaves and soldiers who had received severe blows to the head. In one case which he recorded in his notebooks, a man kicked in the head by a horse was in a sleep-like state for twelve days. After he awoke it took several more days before he returned fully to his senses. Even then his power of speech was permanently diminished. In other cases people were unconscious for only a few hours and suffered no ill effects. My uncle could find no consistent pattern or reasonable explanation for the differences.

With enormous relief I saw Luke reach the landing of the stairs and hurry down to where we were. He examined Chryseis much as I had.

"There's not much I can say," he concluded. "She appears to have hit her head as she fell. Perhaps more than once. I don't think any bones are broken. There's nothing we can do except put her in bed and keep watch over her. There may be some bleeding inside."

"But how will we know?" Marcus Carolus asked anxiously.

"I'll be watching for discolorations and swellings. For now we need to get her into a bed. I'd rather not move her upstairs. She needs to be kept as straight as possible and moved as short a distance as possible."

Tacitus fetched Androcles and we asked if there were any rooms on the ground floor of his inn.

"There are several in the back," he informed us, "but they're all occupied."

"Well, get one of them unoccupied immediately," I said.

"Now, just a minute, my lad! This isn't government business. You can't come in here and start throwing my paying customers out because some clumsy slave fell down the stairs."

I hesitated. He was within his rights. If I were on official government business, I could commandeer his entire inn, his livestock, anything I wanted. As it was, all I could do was ask, or offer money.

Suddenly Marcus Carolus grabbed Androcles by the neck of his tunic and jerked him up so hard that the innkeeper's toes barely stayed on the floor. "I will pay for the room," he said, "and I will flatten your ugly face if it isn't ready immediately."

Androcles pulled free and scurried to the back of the inn. "It rents by the hour," he shot over his shoulder. We heard squeals and protests, then a woman who was past her most glamorous days came running by us, with a blanket almost wrapped around her and her clothes in her hand. A man followed at her heels, pulling on his tunic as he trotted past us. So the noble Androcles was running a whore-house on the first floor of his inn.

"Your room is ready," he said sarcastically.

Carolus scooped Chryseis up in his arms and carried her into the suddenly vacant, windowless room, which still reeked of the old whore's perfume. It contained no furnishings except a bed carved out of stone and covered with blankets and pillows, a common feature in *lupinaria* across the empire. Two small lamps illuminated frescoes of couples engaged in acrobatic sex acts. As soon as Chryseis woke up we would have to move her somewhere else, I resolved. Luke insisted that we all leave.

Tacitus was kind enough to find Damon, the most reliable of my slaves, whom I placed on guard in front of the door. I told him he was not to leave the door until he was relieved. Nor was he to let anyone but me, Tacitus, and Luke enter the room. Under pain of death. Since I never threaten my slaves with such dire consequences, the man realized I was entirely serious.

"Why the guard at her door?" Tacitus asked.

"I find it peculiar that Cornutus is brutally murdered and a few hours later one of his slaves just happens to fall down the stairs," I replied. "And Marcellus is close at hand in both cases."

"Then why don't you put guards on all Cornutus' other slaves? Aren't you afraid something will happen to them? Or are they not blond enough for you?" For those questions I had no ready answer.

I was about to go upstairs and take care of some of my own personal needs when one of Cornutus' slaves brought me a cloth bag.

"Chryseis keeps her things in this, my lord. I thought it ought to stay with her."

He was a young fellow, perhaps the one Chryseis said she liked. But Cornutus must own dozens of young male slaves. No reason for my instant dislike of him.

I took the drawstring bag into Chryseis' room, where Luke was examining her with her gown pulled up under her arms. I turned my head to avoid taking advantage of her, even if only with my eyes. As I started to put her bag down by the bed curiosity got the better of me, as it usually does. I pulled it open and began to look through it. It contained two other dresses, another pair of sandals, and a couple of pieces of glass-and-paste jewelry – things which could be found in any female slave's baggage. At the bottom, though, I came upon a leather pouch sealed with Cornutus' horn seal, the sort of bag one would seal up a document in.

"Now, why," I said aloud without meaning to, "would she be carrying a sealed document?"

Luke glanced up from his examination. "Might it be something she stole?"

I quickly dismissed that possibility. "It wouldn't make any sense for her to steal something like this and then carry it around where it could be found so easily."

"Do you want to open it?" Luke asked.

I fleetingly considered breaking the seal and opening the document, but decided I could not violate Chryseis' confidence by looking at this any more than I could violate her by looking at her when she was unconscious.

"When she wakes up, I'll ask her about it. If I can't get a reasonable explanation from her of what the document is and where she got it, it might be necessary to open it."

"That would be better done in the presence of someone with official status," Luke said.

"That's true." But could I hold everything together until the governor arrived?

* * * *

By now it was approaching noon and I had yet to complete my usual morning ablutions. I found the slave who served as my personal attendant and had him shave me. I longed for a bath to wash away the stench of slaughter, but this early in the day the women would still be using the bath houses, so I had to content myself with washing off in my room and putting on a fresh tunic. Our enforced stopover in Smyrna would enable us to get clothes laundered better than we could while traveling. We started out nearly every day with wet garments hanging over the sides of the wagons. Even as they dried they picked up a coating of dust.

As I left my room I had to stand aside to allow three of Cornutus' slaves to carry his body down the stairs. Glancing from one face to another, I tried to discern any signs of guilt or pleasure in his death. All I could read was fear.

Feeling somewhat refreshed, I returned to Chryseis' room. Marcus Carolus was standing outside the door, looming over poor Damon, who was holding his ground only because of the threat I had given him earlier.

"This gentleman wants to go in, my lord. I told him you had given orders that no one was to be admitted."

"I am paying for the room!" Marcus Carolus rumbled.

The man puzzled me. He stood a full head taller than I, with that yellow hair which so many Roman women envy. They resort to dyes or wigs made from the hair of Teutonic captives to achieve what nature only rarely bestows on Mediterranean peoples. Marcus Carolus' hair bore no hints of gray, so I figured him to be less than forty. He was broad and muscular, and I don't think I had seen him smile in the entire time we'd been traveling together. It was a band of such men who wiped out Varus and his three legions in the Teutoburg Forest. Standing as close as I had ever been to an angry German, I could imagine what fear must have welled up in the hearts of those doomed Roman soldiers, surrounded, cut off, with the noose tightening around them.

And yet Marcus Carolus had shown an almost paternal tenderness when he put the cushion under Chryseis' head and brushed her hair back out of her face. And he was paying for her room. Why?

"I appreciate your generosity, Marcus Carolus," I said. "But it would be better if Chryseis not be disturbed right now. There's nothing any of us can do for her but wait."

"I want to know that she is getting good care," he said stubbornly.

"Is the doctor with her?" I asked my slave.

"Yes, my lord."

"Then she is getting good care," I said to Marcus Carolus. "Better than anything you or I can do for her. It's noon. Why don't we get something to eat? After that we'll check on her. Maybe the doctor will have some word for us by then."

He grudgingly allowed me to take his elbow and steer him toward the dining room. Apparently he had also taken the opportunity to wash. The stable smells had been replaced by an odd, though not unpleasant, scent. We ran into Tacitus as we reached the door, so he joined us. A few people were trickling in for something to eat at the end of their work day and before the midday rest. The way the day was warming up, it would feel good to lie down for a while.

"We've not had much opportunity to talk on this trip," I said to the big German as the three of us found a table in the corner. "I don't know much about you."

"What do you want to know?" His question was more of a challenge.

The question stumped me for a moment. I actually didn't know what I was hoping to learn from talking with him. I just wanted to open a box and rummage around inside until I found something interesting.

"Did you kill Lucius Cornutus?" Tacitus asked impulsively.

Marcus Carolus laughed; I was relieved to know that he could. "The famous Roman wit," he said. "Before this trip I never met Cornutus. In recent days we spoke only briefly."

"And yet you were very solicitous about one of his slaves," I said.

"Her mother was German. She spoke to me during one of our rest stops one day. She's such a sweet girl. She asked Cornutus if she could ride in my wagon so I could tell her about Germany. He agreed once but changed his mind the next time she asked." He leaned back to allow a serving girl room to put bowls of some sort of stew and cups of wine before us.

"Where are you from?" I asked. "How did you come into Roman territory?" And why did you concoct that ridiculous name for yourself? I wanted to ask.

"My family lived north of your Colonia Agrippina, on the lower part of the Rhine. My father traded with the Romans in a small way, and I built up that business. Eventually I moved to Rome itself. For fifteen years now I have been traveling the empire, trading mostly in herbs and spices."

"You're also carrying cloth from India, aren't you?" Tacitus asked.

"Silk, yes. It comes originally from even farther east, from China."

"It must bring a handsome profit," I said.

"As handsome as Adonis. I plan to sell my business after this trip and return to Germany."

"Haven't you fallen under the city's sway?" I asked. Most people who live in Rome, even for a short time, find it too exciting and alluring a place to leave. For all of us 'The City' means only Rome.

"No," Marcus Carolus snorted. "I have endured that stinking sewer of humanity for far too long. Now I have done what I set out to do and I'm a rich man, so I am going home."

Our conversation was cut short as Marcellus swept in with several slaves in his wake. Roman aristocrats don't venture into the streets without a throng of their dependents to clear the sidewalks. Lacking dependents of free status on this trip, Marcellus was making do with his slaves. Like many aristocrats, he dressed his servants better than most free men could afford to dress themselves, as a mark of his own wealth.

"Pliny, there you are," Marcellus said, in the tone of voice that Roman aristocrats use when addressing a servant or a shopkeeper.

"What can I do for you, Marcellus?" I said, standing at my table.

"We need to notify Cornutus' father of his death," Marcellus said, drawing his toga around him in his best formal stance. "Since you've assumed control of this matter, it seems, have you thought of that?"

"I haven't yet taken care of it," I said, mainly because it hadn't even occurred to me until he mentioned it. I'd been so single-mindedly focused on the murder.

"I've learned there is a boat sailing for Rome tomorrow," Marcellus said smugly. "That is, if you'll allow it to leave. We can send word then, under your seal, I suppose. It's most unfortunate that we have to deliver such shocking news to a man already in failing health."

"Thank you for reminding me of this," I said, as though we had finished our business.

Marcellus didn't take the hint. "I also want to send a letter to Regulus, reporting on the outcome of the business I've been conducting for him. Do I need your permission?"

"Are you planning to send the letter by the ship's captain?"

"Certainly not. I'll have one of my slaves carry it. He could also carry your letter to Cornutus' father."

He was offering me a direct challenge. I didn't want anyone to leave Smyrna, but it was essential to notify Cornutus' father. If I didn't take advantage of this boat's sailing, it could be days before another left for Rome. The old man might be dead by then. If I refused to let one of Marcellus' slaves leave, it would be an accusation of Marcellus. But what if one of his slaves had killed Cornutus, or helped Marcellus do it? I could be letting the culprit, or an important witness, go scot free.

"I can't let anyone leave who hasn't been interrogated," I finally said. "Send me the slave you intend to dispatch to Rome, and I'll talk with him."

"That will have to do, I suppose," Marcellus said, turning away. "I'll send the fellow down shortly."

"Before you go, Marcellus, I'd like to ask you a few more questions about Chryseis' fall on the stairs. You said she ran into you – "

"By the gods, man! Why are you making such a fuss over that girl? She's clumsy as a new-born colt. Everyone knows that. We all saw her stumble at lunch yesterday and drench Cornutus with the wine. Those stairs are narrow and dark. Anyone not familiar with them could easily miss a step. I barely managed to keep my own balance after she barreled into me."

"Was there anyone with you? One of your slaves?"

"I have no more patience with your badgering. If you're accusing me of any crime, come right out and say so."

I ran my hand over the edge of the table nervously. Nothing I had uncovered so far would convict Marcellus of anything. He had dinner with Cornutus and was one of the last two people to see him alive. He'd been on the stairs when Chryseis fell. He could be guilty of nothing more than being in the wrong place at the wrong time.

"I have a letter to write," Marcellus finally said in disgust and led his servile entourage out of the room.

* * * *

Carolus thanked us for lunch – though I hadn't realized I was paying – and left. As I forced myself to swallow a few bites of the stew, one of the members of our caravan approached the table. He clearly intended to speak to me, and I had to think for a moment to get all the syllables of his name in the right order. It was Orophernes, one of the two-man delegation from somewhere east of Antioch.

"My lord, pardon the intrusion during your meal."

"It's quite all right," I said amicably, though I did not attempt to pronounce his name or offer him a seat.

"We were wondering, Rhascuporis and I, if you know how long we're going to be delayed here. You see . . . well, our financial resources are somewhat limited. We hadn't counted on a long stay in an inn."

"I'm afraid I can't say with any certainty. It will be six or seven days at least. Beyond that, it all depends on how quickly we can find Cornutus' killer."

"Oh, my! As long as that?" He appeared to be doing calculations in his head.

"You might shorten the time if you could tell us anything that would help us find the killer."

His eyes widened, as though he thought I was accusing him. "My lord, I know nothing of this matter."

"Have you observed any animosity between Cornutus and other members of our caravan?"

"No, my lord." The poor fellow was fairly quaking. "Rhascuporis and I had little contact with Cornutus. He was such a brusque man, I don't think anyone in our troupe had any love for him. But I saw no open hostility."

"Did you notice anything unusual at dinner last night? Did anyone – of our people or of the locals in the inn – have a run-in with Cornutus, or seem abnormally interested in his activities?"

"Early in the evening, before Marcellus joined him, he was gambling with Saturninus and a few local men. Cornutus won most of the money, it appeared. The other men weren't happy about that. But I saw nothing out of the ordinary, my lord. Nothing at all."

"Do you know their names?"

"No, my lord. But Androcles might. Or Tiberius Saturninus over there." He pointed across the dining room to where Saturninus sat hunched over a bowl of the same stew we were eating.

"All right. If you or your friend should recall anything, please let me know at once. Any little bit of information could be helpful."

"Yes, we will, my lord. Thank you." He made a sweeping bow in the eastern fashion, with one arm folded across his chest and his knees bent, as though I were some sort of monarch. "If I may be so bold, my lord, may I ask whether there would be any financial remuneration for such information? I know it's the custom in Rome to reward people who provide such a service."

"Informers, you mean. Or spies."

"Oh, sir, such indelicate terms." He turned his head away as though I had waved something offensive under his nose.

"But such accurate ones. Yes, I will see to it that your service is gainful."

"Thank you, my lord." He backed away from the table, bowing and sweeping as he went.

"So, you've just hired your first spy," Tacitus said. "Or is he your first?"

"Yes, he is. And I have very mixed feelings about doing it. In order to fight Marcellus, do I have to become like Marcellus?"

"Our army couldn't adapt to fighting the Germans, and look what happened to Varus and his legions. Wiped out to the last man. If Marcellus is as dangerous and devious as you claim, you'll need all the help you can muster."

I shook my head. "I doubt this fellow's going to find out anything really useful, but he seems to need the money. Who knows? He may glean one key piece of information. At the least, he'll be a pair of eyes in places where we aren't."

We had barely resumed our meal when Luke and the man traveling with him came into the dining room. Luke approached our table. The other man hung back.

"Doctor," I said eagerly, "how is Chryseis?"

"She's still asleep. I can find no sign of internal bleeding, no discoloration or puffiness. The young are more flexible. They usually survive something like this much better than someone my age. Your slave is guarding the door faithfully. I'll check on her later." He hesitated.

"Is there something else?" I asked.

"I thought I should tell you that she has a mark on her left buttock, a brand."

"Yes, she told us. A ram's horn."

Luke nodded. "I found it peculiar and didn't know what to make of it."

"How large is it?" Tacitus asked. I wasn't sure whether he was asking about the brand or her buttock.

"Slightly smaller than my thumb," Luke replied, holding up his right hand with that digit extended, "but quite distinct. I've never seen a slave marked in such fashion."

"Unfortunately," I said, "Cornutus is the only one who could explain what he intended by it. Are you gentlemen ready for some lunch?" I wanted to change the subject. There were too many ears around and we were conversing in Greek.

"We're on our way to the house of Apelles," Luke said, "to pay our respects to his family and to extend condolences on behalf of friends from Ephesus. This is my friend, Timothy." He beckoned for the other man to step up beside him. Timothy did so reluctantly and acknowledged Luke's introductions of Tacitus and me. He was a tall, slender man, with a slightly nervous air about him, like a man who knows it's just a matter of time before he's called to account for something he's done.

"When is the funeral?" I asked.

"Tomorrow morning," Timothy said.

"I suppose we ought to attend," I said, "as representatives of Rome. The man was a magistrate of one of our provincial cities." Tacitus nodded without enthusiasm. Standing through a funeral eulogy is bad enough if you know the deceased and if the eulogy is being given by a competent orator. A stranger's eulogy delivered by some provincial youngster was not an enticing prospect.

"I'm sure the family would be honored," Timothy said somewhat sourly.

He and Luke turned to leave but were stopped by the sound of a dish crashing to the floor on the other side of the dining room. A man's voice bellowed, "It's swill! Your own pigs wouldn't eat it."

We turned to see Tiberius Saturninus getting up from a corner table. A serving girl was scooping up his bowl and the remains of his meal.

"I'll get Androcles," the girl said.

"Don't bother," Saturninus said with a scowl.

"It's no bother," Androcles said, hustling up to block Saturninus' exit from the dining room. "What is a nuisance is your constant complaints about our food and service."

"I have every right to complain. This is one of the filthiest inns I've ever stayed in, and this lunch today was rotten. Literally rotten."

"That didn't stop you from eating over half of it." Androcles stood chest-to-chest with Saturninus.

"It took me that long to dig under all the sauce and find out how bad the meat really was." He tried to step around Androcles, but the little innkeeper sidled along with him.

"You have not yet paid so much as a sestertius on your bill, sir. Everyone else in your party has paid something."

"I can't tend to that right now," Saturninus said. "That meal is making me sick." His cheeks swelled up like a man about to vomit, and he pushed Androcles aside and ran out of the dining room.

"You'll find the full charge for this meal on your bill!" Androcles yelled after him. "And I want something paid on the account by tonight."

Then he noticed us watching the little drama. "You see, gentlemen, what an honest businessman has to endure. Deadbeats like that take advantage of us, smash up our crockery. I've a good mind to turn him out on the street this very day."

Luke reached into his purse and took out three coins, tetradrachmas from what I could see as he slipped them into Androcles' dirty hand. "That should cover his expenses for a few days at least."

Androcles' hand quickly snapped shut around the coins, like a trap on an animal's foot, and he bowed slightly. "Thank you kindly, sir. That's most generous."

"Not at all," Luke said. "I'm sure Saturninus will pay me back."

"Hah!" Androcles snorted. "He's borrowed money from almost everybody who comes in here. He acts like a beggar on the street, with his hand always out. Then he gambles every bit of it away."

Timothy and Luke exchanged a look and Timothy rolled his eyes upward.

V

Before everyone settled down for the
midday rest I called all of Cornutus' slaves together in the small dining
room. Besides Chryseis, the group consisted of five men and two women.
I told them they were not to leave the inn under any circumstances. I
would take them under my protection and wouldn't allow anything to
happen to them. In return they would have to accept my authority for
the time being. They agreed and seemed relieved to have someone in
control again. I don't believe, like Aristotle, that some people are servile
by nature, but I have observed that people who've been slaves for a
long time are uncomfortable when they don't know who's responsible
for them. Some of the slaves whom my uncle freed to celebrate his
fiftieth birthday were reluctant to accept the gift. Like many emancipated slaves, they remained in their former master's household as freedmen, doing the same tasks.

Dismissing the rest of the slaves, I asked the big-eared fellow
and Melissa, Cornutus' favorite bedmate, to remain behind. The woman
seemed to regard me with a hint of hatred or contempt in her eye. I
knew no cause for her to have such feelings about me. Big-ears was
named Phrixus. Tacitus didn't have any papyrus handy, but our two
memories together would suffice, I thought. Tacitus sat at the table
while I stood beside it.

"You helped Marcellus carry Cornutus upstairs last night, didn't
you?" I asked Phrixus.

"Yes, my lord. It's my responsibility as my master's personal attendant." He appeared very nervous. I hoped that would make him more talkative. I paced back and forth in front of him, stopping now and then and fixing him with a hard stare. My uncle often used that tactic to unnerve a slave or soldier who was being dressed down.

"How was he feeling when you put him to bed?"

Phrixus looked at the floor and rubbed his hands together anxiously. "I was worried, my lord. I had never seen my master so completely drunk. He's a large man and holds his wine pretty well. Last night he was having trouble moving his legs and couldn't talk clearly."

"He was trying to talk? Could you make out any of it?"

"He said something about being cold."

"In this weather?"

"I thought it odd, too, my lord. I wanted to stay with him, but Marcellus said he would be all right. The wine they'd been drinking – the stuff Marcellus brought – was particularly strong, he said. Let him sleep and he would be fine in the morning."

This bit of information raised my eyebrows. "They were drinking wine that Marcellus brought with him?"

"They drank the inn's wine for a while, my lord, but then Marcellus sent one of his servants to get a special wineskin from his own stores. He said he wanted to toast his new friend with an especially fine vintage."

"A wineskin, you say? Not an amphora?"

"That's right, my lord. A wineskin with Marcellus' seal on it. He said he sealed it up to keep his slaves from getting into it."

"Now think carefully, Phrixus. What did Marcellus do when he got this wineskin?"

The man looked at me quizzically, unable to see where my line of questioning was leading. "Just what you'd expect, my lord. He broke the seal, poured some for himself and my master, and they drank."

"You're certain that they both drank?" That wasn't what I'd expected to hear. If Marcellus poisoned Cornutus with the wine, how could he have drunk it himself? "How much?"

"My master drank two cups, Marcellus only one, I believe."

"Did Marcellus offer Cornutus a second cup?"

"No, my lord. My master praised the wine and asked for more."

His answers didn't fit the theory I was working to prove. It's a nuisance when a structure you're trying to build doesn't fit the terrain. I might have to restructure my theory about Cornutus being poisoned if the landscape continued to pose these kinds of problems. "What did Marcellus do then?"

"Nothing, my lord. What do you mean?"

"Did he stay at the table? Or did he go out, perhaps to the latrine?" One trick a poisoner can use is to ingest a slow-acting poison along with the victim, then go to the latrine and force himself to vomit.

"No, my lord. He stayed at the table until we carried my master upstairs."

Melissa, silent to that point, raised her hand to her lips. "He sealed the wineskin back up. Remember, he made a fuss about not wanting his servants to get into it."

"But there was nothing about his behavior that you would call odd or unusual?"

"No, my lord," Phrixus said, and Melissa shook her head in agreement.

Tacitus put an oar in. "Did Marcellus send any of his servants to the kitchen during the evening, to prepare anything special, or to help out?"

"No, my lord," Phrixus replied.

That line of questioning appeared to have petered out, after such a promising start. "What happened next? All of Cornutus' slaves were locked up for the night, weren't you?"

"Yes, my lord," Phrixus said. "As you know, on this trip whenever space can be found, he locks us up at night. He's a harsh man and doesn't trust us, I'm afraid."

"Did he have reason not to trust you?" I asked quickly.

Phrixus' eyes expanded to match his ears. "Oh, no, my lord! None of us would raise a hand against him. Or against any other master. It's just his nature. He won't have anyone with him at night except Melissa here."

Reality hadn't set in for the poor fellow yet. He was still speaking of Cornutus in the present tense.

I turned my attention to the woman. She was about thirty, with sleek black hair done in a tight bun low on the back of her head, lustrous dark eyes, and an olive complexion. Eastern in origin, of medium height, an attractive woman rather than a raving beauty. Her face evinced more confidence than Phrixus'.

"And you spent every night with your master?" I asked.

"Yes, my lord. Every night." Her voice was warm, throaty. Even with my limited experience in such things, I could imagine its effect on a man as she whispered and moaned softly in the dark beside him. From the way Tacitus sat up and leaned forward I could tell that he was having the same reaction.

"How long were you his favorite?"

"Since he purchased me, five years ago."

"How did you become a slave?" Tacitus interjected.

"My sister and I were taken captive during the war of the Jews against Rome."

"But your name is Greek. The honeybee."

"It means the same as my Hebrew name, Deborah."

"All right," I said. "Last night – "

"What town are you from?" Tacitus asked. It was the question I hadn't wanted raised.

"Emmaus. It's a day's journey west of Jerusalem."

"What a coincidence," Tacitus said, turning to me. "Isn't that where your uncle served with Titus in the war?"

"I believe he served on Titus' staff at some point." I didn't want this conversation to go any further. "That was shortly before he returned to Rome to become praetor."

Melissa's breathing quickened. "He wasn't just on someone's staff, my lord. He commanded the legion that sacked Emmaus . . . the legion that killed my mother and brother. He gave me to one of his subordinates and my sister to another. We were marched through the streets of Rome in chains in Titus' triumphal parade."

Her sharp tone bordered on impertinence. Phrixus took her arm, fear showing in his bulging eyes and quivering mouth. "That's enough, Melissa."

I studied Melissa, her chest heaving in anger. Justifiable anger, I suppose. She hadn't started the Jews' war against Rome, and yet she had lost everything because of it. And my uncle and his troops were the most visible cause of that tragedy, for her.

"War, by its very nature, is devastating," I said. "Not everyone who fights takes pleasure in it. My uncle never talked about his military experience. I know he found no gratification in inflicting suffering on anyone."

She jerked away from Phrixus. "Your uncle – "

"Melissa, no more!" Phrixus stepped in front of her.

"There's no point in talking about this," I said. "We can't change the past. What we're trying to do right now is find out who killed Cornutus. You need to put aside your hatred of me and my family and focus on the events of last night. If you can't do that, I'll have you locked up again. This time in a room without a window."

That last remark took the fight out of her. Anger still twisted the corners of her mouth, but she stood silent, like a horse that has finally accepted the bit. Slaves and horses – they both have to be broken to be useful. But you don't want to crush the spirit entirely.

"Now," I said. "Did you expect to spend last night with Cornutus?"

"Certainly, my lord. I was his wife in all but name."

Ownership of Jewish women had been a kind of craze among the Roman aristocracy for a few years, just as certain kinds of exotic dogs enjoy popularity from time to time. The late emperor Titus started the rage when he brought back Berenice, sister of the Jewish king Agrippa, to be his mistress. Our current emperor, Domitian, dislikes the Jews, so the fad of Jewish mistresses has gone into a sharp decline. Cornutus must have felt some genuine affection for this woman if she still enjoyed such status in his house.

"Why didn't you stay with him?"

"After Marcellus and Phrixus put my master to bed, Marcellus reminded the innkeeper that we were supposed to be confined for the night. Phrixus told the innkeeper that I was supposed to be in the master's room. The innkeeper said he had no such instructions. Marcellus said my master would not be needing my services anyway, so I was locked up with the other slave women." The disapproving tone of her voice and the lift of her chin made it clear she considered that an indignity which she should not have to suffer.

"But you didn't actually stay in the room, did you?"

She hesitated at first. "No, my lord. Phoebe and I were able to climb out through the window and sit on the roof. We were desperate for some relief from the heat."

"Did Chryseis get out of the room during the night?"

"I don't believe so, my lord. At least not while I was awake."

"Has she ever said anything to you about being afraid of high places?"

"I've never heard her mention that, my lord."

* * * *

We dismissed the two slaves with a stern reminder not to leave the inn. I would check on them in the evening and make arrangements about their accommodations. It seemed unfair that they should have to sleep under lock and key for the entire time we were stalled in Smyrna.

"That little Honeybee can sample my pollen any time," Tacitus sighed when Melissa was out of earshot.

I tried not to smile at his vulgar witticism. One shouldn't encourage that sort of thing. Instead I said, "Doesn't it strike you as convenient that Cornutus was cut off from his slaves, including his regular bedmate, on the night he happened to have been murdered? And that Marcellus was responsible for isolating him?"

"Actually it was the innkeeper who refused to let Melissa go to Cornutus' room," Tacitus pointed out.

"But Marcellus backed him up."

Tacitus sighed and ran his fingers through his hair, his most evident signs of impatience. "Pliny, why are you so determined to implicate Marcellus in Cornutus' murder? He just met the man two days ago. There wasn't a cross word exchanged between them. They bathed and had dinner together quite amicably yesterday. What reason would Marcellus have for killing Cornutus?"

"I don't think Marcellus has any reason of his own to kill Cornutus. But Marcellus is Regulus' lap dog. He will bite whomever Regulus commands him to. The question you should be asking is, What reason would Regulus have to kill Cornutus?"

"A more pertinent question," Tacitus said sharply, "might be, What has Regulus ever done to you to make you hate him so much?"

"There is an answer to that question, but you can't have it just yet. I'm going to check on Chryseis and then get some rest. I'll be most eager to get to the bath this afternoon."

"On that we agree," Tacitus said, clapping me on the shoulder. "I can still smell poor old Cornutus in this tunic, in my very pores. And you stink like something out of a slaughterhouse. Marcus Carolus smelled better after rolling around in the stable."

His mention of that word gave me an idea. "As long as we haven't cleaned up yet, why don't we go out to the stable and look around at the wagons of our fellow caravan members."

He looked horrified. "You mean poke around in other people's things? What on earth for?"

"Somebody has a knife hidden somewhere. And somebody has a drug of some sort hidden somewhere. And we still don't know where Cornutus' heart is."

"Do you honestly think the person who mutilated him would keep his heart stashed among his own personal belongings?"

"We won't know until we look, will we?"

Tacitus held his hands up, palms out, as though pushing me away. "You'll have to do that without me. We have no legal standing here. If someone found you going through their things, they could get very upset. And we already know that somebody around here won't hesitate to act when they get angry." He turned toward the stairs.

"I think it's worth the risk," I said to his back and turned toward the door that led to the rear of the inn.

* * * *

The stable was dim, quiet except for soft whinnies and the rustle of horses in the straw. Located on the west side of the inn and in its shadow, it was still cool inside. The travelers' wagons were lined up two by two at one end. I decided to start with the first one and work my way back.

The first wagon I looked through, I concluded, was Luke and Timothy's. I gave it only a cursory glance because I was convinced that neither of them had killed Cornutus. They were carrying no more clothing than you would expect of two men. Two of their chests contained scrolls and individual pieces of papyrus written in Greek. The document on top was a letter from someone named Paul to a man named Philemon, asking him to take back a runaway slave. Nothing extraordinary in that. I've written similar notes myself.

What did strike me as odd about the letter was the way Paul referred to himself as a 'prisoner' and the frequent mentions of 'Christ.' At the end of the letter Paul mentioned several 'fellow-workers', one of whom was Luke. Could this mean Luke and Timothy were members of the group called Christians? Other than the name and its unsavory reputation, I knew nothing about this cult. Perhaps I'd better keep a closer eye on these two.

I had just stepped over into the next wagon and opened another chest when a sharp voice said, "What do you think you're doing?"

I looked up to see Gaius Sempronius storming toward me.

"Get out of my wagon!" he said, doubling up his fist.

"There's no reason to be angry, Sempronius," I said, still standing in the wagon, but he would not be mollified.

"Get out of there!" he ordered again. As I started to comply and had one leg over the side of the wagon, he grabbed my ankle and pulled. I lost my balance and fell heavily on the ground. He pounced on me, his anger fully aroused. With his weight and height advantage he was able to pin me to the ground. He sat on my chest, pinning my arms with his knees, and punched me in the face. "What are you doing in there?" he demanded, adding a punch for emphasis.

"Looking for a murder weapon." I could taste blood running in the corner of my mouth.

"Do you think *I* killed Cornutus?"

"If you have nothing to hide, why object to someone looking through your wagon? I intend to search everyone's." I hoped that would reassure him. It didn't.

"Not mine, you won't," he said through clenched teeth. "If it's a knife you're looking for, I'll show you mine."

He reached into the bosom of his tunic and pulled out a knife. He must have been wearing it strapped around his chest. He waved it under my nose.

"This what you're looking for, you nosy young pup? Shall we test it?" He grabbed my hair and yanked my head back, exposing my throat. With the blade of the knife pressing against it, he said, "There's no one around. One quick flick of my wrist and it's done. I won't be the only one glad to see the last of you."

I believe he would have killed me at that moment if a piece of rope hadn't suddenly slipped around his throat and jerked him back off of me, lifting him up and slamming him against one of the wagons. Tacitus, who had a firm grip on the other end of the rope in the wagon, yelled, "Drop the knife, Sempronius, or I'll choke the life out of you!"

With his free hand Sempronius, gasping and wheezing, tried for an instant to loosen the noose. Unable to do it, he dropped the knife, which I scrambled to pick up. The rope went slack and Sempronius collapsed against the wheel of the wagon.

Tacitus vaulted over the side of the wagon to land beside me, with the end of the rope still in his hand. He tossed it over an exposed beam and yanked it tight, causing Sempronius to clutch at the noose. "Are you all right?" he asked me.

I didn't take my eyes off Sempronius. At least the one eye I could see out of. "Yes, I'm fine. What are you doing here? I thought you were going up to your room."

"I did, but it was intolerably hot, so I came down to get something to drink. I saw Sempronius going out toward the stable and thought he might object to you poking around in his wagon. I sneaked in behind him, in case you needed some help."

We turned our full attention to Sempronius. "You just tried to kill me, Sempronius," I said. "What are you trying to cover up?"

"Nothing!" He tried to remove the noose, but Tacitus tugged on it. "I wasn't going to kill you. I was just going to scare you, teach you a bit of a lesson, you high and mighty little bastard."

"Don't take that personally," Tacitus said.

On one level I didn't take it personally. Sempronius came from an ancient noble family from the city of Rome itself, but one that had fallen on hard times in the last couple of generations. His wasn't the only one. Some members of those families resented the prosperity of families like mine and Cornutus', from other Italian cities or the provinces. We were originally lower in social standing but are now rising in wealth and prestige.

"Did you think Cornutus was high and mighty, too, Sempronius?" I asked. "Did you decide to teach him a lesson?"

"What kind of nonsense is that?" he rasped. "I don't have any reason to kill Cornutus. Saturninus is the one you ought to be talking to."

"Why would Saturninus want to kill him?" Tacitus asked.

"Gambling debts. Saturninus has crippling gambling debts to Cornutus. He's so broke that I'm paying all the expenses for our trip home."

"Why would you do that?"

"He's married to my sister. I made him sign over his house to me, so she'll at least have a roof over her head. Saturninus keeps losing, but he keeps playing. Begging to play, in fact. Thinks he'll win it all back on one lucky throw. But it's Cornutus who has the uncanny luck."

"It ran out on him last night," I said somberly. "And I wonder if this knife could have made the wound in his chest? I'm going to let Doctor Luke have a look at it before I give it back to you. Now you can go."

Before releasing the rope, Tacitus said, "I have one question, while we have your attention, Sempronius." He jerked on the rope and raised the gasping Sempronius almost off the ground. "What did Cornutus mean by that comment at dinner last night: 'If she were my daughter...'?"

Sempronius' lip curled. "I happen to like little girls. A few years ago I offered to buy Chryseis, before she got all grown up. Cornutus told me to climb back under my rock. He said he would sell anything else he owned but not Chryseis."

* * * *

After dismissing Sempronius, Tacitus and I hastily looked through the other wagons but found nothing we could identify as suspicious. The witches' garishly painted black wagon was empty. That in itself struck me as suspicious. When we went back into the inn I decided to check on Chryseis before going up to my room. The sight of my slave Damon sitting in his chair, on guard in front of Chryseis' door, reassured me. Damon was an intelligent, conscientious man, only a few years my senior. With him on guard, Chryseis, at least, was safe. At our approach Damon sprang up, opened the door and stood aside for me to enter.

The little room was warm, musty, and dark. The lamp had burned itself out, so the only light coming into the room was from the hallway. Scant though it was, it was enough to show that the bed was empty. Chryseis was gone.

VI

I glared at Damon. The pain in my left eye and cheek fed my anger. Before I could begin asking questions, the poor wretch began answering them.

"My lord, I don't know what could have happened! I was right here at the door, except for a very brief trip to the latrine."

I exploded. "You left your post? I threatened you with death if you left this door unguarded." I smacked him across the face with the back of my hand. Though I have ordered beatings for recalcitrant slaves on occasion, this was the first time I had ever hit a slave myself, and I immediately regretted it. I had demeaned myself as much as him.

Damon put his hand to the spot where my blow had landed, as though he had to touch it to believe it was real. "But, my lord, I urgently needed to piss, and there was no one around. It took me hardly any time. I swear it!"

"What did you see when you returned?" I put my hands on my hips, to keep myself from striking him again. Right now it was more important to get information than to inflict punishment.

"My chair was sitting in front of the door, just the way it was when I left."

"Did you look in the room to see if the girl was all right?'"

"No, my lord. Everything looked fine. I just sat back down."

"How long ago did this happen?"

"Within the hour, my lord. It's hard to reckon time in here. I can't see the sun."

What a quandary! I regarded this man as one of my most reliable servants. That was why I had brought him with me on this trip and why I had chosen him for this particular job. I had threatened him with death if he left his post. My uncle once told me never to threaten a slave with any punishment which you don't actually mean to inflict. If you don't carry through, you weaken your control over that slave and all your other slaves, for they do gossip and spread stories among themselves.

"I'll deal with the matter of your punishment later," I said, leaving him room to imagine his own terror. "Right now there's a more pressing problem. Get me a lamp."

Damon scurried away and returned quickly with a lamp. I took it from him and Tacitus and I entered the dark, dreary room. The erotic paintings couldn't overcome the gloom of the place. They didn't put me in any mood for the activities they depicted.

"Not much to see, is there?" Tacitus commented, his attention diverted by the artwork.

"Not unless we look closely," I replied, scanning the room desperately. "For instance, the bedcover appears to have been turned back neatly, not thrown back violently or hastily."

"Is that significant?" Tacitus asked.

"It could be." I grew more encouraged as I thought about it. "Think about how people get out of bed. If someone came in and grabbed her while she was sleeping, I don't believe the cover would have been turned back so neatly. Someone in a hurry to get her out of here would have yanked the cover out of the way. Perhaps wrapped her up in it."

Tacitus nodded dubiously, like one of Socrates' students in a Platonic dialogue, as yet unconvinced but willing to be shown the light.

"On the other hand," I continued, "if Chryseis awoke, frightened in the dark, unsure where she was, she probably would have pushed the cover back like this and gotten up quietly. So I would conclude that it's likely she might have left of her own volition."

"But how? The door opens outward, and your slave had his chair up against it."

"Except for the time when he was in the latrine. Let's try something. Damon!" He jumped when I called his name. "Close the door, put your chair up against it, and sit down."

Damon did as I ordered. I knew he would be most eager to obey in the future, if I let him have a future. When he was seated, Tacitus and I sat down on the bed.

"Imagine yourself waking up," I said. "The room is pitch black.

You have no idea where you are, or why you're here. The only light you see comes under the bottom of the door. Wouldn't your natural reaction be to go to the door and give it a push?"

"I think so," Tacitus said. He sounded as if he was nodding. "But wouldn't Damon feel someone pushing against the door?"

"This is a frightened fifteen-year-old girl pushing. I think she would give up at the slightest resistance. The door won't open, so you sit back down on the bed, wondering what to do."

"I would call out," Tacitus said. "Maybe knock on the door. Ask who's there."

"You might, being a free man and accustomed to having your way. Chryseis has been a slave since birth. She's never challenged or questioned anything. You saw how passive she was when we questioned her. At the end she would have stood there all day if I hadn't told her where to go and what to do."

"All right. Granted," Tacitus finally said.

"So, after a few minutes you hear a chair scraping," I said, "as someone gets up, then footsteps fading away. Damon, get up! Now you try the door again. This time it opens."

I opened the door and stuck my head out, looking around like a cautious turtle.

"This is your chance to get out, so you take advantage of it." We squeezed through the slightly opened door, closed it, and put the chair back against it.

"That all makes sense," Tacitus said as we re-opened the door.

"I'm also encouraged that her bag is gone," I said. "Would a kidnapper have bothered to pick it up?"

"Would she even have found it in the dark?"

It took me a moment to reconstruct my actions from earlier in the afternoon. "I'm almost certain that I dropped it right by the bed. She must have stepped on it when she got up."

"But why did she leave?" Tacitus asked.

"That's the difficult question. And it's one thing that makes me worry that someone might have carried her off by force. She had no reason to leave."

"Unless she killed Cornutus. But, I know, you don't think your little goddess is capable of such a thing." He raised a hand to forestall my objections.

"It's also possible she wasn't in her right mind. In his notebooks my uncle recorded his observation that people who receive blows to the head are sometimes addled, not knowing clearly where they are or even who they are."

"Let me see if I understand all of this." Sarcasm built in Tacitus' tone. "We have a slave girl on the loose, who may not know she's a slave, and who may be a murderer but may not know it. Is that an accurate summary?"

"I'm afraid so."

"And you're going to look for her, aren't you?"

"What choice do I have?"

"Several, actually. She's not likely to try to travel in this heat. If she does, we'll find her wherever she drops. More likely she's hiding. I don't think she would risk traveling alone in the middle of the day, even if her wits are scrambled. And how far could she get on her own, without protection, money, or supplies?"

I knew his gloomy scenario was all too likely. Anyone who dared to set out alone on a journey was inviting trouble as surely as if he were to thrust his hand into a beehive. A young woman by herself would stand no chance whatever. If highway bandits didn't prey on her within a few miles of town, lack of food and water would soon do her in. "So you think she's probably hiding somewhere in town?" I said hopefully.

Tacitus nodded. "Let's get Nicomedes the boularch to post guards at all the city gates and make sure she doesn't get out. As long as we keep her confined to Smyrna, we can hunt her down at our leisure."

I didn't like his imagery, but his plan seemed the only reasonable one. It would also allow us to get some badly needed rest and a bath. And I could have Luke look at my eye. I wouldn't be a very effective hunter with one eye swollen shut. Tacitus went to find one of his slaves to send to Nicomedes.

* * * *

After getting a poultice for my eye from the good doctor Luke I was on my way back to my room for an abbreviated rest when I noticed one of the Ephesian 'witches' approaching from the other direction. She was carrying a chamberpot to empty it in the large slop jar at the head of the stairs. She had a cloth draped over the pot, as people sometimes do, out of modesty or from a desire to contain offensive odors. As we passed and she lowered her eyes, a scene from a play by some minor Greek comic writer came to my mind. A woman gave birth to a stillborn child. A slave smuggled the child out in a jar and a live child, purchased from an overly fertile prostitute, was substituted to satisfy the father's desire for an heir. I thought the whole situation absurd when I read the play, but I now had to admit that I could not swear what the woman who just passed me was carrying in that pot. A baby wouldn't fit in there . . . but Cornutus' heart would.

Of course! The missing chamberpot. No one would think twice about seeing someone carrying a chamberpot in the middle of the night, especially if it were covered with a cloth. And whoever took the pot out wouldn't risk going back to return it. The only question now was whether the heart had been dumped in one of the slop jars or hidden away until it was needed in some demonic ritual. After the woman completed her business and returned to her room I lifted the lid of the malodorous, waist-high slop jar and saw that it was barely half full. Androcles, I was sure, wouldn't pay to have it emptied until it was close to overflowing. After the midday rest I would tell him not to have any of the jars emptied until their contents had been inspected. And I knew just which slave of mine I was going to assign that task to. If I couldn't kill Damon, I could make him wish I had.

* * * *

I didn't think I'd be able to sleep. My face hurt and Chryseis was so much on my mind. What if I was wrong about what had happened to her? What if someone – Marcellus, no doubt – had carried her out of the room? But why would Marcellus go to the trouble of kidnapping a slave girl? Where would he hide her? Was she Cornutus' daughter? Could someone else – Marcellus perhaps – know that? Such worries chased one another through my head until they blurred together like the spokes on the wheels of a speeding chariot. I was startled when Tacitus' knock on the door woke me up.

"Pliny, let's get down to the bath before it's too crowded," he called.

I stumbled out of bed and explained my deduction about the chamberpot to Tacitus as we descended the stairs. We stopped by Androcles' quarters to tell him not to empty the slop jars until further notice, then walked quickly to the bath house.

While we were still in the *frigidarium* rinsing ourselves off, Luke and Timothy came in. They hadn't undressed and appeared to be looking for someone. Me, it turned out. Androcles had told them where we were headed.

Luke called me into a corner and spoke in a low voice in Latin. "Friend Pliny, the strangest thing has happened. On our way back from Apelles' house, we ran into Chryseis on the street."

"Oh, thank the gods!"

I had told Luke about Chryseis' disappearance while he treated

my eye. He had urged me to treat Damon with compassion and promised to look for Chryseis as he walked to his friends' house. I was
overjoyed at his stroke of luck but knew it was important to act as
though he had not told me anything particularly important. He'd already
attracted too much attention by coming in here fully clothed. Who knew
what interest others in the room might have in this information?

"Where was she?" I asked in a whisper.

"About three blocks from the inn. Once I'd recovered from my
surprise at seeing her up and about, I spoke to her. She seemed confused, unable to recognize her own name or where she was, or why she
was out in the street. I told her she shouldn't be walking around. She
was injured in a fall. She seemed to think hard for a moment, then said,
'He hit me'."

"Marcellus!" I hissed. "I knew it."

"Now, don't read too much into that," Luke cautioned. "When
the memory is confused like this, the person may recall something from
several years ago more clearly than something from a few hours back.
For a slave to say that someone hit her would not be unusual. Remember the scene with Cornutus yesterday."

What I remembered – with shame – was the blow I had struck
Damon. Would he in his dotage be mumbling, 'He hit me'?

"Where is she?"

"We took her to the house of Apelles and asked them to care
for her for a day or two. If someone did hit her or push her down the
steps, it seemed to me unwise to return her to the inn, where her assailant might have another chance to strike."

"Thank you, doctor." My knees were actually weak with relief. "This is wonderful news. I feel as if a burden has been lifted. Do
you think I could go see her after my bath?"

"I suggest you wait," Luke said, and I knew it wasn't just a
suggestion. "The family is preparing for Apelles' funeral tomorrow
morning. You said you were planning to attend. I'll accompany you and,
after the funeral, we'll go back to the house and talk with her. I'm not
sure how she'll react to you. You aren't a familiar person to her, but you
did have some conversation with her, didn't you?"

"Not as much as I would have wished."

"Sometimes contact with anyone or anything the least bit familiar can help an individual regain memory."

"I'll do whatever you think is best for her."

He clapped my shoulder. "I must remind you that sometimes a
person can recover memory in a few days. Other times the loss of

memory can be permanent. Chryseis is young and the blow doesn't seem to have been severe, so I'm hopeful for a full recovery."

Luke and Timothy then returned to the dressing room, left their clothes there with ours under the watchful eye of Tacitus' slave, and returned to the bath. We waited for them to join us as we went into the main room, to soak in the pool. I don't normally pay any attention to the *membrum virile* of other bathers. It's considered impolite and one is taught from childhood not to notice anything. I could not help observing, however, that Timothy was circumcised, though Luke was not. This form of mutilation is considered so bizarre among Greeks and Romans that few Jewish men uncover themselves completely in the public baths. A few, I'm told, go so far as to have some sort of surgery to reverse the process. The very thought made me cringe.

* * * *

When I returned to my room I found Cornutus' concubine Melissa waiting at my door.

"Have you learned anything about Chryseis, my lord?" she asked. She seemed genuinely anxious.

"Her condition hasn't changed."

She looked confused. "But I heard she'd been lost."

Damn Damon! He couldn't keep a secret in his mouth any more effectively than he'd kept Chryseis in that room.

"She's been found and is safe. For now she's staying at the house of . . . some local people."

"Could I see her, my lord?"

"I don't think that's wise at the moment." Something suddenly made me a bit distrustful of her motives. All I knew about her – that she was Cornutus' mistress and that she hated me and my family – was based on one conversation. "The blow to her head has left her uncertain of some things."

"But you're sure she's all right?"

"So Luke assures me, and I trust his judgment."

"Then I'll be content to know that." She started to turn away, but I took hold of her arm and stopped her.

"Why are you so concerned about Chryseis?"

She obviously didn't want to answer, but her status compelled her. "Since coming to Cornutus' house I have been a sort of mother to her."

"Do you know anything about the incident when she was branded?"

From the way her face went pale, she couldn't deny that she

did. "Yes, my lord. I was there."

An eyewitness! This was more than I had dared hope for. I led her into my room and closed the door. "Please tell me what happened."

She seemed confused by my urgency. "Why, my lord?"

"It's not your place to ask questions. Now, tell me what happened the night Chryseis was branded."

"It was . . . very late one night, after midnight. Cornutus told me to bring Chryseis to his *tablinum*. So I woke the poor child and led her there. She kept asking me what he wanted. I could truthfully tell her that I had no idea. When we entered the tablinum, it was lit by only a few small lamps. The effect was eerie, unsettling. There was another slave woman waiting there with Cornutus. In the center of the room was a charcoal brazier with an iron heating in it. I still didn't realize what he intended to do. It was so incomprehensible. Then he told the other woman and me to undress Chryseis and tie her over the table. Chryseis began to cry. I didn't move at first, until the other woman grabbed her and began dragging her toward the table. I pleaded with Cornutus not to hurt her. He told me to shut up and help tie her up. He wanted her bent over the table, with her buttocks exposed. I honestly thought he was going to rape her."

"Did he say why he was doing this?"

"No, my lord. I asked him. I pleaded with him not to do it." She raised her clenched hands as though asking the favor of me. "He just told me to hold her still. The other woman stuffed a cloth in her mouth and clamped her hand over it. I had to stand right beside her, holding her bottom, with the smell of her burning flesh in my nostrils. I survived the sack of my home in Judaea, my lord, and I have to say this was worse. You expect soldiers to pillage and burn. You don't expect a man to brand an innocent child."

"What happened then?"

"He dropped the iron back into the brazier and ran out of the room. The other slave woman left, too. Her task was completed, and she didn't care. I untied Chryseis, put some ointment on the burn, and stayed with her that night. She was terribly upset by the incident and didn't sleep well for several nights."

I was grateful to know that Chryseis had someone to comfort her. "When she told me about it, it still seemed to affect her deeply. Did Cornutus ever give you any reason for doing it?"

"No, my lord. He would never answer my questions about it. But one day, several months later, we were at Baiae. Cornutus and I were watching Chryseis play in a pool with several other girls. The others were nude, but Chryseis would not undress. One of the girls tried to lift her gown and caught a glimpse of the brand. Chryseis was humiliated and ran back to our rooms. Cornutus must have known from my look what I was thinking. All he said was, 'I did it for her own good. You'll see. It was for her own good.'"

* * * *

Androcles had informed me that the slop jars were scheduled to be emptied the next day, so that if I wanted to go fishing in them, as he put it, I had better get to it. He would not inconvenience himself by asking the workers to make an extra trip.

I did impose the task on Damon, as part of his punishment for failing in his guard duty. But I didn't make him use his hands, as I had first thought I might do. We found a long stick in the stable and began on the second floor, nearest to where Cornutus' room was. Damon used the stick to stir around in the jars, as though he were stirring a revolting sort of soup. He hit nothing solid in any of the jars on the second floor. Only after a search of the third floor jars proved fruitless did my spirits begin to flag. I doubted that the killer had gone down to the more public parts of the inn on the first floor to dispose of his trophy. And our search there verified my hypothesis. The heart was not to be found in any of the jars. I would have someone present to watch when they were emptied tomorrow, just to be sure, but it now appeared that whoever removed Cornutus' heart either found some other way to dispose of it or still had it in his possession.

I dismissed Damon to go clean himself up and was contemplating my next step when I heard angry shouts erupting from the small dining room. Tiberius Saturninus ran out, followed by two men whom I did not know. One of the men – a former soldier or gladiator, to judge from his bulk and scarred face – dived for Saturninus, caught his foot and tripped him. Saturninus landed at my feet and grabbed the hem of my tunic like a suppliant.

"Gaius Pliny, help me!"

The man who had tripped him pounced on Saturninus, grabbing the neck of his tunic and lifting Saturninus to his knees. "There won't be much left to help by the time we get through with you, you thieving scum."

"Gaius Pliny, I beg you! Help me!"

"Hold on!" I barked. "What's going on here?"

"We're going to teach a lesson to a cheater," the other man said from the doorway where he still stood. He reminded me of a particularly bad teacher in my hometown, one whom I'd had the good fortune to avoid.

He was about forty. His dark hair had a slight curl to it. His face might have been called handsome if it hadn't been frozen in a perpetual sneer.

"What do you think he's done?" I asked.

"He switched the dice. Put in some of his own."

"How do you know that?"

"He had been losing steadily until a short time ago."

"So you can use your crooked dice, but if he tries the same trick, it's cheating?"

"There's nothing crooked about these dice. Would you like to try them?" His sneer tried to turn into a smile.

"I'd sooner throw my money in a slop jar," I said. "How much did he win?"

"Twenty tetradrachmas," the second man said. "He dropped most of it when he ran, but there's still a few in his hand."

I reached down and pried the coins out of Saturninus' hand. Tossing them to the second man, I said, "Here's your money back. Now, get out of here."

"It's not that easy," the man said. "He tried to cheat us. He hasn't paid the penalty for that."

Saturninus choked back a whimper.

"Do you have any writing material?" I asked.

The second man looked at me in surprise. The other man released his grip on Saturninus, who sank back to the floor in a heap. The burly gambler went back into the dining room and returned with a small wax tablet, which he handed to me. It had a series of numbers written on it. I used the blunt end of the stylus to smooth the wax and began to write.

"This is my promise to pay you another ten tetradrachmas, in return for your guarantee to leave this man alone. Present it to my servant Trophimus." I pressed my signet ring into the wax.

The gamblers looked at one another. The sinister-looking man nodded once and they left.

I took Saturninus' hand and helped him off the floor. He tried to pull his hair over his bald head with his other hand.

"Thank you, Gaius Pliny. I'm very grateful for your help." He said it, but his voice and face belied his words. "I'll see that you're repaid."

"How do you expect to do that? You're already deeply in debt to your wife's brother, Gaius Sempronius."

His twisted mouth showed his disappointment that I knew his secret. "That'll be taken care of. I have a patron in Rome. He paid off all my debts before I left for Syria and assured me he would do so again when I returned."

"You're fortunate to have such a generous friend. What does he expect of you in return?"

"What every patron expects of a client – to do what I'm told."

"Who is this patron?"

Saturninus shook his head. "Merely saving my worthless life doesn't entitle you to know that, Gaius Pliny." He started toward the stairs, then turned around and took a step back in my direction. "Could you see your way to . . . lending me a little money?"

* * * *

I dreaded the prospect of eating dinner in the inn's dining room but felt I must. How else could I investigate what happened after I left the evening before? There was no entertainment offered this evening, much to my relief. A somber mood hovered over the inn. Tacitus and I sat at the table he had occupied the previous evening and conversed quietly in Latin. A serving girl, one Tacitus hadn't bedded yet, brought us some fish and a pitcher of wine.

"When I left last night," I said, "Cornutus was at the table under the fresco of Baucis and Philemon. Did he stay there the rest of the evening?"

Tacitus nodded. "Marcellus joined him."

"Was anyone else at the table with them?"

"Just their servants."

I surveyed the room, concentrating on Cornutus' table. It was in the center of three tables placed along that wall. There was room behind it and on either side for servants to stand while they waited on their masters.

"It would have been virtually impossible for anyone to walk up to the table and poison their food or wine," I observed.

"I'm still not convinced he was poisoned," Tacitus said. "What makes you so sure?"

I took a deep breath, trying to contain my impatience. I felt like a teacher going over a lesson again with my slowest student. "The condition of his body tells me that he died early in the night. That's what I showed you up in his room. The only logical conclusion is that he was given something in his food or drink."

"As bad as this stuff tastes," Tacitus said, "the extra flavor of a little poison would almost be welcome. Certainly hard to detect. But how could it be administered, with all those people around? You can't just lean over and sprinkle something on someone else's plate, or whip out a vial of something and pour it into his wine."

I had no answer to that.

Tacitus looked smug. "Didn't you say that, if your theory doesn't fit the facts, you have to change your theory? Isn't it time you started looking for someone with a knife?"

"We'll have to do that. But the knife didn't kill him. He wasn't beaten or strangled or suffocated. He was poisoned. And how else could it have been done, if not here? He was fine when we were in the bath. A few hours later, he was dead. This is the only time someone could have given him a poison."

Tacitus slapped the table. "The baths! Remember, Marcellus sent his slave to get us some wine. The girl who brought the wine handed Cornutus the first goblet, Marcellus the second one, and the rest of us – including those two Greek fellows – picked our own."

"But that was too early. And it was a slave girl from the baths, not Marcellus' slave, who brought the drinks." Once again I found myself wishing for my uncle's notebooks, so I could refresh my memory about poisons and their effects. My memory is keen, but I had been away from them for over a year. Some details were not as sharp as they should be.

Tacitus shoved his plate away. "It was only an hour or so before dinner. There are such things as slow-acting poisons. I think this fish is one of them."

"Whether you accept my theory or not," I said, "at least help me get some information to prove or disprove it. Are you certain only the two of them were at the table? Neither of them left for any long period of time?"

"Yes, that much I can attest to."

There was a start. But my inquiry was complicated by the fact that I couldn't ask anyone else if they saw what might have been a poisoning. Everyone thought Cornutus was killed with a knife. The slaves had spread the word all over the inn and, from there, all over town. Local gossip probably had him hacked to bits or skinned alive by now. It might be better to let the poisoner think he was off the hook. If he thought no one suspected, then he might get careless, not cover his tracks as well. The knifer was the one I had to appear to be looking for. But was I looking for one killer or two? What were the chances that two people could both have a motive for killing Cornutus and both decide to strike on the same night? On the other hand, why would one person use two methods of murder?

And what if someone had meant to kill me?

I went over to the table shared by the philosopher Lysimachus and the two small-town emissaries. The three of them seemed to have gravitated to one another, probably because no one else could stand to be around such pompous jackasses.

Lysimachus beamed at my approach. "Please, join us, Gaius Pliny."

He scooted down on the bench he occupied, with his back to the wall.

"Thank you, Lysimachus. I won't take much of your time." I wanted to make it clear I was not settling down for the evening. "I'd just like to ask if any of you saw any argument last night or noticed anyone who seemed to be angry with Cornutus."

The two emissaries shook their heads and quickly assured me that they saw nothing the previous evening.

"What about you, Lysimachus? Did you see anything?"

The philosopher stroked his long, white beard in a downward motion. "Did I see anything? How can I answer that question? Can I know for certain that anything I see is real? Seeing relies on sense perceptions, and sense perceptions can only bring knowledge of what is impermanent and transitory. As the divine Plato says, 'Have sight and hearing any truth in them?' What I saw, if anything, might not have been real. What was real, I might not have seen." He made an 'on-the-one-hand, on-the-other-hand' gesture with his hands and then folded them in his lap.

Rhascuporis and Orophernes were obviously mightily impressed with this display of philosophical clap-trap. I was frustrated that he was dodging the question.

"I see you've imbibed deeply of the Skepticism of Plato's Academy," I said, prompting a diffident smile and a wise nod on his part. "And you're able to regurgitate it undigested, like a man who has drunk wine that is too rich for his stomach." The analogy wasn't quite perfect, but it served to wipe the smug smile off his face.

"Let me ask you again, Lysimachus, did you see anything at dinner last night to make you think someone was angry at Cornutus?"

"This is where I was sitting last night, young sir. From here, as you may observe, I could not see most of the dining room because of this pillar. All I could see was the table where that big German fellow, Carolus, was sitting. Studying his face for an entire meal is no aid to digestion, I can tell you. I think he was very angry about something."

"What sense perceptions led you to that conclusion?"

He ignored my jibe. "His face was contorted most of the evening, and he virtually attacked his food with his knife."

Might Carolus have attacked something else last night? I filed that information away in my head, thanked Lysimachus, and returned to the table which Tacitus and I were occupying. His *enamorata* was giving him particularly attentive service.

"This is Pamphile," Tacitus said. "You met her this morning."

"Yes, I'm sorry there wasn't time for proper introductions," I said, as if there ever could be proper introductions between us. I did at least notice her face this time. She had an upturned nose and a small, cupid's-bow mouth. Her black hair glistened.

"What can I get you, sir?" she asked, bowing slightly.

"I'd like to ask you some questions about last night."

She didn't exactly blush. "Well, I figured Cornelius Tacitus had told you all about it by now. Don't you men share the details of your conquests?" Her demeanor said she wouldn't mind if we did. It would be good advertising for her, I suppose.

I did blush. "No, I was referring to what happened here during dinner last night."

"Oh, it was very busy, very noisy. People ate and drank a lot. And Tacitus was being very nice to me. What is it exactly that you want to know?"

I hadn't really made myself clear, had I? "Did you notice that man last night?" I pointed to Marcellus.

"Yes. Him and the poor man who was eating with him, the one who got killed last night."

"Right, they're the ones. Did you notice anything unusual about their behavior?"

"Well, sir, I can't remember every detail of a busy night like that. I mean, I've got lots of customers to look after. I can't stand around gawking at one table. That one, Marcellus, he was pretty rowdy. The other one, Cornutus, was more quiet like. One thing I do remember, though, is how Marcellus sent one of his slaves to get a wineskin from his own wagon. Said ours was swill. He wanted to toast his friend Cornutus with a vintage worthy of so noble a fellow. Or something high-sounding like that."

At least there was no contradiction with what Phrixus and Melissa had told us. "Did Marcellus also drink from that skin?"

"Of course," Pamphile said. "He poured some into both cups, his and Cornutus'. I watched him because I was so tired of him insulting our fare. I was hoping he'd choke on his own fancy stuff."

Damn! Another witness saying that Marcellus had drunk the same wine he gave Cornutus. Could I be wrong about my poison theory? Or was I looking at the wrong method of introducing it?

Suddenly, just as an entire forest falls silent when a predator stalks past, so a hush fell as the leader of the group of Ephesian women entered the dining room. Her necklaces, bracelets, and amulets clanked like a camel caravan coming into Damascus. Pamphile's playfulness evaporated at the witch's approach, and she scurried away in fear, like one of the little forest animals who was liable to be eaten. I wished I could run, but the witch was advancing straight toward my table.

VII

"Young sir," the witch said, pronouncing it as one word, "I am here to report, in keeping with your request, that my followers and I will be leaving the inn after dark to participate in a religious ritual."

I paused, as though considering a request, then said, "I need to know more precisely where you're going and what you're going to do." It was pure bluff on my part. How could I stop her?

The witch drew herself up to her full height. "There will be a full moon tonight. We are going out in the service of the goddess."

Her answer didn't satisfy me. My uncle taught me that religion is merely a way of keeping slaves and the lower classes under control through fear of punishment extended into the afterlife. I found it difficult to accept that anyone of any intelligence took these rituals seriously enough to go prancing about at night. "What does that service involve?"

"We do not reveal sacred mysteries to profane ears," the witch said. "Nor would you want us to. The goddess guards her secrets jealously and wreaks a terrible vengeance on those who transgress the bounds fixed around them." She swirled her robes around her as she turned away from me. I half expected her to disappear under them.

"Does that vengeance include having one's heart cut out?" I said to her back.

She looked over her shoulder, like a disembodied head floating on a black mist. "There are worse ways to die, young sir. There are worse ways."

Watching her make an exit worthy of a Persian queen, I wondered what connection Cornutus could have with these women and their outrageous cult. I turned to Tacitus, who was still cringing at my bold question to the witch.

"Since those women joined us in Ephesus, have you seen any kind of exchange between them and Cornutus, friendly or otherwise?"

Tacitus shook his head. "As far as I know, when the witch told him not to hit Chryseis, that was the first time she had spoken to him."

"Could his mistreatment of a slave girl be a reason to kill him?"

"That hardly seems plausible. They couldn't go around dealing out retribution to every man who raises a hand against one of his female slaves."

"No. But could she have some other reason to want him dead?"

"If she does," Tacitus said, "she won't tell us and Cornutus can't. I'll be content to let the governor discover it when he gets here."

Once the danger had passed Pamphile returned with another pitcher of wine and Tacitus pulled her onto his lap and asked her if she would spend another night with him.

She kissed him, long and hard. "I'd like to," she said when they came up for air, "but I can't tonight."

"Why not?" Tacitus asked with some urgency.

"There's something else I have to do." She wriggled, trying to get out of his grip.

"I'm not going to let you go until you tell me why you can't stay with me tonight."

The girl's eyes opened wide in alarm. "I'm not supposed to tell."

"Then resign yourself to sitting here the rest of the evening," Tacitus said, tightening his grip to the point that Pamphile's discomfort was evident. "And if you keep wriggling, you're going to be impaled on . . ."

She slumped against his chest. "All right. I'm going to the festival."

"The one that old witch was talking about?" I asked.

"She's not a witch, my lord. She's our high priestess, Anyte. Under the first full moon after the spring equinox, worshipers of Hecate gather on the site of a temple of Artemis in old Smyrna, on the north side of the bay."

"If you're worshiping Hecate," Tacitus said, "why do it at the temple of Artemis?"

"Artemis and Hecate are just different names for the same

goddess," Pamphile said nervously, "a goddess of darkness and power. Women come from all over the area for these ceremonies."

"What do you do?" I asked her as Tacitus continued to hold her tightly.

"I can't tell you," she said, on the verge of tears. "I've said too much already. Please don't ask me any more and don't tell anyone that I told you even this much." She broke Tacitus' grip as he relaxed it. "I'll make tomorrow night very special for you," she promised with another kiss. "For both of you, if you like." She stroked my cheek.

"Well, I guess we know where we're going tonight," I said as Pamphile scurried back to the kitchen.

Tacitus' jaw almost dropped onto the table. "You plan to spy on some wild women's cult ceremony? If they catch you they'll tear you apart the way the Maenads did old King Pentheus."

"That's a myth," I reminded him. "I'm disappointed someone of your intelligence would give it any credence. We won't be in any danger. The women won't know we're there. We'll leave the inn well ahead of them and lie in wait to see what happens. It'll be dark."

"There's a full moon tonight," Tacitus objected. "In case you missed it, that's the whole point of the ritual."

* * * *

We were on our way out of the inn when Melissa called to me. "My lord, may I ask you something?" Her expression said she would rather be doing anything than talking to me.

"If you can do it quickly."

"I don't know where I'll be sleeping tonight. Have you made arrangements?"

"Yes. You and Phoebe will share the same room you had last night, but the door won't be locked."

"Thank you, my lord. You're very generous." She seemed relieved. I wondered if she thought I might expect her to sleep with me. She started to turn away, but Tacitus stopped her.

"I have a question for you, Melissa," he said, "as long as you're here."

"Yes, my lord?"

"I'm trying to reconstruct last night in my own mind, which was a bit clouded with drink, I admit. Where were you when Cornutus returned from the bath yesterday evening?"

"Phoebe and I had gone out to get some supplies for the next stage of the trip. When we returned he was already at dinner."

"Did you join him?"

"First we stored our purchases in one of our wagons. Then we came in to dinner."

"You didn't go upstairs before dinner?"

"No, my lord."

"When you were taken upstairs to be locked up for the night, did you stop by Cornutus' room, perhaps to see how he was doing?"

"No, my lord. I wanted to, but Androcles wouldn't let me."

"So you didn't know that Cornutus and Pliny had changed rooms."

"No, my lord. I didn't learn that until this morning."

* * * *

We had told Androcles that we were going for a ride up Mt. Mastusia, to watch the sun set over the bay. It was a weak excuse, but I felt we needed some pretext, and one that would put us leaving town in a different direction than the women. We took Damon with us, to watch the horses while we spied on the ritual. My plan was to leave the horses well out of sight and walk whatever distance we had to in order to get close to the temple.

We rode about half a mile east, then left the road and cut across country, going north and west until we came in sight of the old city of Smyrna. Finding a secure spot behind a ridge for the horses, we left Damon with them and approached the ruins on foot. The Lydians did a thorough job of razing the city. In addition some of the ruins had been cannibalized for newer building projects. Wind-blown dirt had filled in over part of it. Trees were growing here and there, sometimes out of the middle of what used to be houses. In the fading daylight the city looked like the carcass of a giant beast, picked clean by scavengers. There was no sign of any gathering or procession.

"What if it's all a great joke on us?" Tacitus said.

"That wild-haired witch doesn't joke," I replied. "Of that I'm certain. Whatever's going to happen will take place after dark. We still have some time to look the city over and find a hiding place."

Tacitus followed me as I entered the old city by merely walking up to the ruined wall and stepping up onto it and then over it, like Remus stepping over Romulus' wall at the founding of Rome. Thanks to a broken inscription, it didn't take us long to identify the remains of a temple of Artemis located at a crossroads. From the little I've read of this goddess – whether she be called Artemis or Hecate – I do know that she is somehow connected with crossroads and woods. Though this temple and its sacred precinct were in ruins, the ashes at one spot near its center gave clear evidence that a fire had burned there fairly recently. The ashes lay on a large flat stone, into which had been cut a five-pointed star, similar to one of the symbols on the witches' black wagon.

"This must be where everything will happen. We should be able to get a clear view from up there." The spot I had picked out was what remained of the exterior back wall of the town's theater. It had the advantage of being back in the direction of the place where our horses were hidden.

"If you really want a good look," Tacitus said, "why don't we disguise ourselves as women and mingle with the crowd?"

"Very funny. It's getting dark. Let's get ourselves hidden."

"Just a minute." Tacitus stepped to the corner of the temple platform, where the wall was about waist high, lifted his tunic, and began to urinate.

"What are you doing?"

"If I'm going to hide someplace, I want to go in with an empty bladder."

"But somebody might notice . . ."

He waved his hand dismissively. "People – and animals – use these old buildings all the time. Who's going to care?"

I couldn't undo what he was doing, so I started down the temple steps. He caught up with me at the bottom and we headed for the ruins of the theater.

Greek theaters from several centuries ago, when this one was built, were dug into a hillside. We Romans construct our theaters wherever we please, using our superior skill with the arch to provide the support. This particular theater was situated so that the audience sat looking out over the city. The wall I chose for a hiding place had been the back of the stage. Riddled with nooks and crannies from which actors once played scenes from the upper story of a house or the top of a hill, it offered concealment from all sides.

After what I estimated to be about an hour in hiding, I was beginning to wish I had relieved myself and to wonder if Tacitus had been right about this being some gigantic joke, the sort of prank that local people sometimes play on travelers. The moon had risen, gigantically white on this cloudless night. The tumbled stones of old Smyrna glowed eerily in the soft light, but nothing was happening.

I was on the verge of swallowing my pride and suggesting we go back to the inn when I heard a dull murmur, almost like bees, that seemed to come from all sides at once. Torches appeared on the horizon, a few at first, then dozens. Groups of women were approaching the old city from north, east, and south, chanting as they came. We couldn't have left now if we'd wanted to. The women filed into the ruined city and gathered in the courtyard in front of the temple we had visited. I couldn't estimate their number, with all the movement, but there certainly were several hundred, many of them carrying torches. These they stuck into crevices in the ruins of the temple and the wall surrounding its precinct.

Drums and flutes began to play the most alluring, seductive music I had ever heard. I even caught myself swaying to its rhythm. The women started to dance, slowly at first, then working themselves into an ecstasy as the tempo of the music increased. Some of them shrieked and howled. We watched in amazement as they stripped off their clothes and began anointing themselves and one another with some kind of oil or ointment.

"I'm glad we aren't down among them in disguise," I whispered to Tacitus.

"Just imagine what fun it would be," he said, "until they discovered the trick."

Anyte, our traveling companion from Ephesus, strode regally up the steps of the temple. She wore a headdress with what appeared to be snakes on it. From that distance I couldn't tell if they were moving or if the flickering torchlight made them appear to be. Except for her jewelry she was nude but wore a long red cape with mystical symbols embroidered on it. The cape flowed behind and around her as a light breeze off the ocean caught it. In each hand she carried a scepter.

"Who would have thought," Tacitus whispered, "that so magnificent a body was concealed under all her robes and trinkets?"

When Anyte assumed a ceremonial pose at the head of the steps, with her scepters crossed over her breasts, the music came to a crashing halt and all the women lifted their heads to their priestess.

"O, tri-form goddess," Anyte intoned with her eyes closed. "O, goddess of many names, be present among your worshipers this night! Be present within each of us! Accept our sacrifices and our devotion!"

The crowd parted to allow passage to the five women who traveled with Anyte. Each had a fierce Molossian hound on a leash. The dogs seemed agitated and wouldn't stop barking. Their handlers had difficulty getting them to climb the steps. When they reached the platform, the dogs pulled their handlers from place to place, sniffing as though they were tracking an animal. They showed a keen interest in Tacitus' corner. The handlers pulled them away only with a great effort.

"You wanted to know who would be interested," I said. "That's who."

"Those are the kind of hunting dogs that Artemis set upon Actaeon," Tacitus said with a gulp. "I don't like the look of those dogs."

Some of the women piled up wood which they brought in with them on the flat stone with the five-pointed star cut into it. They all seemed to know their tasks and needed no instruction. At a gesture from Anyte the women with the dogs took up positions at each of the points of the star. The dogs kept sniffing, straining at their leashes, and barking. They all had their snouts pointed in our direction.

"By the gods," Tacitus muttered. "You don't think they've picked up our scent, do you?"

One woman, who appeared from her headdress to have some secondary authority in the group – though it's difficult to determine rank when everyone in a group is naked – threw her torch onto the pile and ignited what quickly became a huge fire. As Anyte chanted an incantation, she waved the scepters over the fire, shaking one or the other hard on each pass. Explosive plumes of colored smoke billowed from the fire whenever she did this. The crowd of women raised a ululating cry every time it happened. I realized that she was shaking some kind of powder into the fire. A cheap trick to inflame the minds of the masses. And it was working.

Now a ram with gilded horns was led forward. Its bleating could barely be heard over the women's chanting and howling. Such animals are usually sedated before being sacrificed, but in this case several of the nude women wrestled the thing down. Anyte handed her scepters to her assistant and drew a knife from a pocket on the inside of her cloak. She stabbed the ram in the belly and split its gut open. The ram jerked and thrashed – the way Cornutus would have if he'd still been alive when he was eviscerated. Blood spurted everywhere.

Anyte appeared to be doing some cutting and sawing on the animal. Then she thrust her hands in and yanked out the entrails. Blood streamed down her forearms. She took a bite of the entrails, raw and still quivering. I thought it was the heart, but in the eerie light I couldn't be sure. The rest she scattered around within the five-pointed star. The women who had been holding the ram down threw the carcass onto the fire.

"Did you see that?" I whispered excitedly to Tacitus. "They sacrificed a *ram*."

"And rather crudely, too," Tacitus replied.

I grabbed his arm, hardly able to keep my voice to a whisper in my excitement. "But don't you see the connection? Cornutus' seal isn't just any horn; it's a ram's horn. And the way this animal was cut open, it's exactly the way Cornutus was cut up."

Anyte extended her arms, and the crowd of women fell silent as one person. Her cape fell back, exposing a body reminiscent of some of the better statues of Aphrodite.

"Release the hounds of Hades!" she proclaimed in a voice so monstrous and deep I thought someone else was speaking. "Let them devour this sacrifice as the dark goddess devours her enemies!" The dogs' handlers untied their leashes. But the dogs surprised everyone by bolting down the temple steps into the crowd of women, cutting their own path through the hysteria as they headed straight toward our hiding place.

"Run for it!" Tacitus cried, but he was talking to my back. Scrambling down a narrow stairway and sprinting over the unfamiliar terrain in the dark – even under the full moon – was almost as unnerving as knowing what was behind me. And gaining on me. I was nowhere near the horses yet and running out of breath when something whizzed past me. The lead dog yelped, stumbled, and fell face-first in the dirt. Again something zipped past me and the dog closest to Tacitus dropped without a sound. A third dog was taken down by some force, and the remaining two slowed their pace, sniffing at their fallen brothers and whimpering. Tacitus and I dropped over the low ridge and grabbed our horses' reins from Damon.

By now the women were taking up the cry. An unearthly shriek pursued us, like the wind howling through a crack in a wall. Having narrowly escaped Actaeon's fate, I had no intention of being torn apart like king Pentheus by this bunch of crazed women.

"Ride east!" I yelled. "Ride east!"

VIII

A low-lying valley runs east of old

Smyrna, so we had easy going, even in the moonlight, and were able to outdistance the naked mob. When they were out of sight, we turned southwest until we picked up the main road back to the new city of Smyrna. Only then did we slow the horses to a walk and spare enough breath to talk. My first question was for Damon.

"What did you do? How did you stop those dogs?"

From under his tunic he pulled out a small pouch on a string around his neck. He opened it and showed me a leather strap, broader in the middle and tapering at each end. "It's a shepherd's sling, my lord. You can hurl small stones with it. I doubt I killed the dogs from that distance, but at least I stunned them."

"Where did you learn this skill?" I asked in amazement, wondering how a master could ever know all he needs to know about his slaves. I had known Damon since my early childhood. He was no shepherd, even if he was named after a mythical one. His duties had always been carried out in the house.

"It's something I picked up from a story I heard, my lord. I practice when I've finished my other duties. I carry it with me whenever we travel."

"Well, we owe you our lives," I said. "There'll be no more talk about punishing you, I assure you."

"Thank you, my lord."

I wished I was as sure that the Ephesian witch would be so forgiving of the men who profaned her holy rites.

* * * *

Sleep was a stranger to me that night. Every noise I heard sounded like a threat. Was that Anyte's foot on the stairs? Or was Melissa coming back for another try at avenging her family, now that she knew which room I was in?

At some time well before dawn I despaired of sleep and went upstairs to roust Glaucon, the slave who served as my scribe. He was sleeping in the room next door to Melissa and Phoebe. Their room, I noted, was on the back of the building, the same side as Cornutus'. Where exactly it was in relation to Cornutus', I couldn't be sure. Could Melissa have lowered herself somehow – perhaps with Phoebe's assistance – and entered through the window, thinking she was about to kill me? But wouldn't she have recognized her own master and lover, even in the dark? Cornutus and I did not remotely resemble one another, and she had intimate knowledge of his body.

Glaucon didn't grumble as much as he might have when I woke him. He had been my uncle's scribe for ten years. My uncle habitually got up several hours before dawn and dictated correspondence or worked on whatever book he was writing. Glaucon had led a relatively easy life since he began working for me. I usually rise early, but I write by myself for a couple of hours before calling Glaucon in to take down a revised copy of my work.

By the time the sun came up I had composed the letter which I had to send to Rome today. I took the version I had dictated to Glaucon and read it one final time, just to be sure the tone was right. It would have been a difficult letter to write, even if I had known the recipient. It needed a sympathetic tone, yet one that was also straightforward, since I was a stranger to both the victim and his father. I did know the older man by sight, in the way everyone in our circle in Rome knows everyone else, but we had never met formally. I couldn't remember ever struggling with a letter this much.

G. Plinius Caecilius Secundus to L. Manilius Quadratus, greetings.

It is my unpleasant duty, sir, to report to you the death of your son, Lucius Manilius Cornutus, un-

*der the most unfortunate circumstances. While re-
turning from Syria to Rome to be at your side, he
was murdered in an inn in Smyrna. An investigation of this heinous crime is underway, and I am
confident that the guilty person or persons will be
brought to justice by the time you receive this letter.
Cornutus' body is to be burned today. I myself will
assume responsibility for delivering his ashes to you
for burial. I am also taking responsibility for your
son's slaves and his other personal belongings and
will see to it that those are delivered to you as soon
as possible.*

*Given at Smyrna this tenth day before the Kalends
of May.*

After Glaucon made a copy for my records, he rolled up the
sheet of papyrus, tied it securely with a piece of wool cord, and sealed
it with wax into which I pressed my seal. The action reminded me of
the mysterious document which Chryseis was carrying in her bag. Or
was I making too much of it? No slave of mine would have any reason
to be carrying a sealed document unless he was delivering it to someone. My curiosity about the contents of the document was strong enough
that I was tempted to take advantage of Chryseis' lack of memory to
open it . . . What was I thinking? I couldn't do that. To violate her trust
would be tantamount to violating her.

Glaucon retrieved a small leather pouch from among his supplies.
I enclosed my letter and applied my seal to the cover of the pouch as well.

The slave whom Marcellus proposed to send as a messenger
was waiting downstairs. I had interviewed the man the previous afternoon. All he could tell me was that he helped Marcellus to bed before
midnight. It's difficult to get accurate reports of times during the night.
Everybody says that things happened 'around midnight.' The slave reported that Marcellus was as drunk as he had ever seen him. He ordered one of his slave women to be sent to his room to sleep with him.
That led me to talk to the woman. She informed me that Marcellus did
not have sex with her. He was asleep by the time she got into bed with
him. She did claim that she was in the room all night. She had difficulty
sleeping because of Marcellus' snoring. I wondered how someone could
verify that, since the only other person in the room was deep in a drunken
stupor. Why had Marcellus sent for this woman, when he probably
knew he wouldn't be able to do anything with her? Did he just want

someone to verify where *he* was during the night?

Wasn't that the way a murderer would think?

I found the messenger waiting in the dining room of the inn, which was dimly lit and cave-like in the early morning light. As I handed him the letter I asked, "Do you have anything to add to what you said last night? Sometimes a good night's sleep sharpens the memory."

"No, my lord."

"Torture can also sharpen the memory," I reminded him.

He drew himself up with some dignity, a tall, thin man, about thirty-five, with a broad nose and large eyes in a face made more thoughtful by his receding hairline. "My lord, my testimony would be no different under torture. I told you all I know last night."

I could have badgered him some more, but I reminded myself that a man's slaves aren't all scoundrels just because the man himself is one. This fellow had more nobility in his bearing than the 'noble' Marcellus himself could muster on his best day.

"Would you also see that this letter is delivered to the wife of Cornelius Tacitus?" I handed him the sealed document which Tacitus had given me last night and a few sesterces for his trouble. "She's staying in the house of her father, Julius Agricola, on the Aventine Hill."

The man bowed slightly. "Certainly, my lord. Will there be anything else?"

"No. You'd better get down to the dock. I'm sure the ship is about ready to sail. I hope your journey is a speedy and a safe one."

As I watched him leave I silently wished him well. While travel of any sort is difficult, travel by ship involves enormous risk. Rome has eliminated pirates but cannot control the weather. This man's ship could sink and no word of Cornutus' death reach Rome until we arrived. And we would have no way of knowing what happened for almost a month.

* * * *

Tacitus, Luke and Timothy were waiting for me near the door of the inn, ready to attend Apelles' funeral. I was disappointed to see Marcellus standing alongside Tacitus. Surely this scoundrel hadn't invited himself to a stranger's funeral.

"Pliny, there you are," Tacitus said. "Marcellus has volunteered to see to burning Cornutus' body this morning, so that's taken care of."

Along with any possibility of learning any more about how Cornutus died, I thought. But I just said, "That's very generous of you, Marcellus." And it was. The wood for the pyre, the hired mourners — the whole business would run into some money. "What provisions have you made for the ashes?"

"I will provide a suitable urn for them. Would you like to take charge of them?" His tone was almost as sarcastic as his expression.

"Yes. In the letter I wrote to his father this morning I promised to return the ashes and all of Cornutus' belongings to him as soon as possible."

"Then if that's all taken care of," Luke said, "perhaps we should leave for Apelles' funeral. I believe it will start soon."

As soon as we were out of the inn, Luke handed me Sempronius' knife, which I had delivered to him the previous evening. "It couldn't have made Cornutus' wounds," he said. "The blade is too thick and not nearly sharp enough."

I dropped the knife into the *sinus* of my toga. The only advantage of the garment is this pocket formed by the way the material is draped over the left arm and around the wearer's back and over the right shoulder. "I'll return it to Sempronius. Thank you for checking on that point before the body was burned."

Apelles' funeral ceremony was held in the market square in the center of town. It appeared to me that virtually the entire population of the town was in attendance. The committee of boularchs, twenty-three now, stood in the front row. Tacitus and I were treated with great deference, even though the purple stripes on our togas were of the narrow, equestrian variety. The dignity which our presence bestowed on the proceedings was recognized, and we were invited to stand near the bier on which Apelles' body was laid out. A man of about fifty, he must have died from some wasting, consumptive disease. With his sunken cheeks and wispy hair, he looked thin and drawn, even older than his years.

The funeral oration, which the Greeks call an *epitaphios*, was given by Apelles' son, who was about my age. Watching him take his place beside the bier and collect his thoughts, I was carried back to the time, just four years ago, when I gave the oration at my uncle's funeral. The custom is demanding, but I wouldn't change it. Expecting the son to speak at his father's funeral gives the younger man a chance to reflect on his father's accomplishments and on his contribution to the growth of the family's patrimony. That had been an easy task for me, given my adoptive father's success in so many areas – the military, government service, and scholarship. When the deceased himself hasn't amounted to much, the eulogies tend to become recitals of family history.

Apelles' son did a commendable job. I suppose he'd had some time to think about what he was going to say, since his father had obviously been sick for a while. Part of the problem for a son in this situation is that he doesn't have a lot of time to prepare for this task, unless he's a little ghoulish and thinks about it a lot in advance. Apelles' son had had adequate rhetorical training, though in the florid Asiatic style popular in the eastern part of the empire. I found it excessive and could tell that Tacitus, who kept shifting his feet next to me, was longing to introduce the young man to the beauties of the uncluttered Attic style which we had learned in Rome.

With a flourish the young man finished his speech. The bier was picked up by eight prominent men of the city, and the procession headed out of town on the Via Sebaste toward the south, accompanied by women mourners and flute players. We wound our way through the necropolis to the tomb which we had noticed being prepared when we arrived two days ago. The body was placed in a waiting sarcophagus and deposited in the tomb, one of the largest in the necropolis. In art, as in rhetoric, the Asiatic style tends toward heavy ornamentation and overstatement. The sarcophagus was intricately carved with vines, shepherds, and cupids on every side. A central figure on one side depicted a man carrying a sheep over his shoulders, an image familiar to me from temple art, especially that devoted to Apollo.

What struck me as odd, however, were the inscriptions carved on all sides of the stone casket. Inscriptions are common in such a context, but the wording of these was unlike anything I had ever seen before: 'I am the vine.' 'I know my sheep.' 'I am the resurrection and the life.' They must have caught Tacitus' eye, too. He nudged me.

"What do you make of those?"

I shrugged. "Could Apelles have been an initiate of some local mystery cult we've never encountered before?"

People's religious practices intrigue me as phenomena to be observed, but I find no personal meaning in any of them. That the gods exist, I don't deny or affirm. But, if they do exist, why should they concern themselves with our petty affairs? And why should we presume to think that we exist in some other form after this life is over? To use Seneca's analogy, our life is like a flame. Before it is lit and after it's extinguished, is all the same. Our memory of the dead may endure for a while, just as the smoke and the scent from a candle linger briefly in the room, but the dead have no more awareness of us than the smoking candle does. There's no reason to fear what comes after the extinguishing of death, any more than what came before the kindling of birth. We have no memory of the one and will have no consciousness of the other. As Epicurus says, 'Death is nothing to us, for what has been dissolved has no sensation, and what has no sensation is nothing to us.'

"That woman is carrying on like a hired mourner," Tacitus whispered in my ear. I nodded. Apelles' wife was crying a good deal more than is considered fitting for a free person of any rank in society. That sort of wailing is best left to those who are paid to do it.

Still, it's fitting to commemorate a person's death with some sort of ceremony. If he were leaving on a long voyage, his family and friends would gather to see him off. There would be tears – such as my mother shed so copiously when I left for Syria – words of encouragement, promises to care for his family. They would be for the benefit of those staying behind as much as for the one departing. And it makes no difference by what means of conveyance a person leaves. A wagon will carry him away as well as a ship. Entombment in a sarcophagus gets rid of the body as well as cremation. I prefer the fire myself. There's something undignified about the thought of a person's remains putrifying in a dark tomb. Fire purifies, reduces, finishes the job completely and quickly.

Glancing back toward the west, I could see a column of smoke coming from the other side of Smyrna. Undoubtedly Cornutus' funeral pyre. Rising in that smoke was whatever else his body might have told us about the manner of his death.

What difference does it make? The end of both men – of all men – is the same. The day will come when Apelles' wife and children will no longer remember just what he looked like, what his voice sounded like. He will 'live' only in the name which his son bears. Poor Cornutus didn't leave even that much to keep his memory alive. I find each day that my uncle's visage is dimmer in my mind. He was fortunate to have written so much. He is 'alive' even for people, like Luke, who never met him. That kind of legacy is the closest we can come, I think, to immortality. It's what I hope to achieve with my life.

The movement of the crowd jarred me out of my reverie. On the walk back into town the caterwauling of the hired mourners began to grate on my nerves. I would have liked to drop back in the crowd, to get as far away from it as I could. But, as a distinguished guest and representative of Rome, I had a duty to lend dignity to the proceedings. The crowd accompanied Apelles' family back to their house. As a conclusion to the rituals, the son took a new broom and swept the room where the body had lain, symbolically cleansing it from the contamination of death. The family was now ready to begin this new phase of their lives. The front few ranks of the crowd seemed to know that they were invited into the house for food and drink. The rest drifted away.

Luke steered Tacitus and me through the crowd in the front room. "Chryseis is in the back of the house," he said.

* * * *

We found her sitting in a peristyle garden of the Roman sort, carding wool, as virtuous women of every class always seem to be doing something with their hands. Ionic columns supported a roof running around the garden, providing welcome shade. A flagstone path, bordered by boxwoods, meandered across the garden. Several early spring flowers were blooming. My uncle would have chided me for not recognizing them and knowing their medicinal properties. In the middle of the open space a fountain gushed. How sad to think that Apelles would never enjoy another day here with his family.

"Good morning, Chryseis," I said hesitantly. Why did I feel like some lowly peasant approaching my mistress, or like Odysseus, covered in seaweed and brine, washed up on the shore at the feet of the princess Nausicaa?

She looked at me with her head cocked to one side, like a dog trying to figure out whether a stranger is friend or enemy.

"Good morning," she replied. When she did not add the requisite 'my lord', I realized she had no notion of my status or hers. "Do I know you?"

"Yes, though not well. My name is Gaius Pliny. We met recently and talked for a while."

"I'm afraid I don't remember a lot of things," Chryseis said sadly. "These nice people are trying to help me. I do know that my mother was very beautiful. My nurse used to tell me so."

"I believe she was," I said without thinking.

Her face brightened and she leaned toward me. "Did you know my mother?"

"No. But you are very beautiful."

She looked me right in the eye. "Thank you. You're very handsome."

It was like talking to an empty shell. She would echo anything I said to her, but Chryseis herself wasn't there at the moment. Somewhere in there, though, I felt sure she was hiding, like the sun waiting to peek out from behind a cloud or a child playing a game. How could I find her?

Luke took me by the arm and led me across the garden. Chryseis resumed her wool-working.

"As you can see," Luke said, "she doesn't remember anything. She doesn't know who she is or why she's here."

"How long do you think she'll stay like this?"

He shrugged. "I have no idea. It might last a few days, a month. Or, she might never recover. I've seen such cases."

"Is there anything we can do to help her?" I asked urgently.

Luke put his thumb under his chin and his index finger beside his nose. After a moment's reflection he said, "Once, when I was a young doctor, I assisted in the case of a man who lost his memory after a fall from a horse but was otherwise in fine health. His doctor suggested we try to recreate a dramatic scene from his life, to awaken that memory and see if it would awaken others as well, just as a dash of cold water or a slap on the face awakens someone from sleep. His wife described one scene which she thought was important for him. We rehearsed it like actors, performed it with him present, and by the end of it, his memory was returning."

"Well, let's try that with Chryseis," I urged.

"She's so young. What incident in her life would stand out enough to make an impact on her shattered memory?"

I knew instantly. "The night she was branded. I know from the way she talked about it that it was seared into her soul as much as into her flesh."

"That would certainly be dramatic enough," Luke agreed. "But how do we know what happened? Chryseis can't tell us. Cornutus is dead."

"Melissa, Cornutus' concubine, was present at the branding. She described the whole thing to me."

"Could you bring her over here? With her help we'll try to make the re-enactment as accurate as possible."

"Yes, let's do it tonight. It happened in the middle of the night, according to Melissa." I went on to give him a list of 'props' we would need to stage our little melodrama.

* * * *

When we returned from the funeral Androcles met us on the sidewalk in front of his inn. His customary insolence had been replaced by hand-wringing terror.

"My lords," he said, "those women from Ephesus want to see you. They're waiting in the small dining room."

Tacitus and I exchanged glances. "We still have time to run," he said.

I shook my head. "Perhaps they'll kill us more humanely if we just go in and face them. Either way we're dead."

Glancing in the door of the small dining room before we entered, I was relieved to see that they didn't have the Molossian hounds with them.

I wondered if Damon's sling had proved more deadly than he thought. Anyte stood in the center of the room, with her acolytes arrayed in a semicircle behind her. Was the red around her mouth make-up clumsily applied or traces of the blood she had consumed at the ritual last night?

"What can I do for you, lady?" I asked, trying to take the initiative. For once I doubted my uncle's advice about acting as though I was in charge. It wasn't convincing me.

Anyte folded her arms across her chest. I could swear I saw a flame smoldering in her eyes. "Someone profaned our rites last night."

She hadn't directly accused me. She wasn't sure. If she had known for certain, I think she would have killed us last night in our sleep.

"What exactly happened?" I asked with a little more self-assurance. I was afraid Tacitus' blanched complexion had already given us away, but I was determined to keep up my pretense of innocence.

"Three men spied on our sacred rituals," she said, her voice growing deeper as the sentence progressed.

"Do you know who they were?"

"No, we weren't able to get close enough to identify them." She leaned closer to me, as though some lingering scent – perhaps the stench of fear – might give me away. "They rode away on horseback."

"Then why are you coming to me?"

"You claim to be running things since we arrived here."

"Lady, I must remind you that I have no official jurisdiction in Smyrna. I am merely trying to maintain order so that Cornutus' murder can be investigated according to Roman standards. As far as this matter is concerned, you can levy a complaint with Nicomedes, the boularch, if you wish, or wait until the governor arrives."

"Nicomedes, hah! He would shit all over himself if I showed up at his door."

I had to admit that her assessment of the surviving boularch's character matched my own, though she found an earthier way to phrase it.

"Perhaps I'll talk to the governor when he arrives," she continued.

"You may find him reluctant to do anything," I cautioned her. "Roman governors seldom interfere in the internal affairs of religious cults unless they threaten the public welfare."

"Then perhaps I will settle it myself. And woe to those three wretches if they fall into my hands." Her hands trembled as she clenched them in front of my face. Her desire to throttle somebody was palpable.

"Why don't you let the goddess defend her own honor?" I said before I thought.

"The tri-form goddess is not lightly mocked, young sir!" Anyte flung her robe around her. "The men who violated her rites must pay. They will lose something that they value above all else." She stormed out of the room.

Tacitus, aghast at my effrontery, could hardly contain himself until all the women had filed out. He grabbed my toga and jerked me around to face him. "Are you crazy? What if that witch did kill Cornutus? She won't stop at doing somebody else in. Or putting some kind of spell on them."

"I can't think of any way she could hurt me. I have nothing here that it would grieve me to lose. But I do remember that the main character in the *Satyricon* was rendered impotent because he spied on the rites of Priapus. That would certainly be a heavy punishment for you." I couldn't suppress a smile. "Something you 'value above all else'."

* * * *

As long as we already had the dining room to ourselves, we asked Androcles for an early lunch, which Pamphile promptly brought to us. But she practically threw it on the table and ran away without even looking at us. I think she was petrified that Anyte would learn that she had told us about the ritual. At least she hadn't informed on us. Yet.

Before we could begin eating, Orophernes skulked into the room. He stood such a respectful distance from our table that I wasn't sure at first if his business was with us. But we were the only people in the room.

"What is it, Orophernes?" I finally asked. Pronouncing his name made me feel the way Demosthenes must have felt when he put those pebbles in his mouth to improve his oratory.

He took a step closer. "Forgive me, Gaius Pliny, for interrupting your meal, but I believe I have some information that you will find interesting. Even valuable."

Probably, I thought, no more interesting or valuable than something a dog might drag home. "What is it?" I asked.

"Last night, a couple of hours after dark, I observed Lysimachus returning to the inn. He was sweaty and clearly agitated."

"And what significance do you attribute to this?"

"I suspect he was one of the men who spied on the witches' ritual. Should I tell her? Do you think she would reward me?"

I could see that Tacitus was having difficulty suppressing a laugh. "With no more proof than a sweaty brow," I said, "I would hesitate to expose a man to Anyte's wrath. Let's keep this between us for now. Thank you for telling me."

I thought I had dismissed him, but he continued to stand by our table until I caught on. I fumbled under my tunic, fished out a few coins, and handed them to Orophernes. My leading spy bowed and backed out of the room, almost bumping into Marcus Carolus on his way in.

"May I join you?" the big German asked.

"Please, do," I said, sorry that we would have to postpone sharing a laugh over Orophernes' performance.

Tacitus called to Pamphile for another helping of whatever gastronomical disaster we were flirting with. The beefy German settled himself across the table from us and attacked his meal the way his forefathers must have fallen on Varus' legions in the Teutoburg Forest. There would clearly be nothing left but bones.

He paused amid the devastation and asked, "Any news about the girl, Chryseis?"

"I'm pleased to report that she's well and is staying in another location where she will be safe."

Carolus raised his cup in a toast. "That's a relief. She's a sweet girl. Here's an offer for you. Why don't I buy all of Cornutus' slaves? It would save anyone else the trouble of escorting them back to Rome."

There was only one of Cornutus' slaves he was concerned about. Somehow I didn't think his interest in her was sexual. But I was afraid that, if he were to get control of her, I would never see her again.

"I'm afraid no one but Cornutus' father can make decisions about disposing of his property," I said, drawing myself up to exert whatever authority I could against this behemoth. I sometimes wondered how long Rome would be able to resist the power of the Teutons, poised up there above the Rhine and the Danube, like an avalanche waiting to bury us. "All we can do is hope that Manilius Quadratus is still alive when we get back to Rome. Cornutus' will must be read and everything sorted out according to law. Until then I've assumed guardianship, and I assure you that Chryseis is safe."

"You're a fair man, young sir," Carolus replied. "I'll rely on you to keep Chryseis . . . and the rest of Cornutus' property . . . out of the clutches of that villain Marcellus."

He redeemed himself somewhat in my eyes by sharing my low opinion of Marcellus. But I didn't want to continue that topic of conversation, even in Latin, in so public a place. "I gather you've been out this morning," I said, inviting him to tell me what he'd been doing without actually asking.

"Yes, I've been making arrangements to sell my load of silk and spices."

"Wouldn't you get more for them at Rome?" Tacitus asked in surprise, voicing my thought.

"I would, but I'm worried about the safety of my stuff while it's stored in Androcles' stable. Someone has been poking around in it already."

I almost blurted out the truth.

"I don't trust these damn Greeks for the blink of an eye," Carolus said. "Better to get rid of it at a lower price than risk losing it entirely. In fact, I need to go meet the man who's coming to have a look at the silk now." He wiped his mouth on a corner of his tunic and excused himself from the table.

Tacitus leaned back with his mouth twisted in disgust.

"What's the matter?" I asked. "His table manners too crude for you?"

"No, it's this wretched food. I know you think Cornutus was poisoned, but I wonder if this fish might have killed him without any assistance."

"This might have made him sick, but it's not lethal. No one else who ate here that night died. A poisoner can't poison the common pot and expect to kill only one person."

Tacitus turned his food over on the plate with a knife and sniffed at it warily. "Maybe the regular customers build up a resistance to it, like people who take small doses of poison so they can't be harmed if someone decides to do them in. I'd like to have someone who knows about poisons look this over, to see if they could identify what's in it."

I clapped him on the shoulder. "That's the best idea you've had all day."

"What idea? I was joking."

"Oh, I'm not talking about the food. But your suggestion made me wonder if we can see whether someone who knows poisons could make an educated guess about what might have killed Cornutus."

"How could anybody do that? His body's already been burned."

"I know. But we can describe his symptoms. Different poisons have different effects. We have several witnesses, including yourself, so we should be able to put together an account that could enable a knowledgeable person to figure out what was used."

"But you've announced that Cornutus was killed with a knife. If you start asking about poisons, you'll alert everybody, including the person who poisoned him."

Sometimes Tacitus' acuity was as annoying as it was helpful. For the moment the poisoner thought he (or she?) was undetected. That could make him relax and fall into a mistake.

"I've got it!" I said. "Let's find Androcles."

We finally located the loathsome innkeeper in the brothel section of his establishment.

"What can I do for you lads?" he asked unctuously. "Looking for a bit of company during your midday rest?"

Tacitus' eyes brightened, but I said, "No, thank you. I've been having some trouble sleeping at night. Do you know anyone who could mix me up a potion?"

"How long do you want to sleep?" Androcles replied archly.

"Just a few hours during the night will suffice."

"Well, for anything in that line, you want to see old Philyra. Just go down this street to the bathhouse – the one you've been to. Turn left there, go four blocks, then turn right. Her shop is in the middle of that block. She can mix up *anything* you need." He winked.

* * * *

Tacitus and I set out at once for Philyra's shop. I hoped I didn't arouse too much attention by not sending a slave to do this sort of mundane task. By midday the paving stones were heating up. The garbage and human waste dumped in the streets during the night was reeking. A good rain was needed to flush everything into the sewers. As in any town, the merchants displayed their wares on the sidewalks in front of their shops, forcing passersby to walk in the filthy streets. Covering our mouths and noses with scented handkerchiefs, we picked our way very carefully, hopping from one dry spot to another, like children playing a game.

We found Philyra's shop easily enough. The hag sat on a stool inside the door, scratching her right buttock. Her clothes hung on her like rags thrown haphazardly over a scrawny bush. Her cheeks had sunk in over her missing teeth. Jars of various sizes – some bearing arcane markings – crowded the shelves lining all the interior walls of the shop except for a door in the back, which I suspected led to her sleeping quarters.

"Good mornin', my lords," she croaked as she staggered off her stool. Obviously she had already had a considerable quantity to drink. "What'd ye be in the market fer t'day?"

I explained my need for a sleeping potion.

"Got just the thing." She shuffled over to a jar and spooned powder into a packet made of used papyrus. "This'll fix ye right up. Put three pinches in yer wine at dinner tonight and ye'll sleep like a innercent chile."

I paid her and we turned to leave. Then, as if an afterthought, I asked her, "Could you tell me what drug a person had taken, if I described the symptoms?"

Philyra was cagey in her response. "I could make some sorta

guess at it, my lord. Mind ye, I'm no expert on poisons. But some drugs perduce reactions sim'lar to others."

I described Cornutus' symptoms – drowsiness, numbness of the limbs, sensation of being cold – as best I could, considering I was relying on second-hand accounts. Tacitus added a detail here and there. The old crone listened to us attentively, scrunching up her face to focus through the alcoholic fog enshrouding her.

"It sounds to me, my lord," she finally said, "that it were aconite or hemlock. Either one will chill the blood and numb the arms and legs. Aconite can also perduce a tinglin' sensation on the skin."

"How would such drugs be administered?"

"Usually in wine. 'Member the description of Socrates' death by Plato?"

"Of course! The hemlock was mixed in wine, he drank it, and when he began to feel the effects, he lay down."

"Layin' down lets the drug work faster," Philyra said.

"You're very knowledgeable," Tacitus said, a bit nervously. "Do you have such drugs in your shop?"

She shook her head vigorously. "I've studied the lore of herbs an' roots since I were a chile, my lord, but I sell only medicinal ones. There be no aconite or hemlock in this shop." She waved her hand unsteadily around the place.

"How could such a drug be administered in front of other people?" I asked.

"There be a thousand ways," Philyra replied. "Or so I've heard. A poisoner is like a magician. He makes ye look at somethin' over there while he's doin' his business over here. Distracts ye. At least, that's what I've been told."

I took a few more sesterces from my money pouch and gave them to the crone. "You've been most helpful."

"I could be more helpful still," she said.

My damnable curiosity was piqued, and a few more coins jingled into her withered palm to satisfy it.

She looked around as though concerned that someone might overhear her. Then she leaned toward me. The wine on her breath did not quite mask the odor of her body. "Aconite be used to invoke Hecate," she whispered. "Her devotees smears themselves with an ointment containin' the drug. The tinglin' sensation is said to be a sign of their possession by the goddess. Legend is that Hecate created the drug from the foamin' mouth of the hell-hound, Cerberus."

IX

On our way back to our rooms we came to a food shop, what we would call a *taberna* in Rome.

"Lunch at the inn was awful," Tacitus said. "Why don't we get a bite here?"

"I'm not hungry," I said, "but I'll have a cup of wine."

Like most such shops, this place had no room for customers to sit down. Tacitus was given some bread dipped in olive oil and we both got some watery wine in a cheap, undecorated cup, which we were expected to return. We stood on the sidewalk eating.

While we ate I glanced around at the other customers. Some dozen or so people were crowding around the door of the taberna. Groups like this are interesting to observe just to try to figure out their ethnic background. Babylonians, then Persians, then Greeks have dominated this area for so long that the original native population has disappeared as a pure strain. Some of the worst characteristics of each group seem to have been emphasized by this blending.

As I watched today one fellow almost started a riot among the bystanders when he pulled his own wine cup from a bag. The taberna's owner didn't want to let him use it because it was bigger than the taberna's cups and the wine was sold by the cup. The man became quite cantankerous.

"I don't want to drink out of a cup that any pox-ridden whore could have used!" he sneered. The taberna's owner quickly filled his cup just to shut him up because he could see his other customers were getting restless.

"I wonder if that was Marcellus' reasoning," Tacitus said as he and I emptied the rest of our wine in the street and returned our cups.

"What are you talking about?"

"Haven't you noticed? At dinner the last two nights Marcellus has used his own plate and cup instead of the inn's. I thought a man who carries his own strigl with him all over the empire – "

"I'm not going to let you bait me about that again. You heard what doctor Luke said. It's eminently sensible."

"So is bringing your own napkin to dinner. We all do that. Your own plate and cup – doesn't that qualify as eccentric behavior?"

* * * *

When we returned to the inn I settled in my room to make a few notes before resting. Following my uncle's model, I have begun to keep my own records of interesting bits of information and my observations and conclusions about them. Philyra's tidbit about aconite begged to be recorded.

Leaving the door to my room open because of the heat, I was engrossed in my writing when my concentration was broken by Damon's voice.

"My lord," he said solicitously, "I was wondering if you needed anything before the midday rest." He was still trying to make up for letting Chryseis get away. Slaves don't normally come looking for work.

"No, thank you, Damon." I expected him to leave, but he remained standing in the door. "Is there something else?"

"I'm not sure, my lord." He stepped into the room and closed the door. "I just ate lunch with one of Marcus Carolus' slaves. He said some things I found puzzling. I thought I should mention them to you."

"So you two were gossiping about your masters?"

"Slaves have little else to talk about, my lord." How long would I have to put up with his impudence just because he had saved my life? "One can always start a conversation among other slaves by mentioning a few faults of one's master."

"And what faults of mine did you mention?"

He seemed to sense he was treading into dangerous ground. "They need not be real faults, my lord. One can make up anything, just for the sake of conversation."

I had made him squirm enough. "So what did this slave say that you thought worth reporting?"

"His name was Euergetes, my lord."

That was a subtle reminder that he was an individual, a person, someone with a name. One of Damon's constant complaints was that slaves were deprived of their standing as human beings. I guess he'd been listening while he read all those philosophical treatises to my uncle and me. So, this fellow was a Greek. At least the name was. It meant 'Good worker'. But sometimes slaves are given ironic names. He might be the laziest slave Marcus Carolus owned.

"What struck me," Damon continued, "was his complaints about what a poor businessman Marcus Carolus is. He said Carolus had spent the morning selling off his silk and spices at a fraction of what they would bring in Rome."

"Yes. Carolus told me about the transaction. He's afraid of having his merchandise stolen out from under him while we're stalled here."

"But, my lord, Euergetes says this is typical of the kinds of unpredictable decisions Carolus makes. Sometimes he decides to go on business trips that don't make much financial sense. They've spent the last year in and around Antioch, to little purpose. The trip was not really necessary or particularly profitable. Carolus paid too much for the silk and spices. But they could have salvaged something on this trip if they hadn't left so soon, in Euergetes' opinion."

I'm sure the lift of my eyebrow told him what value I placed on this slave's evaluation of Carolus' business acumen. "What makes him so sure of that?"

"Well, my lord," Damon continued nervously, "Euergetes says another caravan was due to arrive in Antioch in a few days with more goods from the east, including some slaves. A servant from the caravan was sent ahead to alert everyone to its arrival and to make arrangements for lodgings. He said they had several extraordinarily beautiful women from China among the slaves – delicate, almost childlike creatures. Such exotic slaves could have been sold for an enormous profit in Rome. But Carolus wouldn't stay. With only two day's notice he decided to return to Rome. His slaves were ordered to pack practically overnight. One was left behind to see to shipping most of their belongings and merchandise. It's as though there was some reason that Carolus just *had* to be in this particular caravan."

"If you miss a caravan, you can't always predict when the next one will leave."

"Euergetes knew of another one planning to leave a week later, my lord. It wouldn't have hurt to wait, but Carolus wouldn't hear of it."

I was growing impatient and ready for some rest, but I could see Damon might prove a source of useful information. He had access to people who would talk to me only under duress. For all that Roman law stresses torture for extracting the truth from slaves, I doubt it actually has that effect. People will admit to anything when their arms are being wrenched from the sockets.

"I appreciate your inquiries," I said, "but what have you learned other than the unsurprising fact that not everyone agrees with Marcus Carolus' business methods?"

"There is one other thing, my lord. Euergetes said they've been on several caravans in recent years with Cornutus. They came to Antioch when he did and have spent the past year there. But Marcus Carolus never said anything to the man. Euergetes thought he appeared to be following Cornutus. 'Like a hunter tracking his prey' – that's the very phrase he used, my lord."

"He wouldn't be the only hunter in Rome after Cornutus. Cornutus had a lot of money and no children. You know what that means."

Damon nodded. "Legacy hunters."

"Yes. A constant stream of sycophants paying court, trying to ingratiate themselves into his will. I'm sure Regulus himself has been on the scent for some time."

"But, my lord, Carolus never spoke to Cornutus, at least according to Euergetes. How could he be looking for a legacy?"

I pondered Damon's question until I fell asleep. No immediate answer suggested itself, but a suspicion grew stronger that Chryseis was at the center of this maze. What I couldn't find was the path leading from her to Cornutus to Marcellus. And Regulus, I was sure, was lurking somewhere, waiting to devour us all, like the Minotaur in his lair.

* * * *

Despite the heat I did sleep for a while. At around the ninth hour of the day I awoke, feeling refreshed enough for a little walk. On a roof.

I knocked on Tacitus' door and heard some scurrying sounds from inside the room. I waited a moment until a handsome young boy opened the door, still adjusting his tunic, and slipped out past me with only a suggestion of a bow. Something about his face seemed familiar, though I knew I had never seen him before.

"Pamphile will be jealous," I said to Tacitus, who was still lying in bed with a blanket pulled up to his waist, his head cradled on his left arm. Sweat beaded around the edges of his brown hair. He could have been a sculptor's model for a resting satyr.

"No, she won't. She sent him to me. He's her brother."

I hoped the shock and disgust I felt didn't register on my face. "Oh, yes. That upturned nose. That's where I've seen it before." I wondered if Tacitus was going to plow his way through the whole family while we were stalled here.

"I'm sure you didn't drop in to congratulate me on another conquest," he said. "Are you looking for company for the baths?"

"Soon. But first I want to examine the room where Cornutus' female slaves were confined the night he was killed."

He threw on a tunic and we climbed the dark stairs to the third floor. Melissa and Phoebe had already left the room. I had told Trophimus, my overseer, to keep them as busy as possible. There were clothes to mend and wash. Beyond that, I wasn't sure what tasks he was assigning them, or what tasks they had any experience with.

The room was a copy of my own and Tacitus', but it hadn't been whitewashed as recently as ours. The rooms on this floor were for poorer guests and the slaves of wealthier travelers. The beds were rickety, the mattresses a bit aromatic. I went straight to the window and poked my head out.

"I thought you were going to search the place," Tacitus said.

"What's the point in that? If Melissa or Phoebe cut Cornutus' heart out, they would hardly try to hide it here. I'm more interested in seeing whether someone could have gotten from here to Cornutus' room."

I pulled the only chair in the room over to the window. When I put my head and shoulders through the opening I found myself looking out over the roof of the stable behind the inn. The peak of the roof met the wall of the inn only a couple of feet below me. I wriggled out the window and tested my footing on the roof. Its slope was gentle enough that I could stand.

Tacitus stuck his head out the window. "You'd get a better grip on those tiles with your bare feet than with your sandals."

I looked up at him and down at the roof. It was covered with rotting garbage and waste which people – too lazy to walk to the nearest slop jar – had tossed out of windows.

"I'll take my chances in my sandals."

"Don't trip over Cornutus' heart."

That crack gave me pause. "Surely whoever cut it out wouldn't just toss it out the window. That act had some significance for the killer."

"Or he needed a piece of meat for a stew."

I let go of the window sill, steadied myself by keeping one hand on the wall of the inn, and began walking down the roof toward where

I thought Cornutus' room was. Some of the second-floor rooms didn't have windows because they were covered by the stable roof. Three rooms over from Melissa's room, under the second window that I came to on the second floor, I noticed the wall was streaked with vomit. Mine and Tacitus', I was sure.

The window of Cornutus' room was at shoulder height. I could see the room was unoccupied. Hoisting myself up into a window at this height proved to be more difficult than lowering myself out of Melissa's window. I scraped my knees and made a good bit of noise in my efforts. But it could be done, I was sure, by a reasonably agile person, someone determined to gain entry to the room. Could a woman do it alone? What if she had someone to give her a boost . . . ?

Without any warning a potful of human waste from a third-floor window landed a few steps farther down the roof, splattering my feet and lower legs.

"Damn you! Use the slop jar!" I yelled. Then I retreated to Melissa's window.

* * * *

I gave my sandals to Damon to be burned or buried. Thrifty soul that he is, he tried to assure me they could be cleaned. Even if they could, I told him, I didn't want them on my feet again.

A bath and a vigorous massage from Tacitus' deaf slave restored my spirits. While the man worked on us we mulled over, in low voices in Latin, the implications of my little expedition onto the roof.

"Clearly Cornutus' female slaves can't be removed from suspicion," I said.

"But," Tacitus countered, "we don't know for certain that the killer entered through the window."

We had agreed to continue to talk about the person who cut Cornutus up as 'the killer', in case anyone should overhear us. I was still convinced the real murderer was the one who gave him poison earlier in the evening. But that secret had to remain among three people – Tacitus, Luke, and me. Finding the person who cut Cornutus' heart out was also important. Especially if I was the intended victim.

"Granted, the killer could have used the door," I said. "It was late at night. But the women are either suspects or they're witnesses to the fact that no one went in through the window. We'll have to find out how long they actually stayed on the roof."

"It would take a fairly small person to get in through the window," Tacitus said. "A woman or a man no larger than yourself. I mean no offense."

"And I take none. I don't pretend to be the epitome of Roman manhood. I don't think a man my size – or a woman – would plan to attack someone as large as Cornutus unless the assailant was sure Cornutus couldn't fight back."

"So you think someone drugged him in the hope of rendering him unconscious, but not necessarily intending to kill him."

I rubbed my eyes, as if that would make the answer to this puzzle clearer. "I remain convinced the poisoner and the knifer were not the same person. Cornutus was poisoned first, and poisoners aim to kill, not immobilize. Then, once you've killed somebody, you don't need to kill him again. So, I believe we're looking for two people. And a missing heart. Beyond that I'm not sure of anything. It's been two days and I don't feel I'm any closer to the answers."

"But," Tacitus said, "what is the likelihood that two different people would decide to kill the same man on the same night? If there were two killers, isn't it more likely there were two intended victims? And if somebody thought you were in Cornutus' room, was one of those victims meant to be you?"

Some of his questions just posed a challenge. That one scared me.

* * * *

Dinner in the inn's dining room started well when Marcellus made no appearance. I had brought Melissa and another of Cornutus' slaves, along with two of my own, to attend Tacitus and me and to give them a break from eating their meals in a corner of the kitchen or in the stable. Instead of making them stand behind us during the entire meal, I had a small table set up so they could eat when they weren't serving us. Melissa had obviously grown accustomed to living like a Roman aristocrat during the last five years, and before the war she had been a free person, apparently of some status. If I could make her a little more comfortable as a reward for her care of Chryseis and in partial repayment for what my uncle's troops had done to her family, I would make the effort.

My mediocre dinner curdled in my stomach when Marcellus and his entourage entered the dining room with a great show. He seemed to have augmented his troop with some local hangers-on. One of his slaves carried a funeral urn, a quite elaborate one, in the gaudy Hellenistic style, overlaid with silver. Nude demigods and heroes, entwined with vines, writhed in contorted positions which the human body couldn't possibly assume. Cornutus' full name was engraved across one side. Marcellus wanted everyone to see that he had spared no expense in packing up the ashes of his 'friend' for the trip to Rome.

"Ah, Gaius Pliny, you're here," he said. "I can deliver this to you and discharge my responsibility." He snapped his fingers and motioned to the slave carrying the urn, who stepped forward and deposited the thing beside my chair. I didn't know quite how to react. An urn filled with a dead man's ashes does nothing to lift the mood in a dining room. I also resented Marcellus' smugness. He had poisoned Cornutus in some way, I was convinced of it. Now he had destroyed all evidence of the crime and was flaunting it in front of everyone, practically daring me to prove it. Because of the 'second murder' later in the evening, he thought we didn't even know about the first.

Laughing with his sycophants, Marcellus settled at a table. One of his slaves ran upstairs and returned quickly with a plate and a wine cup, which he set down in front of Marcellus.

My attention was drawn away from the odd little scene by a stifled sob behind me. Melissa, her hands over her mouth, could not stop her tears. For the first time it struck me that she had lost her lover – her husband in all but name – and yet she could not go through the rituals of mourning which society allows to widows. I caught her eye and nodded her permission to leave the dining room. Everyone fell silent and watched her departure.

Lysimachus' rich baritone broke the trance. "What a waste to weep over the dead. As Euripides says in the *Heraclidae*, 'I don't long to die, but when I leave life I won't grieve at all.' Or, as the divine Plato put it in the *Laws*, 'Death is not the worst that can happen to men'."

"But did Euripides or Plato lose someone very dear to them?" I asked, suddenly thinking of my uncle's death.

Lysimachus ignored me. This was probably some set piece he had rehearsed and he wasn't going to let himself be blown off course. "All the great thinkers remind us that it is our fear of death, rather than death itself, that is our burden. In the words of Euripides again, 'We know what it is to live, but ignorance of death makes everyone afraid to leave the light of day'."

He was making the opening gambit in a game often played at dinners by people who pretend to erudition. One person proposes a topic and quotes a few lines from some poet or philosopher. Other guests are expected to chime in with other relevant quotations.

Tacitus kept the game going. "Our Seneca said something along those lines: 'Death is among those things which are not evil but have the appearance of evil'."

That seemed to give Lysimachus an extra gust for his sails, as if the windbag needed it. "Quite so! In the words of the divine Plato,

'The fear of death is indeed the pretense of wisdom, and not real wisdom, being a pretense of knowing the unknown; and no one knows whether death, which men in their fear apprehend to be the greatest evil, may not be the greatest good'."

Marcus Carolus spoke up, slurring a bit drunkenly. "Cicero said it best, 'The happiest fate is not to be born; the next happiest is to die very early'."

Until that point Luke and Timothy had been eating quietly in the far corner of the dining room. I had noted, with some surprise, Tiberius Saturninus sitting with them. Now Luke cleared his throat and said, "He's not the only one to feel that despair. Consider this line: 'Why did I not perish at birth and die as I came from the womb?'"

Everyone fell silent. To quote an obscure source destroyed the rhythm of the game.

"Who said that?" I asked.

"It comes from one of the holy books of the Jews, about a man named Job."

Tacitus' interest was piqued. "Are you a Jew?"

I had wondered the same thing about both Luke and Timothy. My observation in the bath house made it clear Luke was not circumcised, so he could hardly have been a Jew. That barbaric ritual is performed on all their male infants and on any males who join the cult as adults.

"No, I'm not," Luke replied, "but I have read many of their books. There is much wisdom in them about the whole course of life, and about death."

Orophernes – my chief spy – who was dining with Lysimachus, picked up that theme again and said, "Cornutus' was such a tragic death. Gaius Pliny, have you learned any more about who's responsible?"

I knew I had to phrase my answer very carefully. Appear to be doing something without letting everybody know what we were doing. "We will report our findings to the governor when he arrives, probably tomorrow."

Gaius Sempronius caught me off-guard with a question, damn him. "What about Cornutus' slave girl, the pretty golden-haired one, who disappeared? Have you found her?"

"We're working on that," I replied. "I believe we'll get her back soon." It wasn't an entirely dishonest answer. If our plan to restore her memory proved successful tonight, we would in fact have her back whole.

"But, my lord," said Pamphile, plopping a plate on a nearby table, "she's at the house of Apelles the boularch. Half of Smyrna knows that."

And now, thanks to you and a bunch of gossipy slaves, I thought, so does Marcellus.

* * * *

My anger at Pamphile for spilling what I thought was a carefully guarded secret curbed my appetite entirely, so I got up and left the dining room. On the second-floor landing of the stairway I found Melissa. Her face was streaked from crying and the front of her dress was torn.

"Is there anything I can do for you?" I asked.

"No, my lord. Thank you." She sniffled several times and wiped her eyes on a corner of her gown. "I apologize for being upset. I know slaves aren't supposed to feel anything. But he wasn't just my master. I loved him so much."

I had never before found myself in such a dilemma. This woman hated me and my family, with some justification. She might have tried to kill me. She was someone else's slave. I had no reason to feel any sympathy for her. I ought to squeeze my way past her and go on to my room. Instead I took her in my arms. She kept her arms folded across her chest but accepted my embrace.

"They wouldn't . . . let me go to his funeral," she said as the tears started again, dampening the right shoulder of my tunic. I could appreciate the uncertainty of her situation. She was supposed to show only a slave's sorrow for a dead master, but she felt the grief of one who has lost a lover and the fear of a slave who doesn't know what the future holds for her.

"Who wouldn't let you go?" I asked, though I knew the answer.

"Marcellus and his people."

When her crying subsided again I said, "You're obviously very upset. Should we postpone our re-enactment of Chryseis' branding scene to another time? Are you up to it?"

She pulled away from me and straightened her clothes and hair. "Thank you for your concern, my lord. I can be ready. I just don't think it's wise to put her through that. I know you and the doctor believe it's a good idea, but I wish you could give her a little more time to recover on her own."

"You're being too presumptuous," I snapped. "Luke thinks this is what we should do, and it's not your place to question his judgment." I was glad she wasn't my slave. Her spirit would make her very difficult to handle.

She bowed her head. "Forgive me, my lord, but Chryseis is like a daughter to me. I will do anything to protect her. Can't we see if her memory returns gradually? That sometimes happens, doesn't it?"

"Luke says it might take days, even months, if it ever happens that way. We don't have time to wait. If she knows something that might lead us to Cornutus' killer, we have to find out what it is."

"But, my lord, she's only a child."

"Hardly. If she were a free woman, she'd be married by now."

I could see instantly that my remark had the effect of a flint struck against a pile of dry grass. A flame flashed in Melissa's eyes.

"Yes, my lord. *If* she were free . . ."

"I won't argue with you, Melissa. Luke and I have decided what is to be done. We will be as gentle with Chryseis as we can. You need to help us – and her – to make this experiment as effective as possible. Now, that is the end of the matter."

She bit her lip. "As you wish, my lord."

It's funny how a slave can say exactly the words she's supposed to say, but convey an entirely different message in the tone of her voice, the look in her eye, the very way she moves.

* * * *

Since our presence would be required at Apelles' house in the middle of the night, Tacitus, Luke, Melissa, and I walked over there not long after supper to avoid being on the streets after dark. A smaller city such as Smyrna must be safer than Rome, which falls into the hands of cut-throats and bandits after sunset, but no city of any size affords real security for those who venture onto its streets after dark. I observed Melissa closely as we walked. She seemed composed, almost resolved. Time alone to vent her grief seemed to have settled her.

Upon our arrival we were assured by Apelles' widow, a pudgy, sad woman named Kallisto – though I doubt anyone but the most doting parents would have considered her 'the most beautiful', as her name indicated – that Chryseis was in another wing in the back of the house and would not be aware of our presence.

I hadn't taken much notice of the house on my previous visit, but I now realized it was quite large, and built on the Roman model. Apelles, Luke told me on the way over, had lived in Rome for a number of years before returning to his hometown. The house boasted not one peristyle garden but two.

Melissa and I inspected the tablinum, where our little drama would be acted out. As she suggested some rearrangement of furniture to make it look more like Cornutus' tablinum I could imagine her as a free woman, in her own home. She had never lost that poise and self-confidence. Kallisto had her slaves carry out Melissa's directions. Then there was nothing for us to do but wait. We retired to the same peristyle garden where I had talked with Chryseis earlier in the day. Torches had been lighted, and several slaves were ready to serve us.

Conversation soon dwindled, since Luke and Timothy on the one hand were not well acquainted with Tacitus and me on the other. "We need a bard to sing us the tale of the Trojan War," Tacitus finally said during an awkward pause, drawing a chuckle from the rest of us. A long story would certainly help ease the social awkwardness and pass the time we had to wait.

"Your uncle died in something just as devastating as the Trojan War, didn't he?" Luke said to me.

"Yes. He was overcome by the fumes from Mt. Vesuvius while he was trying to rescue people from the eruption."

"Would it be too painful for you to tell us about it?" Luke asked.

"It would be painful for us if he were to sing it," Tacitus said. "Believe me, I've heard him sing."

"Tacitus is right about that. But I can tell the story." I glanced apologetically at Tacitus. He had heard parts of the narrative while we were traveling, but he was the one who brought up the idea of a story-teller. I was secretly pleased to have the opportunity to relate my tale to a new and appreciative audience.

"It began one afternoon in late August, four years ago. We – my mother, my uncle, and I – were relaxing on the terrace of my uncle's house after lunch. He had command of the fleet in that area. The house is on the peninsula of Misenum, at the extreme west end of the bay of Naples, where it joins the open sea. My mother noticed a cloud rising from the other end of the bay, some twenty miles away. My uncle, because of his scientific interests, decided to take a boat and go investigate. There seemed no reason for haste, and by the time he got the little expedition organized, a messenger arrived from Naples to say that disaster had struck. Mt. Vesuvius, which no one had ever suspected was volcanic, was erupting. The towns along the coast – Pompeii, Herculaneum, and Stabiae – were in mortal danger, as were the numerous private villas which lined the coast. What had begun as a leisurely voyage prompted by curiosity became a rush to save as many lives as possible.

"We decided that I would stay at the house, to watch over my mother and the slaves. We had no way of foreseeing how widespread a catastrophe this would become, but my uncle always stressed the importance of protecting one's home base in a military operation, which this was now turning into."

As I slipped into the rhythm of my story I could see my audience falling under its spell, too. From the accounts of those on the ships I had compiled my own 'bardic' version of the disaster. Now I led this small circle of listeners through the terrifying voyage of the ships across the bay, with ash and bits of pumice raining down on them like flaming projectiles from an enemy ship as they sped into ever-thickening darkness.

Nor was I ashamed to mention my own part. At Misenum, I attempted to keep everyone in our household calm, but that night the house began to shake and ash began to fall on us. We joined the flow of refugees heading north. Some were crying for family members who'd become separated from them. Others were cursing the gods and bewailing the end of the human race.

"'There shall be weeping and wailing and gnashing of teeth'," Luke said softly.

"Where did you get that line?" I asked.

"Oh, from something too obscure to have come to your notice," he replied quickly.

"The author could have been with me that night," I said.

"Please continue, friend Pliny," Luke said. "I shouldn't have interrupted you. We're all enthralled by your story. I'm sorry you were interrupted."

"There's not much more to tell," I said, picking up the thread. "My mother proved too frail to travel far, so we tried to take refuge beside a tomb, but if we sat still for even a short time, the ash threatened to cover us. When we first stopped by the tomb, the top of it was even with my head. By the next morning the top of it was below my waist. Most frightening of all was the darkness. I've never known a night of such thick, suffocating darkness. Morning in this case was just slightly less darkness.

"The next day we received the terrible news of my uncle's death."

As I finished the story and fell silent my listeners seemed to remember that they could breathe again.

"That was an unimaginable horror," Timothy said. "I had friends in Pompeii. The entire family was lost. I'm glad to know something of what it was like."

One of Kallisto's slaves brought a fresh pitcher of wine. We all drank and sat alone with our thoughts for a few minutes.

"My lord," Melissa said, "the moon is visible above the roof of the house now. I think it's late enough for us to begin."

X

We filed out to our several places. Luke, Tacitus, and I concealed ourselves in a room next to the tablinum. After Chryseis entered the room, we would take up positions outside the door, to be able to hear what was going on and to allow Luke to intervene if he felt Chryseis was being endangered. Melissa had selected two of Apelles' slaves who matched the general size and appearance of Cornutus and the other slave woman who had assisted her. In that poorly lighted room, she said, they would serve the purpose. She had given them specific instructions about where to stand, what to say and do. A brazier had been filled with hot coals and a branding iron was glowing in it. With all of us in our places, Melissa went to fetch Chryseis.

They returned in a few moments. I could hear Chryseis asking tiredly where they were going. Melissa, according to the script, told her that her master wanted to see her. Once they were in the tablinum, Luke, Tacitus, and I tiptoed over to the door and flattened ourselves against the wall. What I heard cut into my heart.

Chryseis was crying. "What are you doing? Please, let me go." In the original incident she was gagged, but we couldn't gag her here. We had to hear what she was saying, to know if her memory was returning.

She let out a scream so piercing I could hardly bear to listen. I stood away from the wall and turned to the door, about to rush in and rescue her. Luke, on the other side of the doorway, made a gesture with his hand as if to hold me back. His face displayed as much anxiety as I felt.

"No!" Chryseis cried again. "No!" From the thuds of furniture being kicked around, I realized that they were trying to tie her to the table. If the real Cornutus was her father, how could he have stood to put his child through this?

"Shut her up," I heard the fake Cornutus tell the other slave woman. He spoke his lines with no conviction at all.

But then Chryseis called out, "Mel . . . Mel . . . Melissa!"

Luke's face brightened as Melissa said, "Stop! She knows me."

I bolted into the room ahead of Luke and grabbed the branding iron from the hand of the fake Cornutus. He was holding it just inches from Chryseis' face. Unfortunately, I didn't have my hand wrapped in a cloth, as he did, and the handle was almost as hot as the brand. The searing pain helped me to avert my eyes from the sight of Chryseis nude, stretched over Apelles' table, her ankles and one of her wrists tied to its legs. Melissa threw a blanket over the sobbing girl and untied her.

I dismissed the two slaves. Luke told the woman to bring some oil for my burned hand. Melissa wrapped the blanket around Chryseis and hugged her. I longed to hold her myself, but I knew she needed the comfort of Melissa's familiar presence.

When she had settled down, Melissa said, "Let me help her get dressed and gather her wits for a moment. We will return."

I put a hand on the girl's shoulder. "Chryseis, I am so sorry we had to put you through this. We had to risk it to help you get your memory back. You know I would never hurt you."

She looked me straight in the eye. "Yes, my lord, I know." She turned to Melissa and said, "I'm all right. I can talk with them now."

We all took seats around the table which sat in the center of the room. Melissa moved her chair close to Chryseis' and placed her hand on the girl's arm. As in any aristocrat's tablinum, shelves around the walls held Apelles' collection of scrolls, and bits and pieces of papyrus with household accounts and other necessary information. Luke glanced at me in a way that put me in charge of the questioning.

"Can you tell us what happened on the stairs in the inn?" I began. "What, or who, made you fall?"

Chryseis hugged the blanket tightly around her. "All I know for certain, my lord, is that a man hit me and I fell."

"You didn't fall accidentally, or stumble?"

"No, my lord. I was being very careful because the stairway was so dark and narrow."

"Marcellus claims that you stumbled on the stairs and bumped into him as he was coming down. Think very hard. Can you see anything in your mind?"

She looked down and really did appear to be trying to concentrate and remember something. Finally she looked up at me. "I'm sorry, my lord. It was dark and everything happened so quickly. I don't remember bumping into anyone, but if Marcellus says I did . . . maybe I did. I had my head down, watching my footing. My master was right, actually. I am a bit clumsy."

"But you said before that he hit you," I persisted.

"Somebody did . . . I think." She rubbed a hand over her eyes. "It's all very confusing to me now."

"Could Marcellus have been reaching out to grab you," Tacitus said, "perhaps to keep you from falling?"

I glared at him in disbelief and anger, made even stronger by the pain in my hand. "When did he hire you to defend him?"

Tacitus shrugged. "Do you want to find the truth, or do you just want to construct your own version of what happened?"

I broke away from his gaze because I realized he was getting to the core of the problem. In investigating any sort of puzzle one must have a theory, as a sort of guide. But one must also remain open to any other possible explanation that might develop.

"I have no wish to defend anyone either," Luke interjected quietly, "but it does seem unlikely to me that Marcellus could have been planning to attack Chryseis. First, what possible reason could he have? Secondly, how could he have known she would be coming up those stairs at that particular moment? The stairs are narrow and dark, as we all know. Isn't an accident the simplest explanation for what happened?"

"It's clear we're not going to get any further on this path of questioning," I said. "You, my supposed colleagues, are now speaking for the other side and sowing such confusion that Chryseis is no longer even certain about what happened."

"You need not get so huffy, friend Pliny," Luke said. "We're simply trying to be certain that, in your zeal to convict Marcellus, we don't allow the real culprit to escape."

Before I could object, Tacitus said, "Marcellus may well be the guilty one, but there is no compelling evidence against him, for either Cornutus' murder or for trying to harm this girl. Why don't you look at some others who had perfectly good reasons to kill Cornutus? I'd like to know more about Tiberius Saturninus' gambling debts myself. Or where the witch Anyte was at the time Cornutus was killed."

I had to admit they were right. I could almost hear my uncle's voice in their admonitions. "All right. For the sake of argument, let's cast the net a little wider. But before we finish here, I want to ask Chryseis about something else."

The golden-haired slave girl sat up straight, nervously alert. "Yes, my lord?"

"Where did you get the sealed document that you carry in your bag?"

The way she looked at me is the way I imagine Hera glared at Zeus when she discovered one of his infidelities. I knew she wanted to ask me by what right I was rummaging through her bag. Even if she was only a slave, she was someone else's slave, not mine. She clipped her words as she said, "My master, Cornutus, gave it to me the day after he branded me. He told me not to open it myself under any circumstances. If something happened to him, I was to take it to the nearest Roman magistrate and have him open it. The document would protect me, he told me, but I must never break the seal."

"Do you want to open it now?" I hoped she would say yes, just to satisfy my own curiosity. Sometimes that characteristic of mine seems almost a flaw.

"You aren't a magistrate, are you, my lord?"

"No."

"Then I'll wait until the governor arrives, my lord. I don't mean to be difficult, but those were my master's instructions and I believe I should carry them out."

The lift of her head could have seemed arrogant in a slave. It struck me as self-confident, worthy of a noblewoman.

I sensed it was time to quit. "I think that's all we're going to learn tonight. It's very late. Melissa, why don't you put her to bed? Then there are a few things I'd like to ask you. Would you meet me in the garden?"

She looked a bit irritated, but just said, "Yes, my lord."

* * * *

Since we knew in advance that it would be late before we were finished, we had made arrangements with Apelles' family to spend the night there. Luke put a salve on my hand and wrapped it. Then he and Tacitus had gone to bed by the time Melissa found the bench where I was sitting in the garden. She stood before me until I motioned for her to sit with me. The torches had been extinguished. The moon, just one night past its fullest point, provided all the illumination we needed. Melissa's gown, a pale green, took on a lustrous sheen. It was almost as though she was moving through a waterfall.

"Thank you for your help tonight," I began. "We couldn't have pulled her through without you."

"I'm sorry to have doubted you and the doctor, my lord. And I am pleased to do anything for Chryseis."

"Can you put aside your hatred of me, for her sake?"

She sighed, as though expelling some of her animosity. "I will try, my lord. I've been telling myself these last few days that you aren't your uncle. You have been very fair, even gracious, in your treatment of me. And your concern for Chryseis goes beyond anything we have a right to expect."

"I want to continue to help you. But to do that I need information that only you can give me. Now, I know it's late, and this probably could wait until tomorrow, but I'm too excited to sleep right now."

"I can understand, my lord. I doubt if I will sleep tonight."

I wasn't quite sure that she was referring just to the excitement of the evening. I wished I could knock down the fortifications she had erected around herself, fortifications held together by resentment of men like me and my uncle. I wondered how Cornutus had breached the wall.

"I don't mean to frighten you," I said, "but I believe whoever killed Cornutus may intend to harm Chryseis." Actually, frightening her was exactly what I hoped to do. If she was a bit scared, I thought, she might be more open with information. "I want to protect Chryseis, but to do that I need to know as much about her background as possible. That may help me figure out who would have a reason to hurt her. Since you were so close to Cornutus, I thought he might have told you something he wouldn't tell anyone else."

She began cautiously. "Very soon after I arrived in his house I saw that Cornutus took a special interest in Chryseis, but in a funny way. At times it seemed he doted on her. She was a kind of pet, the way many Roman aristocrats treat a favorite slave child, especially when they have no children of their own. But, at other times, he seemed to hate the sight of her. As he and I grew closer, I asked him why he treated her that way. He told me that her mother was a German captive, taken in a battle across the Rhine, north of Colonia Agrippina. He purchased her in the aftermath of the battle. She died in childbirth. Cornutus felt she hadn't had proper care during the birth, and that was his fault, since she was his slave."

"Do you know if this German woman was his . . . concubine, if you'll pardon my using that term?"

"It's all right, my lord. I have accepted my status. Cornutus loved me, no matter what anyone may call me. I was his wife in all but name. He was married at the time he took this German woman captive. I don't know if he had any relationship with her. He told me nothing more about her."

"Is there anything else you can tell me about Chryseis, anything that would give someone reason to harm her?"

"No, my lord. She's a sweet, loving child."

"Do you know anything about the sealed document Cornutus gave her?"

"No, my lord. That was a secret both of them kept from me."

"I guess we'll have to wait until the governor arrives to get to the bottom of that."

"My lord, I'm very worried. What's going to happen to us? Will we be sold?" She forgot herself enough to clasp my unburned hand in both of hers.

I laid my bandaged hand over hers. "Melissa, I promise I will do whatever it takes to protect you and Chryseis. I've taken on the responsibility of returning you to Cornutus' father in Rome. That gives us some time."

"Thank you, my lord. Is that all you need from me?" She withdrew her hands and assumed the more servile posture, with her hands clasped in her lap.

"Yes. And I thank you for your forthright answers." I wondered if I dared to ask her if she had tried to kill me and cut Cornutus up by mistake.

"With your permission then, my lord, I will spend the night in Chryseis' room."

"I think that's an excellent idea, since that's what happened before and Chryseis has been through quite an ordeal tonight."

* * * *

The next morning I awoke well before sunrise, as is my habit, partly learned from my uncle and partly a family trait, like big ears or red hair. My uncle was always up while it was still dark, dictating replies to letters or doing other official business. Once I remembered where I was, I walked around the house a bit. It appeared to have been enlarged several times, to judge from the way doors had been cut into walls and roofs extended here and there. I was tempted to look in on Chryseis and Melissa but decided not to bother them. They were sure to be sleeping soundly after the exhausting ordeal of the previous night.

Finally I found a spot in the larger garden, behind a bush and a column, where I could sit and reflect. I had been doing that a lot while plodding along in the wagon on this trip. Like the mules pulling the wagon,

I was on a long journey, but not entirely sure where it would end. Perhaps I would be happier if, like the mules, I gave no thought to the ultimate destination and simply focused on the trip, the metaphor for my life.

What was I going to do with my life? Would I ever accomplish as much as my uncle did? In addition to his research and writing, he held a number of government posts and undoubtedly would have been rewarded with the consulship if he had lived a few more years. Could I follow in his footsteps? Could I aspire to that honor? Cicero, whom I also try to emulate, had served in the provinces and then achieved the consulship. And Cicero was not from Rome itself, but from a small Italian town, like my family. The aristocratic families of the city itself no longer seem strong enough to provide men who possess the qualities of leadership on which Rome was built. Too many of them are like Marcellus – dissolute, dissipated, interested in nothing but their own advancement. Younger, more vital, parts of the empire must pick up the slack.

In that regard I'm like the provinces, I realized. So much has been thrust on me, so young. I wish my uncle had lived at least another five years. I haven't had time to consider what direction my life ought to take, as most Roman men do at this stage. Legally we become adults at age seventeen, but social custom allows us several years to continue our education, travel. Or just waste our lives. I'll have to make some decision about a marriage in the next year or two. That will be difficult because I have no father or older male relatives to negotiate arrangements with another family. I am my own *pater familias*, far earlier in life than most Roman men.

Cornutus' approach does have simplicity on its side: buy a woman and compel her to sleep with you. But I could never do that. Chryseis, for example. In spite of how much I want her, the thought of forcing myself on her is repugnant. Besides, in this society she could never be my legitimate wife. I would have to marry someone of my social class, someone with a sizeable fortune.

Once I've done that, what am I to do with my life? Make myself richer than I already am? Managing the estates my uncle left me requires much of my time and energy. I'd like to be rid of them, but I have to worry about supporting my mother. The eruption of Vesuvius shook her badly; she's not fully recovered. She won't set foot south of Rome. Living in Rome requires money, which must come from my country estates. But I don't want to get sucked into the whirlpool of meaningless social engagements that make up aristocratic life in Rome – afternoons in the baths, evenings spent exchanging dinner invitations with people you don't really like, and seasonal moves to whatever resort is currently in fashion, dragging along all the servants and freedmen attached to the family.

My uncle gave me a model of living a meaningful life, a life that adds to the sum total of human knowledge or makes the world better in some way. Government service bores me, but I feel obligated to do it. 'If sensible men don't do it,' my uncle used to say, 'it will be left to fools and men set on self-advancement.' But being an advocate for my dependents and their families in their endless petty suits is unspeakably dull. It means insufferable hours in court, trying to out-orate the other side's advocate.

In my uncle's notebooks I found his ruminations on this fundamental weakness of the Roman legal system. It relies on an orator's ability to persuade a jury. And the orator is not trying to persuade the jury alone. He speaks to the crowd standing around listening to the case. The jury often votes on the basis of the crowd's reaction to one side or the other.

This lesson was brought home to me in one of the first cases I tried. The brother of a client of mine had been murdered. The man we were prosecuting was found practically standing over the body, with a bloody knife in his hand. But he was a client of Regulus'. And Regulus persuaded the jury that his client just wasn't the kind of person who could have committed that murder. Look at his political record. You all know what a fine young man his son is. How could this man have killed anyone?

In my prosecution of the case I tried to make a few scientific observations – such as when the murder took place, what type of weapon was used – and to ask about the defendant's motive for committing the crime. Some members of the jury went to sleep during my speech. No one sleeps through one of Regulus' perorations. I still regret that my ineptness in that case allowed a killer to go free. In a rational legal system, based on scientific observations and not on the advocate's ability to manipulate the emotions of the crowd, he would have been convicted.

What is exciting about investigating Cornutus' murder is that unless rational principles are applied, the murderer (or murderers) will never be found. No amount of rhetoric could convince a jury that Marcellus killed Cornutus. Finding out what poison was administered and how it was done could convict him. I also have to find out who cut out Cornutus' heart and what connection, if any, that 'murder' had to the poisoning. And I must do it quickly to protect Chryseis.

The first harsh, cutting rays of the sun slashed over the top of the roof. I averted my sensitive eyes to avoid the pain which bright light often causes them. Others would soon be up and about the day's business. In fact, I could hear people moving past me in the garden and gathering in a room nearby. It struck me as an odd time for a group of people to be assembling in someone's house. Through the shrubbery which concealed me I glimpsed several of them, a little knot of five.

One of them was my own slave, Damon! Another was Tiberius Saturninus. I recognized that bald pate shining out through his thin, dark hair. What on earth was going on? How dare Damon sneak away to some sort of clandestine gathering? And why was Saturninus talking to him as though they were equals?

Roman law forbids unlicensed gatherings because they might hatch a criminal plot. I was obligated to find out whatever I could and report it. The shrubbery in the garden allowed me to move under cover until I was almost outside the room where they had gathered. The door had been left open. They were singing something in Greek, and I crouched down to listen. The group had divided themselves, as the chorus in a play will sometimes do, to sing antiphonally. The men sang one line, the women the next. The song was something about Jesus the Christ, the son of God.

I had stumbled onto a nest of Christians! And my own Damon was one of them!

A deep breath calmed me and I willed myself to act like a Roman. I needed to keep myself under control so I could gather accurate information for the governor.

After the song concluded, someone began to read, in a nice, clear voice, from what he called the songs of someone named David. The piece contained some bucolic imagery. David compared his god to a shepherd leading his flock into green pastures and beside still waters. Then it abruptly shifted metaphors. The god seemed to be anointing the singer and preparing a table for him. I had difficulty seeing the connection between the two parts. The same speaker then addressed a prayer to the god, with the others joining in at certain points.

After a moment of silence another man began to speak, but, with his softer voice, I couldn't hear him as clearly as I had the first man. As he warmed to his theme and increased his volume a bit, I began to pick up more of what he said. It was something about a table.

Then it struck me – the speaker was Luke.

I strained to catch every word. Luke, a Christian! But, of course. When we were examining Cornutus' body and I said something about their rituals, he defended them and admitted he knew some of them. Knew them! That was putting it mildly. He must be a leader in the conspiracy. But what was its objective? What about the letters Luke was carrying? Who was this man Paul? Was there some revolution brewing? I shifted as close to the door as I dared.

"And now," I heard Luke say, "as we prepare to gather around this table, let us recall the words of our Lord Jesus, when he said, 'This is my body, take it and eat. This is my blood, take it and drink. Do this in remembrance of me.'"

By the gods! I was trapped in a den of cannibals! Whose body were they eating? Whose blood were they drinking? If they found me out here, it was likely to be mine.

I broke into a nervous sweat as I backed away from the door. This is how Odysseus must have felt when he watched the Cyclops wolf down a couple of his crew members for dinner. I made for the passageway which opened off the other side of this garden and led into the rearmost garden. Tacitus' room was down that way. Was he still alive, I wondered?

His slow response to my knock on the door did nothing to ease my mind.

"What's the matter?" he asked groggily, scratching his head and leaning against the door.

"We've got to get out of here," I said in a hissing whisper. "At once."

"Why? What's wrong?" He had to lean his head back to look at me through eyes which wouldn't open more than halfway.

I shouldered my way past him into the room. Some things I could not say while standing in the open. He had apparently spent the night alone, an unusual event for him, but I was too upset to tease him about it.

"These people are Christians. I've just overheard one of their meetings."

"Why are you so upset?"

"Because the rumors we've heard are true. They *are* cannibals. And Luke is one of them. So is Damon. And Tiberius Saturninus."

"By the gods! You can't mean it!" Now he was awake.

"I'm telling you what I saw and heard. We've got to get Chryseis and Melissa and get out of here at once."

"Yes, of course." Tacitus slipped on his sandals. "Let's go!"

Fortunately there was no one outside when we stepped out of his room. I pictured the entire household in that room off the main garden with gore smeared all over their mouths, and I shuddered. Chryseis' room was at the very rear of the house, close to a service entrance that was used only during the day. Melissa had asked for a room there so it would be quiet.

There was no answer when I knocked. That frightened me. I knocked louder and called as loudly as I dared, "Melissa! Chryseis!"

Still no answer. Tacitus and I looked at each other with a sense of foreboding. I opened the door. The room was empty.

XI

"You do have trouble keeping track of this girl," Tacitus said as we stared into the empty room in amazement.

I turned on him as I never had in the month that I'd known him. "This is no time for jokes! I'm sure the Christians have her. There's no telling what unspeakable things they've done to her. Damn Luke! Damn all of them!"

"Now, calm down," Tacitus said, grabbing my shoulders and shaking me. "You're making a very big leap there. I thought you like to approach problems rationally."

"But this isn't just an intellectual problem." This was a matter of the girl I was falling in love with, as utterly irrational as that was. And those horrible words were still ringing in my ears: 'My body . . . eat; my blood . . . drink.' This wasn't a time for cogitation; it was a time for panic.

Tacitus pressed me against the wall, his hand on my chest, as one might try to get the attention of an unruly child or an obstreperous slave. "First, Pliny, consider this. Have you seen any evidence that Luke is anything but a pleasant old gentleman and a knowledgeable doctor? Do you really think he could hide such a monstrous character under that unassuming facade?"

That slowed me down. I realized I was rushing out of control, like a wagon careening down a mountainside. I needed a steady hand on the drag. "You're right. It hardly seems likely. The evil in a man is always going to ooze out at the edges, no matter how he tries to bottle it up. Like Marcellus. By the gods, yes! Marcellus must have her."

Tacitus threw his hands up in disgust. "There you go with Marcellus again! Before you convict and execute the man, consider this. Has Chryseis ever run away before?"

The drag took hold. "Yes, of course she has."

"And the last time she did, you examined her room carefully. Why not do that now?"

We quickly searched the sparsely furnished room, but found no trace of any of Chryseis' possessions. Or of anything that might have belonged to Melissa. Melissa was carrying a bag when we walked over here last night. That I distinctly remembered now, though I thought nothing of it at the time. "She said there were some things she would need to tend to Chryseis, didn't she? She must have been planning this all along."

Tacitus nodded in agreement. "If anyone took these women to do harm to them, they would not likely have tidied up the room this way, as you pointed out to me when Chryseis disappeared the first time. I don't think these beds have even been slept in."

So he was capable of learning! "Exactly. If anyone had tried to harm Chryseis or take her away, there would be evidence of a struggle, probably even Melissa's dead body on the floor. So let's work on the more logical assumption that she has run away again."

"But why would Melissa have run away with her?"

"For two reasons. She's a proud woman who resents her enslavement, and she's determined to do anything necessary to protect Chryseis. Even lie to me to put me off-guard. But I'm glad she did run away. It means Chryseis will be safer, and two people are easier to track than one."

"Then we ought to start looking for them at once," Tacitus said. "They obviously left during the night and have had time to put some distance behind them or find a safe place to hide. Let's alert Kallisto and her son and get the search started."

I grabbed the front of his tunic as he turned away. "Wait! How are we supposed to act around these people, now that we know they're Christians?"

"They don't know that we know, so just act like you did yesterday, starting now." He nodded his head to his left. I followed the gesture over my shoulder to see Kallisto coming across the garden, accompanied by a slave girl carrying a tray with bread, cheese, and water on it.

"Good morning, my friends," she said. "I brought a little something to eat for the women. There's more in the dining room, if you're inclined to eat in the mornings."

"I'm afraid you're too late for that," I said. "It appears they've run away." I watched her face closely to gauge her reaction. Her surprise appeared genuine. A simple soul such as herself hardly seemed capable of dissimulation.

"Run away? Why would they do that?" She motioned for the slave to set her tray on a three-legged table by the door of a neighboring room. The girl peered over her mistress' shoulder as Kallisto glanced into the room. A hint of suspicion crossed her eyes. Did she think we had done something with them?

"We don't know what happened to them," I said. "But, as you can see, the room is empty."

"But where could they have gone?" Kallisto asked.

"The first thing I want to do is determine if they really are gone," I said. "I'd like permission to search your house, to see if they're hiding somewhere else in it." Or if you and your cannibalistic friends have their remains hidden somewhere, I was thinking.

That permission was quickly given, and Tacitus and I spent over an hour going through the house. Luke joined us, though I wished he hadn't. His presence unnerved me, and I didn't want him to misdirect us if he was somehow involved in the disappearance of the two women. But he let us search everywhere without any sort of objection.

Our search turned up nothing and finally brought us back to the room which Melissa and Chryseis had shared.

"If they're not here," I said, "they most likely left through this door."

Tacitus opened the rear door, just outside Chryseis' room, which let out onto a narrow street, hardly more than an alley, running between two blocks of houses. It was for the convenience of tradesmen and service people, such as those who emptied the latrines in the houses of the wealthy. On the outside of the door we found painted a pentagram, the sign of Hecate. The sign on the witches' wagon and in Artemis' temple. Kallisto's slavegirl squealed in fright. I felt like joining her.

"Heaven help us," Luke muttered. "They're in the hands of that witch."

As unsettling as that news was, I was relieved on two counts – the Christians hadn't eaten her and Marcellus hadn't kidnapped her.

"Did they leave of their own volition, I wonder," Tacitus said.

"They must have," I replied. "The door locks from the inside, and it hasn't been forced open, so the women had to open it. They wouldn't have opened it for anyone they didn't trust."

"What reason would the witches have to kidnap her?" Tacitus asked, running a finger over the pentagram. "Or to help her?"

"To take vengeance on us for . . . you know."

"But Anyte didn't know that Chryseis was going to be here."

"This is Melissa's planning. She must have contacted Anyte for assistance. She's devoted to Chryseis, and she's afraid they'll be sold to different owners."

"Two runaway slave women shouldn't be hard to find," Tacitus said.

"You don't quite see the problem," I said. "They're not just running away by themselves. They have help, people who will give them places to hide. And we're not the only ones looking for them. We've got to find them before Marcellus does." I shifted my attention to Kallisto and her slavegirl. "It's *very* important that you say nothing and caution everyone in this household to keep quiet about what has happened. The fewer people who know, the safer Chryseis will be." I knew my admonition was futile, even as I gave it. The only way I could keep them from talking would be to cut out their tongues.

* * * *

Tacitus, Luke, and I returned to the inn and found Anyte and her acolytes leaving the dining room. I stepped in front of her to block her passage but nearly retreated when she folded her arms across her chest. I knew what magnificent breasts she was covering. What I didn't know was what other surprises she might have hidden in there. I reminded myself of my uncle's teaching that all religious spectacles are shams, cheap illusions staged to impress the gullible and undergird the power of charlatans. If he had ever stood this close to this practitioner, he might have revised his opinion.

"Excuse me, my lord," she said with just a hint of sarcasm on the honorific. "Will you let us pass?"

"I need to know where you were last night," I said too rapidly.

"The nights are long," she replied, drawing a smile from her leading acolyte. "Could you be more specific?"

"After midnight. During the last watch."

"I was blissfully asleep by then, my lord."

"Can anyone verify that?"

"Why should anyone have to? Has someone else been murdered?" She lowered her heavily colored eyelids and her voice. "Something you value gone missing?"

"That is none of your concern." I tried to throw a little swagger into my voice but failed miserably. Even I could sense that.

"My whereabouts last night are none of your concern, young man!" she snapped. "I resent this interrogation. You are not a magistrate and you have no authority to detain or question anyone. I have stayed this long only in deference to Rome's power, but I'm not sure how much longer I'll feel that way."

"Before you change your mind entirely," I said, "may I ask another question that has been bothering me?"

"You may ask. I'll decide then whether I'll answer."

I could sense Tacitus edging toward a pillar for protection.

"You came from Ephesus to Smyrna to worship Artemis, did you not?"

"You know that."

"I also know that there is a magnificent temple of Artemis in Ephesus. Why come all this distance to worship her in the ruins of an ancient temple?"

She studied me intently before she answered. "Artemis is worshiped in many ways, young sir. Some places are sacred to her under one name, others under another name. She is the tri-form goddess. And now my patience is almost at an end."

She gathered up her robes and I cringed, half expecting her to disappear beneath them in a puff of smoke. But she pushed past me and headed for the stairs in a much more mundane sort of exit.

Tacitus emerged from hiding. "She's right, you know. If she left right now, there's nothing you could do about it." He can be so supportive sometimes.

"I'm well aware that she's right," I groused. "I just hope the rest of the members of the caravan don't start thinking about it."

"I think she knows something, though," Luke said. I had almost forgotten he was there, he had been so quiet.

"You mean because of the crack about someone missing? That could just be a lucky guess, given Chryseis' recent behavior."

"No. I was watching her acolytes," Luke said. "The way two of them glanced at one another, they know something. I guarantee it."

"Well, I don't have any authority to arrest her or to have her servants tortured. We'll just have to keep an eye on them and start searching for Melissa and Chryseis on our own. I think we have to assume that Anyte made contact with devotees of her cult in the city and that they have spirited Chryseis and Melissa away."

"But where?" Tacitus asked. "There are roads leading out of Smyrna in all directions and boats ready to sail at any time."

"East," Luke and I said together. I looked at him in surprise. Could this cannibal and I be thinking alike?

"Why east?" Tacitus asked.

"The only way a runaway slave can be truly free," Luke said, "is to get out of Roman territory entirely. The roads north and south, and the sea to the west, only lead to other parts of the Roman empire. But to the east lies Parthia. And there lies freedom for an escaped slave."

"It's a long and difficult journey, though, isn't it?" I said. The geography of this region was vague, at best, in my mind.

"Their most likely route," Luke said, "would be to Sardis, almost due east of here. Then through Philadelphia and Antioch of Pisidia. From there the road runs northeast along the base of the Taurus Mountains until it reaches the border with Armenia."

"You know this area well," Tacitus said somewhat suspiciously.

"A friend and I traveled extensively here when I was younger."

"How long would it take them to make this trip?" I asked.

"Under ideal conditions, at least a month. But I suppose they're going to be hiding out, perhaps even keeping off the main road. It could take twice that."

"What will they find in Armenia?" Tacitus asked.

Armenia is one of our client kingdoms, semi-independent and kept that way intentionally as a buffer between our empire and that of the Parthians. The Armenians would not encourage Roman slaves to flee to their territory, but they would feel no obligation to return those who did.

"There are settlements of Jews there," Luke said, "and on down into the Mesopotamian Valley. They've been there for several hundred years. These two women could be absorbed into that community, although Chryseis' hair would make it hard to hide her among those darker-skinned races."

"That's it!" I said, grabbing Tacitus' arm. "They'll have to lie low for a day or two to do something about Chryseis' appearance. They'll dye her hair or get a wig, something to disguise her. I think we've still got time. Go roust out the boularch Nicomedes. Tell him we need to look for a runaway slave. We'll need some dogs. Anything that's good at picking up a scent."

"Some big Molossian hounds, perhaps?"

I cringed. "I can't make jokes about that yet. Have them assemble at Apelles' house." I turned to Luke. "Will you come with us, doctor? If we find her, she may need medical care." And if we don't, I may, I thought.

Luke assented, but before we could set out for Apelles' house

I was accosted by Orophernes.

"Excuse me, my lord," he said with his customary bow. "Could I have a private word with you?"

"I need to speak with my chief spy," I said to Luke in Latin. He appeared thoroughly confused.

All I could do was take a few steps away from Luke and huddle on the street corner with Orophernes, who dropped his voice to a whisper. "I thought you'd like to know, my lord, that Lysimachus was seen coming in shortly after dawn."

"You do seem to take a peculiar interest in that man's comings and goings."

"His room is across from mine, and I can see through a crack in my door."

"So his activities interest you. Why should they interest me?"

"Oh, my lord, I saw something unusual this morning. Lysimachus looked entirely worn out and had scratch marks on his face and arms."

I wasn't sure what that information meant, but it seemed worth the couple of coins I fished out of my money bag.

* * * *

My request that Luke accompany me was made impulsively, due to my distraction over my concern for Chryseis. I regretted it by the time we had crossed the street. This man was a Christian, a member of an unrecognized cult. If I had knowledge of his participation, wasn't I obligated to report it to the governor? Now I had saddled myself with him when I wanted to get as far away from him as possible. I didn't even know how to begin a conversation as we walked. And I had to walk more slowly than I wanted to, so he could keep up with me.

"So, you were eavesdropping on our service this morning," he said with a slight smile.

I spun around. "How did you know?"

"One of our group saw you crouched outside the door."

"I suppose I should be grateful you didn't kill me."

"Why would we do that?" He appeared to be genuinely surprised.

"Most secret cults don't appreciate having people spying on them. That witch from Ephesus certainly doesn't."

"We're not a secret cult. We proclaim our message openly and would prefer for you to hear it and receive it."

"What message is that?"

"The message about Jesus of Nazareth."

"Jesus? Yes, I've heard a bit about him. Some sort of revolutionary or bandit, wasn't he?"

"I suppose he would look like that to a Roman official," Luke said.

"He must have been. Wasn't he crucified?" That particular form of execution is reserved for the lowest sort of criminals and rebellious slaves. Like Chryseis and Melissa! The government would be within its rights to crucify them if they were captured.

"Yes, he was crucified." Luke sounded almost proud of the fact.

"Who ordered it?"

"Pontius Pilate, governor of Judaea when Tiberius was emperor."

Pilate's name struck a faintly familiar chord. I was acquainted with two of his grandchildren. They weren't prominent people in Rome but did mingle on the fringes of my social circle. Perhaps I could ask them about this matter when I got back to the city.

"But what you don't understand," Luke said, "is that God raised him from the dead. He is the son of God." His face began to glow.

"Another one of those, eh? Like Hercules?"

"Could Hercules heal the sick, or calm a storm? Did your gods raise Hercules from the dead?"

"Everyone knows Hercules is just a myth. If you start claiming that a historical person was the son of God and was raised him from the dead, those claims are hard to verify," I pointed out. "If not impossible."

"Hundreds of people witnessed his miracles and saw him after his resurrection."

"Were you one of them?"

"No, I was just a boy at the time. But I trust the testimony of those who did."

"Where are they?" I said, looking around as I would do in a courtroom to emphasize the absence of the witnesses.

"Their accounts have been written down for all to see. I've written a book about Jesus myself."

"Anyone can write a book about anything," I said.

He put a hand on my shoulder. "My young friend, you've read too many books by Skeptics and Cynics."

"Regardless of that, what is the significance of eating the body and drinking the blood? Whose body? Whose blood?"

"The body and blood of Christ. That's what we see in the bread and wine." His urgent tone indicated it was very important to him that I understand, even if I couldn't accept, his message. "Jesus himself ordained the ritual which you overheard us performing. It commemorates his sacrificial death on the cross."

"There you are back to his being crucified."

"Of course. It's the heart of our message."

"Didn't Nero execute some Christians in the aftermath of the great fire? So you've got the founder of your group executed as a criminal and a recent emperor condemning you as arsonists. Hardly an impressive pedigree."

"I'm surprised you cite Nero as an example of anything. That's the only case where the government has taken action against us, and everyone knows that Nero was deranged and looking for a scapegoat. The governor of Achaia, Lucius Junius Gallio, refused to hear charges against my friend Paul, who was a Roman citizen, as I am. Gallio was the brother of Seneca, whom I've heard you quote to good advantage."

"A governor's decisions," I pointed out, "hold force only in his own province during his tenure. They don't set policy for the entire empire, or even for the next governor of that province. The government has the right to inquire into the activities of any group, if it may pose a danger to the common safety."

"But," Luke replied with more heat, "what threat do we pose? You Romans simply don't know who or what we are."

"How can we know? The only information we have comes from rumors and charges from your enemies."

"I can let you read the book I've written about Jesus."

One of those in his wagon, I assumed. "And what would that tell me?"

"You seem to have a scientific mind. A true scientist should examine various sides of a question before he commits himself to one, shouldn't he?"

He had me there. Chagrined, I agreed to read his book.

"I'll get it to you later today. Apelles' scribes have been making a few copies. I'm now writing a second book, about the early days of the church and the activities of my friend Paul. He was a leader in spreading the good news of our faith across the Roman world. I'm traveling with Timothy to gather material for that book. Timothy and I both traveled with Paul twenty years ago. Now that generation is dying off. Apelles was one I especially wanted to talk to. He knew Paul in Rome years ago. Our history needs to be written before all the witnesses are gone."

"It sounds like an ambitious project."

Luke nodded sadly. "I wish I had started a few years ago. People are dying off, like Apelles, and my own strength is not what it was."

I needed to ask one more question. "I was especially surprised to see Tiberius Saturninus in your group. He's from a noble Roman family. Are there many like him?"

Luke pursed his lips in thought. "There are more Christians in Rome, and more highly placed, than you suspect. Saturninus is a recent convert. He accepted the faith while he was in Syria. He still has much to learn and some old ways to unlearn."

"His gambling, you mean?"

"Precisely. Its grip on him is more powerful than any disease I've ever seen attack a man. He can fight against it for a while, like a man on his way to recovering from an illness, but then it seizes him again. As Jesus once said, you cannot serve two masters. Saturninus has yet to learn that."

"He is deeply in debt, I gather. Someone, he told me, had paid off his debts to various individuals, leaving him heavily obligated to this one person. He wouldn't name him."

"Yes. He has told me that this man now lords it over him like a little king."

A little king! Luke might have missed the pun in Greek, but in Latin it would be Regulus! That's the very meaning of the name.

* * * *

In the alley behind the house three strong hunting dogs soon strained at their leashes, yipping excitedly. The man in charge of them explained in a Greek so ungrammatical it would have made Sophocles weep that 'all they needs is somewhat to pick up the girlie's scent.'

"What about the blanket she was wrapped in after . . . last night?" I said. "She was sweating heavily."

Standing at the back door of the house, with the witches' pentagram glaring at us, we let the dogs pick up the scent from the blanket. They turned right out of the alley, headed south. Tacitus and I trotted to keep up as they passed through the city gate by which I had first entered Smyrna and into the necropolis on the south side of town. There the scent gave out, leaving the dogs circling and baying hopelessly.

"She must have gotten into a wagon or on a horse," I said.

"So we have no way of knowing where she might have gone," Tacitus said glumly.

"There's no guarantee," I said, "but I'm willing to bet they didn't go south."

"Then why come to this side of town?"

"To get us headed in the wrong direction."

* * * *

As we returned to town the traffic around us grew heavier. The dogs' handler explained that everyone was turning out for the funeral games in honor of Apelles. He was eager to be finished with our business so he could get a seat. We dismissed him with our thanks and a few coins.

Near our inn we ran into the boularch Nicomedes, giving orders and sending slaves bustling this way and that. "Any luck?" he asked us.

"Not yet," I replied. "We'll keep looking."

"But now you must take some time to attend my games," the oily weasel said.

"Your games? Aren't they being given by Apelles' family?" That would be the normal protocol. The family of the deceased would put on games to propitiate the gods and to insure that the name of their loved one would not soon be forgotten.

"Apelles and his family . . . have some peculiar ideas," Nicomedes said. "They did not wish to sponsor any games, so I've decided to step in. The people expect it."

It suddenly struck me that the family probably refrained from sponsoring the games because they were Christians and so not concerned with what our gods thought of them. But Nicomedes could stage them as a way of boosting his own popularity, maybe even get himself re-elected. And perhaps quell popular unrest. The crowd would be expecting some such entertainment after the death of a prominent person. He was right about that. And disappointed crowds can turn nasty.

"I've added a few special touches in honor of our guests from Rome," Nicomedes announced proudly. "And I've saved seats for you where you'll have an excellent view."

I groaned inwardly. Even if I were not distracted by the loss of Chryseis, the last thing I would want to do would be to attend one of these inhuman spectacles. I find the blood and gore repulsive. I was stymied, though. With no idea where to begin a search, I could not authorize enough men to comb the entire city. Perhaps I should curry favor with Nicomedes by going to the games. I would try to block out what was happening in front of me and consider my options in the search for Chryseis.

Tacitus, on the other hand, was eager for the bloodletting to begin. "If we expect to get cooperation from the local authorities," he pointed out in Latin so Nicomedes wouldn't understand, "in this search for Chryseis and for Cornutus' murderer, we'd better make a goodwill gesture and attend the games." He dashed into the inn to put on his toga, the requisite garment for any upper-class Roman on such an occasion.

I stood by the door, as though I could postpone the inevitable. Luke nodded his head. "I suspect Tacitus is right," he said, also in Latin. "I share your disdain for the games, my friend. In some ways you are a person with a kind of godly spirit, but your position in society requires you to go this time."

"You, of course, have no such obligation," I said drily.

"None whatsoever." Luke smiled without being smug. "I will retire to my room and give some thought to the puzzles besetting us."

"At least the time won't be entirely wasted," I said. "Oh, please tell Tiberius Saturninus I'd like to talk to him this afternoon."

I trudged up the stairs, rousted Damon, and got into my second-best toga. I hadn't anticipated that I would need even one of the cumbersome things during this trip, so I had sent most of my wardrobe home by ship. I hoped there was a laundry nearby equipped to handle this type of load. Washing and drying a toga is not a task to be undertaken on the fly.

I decided to have my slaves and Cornutus' accompany me to the games. They would provide an escort through the crush of the crowd and I could keep an eye on Cornutus' people more easily than if they were being held somewhere in the inn. Allowing them this diversion might also improve their attitudes toward me. I sent my overseer Trophimus to assemble everyone on the street in front of the inn.

Coming down the stairs I ran into Marcus Carolus. He jumped right over the usual formalities and courtesies and asked, "Is there any news about the girl?"

I pondered my reply carefully. Carolus's concern for Chryseis was endearing in a way but also unsettling. Other than a bit of shared Germanic ancestry, what was there about her that was causing him to fixate on her? I decided to heed the advice I had given Kallisto and her slave. "She has recovered completely from her injury on the stairs. The last time I spoke with her she was feeling well." I felt like a slave, telling enough of the truth to serve my purpose but concealing a lie that could lead to the necessity of an even bigger lie.

"Would it be all right if I visited her?" Carolus asked.

That quickly was I caught. How much could I tell him?

Carolus sensed at once that something was not as it should be. "What is it?" He pressed his broad face close to mine. "What's wrong?"

"All right." I looked around to be certain that no one was within earshot. "The truth is that Chryseis and Melissa have disappeared, sometime during the night."

"Again?" Carolus exploded. "By the gods! How do you Romans rule an empire when you can't keep track of a single slave girl? Is anyone searching for her?"

"We hired some dogs this morning and tracked her to the necropolis on the south side of town. The dogs lost the scent there. She may have gotten onto a horse or into a wagon."

"Why would they go south?"

"I'm not sure they did." I was taking him more and more into my confidence without making a conscious decision to do so. "Perhaps they started in that direction to throw off anyone who might be searching for them."

"Who is searching?" Carolus' voice rose in anxiety.

"At the moment, no one," I said, putting up my hands to fend him off. "I would be if I didn't have to attend the funeral games for Apelles. I expect to be back on the hunt by this afternoon."

"But you're wasting precious time!"

"Calm yourself, Marcus Carolus. I'm in a difficult situation here. I have no authority to order an extensive search. With these games about to begin, I'm not sure I could even find anyone to help me. I doubt the women are going to get far in the next few hours. Most likely, they will travel by night and hide during the day. A few hours' delay isn't going to make much difference in finding them."

"Perhaps not to you," he said in disgust and turned on his heel and stormed out.

XII

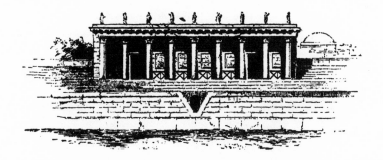

We were barely in our seats when
Nicomedes, directly across the stadium from me in the box reserved
for the sponsor of the games, waved a white cloth, signaling for the
games to begin. A roar went up from the crowd, including Tacitus in my
right ear, as a massive gate, at the end of the arena to my left, slowly
opened and the procession began to wend its way around the arena.
Behind wagons carrying images of the gods the performers – gladiators, animal trainers, acrobats, and athletes – marched proudly and
saluted the crowd. This much was familiar from the few times I had
attended the games in Rome.

Nicomedes' games were small by comparison with those staged
in Rome, but then everything is small by Roman standards. Like the
Circus Maximus, this elliptical stadium was more suited to horse racing
than to the type of games to be staged today, but it seated only twenty
thousand, barely a tenth of what the Roman Circus held. The divider
running down the middle blocked our view of what was happening on
the other side, so we saw only the half of the procession at a time.

In deference to Greek tradition, and while people were settling
into their seats, he began with athletic competitions going on simulta-
neously in different parts of the arena. Any reader of Homer could
recognize the allusion, as it were, to the funeral games of Patroclus in
the *Iliad*. First several chariots ran a short race, followed by contests in

archery, footraces, and a boxing match. The only one that interested the crowd, though, was the boxing. It was the only one that offered the prospect of any blood being spilled, especially since the combatants were outfitted with the Roman – and definitely not Homeric – *caestus*.

Nicomedes gauged exactly how long to let these rather benign competitions run. It was as though he sensed the precise moment when the crowd began to shift in their seats. At his signal, six prisoners were then brought in, stripped naked and forced to carry pieces of the crosses they would be crucified on. Each prisoner was held down by two guards while a third drove the large nails into his flesh, just behind the wrist bone and above the ankle. One poor fellow resisted violently and almost broke away, to the delight of the crowd. One of the guards brought his knee up to the man's groin and put an end to his struggle.

The crosses were hoisted upright and three were set up facing our side of the stadium, with the other three facing the other side, so that everyone would have a splendid view. A herald announced the crimes for which these men were being executed and signs were nailed on the crosses beneath their feet. One was a murderer, two were slaves who had assaulted their masters, and the other three were highway bandits who had preyed on caravans such as ours. I wouldn't deny that they deserved punishment, perhaps even death, but why this way? The wretches on the crosses wept, pled for mercy, or cursed the crowd. Some in the crowd taunted them back and threw messy bits of food at them. I noticed that Damon was moved to tears by this display. He muttered something about forgiving people because they didn't know what they were doing.

One thing did puzzle me. Victims of crucifixion can sometimes take two or three days to die. I didn't think even the most blood-thirsty crowd would find much entertainment in that long a wait. I leaned over to Tacitus. "They won't be dead by the end of the games, will they?" I asked.

"Oh, their throats will be cut later in the day," he replied as matter-of-factly as if he were explaining some aspect of the stadium's architecture. "Or maybe they'll be disemboweled. Whatever the crowd wants."

And it would be done without my presence, I resolved at once, no matter how big an affront to our host that might be.

On Nicomedes' next signal the gates at both ends of the arena swung open. From my left emerged a band of fifteen or twenty men and women – more condemned prisoners. Out of the opposite gate the animal trainers brought their charges into the arena – a pack of lions, tigers, and other ferocious hunters. The trainers released the big cats from their leashes and prodded them with sharp sticks toward the miserable little band, who just then realized the enormity of what was happening to them.

Some pounded on the gates behind them, but they were closed as irrevocably as our yesterdays. Others ran around the arena as though they might find some cranny where they could take refuge. The ones who were running attracted the animals' attention first. A woman actually tried to climb one of the crosses, but a tiger caught her by the heel and dragged her down. The crunching of her bones could be heard at least as far as our seats.

To distract myself from the mayhem, I surveyed the crowd. Their faces displayed a kind of rapture, or ecstasy, similar to what I saw on the faces of those women worshiping Hecate. Why are people so drawn to this form of 'entertainment'? Why am I so repulsed by it? Am I being arrogant? Is love of the games a measure of one's lack of education or sophistication? Then why is Tacitus, every bit as educated and sophisticated as I am, screaming like a madman over every drop of blood that soaks into the sand? And why is Damon, the slave, covering his ears with his hands and keeping his eyes fixed on his lap?

I was relieved to note that Marcellus was also at the games, seated prominently next to the sponsor's box. At least he couldn't be up to any mischief as long as he was here. Or was I being too optimistic? (I couldn't let myself say 'sanguine' in these circumstances.) Regulus was in Rome, but he was creating trouble here in Smyrna. I was sure of it. People of his sort don't need to be physically present in a spot to exercise their baleful influence.

As I observed Marcellus, a man came up to him and whispered something in his ear. Marcellus listened intently and nodded his head but appeared displeased. Good. Whatever displeases Marcellus must have some virtue to it.

Pairs of gladiators were next on the program. Much as I hate to admit it, that type of display even had Homeric sanction, although Achilles did specify that the fight would end when blood had been drawn, not when one man stood over another and slit his throat from ear to ear.

I endured the slaughter until the midday break. Even then, while the crowd was getting something to eat or relieving themselves and an awning was being drawn over the seats to protect us from the sun, Nicomedes had arranged for one of the crudest forms of combat. A group of condemned men and women were brought into the arena wearing leather headcoverings which blindfolded them and which they could not remove. Each person carried a sword or club but no shield. At the signal they began flailing around blindly. When these random blows found a mark, the crowd hooted and yelled instructions such as, 'Look out to your right!' Sometimes the crowd would deliberately mislead the combatants. The purpose of this little exercise in barbarism is to force the criminals to execute one another. The sight brought to mind Seneca's comment that 'In the morning men are thrown to the lions and bears; at noon they're thrown to the spectators.'

When Tacitus returned to his seat I told him I was leaving. Damon immediately asked if he might accompany me. I agreed and asked Tacitus to look out for the slaves who chose to remain.

I walked rapidly back to the inn, regretting that I was wasting time when I could be searching for Chryseis. Damon kept pace, walking alongside me more like a friend than a slave accompanying his master. To blunt his presumption a bit I asked him, "How long have you been a Christian?"

Damon was as frightened as he had been when we discovered that Chryseis had gotten out of the room he was supposed to be guarding. "How did you know, my lord?"

"I was in the garden at Apelles' house yesterday morning when your group was gathering for your ritual. I saw you and the others, Luke among them, assembling. Luke and I have talked a bit about it. How did you become a part of this group? You've been a slave in my uncle's house and in mine for most of your life."

"A slave your uncle purchased about ten years ago was Christian. She talked with others of us about it."

"You mean there are other Christians in my household?"

"A few, my lord."

I knew I could ask him who and where they were – either in my house in Rome or on one of my estates – and he was expecting me to, but at the moment I didn't feel like pressing the point.

My silence unsettled him. "What are you . . . going to do, my lord?"

"I see no reason to do anything. I'm unsure of your group's legal status. I'll inquire about that when we get back to the city, you can rest assured. I am more concerned that you deserted your post when guarding Chryseis' door than that you follow some obscure cult. As long as the cult doesn't teach slaves to rise up against their masters, I see no immediate reason for concern."

"I assure you, my lord, it doesn't. Christians are taught to accept their position in life as ordained by God."

"Then how are you different from the Stoics?" I asked.

"We believe that God cares for each of us," Damon said, "not that he is an impersonal force dishing out fortune or misfortune at random."

"What proof do you have of this belief?"

"That he sent his son to teach us and to die for us."

"This son, that would be Jesus, the one you call the Christ?"

"Yes, my lord." He glanced at me with a look of amazement and distrust that I knew something I wasn't supposed to know.

"He was crucified, wasn't he? Just like those men we saw back there?"

"Yes, my lord. I'd never seen a crucifixion before." He clutched his stomach. "I had no idea of the horror of it, of what Jesus must have gone through."

"And you worship someone who was put to death like a common criminal?"

"I don't worship him. I worship God."

In answer to my quizzical look, he continued, walking sideways and gesturing as if in his rising excitement at being allowed to speak freely, he was totally forgetting his place as a slave.

"I believe Jesus is the ultimate messenger of God, a means of expressing God's will to us in a way humans can grasp. By calling him God's son, we mean he is closer to God than anyone has ever been and speaks for God in ways that no prophet ever has. How can we comprehend God himself unless we can see him in a form that makes sense to us? Even in the Greek and Roman myths the gods take shapes that humans are familiar with in order to communicate with us. And Jesus was raised from the dead on the third day, my lord." he suddenly clasped his hands together and looked down, remembering who and where he was. " I'm sure Luke explained that to you."

"He told me what you claim. I'm not sure anyone can 'explain' something so totally illogical. I'm surprised that a man as learned as Luke would be taken in by such a pack of lies. The simple fact, Damon, is that the dead do not rise. Not one of those men we saw crucified today will ever see another sunrise."

"With God all things are possible, my lord."

* * * *

My plan was to get out of my toga, eat a quick lunch, and assemble a few people to help me search for Chryseis. Three seemed the minimum number I could get by with. I knew we would be going into the temple of Artemis in old Smyrna. If the witch was involved in this disappearance, Chryseis was there or had been there. Damon could be trusted to hold the horses, but whom would I get to go into the temple with me? All of my slaves and Cornutus' would be at the games until dinner. Marcus Carolus would assist me, I was sure, but Androcles, the innkeeper, told me he hadn't seen Carolus in several hours. Shortly after my conversation with him before the games began, Androcles reported, Carolus had stormed out of the inn, not to be seen since.

As I was pondering my dilemma, Luke and Timothy entered the dining room and sat down with me.

"I've been trying to find Tiberius Saturninus for you," Luke said. "But no one has seen him since he left Apelles' house after our worship this morning."

"We're afraid he may have found some gamblers," Timothy added.

"Or some gamblers may have found him," I said. The sinister-looking man and his muscular companion had not yet redeemed my pledge of ten tetradrachmas. Perhaps their scruples demanded that they take it out of Saturninus' hide.

"If we find him," Luke said, "we'll try to keep him here until you can talk to him. May we know what you want to ask?"

"It's a money matter."

"Better not tell him that," Timothy said tiredly. "He'll just go back into hiding."

"I gather he's not one of your more successful . . . students? What do you call people who join your group?"

"We call them our brothers and sisters in Christ."

I could see Timothy getting more nervous with each word Luke spoke. He obviously didn't like to talk about such matters openly. But Luke, like any old man who can see the end of his life drawing nearer every day, was less and less concerned with what a Roman magistrate might think about his cult. Or do to him for belonging to it.

"Jesus once told a story," Luke said, "about a man sowing seed. It was a parable about how people receive our message. I'm afraid Saturninus is one whose faith sprang up quickly, like a seed that has a shallow root. It withers in the heat. You can read the whole story in my book."

"I'll look forward to that. Right now I'm looking for someone to accompany me on a short ride. I think I know where Chryseis is. Everyone else is too consumed with Nicomedes' games to go with me now. I don't want to lose any more time than I already have."

"You know I'll help you in any way I can," Luke said.

"It may involve a confrontation with Anyte and her acolytes."

After a moment of silence Timothy said morosely, "I'll go with you." I think I felt Luke kicking him under the table.

"Thanks. Finish your lunch. I'll ask Androcles to get us some riding gear for our horses."

I found the innkeeper coming out of the steaming kitchen. "It's riding gear you're wanting?" he said with a grin. "Going after that bit of blond stuff, are you?"

"What are you talking about?"

"The blond slave girl, my lord. The one you was hiding in Apelles' house. The one that's gone missing again. Aren't you going after her?"

"How did you hear about that?" I demanded.

He wasn't the least afraid of me. Instead he was proud of his clever ears. "One of my slaves was talkin' to a friend of hers down the street who knows one of Apelles' girls. And there was that witchy sign on the door, I hear."

"Damn!" I said. "Who else knows?"

"You mean, who doesn't know, my lord. By now the whole town has news of it."

He didn't have to remind me. Our society is cursed with one of the most efficient means of communication ever devised. If you want information made public, just tell it to a slave and order him or her to keep it secret. It'll be all over town within the hour. And, as Herodotus said about the Persian king's messengers, 'Neither heat nor snow nor gloom of night' could stop them. I was reasonably certain this was the news that had been whispered into Marcellus' ear during the games. The disappointment he registered on his face gave me some hope that his plans had been thwarted as abruptly as mine.

"Well, in any case," I said, "I want gear for three horses." Androcles ordered one of his servants to bring my animals out.

The servant was assisting us onto the horses when we began to hear a distant murmur, a noise rumbling through the streets like stones rolling down a hill. First it became distinct as a drumbeat, then as a human noise but still indecipherable. Finally someone turned a corner and the words fell intelligibly on our ears: "Make way for the governor! Make way for Lucius Mestrius Florus!"

The governor was here already? How could the message have gotten to him and he made the return trip so rapidly? I hadn't expected him until tomorrow evening at the earliest, if the messenger hadn't been delayed and the governor had set out immediately. Now here he was and we would have to postpone our search for Chryseis.

* * * *

An impressive entourage now marched into view. The governors of senatorial provinces, such as Asia, have only a handful of troops under their command, usually no more than a century or two. Only in frontier provinces which face the threat of attack, such as Syria, do we keep significant forces, and those under the command of men personally loyal to the emperor. Florus appeared to have brought about thirty of his soldiers with him, enough to make an impression but not so many as to frighten the good citizens of Smyrna. A burly centurion – I'm not sure there is any other kind – barked out orders and brought the column to a halt in front of our inn. Florus himself, I assumed, was being carried in a closed litter, trailed by a pack of a dozen or so slaves. Half of his soldiers marched in front of him and the rest brought up the rear. The messenger whom Androcles had sent trailed the party.

The litter-bearers set their burden down and the curtains parted as a small man of about fifty stepped out. Florus had been consul about a decade ago, when I was still a boy. I knew nothing of him. At first glance he appeared a man one could like, with a pleasant round countenance with eyes dark and inquisitive, but nothing grim. He had light-colored hair, with a bald spot on his crown. There was an awkward moment of silence as he dusted himself off. Since no one was prepared to offer a formal welcome, I stepped forward and addressed him in Latin.

"Excellency, welcome. I am Gaius Plinius Caecilius Secundus. It was my message that requested your presence here. This is Timothy of Ephesus." By not introducing Damon I identified him as a slave and of no concern to Florus.

The governor's face brightened as I said my name. "Yes, Gaius Pliny! What a delight to meet the son of the illustrious Pliny. His death was such a tragedy."

"Yes, sir. Thank you. We're surprised to see you so soon. I thought it would be tomorrow before you could get here from Pergamum."

"From Pergamum it would have been," Florus said. "But your messenger ran into my party up the road in Cyme. I'm on my first circuit to hear judicial cases around the province."

I nodded. Making the rounds to hear court cases in various towns in the province was perhaps the governor's most important task. A conscientious governor would spend most of his term away from his residence in the capital city. A slacker would spend his time enjoying whatever luxuries the province had to offer. The fact that Florus was already at work, less than a month after his arrival, boded well for our investigation.

He gave orders for his slaves to find a place to store his litter and for the soldiers to set up a camp on the outskirts of the city. Their supply wagons had not entered the gates but were already scouting for a spot to bivouac. As the noise of the soldiers' marching faded, Florus looked relieved.

"Those fellows frighten me," he said quietly. "Sometimes I think I'm more their prisoner than their commander. But enough of that!" He clapped his hands together. "I can't tell you what an honor it is to meet you, young man. I have so many questions about your father's work. He spurred my interest in a variety of topics. I've done some scientific writing of my own, as you may know."

If he had done anything worth reading, my uncle would have mentioned his name to me. "No, sir, I wasn't aware of that. But we have a serious situation on our hands here. That's why I sent for you. And, if I may say so, I expected you to bring someone with you to help in the investigation."

"Oh, I left most of my staff in Cyme. They can deal with the cases that were being brought to us. Who stole whose goat, where a sewer line should be put – it's all so exasperating." He fluttered his eyes and put a hand to his forehead.

I was beginning to revise my initial impression of the man. If I didn't know him, I recognized his type. He was a scholarly man, a dilettante, somewhat timid, and not very interested in dealing with a really tough problem. Many Roman aristocrats affect this pose because they want to avoid even the appearance of having political ambitions that might draw the ire of the emperor. Even my uncle took refuge in that sort of thing in Nero's last years. The only book he wrote then was an eight-volume work on grammatical problems. Now Rome has developed a whole class of men who dally in scientific explorations of the sort my uncle loved.

"Excellency, this is quite a bit more complicated than stolen goats and sewer lines. As I told you in my note, a Roman citizen, Lucius Manilius Cornutus, a man whose father and grandfather held the consulship, has been murdered."

"Yes, I know. It's horrible." He shook his head. "Just horrible. And I want you to tell me all about it as soon as I've had a bath and something to eat. I'm much too tired right now to consider such a weighty matter. Is there a good bathhouse near here?"

"Yes, excellency, just a block down that way." I pointed over my shoulder.

"Good. Would you accompany me, please?"

A bath was the last thing I wanted right now. I had delayed searching for Chryseis longer than I should have already. While I was turning wrinkly in the caldarium Anyte and her bunch could be moving Chryseis farther and farther away from Smyrna, and farther away from the likelihood that I would ever see her again. And Marcellus could be sending his minions out to look for her. But I had no choice. I had presumed to take charge because the governor wasn't here. Now the governor was here, so I was no longer giving the orders.

While we made our way through the frigidarium and tepidarium I outlined what had happened to Cornutus, but did not mention my theory that he'd been poisoned before he was eviscerated. Without being able to show Florus the evidence of the corpse itself, I had no proof of that accusation. I also didn't mention Chryseis' fall and disappearance.

"This doctor," Florus said as I concluded my report as we soaked in the pool, "this Luke. What do you know about him?"

I couldn't weigh my response too carefully or too long. Florus was probably good at reading pauses. "He seems quite competent."

"Do you remember what your uncle said about physicians in the *Natural History?*"

"Well, sir, he said quite a bit about them. He took great interest in their work. Is there one passage in particular you have in mind?"

"Yes. In one of the later volumes, I believe, he says, 'Only a physician can commit murder with complete impunity.' Do you think he might have had this man Luke in mind?"

I was so stunned to be reminded of my uncle's dictum that I think my mouth must have opened and closed a couple of times, like a fish taken out of water.

"No, excellency, I've seen nothing to suggest that Luke is anything but a competent and compassionate doctor." Leaving aside, I thought, the fact that he's a member of a dubious cult, a follower of a crucified criminal.

"At any rate, we ought to look at him carefully," Florus said before he submerged himself.

Florus proved to be one of those people who spends a couple of hours in the baths, relishing the experience with all his senses. Unless I've had a particularly difficult day, I view a bath more pragmatically. A bit of a soak to relax, a good scrub, and I'm done. Florus wanted a massage, during the course of which he fell asleep, and he couldn't resist trying some of the items the food sellers were hawking. A sticky pastry made with grape leaves and dates sent him into ecstasies. It nauseated me.

We were still in the bathhouse when Marcellus and Tacitus came in, a sure signal that Apelles' funeral games were over. It disturbed me to see my friend chatting amicably with Marcellus. Nonetheless, I introduced Florus to the two of them.

"I've told his excellency how Cornutus was butchered," I said, hoping Tacitus would pick up on the hint and not say anything about the poisoning and trying to make Marcellus think I suspected nothing. Marcellus smirked.

"Yes," Tacitus said, lowering himself into the pool. "It was a ghastly sight. I hope I never see the like again."

I rolled my eyes. This from a man who'd just spent most of the day watching people being hacked up for the crowd's amusement.

Marcellus, still sitting on the edge of the pool with his towel wrapped around him, began fawning over Florus in a way that would have made his teacher Regulus proud. His performance almost completed the job that the grape leaf pastry had begun in my stomach. I hoped I wouldn't vomit in the pool.

"It's a relief to finally have a legal authority on the scene," he said.

Florus made a mild defense of me. "It sounds as though Gaius Pliny has kept things in order. No one has been allowed to leave; Cornutus' father has been notified; the victim received a proper funeral. That was your responsibility, I understand."

Marcellus lowered his eyes, as though embarrassed to be singled out for praise. "Yes, excellency. I was happy to make some small contribution. Now that you're here, I hope to be able to continue my travels, perhaps as early as tomorrow."

Florus surprised me. "That won't be possible. I think Pliny was correct to hold everyone here until we've gotten some questions answered. I will issue the same order. I don't want anyone leaving town until further notice."

The bath wasn't the only thing steaming now, but Marcellus didn't protest. Instead he launched a more direct attack on me.

"It is unfortunate, excellency, that two slaves of the murdered man have gone missing under Gaius Pliny's regime. It's quite likely one of them killed him."

Florus looked at me with a raised eyebrow. "You hadn't mentioned that."

"I was coming to it, excellency," I lied. "It's by no means clear to me that either of these women had anything to do with Cornutus' death. They were both locked up when it happened."

Marcellus dropped into the water so he could put his physical presence behind his attack. "But we don't know what they know because Pliny refused to torture Cornutus' slaves to get information out of them."

Florus looked at me with disappointment. "Is this true? You refused to have the slaves tortured?"

"Yes, excellency. I saw no point in it. All of Cornutus' slaves were locked up for the night when he went to bed. None of them could have had anything to do with his death." An inspiration hit. "In fact, our friend Marcellus here may have been the last person to see Cornutus alive."

Before Marcellus could do more than splutter, Florus held up his hands. "I don't intend to conduct this inquest in the bath. I'll start my soldiers searching for these women in the morning and will convene a formal inquiry at the second hour. Pliny, I want to see the notes you made about the condition of Cornutus' body."

"I have them, sir," Tacitus said. "I'll get them sorted out tonight."

"Luke, the physician," I added, "also examined Cornutus' body and can corroborate my own findings."

"If he didn't kill him," Florus said. "I expect all members of your caravan to present themselves tomorrow morning. That means no one leaves the inn tonight."

"If I may, excellency," I said, "I have already been invited to dinner at the home of a local dignitary. Luke and Timothy, whom you met on your arrival, were also invited. May we still keep that engagement?"

"Well, yes, I suppose so," Florus said. "Just be sure you don't leave the city."

"Of course," I replied. Now I just had to send a slave over to Apelles' house to inform them that I would be dropping by for a visit in the evening and to please have a few horses ready for my use.

"I'm sorry you won't be present at dinner," Florus said. "I had hoped to talk about your father's writing. I've been particularly impressed by his volumes on *The Scholar*. Such a masterful outline of the training that every public man ought to have."

"I'll look forward to that conversation tomorrow night," I promised as I hoisted myself out of the pool and wrapped myself in a towel.

* * * *

As soon as I returned to the inn I had arrangements to make. Luke promised to take word to Kallisto about our visit and the need for horses. Timothy agreed to go with me, though I hesitated to ask someone else to defy a governor's order. It's one thing to go against authority oneself, quite a different matter to encourage another to do so. I also reminded Luke not to mention the possibility that Cornutus had been poisoned. For now we would satisfy ourselves with an official inquiry into who had murdered him the second time. I still hoped that the poisoner would give himself away in some fashion if he thought no one was aware of his crime.

I caught Tacitus upon his return to the inn and was reassured to learn that he had said nothing about the poisoning.

"Since you didn't mention it," he said, "I assumed you didn't want it brought up."

"Something else I don't want brought up is my real purpose for going out tonight."

"I thought you must have something devious in mind, to pretend that you're going back into that den of Christians."

"Do you want to go with me?"

"Pliny, my friend, you are no longer in charge of this investigation. The governor is here. What you need to do now is to follow his orders very carefully so you don't end up in a great deal of trouble. Your refusal to torture Cornutus' slaves may come back to haunt you yet."

"I think all will be forgotten tomorrow morning when I present Chryseis and Melissa at the governor's inquest."

"You know where they are?"

"I'm almost certain I do. If it hadn't been for Florus' untimely arrival, I might already have found them."

"But why can't you just tell Florus and let him send soldiers tomorrow? That seems the sensible thing to do."

"Because I don't think they'll be there by tomorrow. And Florus isn't going to bestir himself to do anything tonight."

"He isn't a very energetic man, is he? But you're taking an awful risk. This could damage any career you might hope to have in Rome."

"It may be the only chance I'll have to get Chryseis back."

"I hope you won't think me not a friend if I don't go with you."

"You can actually do me a service by keeping an eye on Marcellus during the evening. Don't let him talk Florus into torturing Cornutus' slaves while I'm away. And see if you can find Tiberius Saturninus."

* * * *

We actually did eat a light dinner at Apelles' house, though I was too excited to have much appetite. Conversation around the table was strained, with only one non-Christian in the room. Luke and Timothy spent a lot of time talking to a handsome slave, a boy of twelve or so, named Polycarp, a recent addition to Apelles' household.

At last it was dark enough for us to leave. A slave would be sent later to inform the governor that Luke, Timothy, and I would be spending the night at Apelles' house, since the hour was so late, and to promise our prompt attendance at the inquest the next morning. To avoid attracting attention, we walked to the necropolis on the north side of town and found a servant of Apelles' waiting for us with horses.

The ride out to the old temple of Artemis didn't take long. It seemed longer because we rode in silence. Timothy was a quiet fellow, as he had shown at dinner, and Damon was playing the slave's role, to speak only when spoken to unless danger was imminent. That left me with some time to reflect. And I had a lot to think about.

To begin with, there was the possible danger to myself of riding off into the night, armed only with a short sword, borrowed from Apelles' son, and accompanied by two Christians. But I had unwittingly trusted one Christian for years and no harm had befallen me. How many other Roman aristocrats were harboring these people within their very walls, like some disease or infestation which you don't suspect until it suddenly breaks out and overwhelms you? Or like Vesuvius, sitting there for centuries in the midst of thousands of unsuspecting people, building homes and growing grapes on the slopes of the slumbering volcano. Should the government investigate? Try to stamp them out?

And then there was the question of my disobeying a direct order of the governor. In a Roman province the governor is a virtual king. To go against an order of his is to align oneself against Rome. Never in my short life had I contemplated doing such a thing. Were those green eyes and that golden hair worth this risk?

"I don't see any sign of anyone else," Timothy said as we approached the walls of old Smyrna. "Do you think the witch will come out here tonight?"

"I doubt it. I'm sure she and her people had planned to move Chryseis and Melissa by night away from Smyrna. But I saw them talking in the dining room of the inn after the governor promulgated his order that everyone must stay there tonight. They were obviously irritated."

"They do have local contacts," Timothy said. "They could turn the business over to them."

"I suppose so. But all is quiet, so I think we should count ourselves fortunate and not waste any more time speculating about other people's plans. Let's carry out ours and let them worry about us."

This time we rode right up to the ruined temple. Damon stayed with the horses, his shepherd's sling ready. The moon, just past full, gave enough light for us to walk around the base of the temple until we found an entrance to the storerooms under it. Damon struck a flint to light one of the torches we had brought, and Timothy and I descended into the ruin.

The stairway was reasonably wide, since it was used for moving items in and out of storage during festivals and sacrifices. In the basement of the building we found a long passageway with rooms opening off one side of it. The rats registered their objections to our presence, squeaking and scurrying in all directions. The doors of most of the rooms – made of heavy wood – were still intact. Some stood open; others were closed. The first two that we looked into were empty, looted long ago of anything of value.

In the third room we found the carcass of a dog, one of the witch's Molossian hounds. It had been stabbed several times in the throat and stomach. The blood was dry but it was clear the beast had died within the last day. The flies and rats had barely begun their work on him. There was blood on his teeth, suggesting he inflicted injury on someone before his death.

Turning a corner we came upon a door that was blocked. A beam of wood had been braced between the door and the base of the opposite wall.

"I wonder what's in there," I said.

"Another dog?" Timothy said nervously.

"A very quiet one then. There's no barking. Give me a hand." I threw my shoulder against the beam and Timothy reluctantly pitched in. As soon as we made a noise with it we heard a hard thump against the door from inside the room.

Timothy jumped back. I took out my sword as the thump resounded again.

"I don't think it's a dog," I assured Timothy. "These monsters bark at anything."

One more jolt knocked the beam loose and we opened the door. The torchlight fell on the pitiful sight of Melissa, lying on the floor gagged and with her hands tied behind her and her gown bunched up around her waist. A quick glance around the room confirmed my worst fear: Chryseis wasn't here. I knelt, pulled Melissa's gown down, and untied her.

"My lord!" she cried as soon as I had the gag out of her mouth. "Thank God you've come. They've taken Chryseis. I couldn't stop them." She began to cry.

As I freed her hands it seemed to me that the knot was loosely tied. For a moment I couldn't help but wonder if she might have tied herself up. She had betrayed my trust once; I intended to be hard to fool again.

"What happened?" I said when I had freed her. "Tell me everything, slowly and from the beginning."

"Could we please get out of here?" she begged. "It's so dark, and the rats . . . " She shuddered.

I supported her as we made our way back to the stairs, stopping to pick up her bag and Chryseis', and up into the night air. She took a few steps away from the temple and sat on a fallen block of marble.

"Douse the torch," I told Timothy. "No need to send a beacon to advertise our presence to anyone else." He rubbed the flame in the dirt. "Now, tell us what happened," I said to Melissa.

The slave woman's olive complexion glistened in the moonlight, especially the tears on her cheeks. Her eyes stood out almost like an animal's. She fixed them on me but said nothing. I decided to give her a start on her story, like priming a pump.

"You made arrangements with Anyte to help you and Chryseis escape, didn't you?"

She drew a deep breath, then began to recount what had happened. Her voice was not so much soft as toneless, with no spirit to it.

"Yes, my lord. We were brought to the temple and left here with a dog for protection. I spent the day cutting Chryseis' hair and trying to darken it and her skin so she wouldn't stand out so much as we traveled east. I was going to disguise her as my son. The women were supposed to come back tonight and take us to another hiding place.

"But this morning three men discovered us hiding in the basement of the temple. The dog attacked them, but they managed to kill it. One of the men was bitten rather badly. They seemed confused when they found us. Their orders, one of them said, were to bring the blonde girl back. One, the one who had been bitten, wanted to kill me so I couldn't identify them. Another objected. He didn't agree to do a murder, he said, just to find the girl and bring her back. The leader said if he couldn't kill me, he was at least going to have some fun with me. I begged him not to do it in front of Chryseis. Take me in another room, I said, and I would do anything he wanted without a fight. So he threw me into that room and two of them tied me up and – and they raped me.

"The one who didn't want to kill me left me some food and water and loosened the rope enough that I could work my hands free in time. Somebody would find me in a few days, he said, but they would be far enough away by then that it wouldn't matter."

"Had you ever seen any of these men before?" I asked.

"No, my lord. I have no idea who they were. Believe me, I would tell you if I knew. It's the only way we'll get Chryseis back."

"It sounds as though someone hired them," Timothy put in.

"I agree," I said. "Think carefully, Melissa. Did they say anything that might point to the person who hired them? Or anything about where they were going?"

"No, my lord. I've told you virtually every word they said." She put her face in her hands and began to cry. I think women learn to do that on command so they can avoid saying anything more than they want in certain situations. That phrase 'virtually every word' left me uneasy. Would the words she had left out tell me something I needed to know?

Melissa rode behind Damon as we traveled back to Apelles' house. Several of the women there took her under their wings and hustled her off to clean her up. When she returned to join us in the garden my first reaction was that she looked composed. As we talked I decided that 'defeated' might be a more accurate word.

"We all need to get some rest," I told her. "My dilemma is whether I can trust you to stay in a room by yourself."

She dropped to her knees in front of me and hung her head. "My lord, I promise you that I will stay put. My only hope of finding Chryseis is to cooperate with you."

"You know punishments for runaway slaves can be severe. I can't guarantee I'll be able to protect you. The governor is here now, and my influence over events has been reduced to practically nothing."

She looked up. "What happens to me no longer matters, my lord. Just find Chryseis."

We found a room on the interior of the house for her this time, as far from any exterior doors as possible. And I ordered Damon to sleep on a pallet outside her door in any case.

As I retired for the night I tried to put together some of the pieces of this puzzle which seemed to have appeared for the first time today. Florus suspected Luke, just because he was a doctor. That seemed ludicrous to me, but had I been taking the kindly old gentleman for granted? And Saturninus? He disappeared soon after Chryseis did. No one had seen him all day. He was, it turned out, a minion of Regulus'.

Had I been looking at the right hydra, just the wrong tentacle?

XIII

The sun was barely up when a heavy pounding on the front door resounded through Apelles' house like the blows of a battering ram. The servant who answered it found himself facing a small squad of Florus' soldiers, fully armed and menacing. I, as is my habit, had awakened early and, with Damon, was waiting for Luke and Timothy in the atrium. Damon had assured me, on his life, that no one had gone into or out of Melissa's room last night. I took a few steps toward the door, since I was sure that the soldiers had come for me.

The squad's leader rested his hand on the hilt of his sword and announced, as though he were bellowing an order to a full legion, "His excellency, Lucius Mestrius Florus, proconsul of Asia, requires the presence of Gaius Pliny, the doctor Luke, and Timothy of Ephesus at the inquiry into the death of Lucius Manilius Cornutus, now convening in the inn of Androcles."

I stepped forward. "I'm Gaius Pliny," I said, suddenly nervous for some reason. I felt as if a chilly shadow had passed over me. Superstitious people might have said it was an omen of what was to come. But I'm not superstitious. "We'll be ready to leave in just a moment. Let me get the others."

"Please be quick, sir."

I met Luke, Timothy, and Melissa coming into the atrium. "We'd better go," I said. "Florus has sent us an escort in full panoply. I'm worried that, if we take Melissa in with us, we'll disrupt the proceedings and raise questions about where Chryseis is. I'd rather Florus focus on Cornutus' murder. At the same time I don't want to be accused of harboring an escaped slave."

"She could stay here," Luke said, "until later in the morning. The governor will want to know she's been found but, you're right, it might be better to save that news until a more auspicious time."

"All right, we're agreed then. Melissa, I'll leave Damon here to accompany you. Come along to the inn in about two hours. And you will hold true to your word, I trust."

Melissa nodded. "My lord, I have placed myself in your hands. I'll do whatever you say." Her voice was subdued, and she did not hold herself with the dignity I had noticed before, the carriage that would not let you identify her as a slave if you passed her in the street. She seemed shrunken.

I whispered quick instructions to Damon; then Luke, Timothy and I joined the eight soldiers for the walk to the inn. The soldiers surrounded us so that I felt more like a prisoner being transported than a person who was allowing himself to be escorted. We drew stares from the slaves setting out on their morning errands and the shopkeepers who were preparing to welcome their business. I'm sure they wondered what crime we had committed.

Our route took us down the Golden Street, through the agora with its unusual pillars of red-veined white marble, and then through some of the narrower side streets, where it became difficult for the soldiers to hold their formation. We turned into a disorganized knot of people sidestepping the garbage and waste. Had my uncle, in his *Natural History*, really called this place a 'light of Asia'? He obviously had never been here, and had picked up the encomium from something he read.

A crowd of people was milling outside the door to the inn when we stamped into view. I could hear Androcles' voice, protesting the loss of his morning business. Florus had taken over his dining room to hold his inquiry. The crowd outside the door, I gathered, consisted of his displaced customers. Squawk all he might, there was nothing Androcles could do. The governor of a province has the right to commandeer any facilities he needs to do his job. Androcles might soon wish he was still dealing with me and my pretenses of being a magistrate, rather than with the genuine item, backed by the might of Rome.

The soldiers quickly parted the crowd outside the door and allowed us entry. I thought I heard Luke mutter something to Timothy about the Red Sea, but I had no time for clarification. Florus, with

Marcellus at his elbow, turned a lawyer's smile on us. "Ah, Pliny. How nice to see you. I trust you slept well." I wondered if he knew about the little ride we had taken.

"Yes, excellency, I did. Thank you." I pretended not to notice the sarcasm, but I couldn't fail to observe Marcellus' smirk.

"Are you ready for the proceedings to begin then?"

"I am at your disposal," I said with a slight bow of my head, "except that I'm not properly dressed. I apologize for not having my toga on." Marcellus was wrapped in a toga so white I had to squint when I looked at him, with the purple senatorial stripe prominently in view. I didn't want to appear any less majestic. "If you don't mind the delay," I said, "I will go upstairs and put it on."

"Don't be concerned about it," Florus said, adjusting his own toga. "We aren't in Rome. Let's just get this business settled."

He took his seat in a chair against one wall of the dining room. Normally a magistrate sits on a raised platform. He compensated for the lack of height by establishing a lot of open space around him. The slaves who served as his scribes sat to his right. The tables had been pushed back to the edges of the room, leaving a large open area where people would stand while being interrogated. The rest of us, and as many spectators as space permitted, sat or stood at whatever spots we could find on the periphery. Tacitus worked his way through the crowd to stand beside me. The eight soldiers who had accompanied us assured order by their grim visages and spears, like so many Priapus figures in a garden meant to frighten away malevolent spirits.

Since Androcles had found the body, he was summoned first to tell what he knew, which was precious little. Those who slept in the surrounding rooms were asked if they had heard anything. They all, of course, claimed to have been sleeping like the dead. I knew that Gaius Sempronius had been debauching Androcles' young daughter; I wondered how many others had been engaged in other activities besides sleeping. The questions were pointless. Cornutus had been poisoned before he even got into bed. Of that I was sure. There would have been little, if any, noise when his heart was cut out because he was long since dead when that happened. I wanted someone to ask if any of these people had any reason to want Cornutus dead. Had anyone quarreled with him in Syria and been biding his time until he could settle the score?

I had some trouble deciphering Marcellus' role in this process. Sitting closer to the governor than anyone except the scribes, at a table with several pieces of papyrus scattered in front of him, he frequently interjected questions, with Florus' blessing. But he wasn't prosecuting or defending anyone – except perhaps himself. Roman law provides no formal procedure for such an inquest. The governor or other presiding magistrate has the power of *inquisitio*, the power to ask questions about any matter he chooses. But I had never seen a magistrate rely on a private citizen in this way.

I leaned over to Tacitus and whispered, "What do you make of Marcellus?"

"He and Florus had their heads together over dinner last night," he whispered in return. "I think Florus knows he's completely out of his depth here."

A sick feeling took root in my stomach. Marcellus had had an entire evening to ingratiate himself with Florus, to put his version of Cornutus' murder before him, to poison his mind, in a very real sense. Had I made a crucial mistake by not being present to offer an antidote? Now Melissa was going to walk into an enemy camp, defended only by my youthful enthusiasm for the truth. I should have just given her a horse and wished her well on her journey. But she wouldn't have left without Chryseis.

Tacitus, Luke, and I were next asked to describe our observations of the body. I kept my comments brief and deferred to Luke on account of his expert medical knowledge. The three of us had pledged ourselves not to mention anything about poison. It was the only way we could lull the real killer into a false sense of security. When Luke finished, Florus turned to Marcellus with an eyebrow raised.

"Doctor," Marcellus said, "in your opinion, what caused Cornutus' death?"

"After hearing my description, sir, I'm surprised you would ask that question."

I mentally applauded him for his neat evasion of the issue and his jab at Marcellus. Marcellus smirked. I was sure he thought that not even the doctor was aware that Cornutus had been poisoned.

With the conclusion of Luke's testimony, the process seemed at a standstill. We had learned nothing I didn't already know. Florus appeared to be at a loss as to where to go. He looked expectantly at Marcellus, who was shifting the pieces of papyrus on his table.

Before Marcellus could say anything, a stir ran through the crowd as Melissa and Damon squirmed through them and into the makeshift courtroom. Marcellus fixed on Melissa at once and pointed dramatically at her. "There, excellency," he intoned, "is one of the keys to finding the person who committed this heinous crime." Florus half rose out of his chair.

To keep him from convicting her on the spot, I stepped forward and took her by the arm. "Excellency, this is Melissa, the slave and concubine of Cornutus. I found her last night. She has returned of her own volition to assist in this inquiry."

"A slave has no volition of her own," Marcellus said.

Florus raised his hand for silence. "I thought there were two missing slaves. Wasn't there also a girl?"

"Yes, excellency," I said. "The girl Chryseis is still missing. Three men found her hiding place yesterday morning and took her away. They left Melissa to die." The crowd murmured, starting a new wave of rumors that would be all over Smyrna before lunch.

Marcellus began to sound and handle himself more and more like a lawyer in court. "Excellency, are we expected to believe such nonsense?" he snorted. "How convenient that three men, who I'm sure can't be identified, have taken the girl to some unspecified place. The only way we're going to get reliable information out of this woman is to torture her. Her and all the rest of Cornutus' slaves. Gaius Pliny has been very fastidious to see that Roman usage was followed in his investigation of Cornutus' death, but he conveniently neglected the requirement that a murdered man's slaves be tortured for information and then put to death if the culprit cannot be identified. Now there is a complicating factor of a runaway slave to be dealt with."

I could feel Melissa melting beside me. I wished I could get her into a chair before she collapsed, but a slave dared not sit before a magistrate.

"Excellency," Melissa said weakly, "I will tell you all I know about that night. All of Cornutus' slaves were locked up when he went to bed. We were not let out until the next morning, long after he was dead. By all that is holy, that is all I know or can tell."

"The whip can freshen a memory," Marcellus snarled.

I dreaded that prospect. What if Melissa admitted under torture that she had been able to get out of the window? It was an irrelevant piece of information, but just the sort of thing Marcellus would be looking for.

Florus nodded. "I think we must follow the law here. The law has always been the foundation of Rome's greatness." He gestured to one of the soldiers, who gave an order in Latin to the others. Two of them grabbed Melissa, who was clinging to me in terror. They dragged her to a spot where a hook jutted from the wall. A utensil of some sort normally hung there, I would guess. They tied Melissa's hands in front of her, then raised her arms so the rope on her hands caught on the hook. She was left standing on tiptoe. One soldier gripped her gown at the neck and tore it all the way down. Her bare back and shoulders lay open. The crowd fell silent, almost holding their breath as one person.

One of the huskiest of the soldiers stepped into the center of the room and uncoiled a whip. When he snapped it once for practice, I felt as though it had been laid across my own back. As he drew his arm back to begin the flagellation I lunged at him and grabbed his wrist. He grunted with surprise as the force of his blow was thwarted.

"What are you doing?" Florus yelled at me.

I refused to be shaken off the man's arm, gripping him like a rutting dog. "Excellency! Why must we do this? Melissa has told us everything she knows. Hasn't she suffered enough? Those thugs raped her yesterday. How much more must we subject her to in the name of Roman justice?" I almost spat out the last two words.

It was Marcellus, not Florus, who replied. "Do you have one shred of evidence to support this story, other than this slave's own word?"

I actually managed to wrestle the whip out of the soldier's hand. Some sort of demonic ferocity seemed to have possessed me. Ignoring Marcellus, I faced Florus. "Can we not show Rome's mercy, excellency?"

When he spoke I almost thought Marcellus was playing one of those tricks priests use to make an image of a god appear to speak. His voice was low. His lips didn't quite seem to be moving in rhythm to the words I was hearing. "The law must be obeyed. That is my responsibility as governor of this province. If I can ignore this law, what other law could another governor abrogate? Before long we would have government by personal whim, followed by utter chaos. It's time to put aside your personal feelings, Gaius Pliny. Cease your interference with this judicial process or I will arrest you."

A second soldier had come up behind me. He jerked the whip from my hand and tossed it back to the man appointed to do the flogging. The soldier who had snatched it from me shoved me back into the crowd.

I couldn't get out of the place before the lash whistled through the air and cut across Melissa's back. Her scream followed me like a Fury as I ran away from the inn. Luke, who stayed so he could care for her, later told me that was the only sound she made during the entire ordeal.

* * * *

Not knowing or caring where I was going, I walked the streets of Smyrna for a while. I was disgusted with myself for bringing Melissa back and with Rome's legal system for inflicting this on her. The 'judicial process' seemed to be just another form of the brutality I witnessed yesterday in the stadium. What purpose was served by crucifying those men? Or by flogging Melissa?

There ought to be some rational way to get at the truth rather than subjecting people to inhuman punishments, even death. Rome's system relies on bullying the lower classes who can't protect themselves while the upper classes talk one another to death in speeches that have more to do with the supposed character of the people in the case than with the facts. Why doesn't anyone look at what has happened in any scientific way? Men like Florus brag about their interest in science, but they look only at trivial things that have no impact on people's lives. They're like Socrates in Aristophanes' play *The Clouds*, measuring how far a flea can jump but having no idea how to answer a question such as, Who killed this man?

I came out from between two buildings and found myself looking over the city's Inner Harbor, a kind of bulge in the coastline around which Smyrna is built. Only a handful of ships lay at anchor there. It was still early in the sailing season, when the threat of storms wasn't entirely past. I may hate being *on* the water, but I find that standing beside it, when it's calm and glistening under the sun, restores a sense of well-being in me, even with my sensitive eyes. My uncle's house – now my house – on the Bay of Naples had afforded me that serenity since I was a child. I often sat on the rocks at the edge of the terrace and found answers to my problems in what Homer so aptly called the 'wine-dark sea'. Looking into the water for long produces a kind of intoxication, an easing of tensions.

Today, as I sat down and began to idly toss pebbles into Smyrna's waters, I wondered if they could offer a resolution to my dilemma. Was there any way to see that justice is done in spite of the justice system? Shouldn't something be done for those, like Melissa, who are denied all rights under our law, and not because of anything they have done?

Romans pride themselves on handling their legal matters in the public eye, but might they sometimes be better handled out of the public eye? In the private eye, one might say, if there were such a phrase in the Latin language. The wealthy in Rome have long supported lower-class people, whom we call clients. The word literally means someone who leans on you for support. We often take on as clients those who we think might eventually add to our own prestige or offer us some benefit. I inherited a pack of clients from my uncle and would pass them on to my son someday, if the fates allowed me that privilege.

But now I resolved to take on a different kind of client, ones who needed to rely on me because they had nowhere else to turn. Melissa and Chryseis would be the first. No longer would I assist Florus or expect help from him. In a sense I would be working apart from the government, *against* it if that became necessary.

"I figured you'd eventually end up by the water," Tacitus said behind me. "It's over. Florus finally stopped it."

I didn't look up. I was angry at him because he could stand to watch but thankful he had brought me the news. "Do you know how she's doing?"

"She's alive. Barely. Luke's taking care of her." He sat down next to me, squinting into the glare off the water.

"If she dies, I will hold Marcellus and Florus personally responsible," I said. "I swear it."

He looked at me as though I had cursed the emperor's guardian spirit. "You can't talk like that. Florus was just doing what the law requires, and Marcellus was reminding him of his duty."

"How does flogging an innocent woman help us to find out who killed Cornutus?"

"What makes you so sure she's innocent?" He flicked a rock into the water. "She resents being a slave. She wants Chryseis to be free. It seems to me she had some reason to kill Cornutus. And ample reason to kill you – the son of the man who sacked her village – if she thought you were in that room. And we know she wasn't actually locked up all night."

Shading my eyes with my hand, I looked over the bay toward the west and the open sea. I hated to admit it, but Tacitus was raising questions about Melissa that I couldn't entirely dismiss. Just as this bay led to the boundless sea, those questions might lead to totally unexpected conclusions.

"You're right," I said. "Something about her story does bother me. Marcellus – damn his eyes – raised what might be a legitimate question: the only information we have about the attack by the three unknown men is Melissa's word."

"What if she's making up the whole story to throw us off the trail, to delay us while Chryseis gets farther away? You said that her hands were loosely tied. She could have done that herself. She might even have killed the dog."

"No, actually, that dead dog is the best witness on Melissa's behalf."

"What are you talking about?"

"The monster had blood on his teeth. He had bitten somebody, pretty viciously. And Melissa had no bite marks on her hands or arms. There was somebody else in the basement of that temple. Someone who fought with that dog and killed it."

"Chryseis was there. How do you know she doesn't have bite marks on her?"

"Don't be ridiculous. Can you seriously suggest that she could have fought and killed the dog? I believe Melissa's story about the three men is true."

"That means somebody has now stolen Chryseis from whoever stole her in the first place." Tacitus started enumerating points on his fingers. "It's getting very complicated, like keeping track of all the imperial marriages, divorces, and remarriages. And why is a slave girl – granting her extraordinary beauty – of such interest to everyone?"

"I think somebody besides us strongly suspects she's Cornutus' daughter. And whoever killed Cornutus – and it's the poisoning I'm talking about – seems to want Chryseis out of the way, too. That suggests some kind of legacy-hunting scheme."

"And that leads you to Regulus, I know," Tacitus said tiredly, "the source of all the crime and evil in Rome."

"I wouldn't give him *that* much credit. But this sort of thing is his specialty. And that leads us back to the two men here with any connection to Regulus, namely Marcellus and Saturninus."

"And you have not a shred of proof against either of them, may I point out."

I got to my feet. "Nor will I find any sitting here."

"What do you intend to do?"

"I'm going to see if I can talk to Melissa. Meanwhile, could you see if you can find out where I might locate a couple of gamblers?" I described the men who had threatened Saturninus over the crooked dice. "I pity him if he's fallen into their clutches, but at least he won't be hunting for Chryseis if they have him."

* * * *

By the time I returned to the inn it was about the fifth hour of the day, as nearly as I could judge. Having made a commitment to myself to do whatever I could, with my resources or my intellect, to protect those who were at the mercy of our laws, I felt a sense of renewal. I glanced into the dining room to see if I could play any further role in the proceedings, but the room had been returned to its original function. A few people were already drifting in for an early lunch. They all cast wary glances at the hook where Melissa had been strung up. I thought I could detect a few streaks of blood on the wall. Androcles had probably left them – or daubed them there himself – as a lure to draw customers.

I was crossing the main room of the inn, on my way to the stairs, when Luke hailed me.

"Gaius Pliny," he called. "I've been looking for you. I've gotten permission to care for Melissa. Would you like to accompany me?"

I followed him to the same room in the brothel section of the inn where Chryseis had been placed. Now two sturdy Roman soldiers stood guard in front of the door. Luke showed one of them a piece of papyrus with a seal stamped on it, and they stepped aside and allowed us to enter.

"Florus won't allow anyone in here without permission," Luke said, as he pulled some vials and other tools of his trade out of his bag. "He's determined she won't disappear again. I don't know where he thinks she could go in this condition. She couldn't walk across this room right now."

I finally got up the courage to look at Melissa. She lay on a bed on her stomach, nude. She turned her head to acknowledge our entrance. Even in the dim light from two small lamps I could see that her back was a mass of bloody welts. She would be scarred for life. I was amazed again at her strength. Slaves have been known to tell the most outrageous lies to escape torture when they didn't know anything. Melissa could have saved herself a beating and disfigurement by telling Florus something. Anything. But she didn't. Rome's whole system of justice seemed to be based on faulty premises. Can you hope to reach the right answer when you're asking the wrong questions?

I took her hand and wept. I admit that without shame. "I am so sorry, Melissa. This is my fault. If I had foreseen it, I would never have come looking for you."

"But you weren't looking for me." Her words throbbed with her pain. "You were looking for Chryseis . . . as you should have been. If you hadn't found me . . . the rats would have eaten me alive. Is this any worse a fate?"

She winced and groaned as Luke gently cleaned her wounds with wine and soothed them with oil.

"Take your mind off the pain," I encouraged her. "Tell me again about the men finding you and Chryseis."

She told the same story she had told Timothy and me earlier. I didn't notice any difference in the way she told it or any details added or omitted. The whip hadn't gotten anything else out of her. I had to assume she was telling the truth. I just wished I were more certain about her reliability.

* * * *

It was now about midday, and I was feeling the need to eat something. I returned to my room first, washed off, put on a clean tunic, and made certain my slaves were all accounted for. There wasn't much I could give them to do under the circumstances. Being a slave owner is, in its own way, a kind of burden, though I doubt our slaves would have any sympathy for us. We must always be wondering what a certain number of people are doing, finding tasks for them, seeing that the tasks are done satisfactorily. Even if we appoint an overseer, we still have to oversee the overseer. My overseer on this trip, Trophimus, at least knew where his charges were, even if they weren't doing anything constructive.

I hoped to sneak out of the inn and get something to eat at a taberna. Florus was likely to eat in the inn, and I didn't want to encounter him after my performance at the inquiry. I was lucky he hadn't arrested me on the spot.

I could hear voices in the dining room and was almost out the front door when Tacitus spotted me from where he was sitting. He jumped up and came to the door of the dining room.

"Pliny, wait," he called.

I stopped, expecting that he had some news about Saturninus' whereabouts.

"No, no one's seen him," he said in response to my query. "Those two men you described, Ariston and Miltiades, I located them." The pleasure his success gave him showed on his face, like a schoolboy who's managed to recite his *arma virumque* for the first time. "They frequent a taberna down by the docks. They knew nothing of Saturninus. Oh, Ariston said he'd be around today to collect his ten tetradrachmas. Whatever that means."

"Thanks for checking on that. I was hoping we'd find Saturninus hunched over his dice somewhere. Instead I suspect he's tracking down Chryseis, another of Regulus' hounds. He may already have her." I continued toward the door.

"Come have some lunch," Tacitus called. "Florus is here."

I stepped back toward him so I wouldn't have to speak so loudly. "That's why I'm going somewhere else."

Tacitus lowered his voice. "You really need to apologize to him about this morning. If you don't make amends right away, Marcellus is going to turn him completely against you. Florus has influence to make trouble for you back in Rome as well as frustrate everything you're trying to do here."

He took my arm and escorted me into the dining room. Because I knew he was right I didn't resist. In the normal course of a political and legal career I would make enough enemies. If I could reduce the number by one at the beginning, I should take the opportunity.

Florus sat with two other men – an older and a younger – who looked vaguely familiar for some reason. He eyed me warily as Tacitus dragged me toward him. We stopped a few feet in front of his table. At least Marcellus was nowhere to be seen.

"Excellency," I said, "I want to apologize for my outrageous behavior at the inquiry this morning. I'm afraid I let my personal feelings run riot."

Florus considered his reply for a moment, studying me from under his foppish eyelids. I felt like a slave guilty of some infraction and uncertain whether my master was feeling kind or cruel at that particular instant.

"It was quite a display," he finally said. "But I'm inclined to applaud your conviction and idealism. It's reassuring to see such qualities in one so young. Experience, however, eventually teaches us that the old ways are best. That's why they've lasted long enough to become the old ways. Don't you agree?"

I fought down the urge to tell him what I really thought. "I can't argue with that line of reasoning, excellency."

"So you won't be distressed to learn that Cornutus' other slaves are now being tortured?" The question, delivered with his head cocked to one side, was a challenge. We Romans can be a perplexing mix of erudition, civility and cruelty.

"I'm not surprised to hear it. I certainly won't attempt to interfere."

"Good. So far all we've learned is that the two women, Melissa and Phoebe, actually got out of the room they were supposedly locked in. We're continuing to question Phoebe. I hope we'll learn something more useful, but if not, then they'll all be put to death. At least we'll have the satisfaction of knowing we have observed the law. No one can challenge us on that score."

From something in his voice I suspected Florus had no real heart for executing the slaves. He seemed to be defending himself against himself. I decided to take one more risk.

"Excellency, why not send them back to Rome for execution?

The emperor is always looking for victims for the games. It's difficult to keep up with the demand. Tacitus and I could insure their delivery since we're going there anyway."

Florus studied me suspiciously, like a child trying to divine which hand holds a prize. "That might not be a bad idea," he finally said. "It would show my adherence to the law and provide the emperor with something he needs as well. Yes, let's do it that way."

I sighed with relief that I had bought Melissa some time. Of course, she might not consider that a favor after her beating.

"Now," Florus said, "so much for business. Please join us, gentlemen."

Tacitus and I settled ourselves in chairs between Florus and his two guests.

"This job is so demanding," Florus said. "I hope neither of you ever have to be governor of a province. It's an honor I wouldn't wish on my worst enemy. If I'd known what a burden it was going to be, I don't think I would have stood for the consulship."

His comments surprised me, to put it mildly. The consulship is the pinnacle of a Roman man's political career. After holding it, we are required to govern a province somewhere as a proconsul, unless health or some other complication prevents us. But our focus is always on the glory which the consulship brings to us and to our families. I had known from the day I made my first appearance in court, four years ago, that the consulship was my goal. The minor offices I'd held so far were just stepping stones toward that objective. But if it wasn't a desirable prize . . . ?

"Let me introduce you to these distinguished gentlemen." Florus gestured to the other two men at the table. "This is Callicrates, head of the local library, a man who shares my own interests in scientific research." He indicated the older man. "His companion is Plutarch from Chaeronea. He is on his way to study in Alexandria."

"Our paths have crossed," Callicrates said, "though you may not remember. We were in the bath a few days ago when you came in, shortly after your arrival in Smyrna, I believe."

"I thought you were familiar for some reason," I said.

"We were sorry to hear of the death of your friend, Cornutus," Plutarch said. "He was an impressive, vigorous man. It's hard to imagine he was so brutally murdered only a short time after we saw him."

"That reminds me," I said. "Did either of you suffer any ill effects from the wine Marcellus bought for us?"

Tacitus' eyes bulged. I thought he was going to choke on his bread.

"You see, I was a bit ill later that evening," I continued, "and I was wondering if it might have been something I ate or drank."

Callicrates and Plutarch shook their heads and looked at one another.

"Just to refresh my memory," I said as Tacitus coughed, "Marcellus' slave went out to order the wine, didn't he."

Callicrates and Plutarch nodded.

"But a slave girl from the bath brought it in and handed a cup to Cornutus and one to Marcellus."

"That's correct," Plutarch said. "Then the rest of us took whichever cup we wanted."

"That's as I remember it," I said. "Thank you for confirming that."

Florus looked at me impatiently. "Is there some point to these questions, Gaius Pliny?"

"Probably not, excellency. Please, continue with whatever conversation you were having before I came in."

"We were discussing natural phenomena," Florus said. "The sort of thing your father wrote about so brilliantly. Callicrates was describing a place on the bay where the rising waters behave in a most peculiar manner. I want to go out to see it. Would you like to come along? I'm told it's a short ride. We'll be back in time for a bath and dinner."

Since I had missed dinner the previous evening and deprived Florus of the opportunity to discuss my uncle's work, I felt myself under a kind of imperative to make amends by accompanying him. Perhaps an afternoon's diversion would help clear my mind. I was making no progress in finding Chryseis or determining who killed Cornutus. This jaunt would be a complete waste of time, I was sure. My uncle would have been eager to see the thing, but what could I possibly learn from some hole in the ground?

XIV

It was all I could do to force myself to eat so I would be fortified for the trip out to the bay. Hearing that Cornutus' slaves were being tortured sickened me. What had poor Phrixus ever done to deserve such treatment? And Phoebe, I knew from my own conversation with her, was good-hearted and perhaps a bit simple-minded.

Florus, Callicrates, Plutarch, Tacitus, and I set off on horseback just after noon. We were accompanied by some of Florus' soldiers and Callicrates' slaves. Sometimes I wonder what it would be like to actually travel *alone*. Most Roman aristocrats can't even go to the latrine without an entourage. On this day, though, what I most longed for was a hat to shield my sensitive eyes from the sun. At least the breeze off the water diminished the heat.

It was in fact a short ride west along a road that ran beside the bay toward the town of Clazomenae. After a couple of miles Callicrates called us to a halt, and we dismounted. The coastline at this point was a low cliff with no beach at all. The waves breaking on the rocks below were close enough to spray us.

"Lovely view," I said. "But I don't see anything unusual."

"Follow me," Callicrates said, gathering his cloak around him against the sea breeze.

He led us twenty paces or so farther up the coast to a spot where the ground appeared to have collapsed, leaving a hole shaped like a letter C. The ground around the hole was the lowest spot on the shore as far as we could see in either direction. The soldiers and slaves stood back while we stood on the rim and looked down into it at the water lapping at the rocks.

"I wanted to come out here now," Callicrates said, "because this phenomenon can only be observed when the water is rising, as it does in the spring when the rivers are running full. For whatever reason, it's especially noticeable at the time of the full moon."

The little basin or cup-like enclave continued to fill, as the water approached the lip of the hole. I studied it intently, waiting for some surprise. Tacitus was less patient.

"What's so amazing about rising water?" he whispered. "In Rome we wouldn't walk across the street to watch this."

"Well, this is the provinces," I replied, provoking a short laugh from him.

"I wonder what they do when it rains?" he said. "Declare a holiday so everybody can celebrate the miracle?"

Callicrates silenced us with a glance, as he might talkative students in the back of his classroom. "When I bring students out here," he said, "I like to show them the power of my learning, for I now forbid the water to rise any further." He held out his hands as if to stop it, like a magician.

And it stopped! The water was still coming into the basin. That was clear because it was still rising along the rest of the shore, but it wasn't coming up any higher in the hole. By now it should have been almost up to the rim of the basin and in danger of overflowing onto the land. Even Tacitus was awed into silence. I knelt as close to the edge as I dared and peered over.

"Your father, the great Pliny, would have enjoyed this, wouldn't he?" Florus asked.

"He would have taken a keen interest," I said. "No offense to your magical powers intended, Callicrates, but what is the secret?"

Callicrates laughed pleasantly. "A disbeliever, are you? Well, I wish I could tell you the secret."

"Oh, come now," Florus said. "You brought us all the way out here, and you refuse to divulge the secret? That's no way to treat your guests."

"No, I mean I wish I knew the secret so I could tell you," Callicrates said.

I stood and brushed my hands together. "Are you serious? You don't know why the water doesn't rise any farther?"

"No one does," Callicrates said, and he seemed almost proud of his ignorance.

"How long has this basin been here?" Florus asked.

"It appeared in the last year of Nero's reign. There was a particularly bad storm that winter, and the ground collapsed at this point."

"And in fifteen years no one has discovered the cause of this phenomenon?" I asked.

"Not for lack of trying," Callicrates replied. "I myself have tied one of my slaves to a rope and lowered him into the water to try to gain some understanding of it."

"Have you gone into the water yourself?"

He stepped back, as if he thought I might be about to throw him in. "Why would I do that?"

"Because you're interested in finding the cause. Your slave's only concern was to keep from drowning."

"Surely you aren't suggesting that I put *myself* in danger of drowning," Callicrates said.

"My uncle put himself in the path of an erupting volcano. A pool of water hardly seems a challenge in comparison to that."

Callicrates drew himself up, as though I had offended him deeply. "Young man, you have some very peculiar ideas."

"I suppose they appear that way," I said, "but I'll have an explanation for this before we leave today."

I pulled off my tunic and handed it to Tacitus, who draped it over his shoulder. Then I jumped into the water, feet first.

"You fool!" Florus shouted. "What are you doing?"

The water was much colder than I expected, and I gasped. The sound I made must have startled Tacitus. He stepped toward the rim of the pool.

"Gaius Pliny! Are you all right?"

"Yes!" I shouted back. "I'm fine." If my voice hadn't been quavering so much, I might have sounded more convincing.

I swam the few feet toward the edge of the pool. A ring of rock protruded most of the way around the basin, about a foot below the rim. I became aware of a current in the water pulling me toward that ring. The water came up to the ring but would not rise above it. Taking a deep breath, I submerged myself and tried to inspect the ring by sight, but the water was swirling too much for me to see anything.

I surfaced and, like a stick floating wherever the water wants to take it, let myself be carried to the point where the current seemed strongest. There I braced myself against the rock with my feet and left hand and ran my right hand along the lower side of the rock ring. Even with my teeth chattering, I smiled.

Now I became aware of commotion around me. Florus must have ordered his soldiers to rescue me. Several of them were kneeling on the rim of the basin and extending their spears. "Grab on, sir!" they shouted.

I waved them off and swam over to a spot where the rocks in the wall of the basin provided sufficient footing for me to climb. When I emerged on land I was surrounded by soldiers and scholars like nymphs attending Aphrodite. Tacitus toweled me off with my tunic, and then I slipped it on. Florus commanded one of his soldiers to give me his cloak. For that I was grateful, since I couldn't stop shivering.

"I thought you hated the water," Tacitus chided me.

"I do. But my uncle insisted that I learn to swim. Any Roman who expects to make long sea voyages should know how, he said. It might save his life in the all too likely event the ship sinks."

Florus regarded me with his arms folded across his chest. "You do have a flair for the dramatic, young man. Do you ever do anything in the traditional way?"

I met his gaze. "If it will achieve the results I need," I said, "I have no objection to following tradition."

"You promised us an explanation," Callicrates reminded me.

I let him wait another moment while the chattering in my teeth subsided a bit more. "It's quite simple, actually. There's a narrow fissure under that ring of rock. The water runs in there, down through a series of channels, I suppose. It may drain back into the bay. Or maybe there's a grotto. The ground under our feet must look like a piece of rotten wood or a honeycomb. Considering the erosive power of water, there will certainly be further under-mining of the shore along here and the area we're standing on will eventually collapse, as this section did."

Several of the soldiers stepped back immediately.

"So that's how it's done!" Callicrates said.

"Yes," I said. "That's how it was done."

"You seem to be taking particular pleasure in your discovery," Florus said.

"Oh, I was just thinking . . . how my uncle would have reacted to it."

Callicrates put a hand on my arm. "May I offer my condolences on your loss, even at this late date? It was a great loss for everyone who loves learning. Your uncle's books hold an honored place in our library. We have a lovely illustrated copy of the *Natural History*. We would be pleased to have you visit us while you're here."

"Thank you," I said. "You're very kind."

On the ride back to Smyrna I signaled to Tacitus and he and I dropped behind the others.

"What's on your mind?" he asked.

"Since you've proved so adept at making inquiries in low places, could I ask you, when we get back to Smyrna, to see if you can find the slave girl who brought us the wine that first afternoon in the bath?"

* * * *

My mind was still spinning with my inspiration – it felt like a kind of madness, just as Plato said – when we returned to our rooms to gather our bath necessities. I had formed a plan to prove how Marcellus had poisoned Cornutus. My only frustration now was that the assistance I needed wouldn't be available until tomorrow; all the shops were closed as people made their way to the baths. This was one of those times when I wondered how anything gets done in our society, given the amount of time we spend eating, bathing, and attending games, plays and other forms of amusement.

When I reached my door I found a slave standing there, shifting from one foot to the other as though he had been waiting for quite a while. "My lord, my master, Marcus Carolus, requests that you honor him with a visit to his quarters."

"Now?" I protested. I really did want a bath.

"It's a matter of the greatest urgency," the slave said, "about the girl Chryseis."

That name was all it took to get me to follow him to Carolus' room, which was on the same floor as mine but in a wing running at a right angle to my section of the building. This section, on the north side of the building, was cooler than where I was staying. Carolus jumped up as soon as the slave opened the door. The two slaves with him in the room scrambled to their feet. He looked like a man in genuine distress, his eyes red and vacant, his hair a mess.

"At last!" he said. "Thank you, Gaius Pliny, for coming."

"Do you know something about Chryseis?"

He groaned so loudly – almost a roar – I thought he must be in pain. "I have done . . . an incredibly stupid thing. And now Chryseis is in danger because of me."

He was making me agitated. "Please, Carolus, tell me what has happened. Is Chryseis all right?"

He slumped down on his bed and held his head in his hands. The two slaves resumed their seats on the floor in a corner. "Young sir,

I foolishly sent some men to find her."

"What? Why on earth would you do such a thing?"

"Because no one else was doing anything. You were going to games. The governor was taking his time getting here. I thought I knew where she might be, because of the witches' sign that was left on the door. I decided to take matters into my own hands."

"Then those were your men who raped Melissa? These men?" I gestured angrily toward the two slaves.

"No. No. I hired some local thugs." He began to cry. It amazed me to see tears flow from a man so big and intimidating, like discovering a waterfall at the top of a mountain.

"I never intended for anything like that to happen. Or for her to suffer the beating she did. I would gladly have taken her place under the lash."

"It's as much my fault as anyone's. I found her. I didn't have to bring her back here. But none of that will be much comfort to her. We're both a couple of stupid bastards."

He wouldn't even look up. "I deserve every insult you can throw at me. But no one was doing anything."

"If you knew where Chryseis was, why not just send your own slaves to get her? Why hire someone?"

"I couldn't keep her here. I needed someone who could hide her for a couple of days until this mess is cleared up and I could get her out of here."

"All right. Let's get to the point. What has happened?"

"My plan backfired. The men I hired were supposed to take Chryseis to a hiding place of theirs and notify me. Instead, they're demanding a ransom for her. They're threatening to cut off one of her fingers if I don't respond by tomorrow. And another finger for each additional day that I delay paying them."

He held out a sheet of papyrus with a swatch of golden hair held to it by a glob of wax. I took it and read a crudely written note. "Who delivered this?"

"It was slipped under my door while we were eating lunch today. No one saw who brought it."

"Whoever wrote it barely knows Greek."

"The man I dealt with wasn't Greek. He told me his name was Matthias. We had some trouble settling the deal because his Greek was even poorer than mine. He talked to the other two in some other language."

"Matthias is a Jewish name."

"We didn't discuss religion. This man looked and sounded like every other cutthroat I've ever dealt with."

"Do you have any idea where they're holding her?"

"No. I told them not to tell me, so I could lie better if somebody asked me if I knew where she was. I don't think I would hold up under questioning as well as that dear, brave woman endured the whip this morning. And that Marcellus can make anyone trip over his own words."

"Why would you trust unknown men that way?"

He yanked at his hair and made a funny growling noise in his throat. "It was a business deal. I paid enough, I thought, to buy their loyalty. Please help me. They'll mutilate her, even kill her, if we don't do something."

We seemed to be aiming at the same goal, and neither of us felt any confidence in the government's ability to help us. One question still bothered me, though. If I could get an answer to it, I might gauge the depth of Carolus' commitment to getting Chryseis back.

"Why does this girl matter so much to you?" I asked.

With a quick motion of his head Carolus sent the two slaves out of the room. He sat on the bed and indicated that I should sit in the chair facing him.

"During the early days of the German uprisings against Nero, my sister, Helga, was among a group taken prisoner. Our village was attacked while most of the men were away. My mother and Helga and I ran into the forest to escape. Helga got separated from us and was captured. I swore to my mother that I'd find her and do anything I had to, to free her. My father had traded with the Romans and I knew a bit of Latin, so I crossed the Rhine. I managed to find out the name of the man who had my sister – Lucius Manilius Cornutus. But I couldn't get close enough to him to do anything about it at that time. I did whatever it took to keep myself where I could watch him. In the process I became a successful merchant. I've traveled the empire since, tracking Cornutus. I've spent a great deal of money bribing his slaves to learn what he's doing."

I could appreciate his quandary. A Roman aristocrat is constantly surrounded by slaves and family dependents. It's very difficult for a stranger to get close enough to have any contact, much less to attack him.

"What happened to your sister?"

"I learned that Helga died giving birth to a child."

"And that child was Chryseis?"

He nodded. "She is my niece. I'm certain of it. One thing that has kept me going is the few glimpses I've had of her. She resembles her mother – and mine – more and more closely as she grows up."

"Then you must know that it's very likely that Cornutus was her father."

"No! By the gods! That possibility hadn't occurred to me. But it would explain Cornutus' attitude. On this trip I offered to buy her from him, but he refused. He said he wouldn't sell her for any price."

"Is there any chance your sister could have been pregnant when she was captured?"

"No. Chryseis was born over a year after Helga was taken captive."

I tensed as I prepared myself for what I needed to say next. "Carolus, I have to ask you another question. I'm not sure what I'll do if your answer is yes, but I have to ask anyway. Did you kill Cornutus?"

"No. I swear by the shades of my mother and sister that I did not kill him."

His oath meant nothing to me, since I don't believe in the survival of the dead, but it obviously meant something to him. I decided to take him at his word.

"Do you have enough money to pay the ransom?" I asked.

"Certainly. That's not the problem. What bothers me is whether these scum will keep their end of the bargain. I think if we pay them, we might end up with no money and no Chryseis."

"Why wouldn't they give her back?"

"They could sell her to someone else. Then they would have my money and more besides."

"Perhaps we could arrange to follow them when you pay the money. If we can find out where they're hiding, we can simply take Chryseis, maybe even get your money back."

"I like the sound of that," Carolus said. "Better to take action than put ourselves at their mercy."

"All right. Tacitus and I will be at the taberna where you're supposed to meet them. We won't be with you, but we'll follow them. I want to know who they are and I want them punished for what they did to Melissa."

"How can they be punished? They raped a slave. She can't take action against them because she's a slave, and she's not *your* slave, so you can't take them to court."

I mulled over his very good points. Just one more ludicrous feature of Rome's judicial system. "But they also killed the witch's dog.

Don't you think she might want to know who killed her sacred hound? She and her tri-form goddess might exact their own revenge if we point them in the right direction."

Carolus smiled broadly. "Gaius Pliny, may I never find you numbered among my enemies."

* * * *

Tacitus greeted my plan with something less than enthusiasm. "The governor is here now," he said. "It's up to him to conduct the investigation the way he sees fit. I thought you realized that after this morning."

"All right," I said, "let's go see Florus and ask what kind of help he might give us."

We found Florus just outside the inn. I explained to him that I thought we could recover Cornutus' other slave and how important I believed she was to understanding what had happened, although I didn't mention the possibility that she might be his daughter. He appeared to be listening attentively, but when I finished he shook his head.

"Pliny, my friend, you're on the wrong trail. I have taken your lesson from earlier today to heart and have thrown myself into the questioning of Cornutus' slaves, not merely leaving it to my soldiers. I think we'll get a confession out of one of them in short order. Come, I'll show you."

He led us around to the back of the inn, to the stable. As soon as we turned the corner we heard a woman scream. I stopped, but Florus took my elbow and pulled me through the door. The place that had smelled so sweetly of hay and horses the last time I was in here now reeked of sweat, of human effluence – of fear.

"It's not so different from plunging into that cold water," Florus said. "You may be shocked at first, but I think you'll be impressed by the results we're getting."

In the center of the stable the soldiers had set up a device which I had heard of but never seen in use. Called the wooden horse, it consisted of a board, about as long as a man is tall, set sideways in braces that raised it off the ground to the height of a man's chest. The top side of the board had been planed until it had an edge on it. Phoebe was straddling that board, nude. Her feet, which could not touch the ground, had weights attached to them. Blood was running down her thighs. Her hands were tied and raised over her head by a rope which ran over a beam and was held by two soldiers. On a signal from a third soldier, they pulled her up a distance of about a man's pace, then released the rope. I cringed when she hit the board.

I heard a whimper and noticed three of Cornutus' male slaves standing beside one of the stalls, under guard by more of Florus' soldiers. They were all nude with their hands tied in front of them and all bore the marks of the whip, but none as severe as Melissa's beating.

Florus walked up to Phoebe, showing pride in his new direct approach. To think that I was responsible! Had any teacher ever been so badly misunderstood by his first pupil? Phoebe's eyes were open, but they were rolling back under the lids.

"Just tell me what happened the night your master was murdered," Florus said. "You were on the roof. You've admitted that. What did you do? What did you see?"

Phoebe's head lolled forward and she said something which I couldn't hear from that distance. Florus turned and glared at the male slaves.

"Gyges," he said. "Which of you is Gyges?"

One of the slaves fell to his knees. "Please, my lord! I've done nothing. I was locked up all night with the rest – "

Florus gestured and two of the soldiers grabbed Gyges by the arms, dragged him forward, and threw him down at the governor's feet.

"That's what this one claimed at first," Florus said. "But we got some truth out of her. I'll bet you have something more to say after your ride on the horse."

The soldiers began removing Phoebe from the torture device and fastening the weights on Gyges' ankles. "But, my lord," the slave cried, "Phoebe and I were lovers. That's the only reason she called my name!"

I pulled Tacitus back toward the door. "Do you think we're going to get any help from him?"

He shook his head and we left the stable. "When should I be ready to go with you?" he asked.

* * * *

The note demanded that Carolus meet the kidnappers in a place called Miriam's taberna at the eleventh hour. That gave me time to make some inquiries. I went first to Philyra's shop, even though I didn't think it would be open during the midday rest. The heavy wooden door was closed, but I knocked on it until the old crone's head and long, skinny neck appeared in a window above me. I had the eerie sensation I was the prey being eyed by a vulture.

"Go away!" she croaked. "I'm sleeping. Come back later."

"I need something right away. Open up! I'll pay you handsomely."

She stumbled down the stairs and opened the door but wouldn't let me in at first. I didn't want to discuss this business on the sidewalk. I slipped a coin in her hand. "Just let me in, please."

Philyra squinted at the coin. When she realized it was a tetradrachma, she sobered up a bit and stepped back to let me come in. "What kin I he'p ye with, m' lord? Somethin' to make a lady more eager?"

"I want to buy a cup. A kantharos."

"As ye kin see, m' lord, I doesn't sell cups of any kind, just herbs and potions. Ye'd be lookin' fer a potter or a silversmith."

"But I'm looking for a special kind of cup."

"I'm sure a potter or silversmith could make ye anythin' ye'd be wantin', m'lord. Their shops is north of the agora."

I slipped another tetradrachma into her hand, which closed around the coin like a crow's foot. "What I need is a cup that someone could drink from and still be thirsty."

"Now ye be talkin' in riddles, m' lord." But her expression gave her away.

"I'm not going to poison anyone," I assured her. "I just want to figure out how someone else might have been poisoned."

"No one's bought any cups or poisons from me!" the crone squawked. "I swear it."

"I'm not saying that anyone did. And I'm not trying to get you in trouble. I promise I'll not tell anyone we've done business together." I slipped another tetradrachma into her hand. She seemed to be calculating how much wine it would buy.

"And ye'd be wantin' a kantharos? Is that what ye said, my lord?"

I nodded. "On the large side."

"I ain't promisin', but let me look in the back."

After a few minutes she returned, carrying exactly the kind of cup I wanted. It was made of silver, with embossed figures showing Socrates, surrounded by several students and drinking the hemlock on one side, and conversing alone with one of his students on the other side. I was in no mood to bargain, so we quickly agreed on a price.

As I turned to leave, Philyra said, "Ain't ye fergettin' somethin', m' lord?"

"What would that be?"

"The secret. That cup don't do ye no good without the secret."

I examined the cup carefully but found nothing to distinguish it from any ordinary kantharos. "All right. So what is the secret?"

She held out her hand for another tetradrachma.

* * * *

Elated by the quick success at my first stop, I returned to the inn and turned my prize over to Trophimus, my steward, for safe-keeping. Then it took me longer to find Luke – my second task – than it had to purchase the cup. Damon finally brought him to me. Luke was carrying a freshly polished scroll, which he held out to me.

"This is the copy of my book about Jesus which I promised you. Apelles' scribe just finished it."

I took the scroll distrustfully. Having a Christian book in my possession might put me in a compromising position, but I didn't want to be rude to a man who had proved very helpful in a difficult matter. I unrolled the book enough to take a polite glance at the first page. It began with some gibberish about an elderly Jewish priest and an angel. Not the sort of thing I would want read at my next dinner party. I handed it to Damon.

"Thank you, doctor. I'm sure it will make interesting reading. Damon, please ask Glaucon to put that with my other papers and take good care of it."

"May I read it first, my lord?" Receiving my consent, he hurried off toward the stairs.

"And now, doctor," I said, "I need to talk to Melissa. Since you are the only one with permission to visit her, I wonder if I could accompany you when you go again."

"Certainly. Let's do it now. I need to check on her anyway. I had to sew up a few of the worst lash marks on her back."

"Is she going to live?"

He nodded. "I think she's past the crisis. She's a strong woman, and her concern for Chryseis is a powerful incentive to keep her alive."

"Will she be able to travel back to Rome?" Back to a probable execution.

"It would be better if she had some time to rest here. I don't know if there will be some way to arrange that."

"If we don't find Chryseis and solve Cornutus' murder, we'll have little say over what happens to her. I hope Melissa can help us do that."

"By the way," Luke said, "how is your eye and your cheek?" He stopped me and stepped in front of me, peering at my face and touching the area under my eye.

"It feels a lot better," I said. Then I jerked back when he touched a particular spot on my cheek.

"You may have a cracked bone under there," he said.

"Is that going to cause me a problem?"

"No. It will heal in its own time. But it will be very sensitive until it does."

When we got to Melissa's room the guards stood aside. "It's good to see you, doctor," the bigger one said. "Maybe you can get her quieted down."

"I don't hear anything," Luke said.

"I guess she has been quiet for a little while now, but she's been crying most of the afternoon."

His companion nodded in agreement. "When she wasn't crying, she was cursing like a Fury in some strange language."

"It's called Hebrew," Luke said. "And she was probably praying." Then he turned to me. "Let me check on her first."

When he emerged from the room he said, "She's asleep now. I think she's completely exhausted from the pain. I don't want to wake her up. Let's talk to her later."

"All right. I'll use the time to try to find Tiberius Saturninus. It worries me that no one has seen him all day."

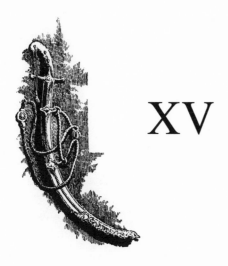

XV

Androcles jumped back when Tacitus, Carolus, and I met him coming around a corner near his kitchen. As big as Carolus was and as beaten up as I looked, we must have given the appearance of a band of thugs to someone who came upon us unexpectedly.

"What can I do for you gentlemen?" he asked when he had recovered himself. "Incidentally, do you know yet how long you're going to be staying?"

"We pray to the gods each day," Carolus said, "that it will be our last here."

"Are we hurting your business?" I asked.

"Oh, no! Quite the opposite. The excitement surrounding your stay has drawn good crowds to my dining room."

"Are you suggesting," Tacitus said, "that if you had realized how well it paid, you might have murdered one of your guests long before now?"

"What? I . . . ? Whatever makes you think . . . ?"

"He doesn't think," I said. "Sometimes he just talks. We do need to ask you something. How do we get to the taberna of Miriam?"

Androcles sighed and pursed his lips. "I doubt I could give you directions that you could actually follow. Her place is located in the Jewish quarter, near their synagogue. You have to make a number of turns to find it. It would be simpler if I let one of my slaves guide you there."

"If that's what it takes, we would appreciate it."

"Have you grown tired of my cooking?"

"Yes," Tacitus said.

"But," I put in, "that's not the reason we're going to Miriam's. We have to meet someone there."

"They certainly won't have any trouble spotting you."

"What do you mean?"

"The big blond fellow here can't do anything about his appearance, of course. But it takes a brave man indeed to wear the purple stripe in that part of town. Since the war, reminders of Rome are not taken kindly by some Jews. I'll get a slave to guide you."

While he went to find the slave, Tacitus, Carolus, and I put our heads together.

"I think Androcles is right," I said. "If we're going to follow this Matthias, we need to be as inconspicuous as possible. If we frighten him off, he could hurt Chryseis."

"I don't have any tunics that don't have the stripe on them," Tacitus said. "Do you?"

"No. But my slaves do. And so do yours."

Damon looked up from the scroll he was reading and could barely suppress a smile when I asked him to lend me one of his tunics. "Forgive me, my lord, but do you think a change of clothes will really disguise you?"

"Why shouldn't it?"

"Since you were a child, you've been taught to carry yourself like a nobleman. Have you ever tried to force your way down a crowded street without your clients and slaves around you? What will you do when some tradesman pushes you out of his way? Or runs over your foot with his cart?"

"Saving my life from those dogs has made you impertinent, Damon."

"I mean no disrespect, my lord. Perhaps I should come with you, to show you how a slave or a freedman acts. How to breathe without a scented handkerchief over your nose."

* * * *

We decided to let Androcles' slave guide Carolus to Miriam's taberna. Tacitus, Damon, and I hung back, following Carolus' blond head like ships keeping a beacon light in sight. Removing the purple stripe from my chest seemed to have rendered me invisible. The streets of any city of any size are crowded, especially in the late afternoon, as people resume

their activities after the midday rest. I had never been shoved and pum-
meled in this fashion. Did all these people somehow recognize that I was a
nobleman without my clients and decide to get a bit of vengeance for all the
times they — or those like them — had been pushed out of my way? I
marveled at Damon's ability to anticipate people's moves and evade them.
He looked like a dancer in a pantomime play.

When we reached the taberna we let Carolus go in first. Then
Tacitus entered and sat at a separate table. We wanted someone inside
in case there was another exit Matthias might use. Otherwise Tacitus
was to come out of the taberna after Carolus had paid the ransom and
point Matthias out to us. We had no way of identifying the man except
by a scar on his left cheek. And that in itself was not a particularly
distinguishing mark in this district.

Damon and I milled around on the street, pretending to examine goods at a neighboring shop. Androcles had told us our Greek would
suffice with the merchants of that quarter, indeed with most of its popu-
lace. Jews have their own language, but those who live outside Judaea
have long since had to learn Greek to survive. By all means, he warned
us, avoid using Latin.

Finally Tacitus emerged from the taberna. Trying to remain
inconspicuous, he gestured toward a man walking a few paces in front
of him. I was sure I hadn't seen this man enter. He must have arrived
before us. I was on his left side and could see the scar, a rather nasty
one. He also wore a cloth wrapped around his head. The more recent
Jewish immigrants, I gathered, clung to this native style of clothing.
Those who had lived in Smyrna longer had given it up in favor of the
Greek style of dress. Matthias wasn't the only man in the street right then
wearing a head-covering, but it did make it easier to keep him in view.

We followed him for two blocks. Then he turned a corner. By
the time we could elbow our way through the crowd and reach that
corner, he was no longer in sight. We saw only two men in head-cover-
ings. Both were walking toward us. Neither bore a scar.

Tacitus caught up with us and we searched up and down the
street, to no avail. There was an alley on either side of the street. A
cart, loaded with a cloth merchant's wares, emerged from one of them
and turned away from us. Its driver wore no head-covering. The horse
looked as if it might not make it to the end of the block.

I slapped my forehead in frustration. "He could be anywhere!
He could have slipped through one of these alleys. Someone could be
hiding him in one of the shops."

"My money's on the brothel at the next corner," Tacitus said.

"Do you want me to check it out?"

I would have liked to search each building on the block thoroughly, but Damon tugged on my – actually his – tunic and said, "My lord, I think the crowd is growing suspicious of us. We'd better go."

He was right. People did suddenly seem to be finding our Greek incomprehensible. Their noses were crinkling at us as though we were fish that had gone bad. Without the purple stripe on my tunic I was unable to compel any kind of obedience from them. Is that slender line of color all that Rome's power rests on?

We rejoined Carolus at the taberna. I apologized to him for letting Matthias slip away, and with him perhaps our last chance of getting Chryseis back.

"Before we give up hope entirely," he said, "let's see how my men did."

"Your men? What. . . what do you mean?"

"I had two of my slaves watching for him, too. They came over here in the crowd along with us, though you didn't see them."

"Why?" Tacitus asked.

"I didn't really think two noble lads like you could track a man in all this confusion."

Was that contempt or pity I saw in Carolus' eyes? I felt my ears redden.

"Uh-oh," Carolus said. "Here they come, and empty-handed."

A very small part of me was gratified, for just an instant, by that news.

* * * *

We returned to the inn and gathered what we needed for a late bath. Damon and one of Tacitus' slaves carried fresh tunics for us, complete with the purple stripe. At the entrance to the baths we ran into Florus and Marcellus. If I could have avoided any two people in Smyrna, it would have been these two. Their faces registered their surprise at our appearance.

"Cornelius Tacitus, Gaius Pliny," Marcellus said, "have the censors reached all the way to Smyrna to demote you from the equestrian ranks?"

"We'll be restored to the order shortly," I said, pointing to the tunics our slaves were carrying. I didn't offer any explanation for our appearance.

"You'll also be back on your way to Rome in a day or so," Florus said.

"I thought you were keeping everyone here until you found Cornutus' killer."

"He's done that," Marcellus said proudly. "By following traditional procedures."

"What? I don't understand."

Florus looked very satisfied with himself. One corner of his mouth even turned up in a modest smile. "Under torture the slave Gyges confessed that Phoebe had talked about how much she hated Cornutus, even expressed her desire to kill him."

"And that makes you think she actually did it?"

Marcellus jumped in. "We are satisfied with the results of the investigation."

"I'm sure *you* are," I said to Marcellus. Then I faced Florus. "What are you going to do to her?"

"There's nothing more I can do. She died as a result of her bumpy little ride on the horse."

He would have expressed more feeling, I think, if he'd been talking about the death of his favorite race horse in the Circus Maximus. But this was an innocent human being, whom he had killed as surely as if he had plunged a knife into her heart.

"Excellency, you still don't know for certain that she killed Cornutus." Of course, he didn't know Cornutus had been poisoned. "She never confessed. No one saw her go into his room. You haven't found the knife that was used. Or Cornutus' heart."

Florus held up his hand to silence me. "She was able to get out of the room where she was supposedly locked up. She had expressed her desire to kill him. Those minor details you mention don't matter. I consider my inquiry closed. You and the members of your caravan can have tomorrow to pack and be on your way the next day."

I wanted to grab his tunic and shake him. The fool! Cornutus' killer was standing right beside him. He'd just taken a bath with him. May the gods in whom I do not believe grant that I never be in a position where I must inquire into a crime using Rome's traditional legal methods! The 'minor details' I'd mentioned were the heart of the matter.

Florus and Marcellus brushed past us. Marcellus even gave me a surreptitious shove with his elbow.

* * * *

After the quickest bath I'd ever taken I dashed back to the inn, only to be accosted by that fool Orophernes. He had more 'vital information' about Lysimachus' doings. I left Tacitus to deal with him and continued on my mission, starting with another conversation with Melissa. Luke and Timothy were already in the dining room. I explained the new urgency with which we were faced due to Florus' inane decision. "We now have two nights and the intervening day to uncover the killer and to find Chryseis," I concluded.

"You've had no luck so far," Timothy said. "You've lost the girl twice. What do you propose to do differently now?"

"We're missing something vital," I said. "It's there, but we just haven't seen it yet. I want to talk to Melissa again. She's our only link to Chryseis right now."

"What more do you think she can tell you?" Luke asked.

"I won't know until I ask."

When we entered Melissa's room Luke lit a lamp. I would have preferred the room remain dark so I wouldn't have to look at her disfigured back. But I also needed to be able to read her face.

Melissa still lay on her stomach, her head cradled on her arms. Her face was to the wall when Luke and I entered her room. She raised her head slowly and turned it to face me.

"Forgive me if I don't rise, my lord," she said. She might as well have laid the lash across my back.

I sat on the stool that Luke kept by her bed and tried to keep my eyes on her face. "Melissa, I need to clarify some of what you told me before about the men who attacked you. It shouldn't take long. I don't want to tax your strength."

"I don't know what else I can add, my lord. I told you everything I heard them say."

"What you heard is exactly what I have to ask you about. You see, Carolus says the men he hired spoke Greek poorly. They used it because it was the only language they and Carolus had in common. These men preferred their native dialect, which Carolus couldn't identify. You reported a lot of their conversation. I don't imagine they were speaking Greek under the circumstances. How did you understand what was said?"

Something about the way she paused told me I was about to get the entire truth. I just hoped it wasn't too late to help me save Chryseis.

"They were speaking Hebrew, my lord. My native tongue."

"Did they realize you could understand them?"

"I don't think so. When they spoke directly to me, they spoke in Greek – two of them poorly, the other somewhat better. Among themselves they spoke Hebrew."

"So, what else did you hear them talk about? Did they mention a place where they were going to take Chryseis?"

"No, my lord. But the leader, Matthias, called her a pretty filly and said he'd find a comfortable stall for her."

I pondered that odd comment for a moment. "Could he be hiding her in a stable?"

"That was my guess, my lord."

"Why didn't you tell me this before?"

"I hoped I could get word to Anyte and she could rescue Chryseis and get her away from Roman territory. No matter what happens to me, I want Chryseis to be free. But I'm so closely guarded that none of Anyte's acolytes can get to me."

I jumped up in anger. "Confound it, woman! You're still scheming behind my back."

She was unmoved by my outburst. "I felt I had to do what was best for Chryseis, my lord. Rome isn't going to take care of her. The only man who could look after her is dead. What could I do?"

I sat back down and put my face close to hers. "Melissa, you promised to put yourself completely in my hands. I've done everything I can to protect you."

"Oh, yes, my lord. I appreciate your protection." She turned her head back to the wall. That little movement caused her to moan.

* * * *

I bolted out of Melissa's room yelling for Androcles. The guards at her door jumped to attention.

"He was in the dining room a few moments ago," Timothy said.

He and Luke stayed a step or two behind me, probably out of fear. I was as angry and agitated as I could ever remember being. The innkeeper came out of the kitchen, wiping his hands on his tunic.

"Yes, my lord? Do you need something?"

"I need a stable. Are there a lot of them in Smyrna?"

"Well, yes, there are. Most of them are attached to inns, like mine."

"Are there are many in the Jewish quarter?"

"Several."

That was unfortunate. But I guess Jews need horses and pack animals like the rest of us.

I lowered my voice and put my hand on his shoulder, as if taking him into my confidence. "If a man had some unsavory business to do in that part of town, which of the stable-owners there do you think would be most likely to cooperate with him?"

"I don't know them personally," Androcles said. "Only by reputation. But, on that basis, I think Bar-Jonah is the man you're looking for."

"Could I ask your slave to guide me to his place?"

"Certainly, for all the good it'll do you."

"What do you mean?" I snapped at him. I had no time for riddles.

"He doesn't like to deal with . . . non-Jews. What do they call us?"

"Gentiles," Timothy said.

"Yes! He doesn't like to deal with Gentiles. He speaks only Hebrew. He's still bitter over Rome's destruction of the Jews' temple."

"I'll go with you," Timothy said. "I speak Hebrew. My mother was Jewish," he added before I could ask for an explanation.

"You'll need to be very careful," Androcles cautioned. "And armed. There are rumors that he harbors refugees and potential rebels. He's a dangerous man."

We quickly gathered a few of my slaves and Tacitus and his slaves. Tacitus and I switched back to our slaves' tunics. I wanted to get underway before Carolus found out what we were up to. I knew he would insist on going, and his size and blond hair would make this Bar-jonah clam up immediately.

We walked rapidly, roughing out a plan as we went. The rest of our people would take up positions around the stable as quietly as possible. Timothy and I would try to talk to Bar-jonah.

"Just say '*Shalom*' when we go in," Timothy instructed me. "Then leave the rest to me."

"What will I be saying?"

"It means 'peace'. It's a traditional Jewish greeting."

I practiced the word several times. It had a funny feeling on my tongue, like some of the exotic foods I had eaten in Syria.

"We'll have to be extremely careful," Timothy said. "The Passover, the great festival of the Jews, ended just a few days ago. It commemorates the Jews' deliverance from bondage in Egypt. Since the war it has become a time when feelings about the destruction of the temple run high."

Even though it was already dark, the streets were not entirely deserted when we arrived at Bar-jonah's stable. The door to what looked like the owner's living quarters was closed, but light could be seen under it. Timothy knocked. A squat, broad man with a curly beard which was going gray opened the door. He and Timothy exchanged *Shalom*s and I added mine. Then he and Timothy began to converse in Hebrew. Timothy and I had rehearsed what he would say, but only later did he relate the conversation to Tacitus and me so we could make a record of it.

"Greetings, Bar-jonah," Timothy said.

The bearded man nodded but said nothing.

"I'm looking to make a purchase," Timothy said. "To be exact, a young filly that has never been ridden. I understand you might be able to supply something in that line."

"And where did you get that notion?" Bar-jonah said.

Timothy nudged me. That was our signal for me to show some money. I reached into the neck of my tunic for my money pouch, which was tied to a strip of cloth around my chest. My knife also snuggled in that same strip of cloth.

Bar-jonah took the coins I offered and grunted. He put the coins in his own money bag. However deep his resentment of Rome, it must not have extended to our money.

"I don't deal with Gentiles," he said. He began to close the door.

Timothy pushed against the door. "I bear the mark of circumcision," he said.

Bar-jonah stopped, the door half-open. "It's easy to make that claim."

Since I didn't know what was being said at the time, I was shocked when Timothy lifted the front of his tunic. Bar-jonah glanced, then nodded his approval. "What about him?" he asked, waving his hand at me.

"I vouch for him," Timothy said. "Now, do you have that young filly?"

"I don't, but I know someone who does," Bar-jonah said. "If you don't mind waiting just a bit, I'll send a slave to fetch him."

Timothy and I stepped into what was little more than a peasant's hut with a stone floor. As soon as Bar-jonah closed the door I felt trapped. We had reinforcements outside, but I didn't know who was inside or whether our people could even get in. Bar-jonah said something through a doorway at the back of the room and a young man slid past us and out the front door.

"Would you like something to drink?" Bar-jonah asked.

"Thank you," Timothy replied. He took a seat on a cushion on the floor and I imitated him. A slave brought some well-watered wine and some sort of stale, tasteless bread.

"My associate should be here very soon," Bar-jonah said. "He's at the taberna on the corner. You're strangers to Smyrna, aren't you?"

"Yes," Timothy said. "We've recently arrived from Ephesus."

"And how did you hear of me?"

Before Timothy had to answer that question the door opened and three men entered. The scar on his cheek identified the first as Matthias. It took me an instant to recognize the second as the driver of the cart who passed us when we were searching for Matthias. Of course! He had ducked into the alley and hidden himself under the cloth. He had his escape planned all along.

The second man pointed at me and said (as Timothy reconstructed it later), "He's one of them. In the street today."

Matthias locked the door, then pulled a knife, I think through a slit in the outer cloak he was wearing. "Bar-jonah, you old fool! They're Romans! They're with Carolus."

He lunged at me as the second man and Bar-jonah drew their knives. Because of the way I was sitting all I could do was roll backwards, causing Matthias to miss with his knife thrust and roll over me. I did manage to land a solid jab of my knee to a sensitive part of his body.

Timothy and I struggled to our feet. With two men guarding the locked front door, escape by that route seemed unlikely. I drew my knife and brandished it at Bar-jonah while Timothy and I backed through the inner doorway into the next room. The odor of a stable led me to a door on the other side of that room. Bar-jonah's slaves offered no resistance, other than being obstacles that we had to avoid tripping over.

We broke into the stable and I began to yell. "Tacitus! Damon! Help!"

Bar-jonah, Matthias, and the other two had regrouped and were right behind us. Matthias was still hunched over. Bar-jonah lit a lamp by the door. The small flame showed us our enemies but did not reach far enough to help me assess our surroundings. Matthias and the second man looked like formidable foes. The third man's sad eyes showed little stomach for a fight. I wondered if he was the one who persuaded the other two not to kill Melissa. Bar-jonah's eyes, on the other hand, glinted as eagerly as his knife blade for Roman blood.

In the dark I had no idea where the exterior door of the stable was. Nor did I know how many animals were around us or where they were tethered. We were as likely to be tripped by an ox or a horse as felled by our assailants.

Matthias started to say something, but Bar-jonah cut him off. "The tall one speaks Hebrew. We're not going to be able to surprise them."

"Then let's just rush them and be done with it," Matthias said.

But, as he took his first step, a crash resounded through the house. Even though I'd never heard the sound before, I knew it was a door being knocked off its hinges. Bar-jonah's slaves came running into the stable in a panic, followed by Tacitus and Damon and several other of our slaves. Even with numbers on our side, the struggle that followed was still in doubt. Bar-jonah, Matthias, and the other two had considerable practice in using their weapons. No one on our side had ever pointed a knife at another human being.

The four cut-throats had forced their way through our ranks, leaving two of our slaves writhing on the floor and Tacitus with a gash on his arm. They were about to break completely away from us when a Herculean figure loomed in the doorway leading into the living quarters.

Marcus Carolus!

* * * *

The fight was soon over. Bar-jonah and the second of the three cut-throats lay dead at Carolus' hand. One of Tacitus' slaves appeared to be seriously wounded. Tacitus and another of his slaves had suffered cuts that were quickly bound up by one of Bar-jonah's slaves. Using the litter and bearers which had brought Carolus to the stable, we sent the wounded slaves to Apelles' house. Timothy knew Luke had been planning to visit the family. He sent along a note explaining that we would all be arriving there soon.

"Your transportation came in handy," I said to Carolus as the bearers set off.

"It was the only way I could get through the streets in this part of town without drawing attention to myself," Carolus explained. "I thought you might need some help. Why didn't you tell me what you were planning?"

I resented feeling like a child always in need of rescue. But I could only watch in awe as Carolus had tossed our attackers around like a bull in the arena tossing condemned criminals. I posted Damon to watch the stable door that led onto the next street and put a couple of the slaves Carolus had brought with him at the door of Bar-jonah's living quarters. Now there was just one matter left to settle. I turned to the surviving assailants, who were seated on the floor with their backs against the wall.

"Where is the girl?" I demanded of Matthias.

He snorted and refused to look up at me.

"Tell them," the other man urged him. He had said his name was Simon. He was the one who spoke the best Greek in the group.

Matthias replied in Hebrew, which Timothy translated. "Why should I help Romans find their precious little pet?" He spat at my feet.

Carolus grabbed him by the beard and jerked his head back hard against the wall. "Tell us where she is or I'll yank your ugly head right off your shoulders."

"Why are you with them?" Matthias sneered, forced into Greek. "The Romans have burned your homes, enslaved your women. You

Germans should rise up against them, as we did."

"We tried that," Carolus said. "And it got us exactly what it got you. But we're not here to talk politics. Where is the girl?" Matthias' head hit the wall hard on each word.

"I'll tell you," Simon said.

"You dog's vomit!" Matthias said. "Don't betray our cause."

"Your only cause is your purse," Simon said. "Kidnapping this girl had nothing to do with Rome or Jerusalem. You just wanted to make yourself rich. That's all you've ever wanted."

I turned my attention to him, determined not to resort to traditional Roman methods to get the information I wanted.

"Simon," I said, "I'm a reasonable man. I don't want to hurt you. In fact, I want to thank you for not letting Matthias kill Melissa."

"Was that the woman we left tied up in the old temple?"

"Yes. The woman you raped."

"I had no part in that. I swear it. That was Matthias and Benjamin."

I pulled his hands toward me and examined them and his forearms.

"What are you looking for?"

"Dog bites," I said.

"Check Matthias' arms. He fought with the dog, and Benjamin helped him kill it. I've never seen anything so ferocious."

"What were you doing all that time?"

"I was holding the women, to make sure they didn't run away. But I didn't hurt them. It was those two thugs."

"That's not a nice thing to say about your family."

Simon shook his head. "They're not my blood. They're my wife's cousins. Matthias always has some scheme going, something that will make him rich without any hard work. He killed a man in Antioch. We barely escaped crucifixion and didn't stop running until we reached Smyrna. Matthias has made us notorious here as men who will do any job, no matter how despicable."

"That's true," Carolus said. "His was the first name that came up when I started looking for someone to find Chryseis."

"But he had no intention of giving her back, did he?" I asked.

"No. As soon as he heard the description of her, he started this plan. He knows that a blond virgin slave will bring a high price in some palaces in Mesopotamia."

"But right now she's not blond," I said. Carolus' head jerked toward me in surprise. "Melissa cut her hair quite short and dyed it," I explained. "She also applied some kind of coloring to her skin."

Simon nodded. "She looks more like a Jewish boy than a Greek girl. I wasn't sure we had the right one. Matthias was furious. He would have to wait months for her hair to grow out and the dye to wear off."

"Has he hurt her?"

"Not that I know of. I'm so tired of it all. I just want it to end." I think I saw tears in the poor man's eyes.

"Do you know where she is?"

"We brought her here. Matthias and Bar-jonah took her out into the stable and hid her. I think they put her in some sort of cellar. I don't know exactly where it is."

Carolus jerked Matthias to his feet. "Come on, scum. You're going to show us right now."

I helped Simon up and we all trooped out into the stable. The slaves brought lamps. With their dim illumination the stable appeared to be cavernous. The earth floor was covered with a thick layer of straw. The dozen or so tethered animals – a conglomeration of horses, donkeys, and oxen – moved nervously.

"Where do we begin searching?" I asked.

"I could make this one talk," Carolus said, tightening his grip on Matthias' beard.

"He won't tell you," Simon said. "He'd let you kill him out of spite."

"Don't you have any idea where they hid her?" I asked Simon.

"No, but one of Bar-jonah's slaves has been tending to her." He looked around, then pointed. "That one."

Carolus pushed Matthias away and stepped toward the slave. But the fellow was already scampering across the stable. At first I thought he was trying to escape, but he shooed some animals out of his way and began brushing back the straw at one spot on the floor.

We all had our attention turned in that direction, so I don't know exactly what happened. And it all happened so fast. Simon, standing right next to me, gasped and let out a groan, then dropped to his knees. Out of the corner of my eye I saw Matthias pull a knife out of his back and strike him again. Simon crumpled to the floor and Matthias stepped back, brandishing the bloody knife.

"He's got a knife!" I yelled. Then I realized it was my knife. I had carelessly laid the thing down instead of putting it back in my chest band.

Matthias grabbed a lamp from a slave standing near him. He threw it hard onto the floor a few steps away from me. The clay shattered and burning oil spread quickly into the straw.

Fire! It would be a raging inferno by the time it consumed Bar-jonah's stable, I wanted to catch Matthias, I had to put out the fire, I had to get Chryseis out, and I was paralyzed by indecision.

Matthias turned to run. I felt a vaguely familiar sensation of something whizzing past my ear. Matthias dropped like a child's doll cut loose from a string. Damon, across the stable, tucked his shepherd's sling under his tunic.

"All right, everyone, don't panic!" I shouted. I grabbed the two slaves standing closest to me. "Get water and blankets! Put that fire out." They didn't move until Timothy repeated my commands in Hebrew.

Through the smoke, I thought I saw Matthias' leg move. "Timothy," I called, "check him. He may still be alive."

Carolus was digging in the earth where Bar-jonah's slave had cleared away the straw. I joined him to see the outline of a door emerge. Carolus found a ring attached to the wood and pulled. There, in a hole not much bigger than a bed, lay Chryseis – a brown-haired, dark-skinned Chryseis – bound and gagged. Before Carolus could let go of the door, I dropped into the hole, picked her up, and handed her up to him. He put her on the floor and started to untie her.

"Get her out of here!" I barked. "Do that outside."

Tacitus and Damon helped me out of the hole. The fire was getting beyond the point where we could put it out. The doorway back into the living quarters was blocked by flames and thick smoke. Timothy dragged Matthias over to us. "He's still breathing."

I glanced at Damon.

He shrugged. "I don't carry large stones, my lord. I don't really want to kill anything."

"We'll take him with us," I said. "Timothy, tell these slaves to call the night watchmen." He translated and the slaves scampered away.

"Let's get out of here," I said. "I don't think we can save the place."

"But, my lord," Damon said. "What about the animals?"

"I guess they'll be consumed along with everything else."

"Please, my lord, we can't leave them to suffer like that." He ran to an ox and struggled with the tether. Tacitus and I looked at one another and then began untying the animals or cutting them free and herding them out the stable door.

XVI

Full darkness had settled by the time we were all safely ensconced in Apelles' house. I had been half afraid Carolus would take Chryseis and run once he got out of Bar-jonah's stable. Every time I got her back, it seemed, someone was waiting in the shadows to snatch her away again. I insisted that Damon stand guard outside the room where the servants helped her clean up. Matthias was trussed up in a neighboring room, complaining of the pain in his head. Luke examined him and pronounced him fit to stand trial for his actions. I didn't tell the doctor, but a trial wasn't what I had in mind for that cut-throat. I was concerned about keeping him confined. Kallisto had no chains in the house. She and Apelles would never chain a slave, she told us, so we had to settle for a couple of pieces of rope and some vigilant watchmen.

After what seemed too long a time Chryseis entered the large peristyle garden, where food had been set out for all of us. Kallisto and one of her slaves tended to our needs. In the flaring light of torches the plain white gown Chryseis was wearing made her darkened skin seem even browner. She kept looking at her hands and arms in dismay. Among Greeks and Romans the whiter a woman's complexion is and the longer her hair, the prettier she is considered to be. Chryseis must have felt like some deformed creature.

"Come and eat, Chryseis," I said.

She knelt in front of me. "Thank you, my lord. And thank you for saving me. I know I'll be punished for running away, but – "

"There'll be no talk of that," Carolus said. The challenge in his eyes when he looked at me was unmistakable.

I took her hand, pulled her up, and seated her between Carolus and myself. I thought everyone in the garden, slave and free, would be taken aback by this breach of etiquette. "Seneca invited his slaves to recline on the couch with him," I started to say in my defense. "After what Chryseis has endured, she certainly deserves to be treated with some consideration."

"In this house," Kallisto said, "we see no difference between slave and free."

That was the same claim Luke had made when Cornutus and I were squaring off over lunch a few days ago.

"How do you get your slaves to do their work?" I asked.

"We work together because we love one another," Kallisto replied.

"You'll understand more," Luke put in, "when you've read my book about Jesus."

"I'll do that as soon as we've cleared up the matter of Cornutus' murder." Turning to Chryseis I said, "I'm not sure what's going to happen to you, Chryseis. Given Florus' eagerness to torture slaves, I'm hesitant even to let him know we've found you."

"Florus? Is he the governor?" she asked.

"Yes. He arrived yesterday."

"He's a Roman magistrate, isn't he?"

"Yes."

"Then I have to see him, my lord."

"I'm not sure that's wise."

Carolus put a hand on her arm, alarm on his face. "He's right, my child. Florus has found he has a taste for blood."

"He's a weak man who has discovered that being cruel makes him feel strong," Luke said morosely.

"But I have to see him, my lord. That's what my master told me to do if anything happened to him. Oh, do you know where my bag is? The one I was carrying when I ran away?"

"It's in my room at the inn," I assured her. "Melissa made sure I retrieved it when we found her at the old temple."

"Is everything still in it?"

I knew what she was asking: Have you been meddling in my things again? "I couldn't say what is or is not in it. I haven't opened it."

"Thank you, my lord."

* * * *

Chryseis was so exhausted from her ordeal that she nearly went to sleep while she was eating. Her head drooped onto my shoulder. She would have stayed there all night if I'd had my way, but I knew she needed good rest. I sent her, under Damon's aegis, off to the room which had been prepared for her in the interior of the house. Damon would see to it that the slaves assigned to stand watch at her door and Matthias' understood the importance of their task. Of that I was sure.

After Timothy and Luke retired as well, Carolus let out a long sigh. "Well, Gaius Pliny, we have had some excitement tonight, haven't we?"

"Yes, Marcus Carolus. Thank you for your help. Your arrival was well timed. It's good strategy in battle to hold fresh troops in reserve until a crucial moment."

He dismissed my compliment with a wave of his hand and a modest smile. "I wish I could take credit for being so clever. Tonight I just happened to blunder in when I was needed."

"You certainly didn't make any blunders with that knife of yours," Tacitus said from the bench where he was sitting across the table from us.

"Yes, about your knife," I said. "May I see it?"

Carolus' smile faded. If Tacitus hadn't been present, I'm not sure what the big German would have done. As he hesitated, I put out my hand. He reached inside his tunic, pulled out the knife, and laid it in my hand, hilt first. "My father purchased it," he said, "on one of his trading trips. It comes from somewhere in the east, beyond India."

I held the knife up to the light of a torch that was fastened to a column on one side of me. The hilt was carved of ivory and shaped like some mythical beast. I had never seen anything so exquisite. I ran a finger along the blade, looking at it rather than Carolus as I spoke. "It's an unusual design. I've never seen one with such a slender blade. Is it the one you used to cut out Cornutus' heart?"

"Yes," he said matter-of-factly as Tacitus gasped. "But I didn't kill him. That's what you asked earlier."

"I know you didn't." I handed the knife back to him. "He was poisoned at dinner."

"But . . . who?" I don't know if he was more surprised by my returning the weapon or my claim of poisoning.

"I think I know, but I need conclusive proof. For now, though, please continue with your story. You cut his heart out. Why on earth would you do such a . . . horrific thing?" I managed to catch myself before I said 'barbaric'.

"My mother was distraught over her daughter being taken captive. She made me pledge myself to getting Helga back or taking revenge on the man who captured her. When I had to tell her Helga was dead, she killed herself. She stabbed herself in the heart. With this very knife."

He held the blade poised between two of his own ribs. If he decided to plunge it in, I would be unable to stop him.

"Losing her daughter was like having her heart cut out, wasn't it?" I said.

"Yes, exactly. I have known for years I would stab him in the heart when I got the chance. I thought I had him cornered four years ago at Baiae, but Chryseis was right there. I couldn't kill him in front of her. Watching Marcellus help him up the stairs that night, I decided Cornutus' defenses were down enough for me to make my move."

"What did you think when you stabbed him?"

"I realized he was already dead when he didn't react to my first thrust. It was like butchering a dead animal. When he didn't resist, I went wild and gutted him. I guess I was so angry at being denied my chance for revenge." Recognition came into his eyes and he lowered the knife. "By the gods! It was Marcellus who poisoned him, wasn't it? It must have been that wineskin."

My glance at Tacitus said, See, it's so obvious that even a German can figure it out. "That's what I've concluded," I replied to Carolus. "The problem is to prove it. Cornutus' body has been burned, and the type of poison he used left no signs that even a doctor could find."

"Why don't you ask Marcellus to take a sip of the stuff?" Tacitus said. "If he refuses, then you can demand to know why."

Carolus must have missed the sarcasm. Too subtle for the German mind. "Good idea! That would prove it, wouldn't it?"

"It's more complicated than that," I said. "We don't know whether he still has the poisoned wine. He could be quite willing to drink out of the wineskin if he's gotten rid of the poison and refilled it with ordinary wine."

"It's also possible," Tacitus put in, "that Cornutus was poisoned earlier in the afternoon, at the bath. The slave girl who brought us wine there is a devotee of the cult of Hecate. I learned that through my inquiries." He was so proud of having gleaned that bit of information that he didn't want to dismiss it, no matter how irrelevant it was.

"Half the women in Smyrna worship Hecate," I reminded him. We'd had this discussion earlier. "That proves nothing. We know now that the witches didn't cut his heart out. And, if they didn't want Cornutus' heart for some ritual, then they had no reason to poison him." I slowed down on the last few words for emphasis.

Carolus shifted his weight and I tensed, but he was just making himself more comfortable. He put his knife away, which made me much more comfortable.

"How did you dispose of the heart?" I asked.

"I still have it," he said as calmly as if announcing he had the man's missing sandal. "I hid it in the chamberpot and took it back to my room."

"The chamberpot! Just as I suspected." I couldn't help but congratulate myself.

"I wrapped it up and put it in a bag. It's hidden under the floorboard in my room. There are times, in the night, when I think I can hear it pounding, the way your heart does when you've run hard. Or maybe it's just my own heart I hear."

"What do you plan to do with it?" Tacitus asked. His fascination with the grotesque had been aroused.

"I'm going to take it back to Germany and burn it on my mother's grave."

"I hope her soul will be comforted," I said. It seemed a barbarous sort of homage, but I didn't want to say so to a large man with a knife at hand. Nor did I want to venture into a discussion of whether or not the soul exists after death. A large man with a knife at hand can believe whatever he wants. If there isn't a proverb to that effect, there ought to be.

"Now that you know, what are you going to do?" Carolus asked.

Tacitus and I exchanged a long glance. What should we do with him?

"Technically," Tacitus said with a shrug, "you can't be prosecuted for murder, since Cornutus was already dead when you attacked him. If you were charged, you could call on our brilliant young friend here to testify to that. But, on the other hand, the intent was there. And you did mutilate the body of a Roman citizen."

"A body which has now been burned," I pointed out, "so there is no evidence of that crime."

"I'm not afraid to face the law," Carolus said. "Don't think I'm afraid."

"We have no doubt of your courage, Carolus," I said. "I myself don't want someone else to fall victim to Roman justice. Bringing you to trial would be a touchy situation. Marcellus would manipulate Florus --"

"But," Tacitus put in, "Florus has already condemned someone for Cornutus' murder, the slave Phoebe. You can't condemn someone and then try someone else for the same crime."

"And Phoebe," I said, "has already paid the price, not for Cornutus' murder but for Florus' stupidity. One is as great a crime as the other."

I poured myself some more wine and offered some to Carolus, who refused. "Several innocent people," I said, "have already suffered horribly in our search for justice under the Roman system. I see nothing to be gained by sacrificing another victim on that altar. You wanted revenge on only one person. You pose no danger to anyone else."

"What about the two men he killed tonight?" Tacitus asked.

"Killing two cut-throats who were attacking Roman citizens is no crime," I said. "I can't imagine that Carolus is going to roam the streets slaughtering innocent people."

Carolus snorted. "My only wish is to get away from you Romans. But I can't leave until I'm sure Chryseis is safe."

"That's the most important thing for me, too," I said. "To do that I think we have to find Cornutus' killer."

"And we have only one more day before Florus allows everyone to leave," Tacitus reminded me.

"I do my best work under pressure," I said.

* * * *

We left Apelles' house before dawn to return to the inn. Acrid smoke from Bar-jonah's stable still hung low over the city. Since the streets were calm I assumed the night watchmen had contained the fire. At the time we left there last night they were beginning to demolish the buildings on either side of Bar-jonah's to prevent the fire from spreading.

I wondered whether the bodies of Bar-jonah, Benjamin, and Simon had been removed or whether they had been left to the flames. The Jews probably have peculiar burial rituals. Everything else about them is peculiar. It saddened me to think all three men suffered the same fate. Two deserved what they got, the other probably didn't. Simon seemed genuinely remorseful about his participation in Matthias' schemes. I owed him a lot. He had kept Melissa alive, and he had helped us in every way he could to find Chryseis. There seemed to be a vein of goodness in the man which circumstances had prevented him from mining to the fullest. If I had been able to protect him . . . But I was proving singularly inept in my efforts to protect those who came under my care.

"These ropes are too tight," Matthias groused. We had his hands tied behind his back and a rope around his neck with Tacitus leading him like a pack mule. Even in his complaints he used Hebrew, forcing Timothy to translate.

"That's going to be the least of your problems," I said.

When we arrived at the inn I sent Damon up to get Chryseis' bag and to request that Anyte come down to meet me. As he dashed off, Chryseis called after him, "Be careful on those stairs." Something was definitely different about her. Had I encouraged a feeling of license by inviting her to sit with me last night? Or was some innate characteristic asserting itself?

When Damon returned and handed over her bag, Chryseis scrounged through it and smiled when she held up the leather pouch with its unbroken seal.

"My lord," Damon said, "one of her acolytes informed me that Anyte is in the stable, overseeing preparations for her return journey to Ephesus."

"Let's go see her then," I said. Tacitus jerked on the rope around Matthias' neck.

"My lord," Chryseis said, "while you're doing that, may I see Melissa?"

I glanced at Luke. "Is that really wise?"

"It will be hard on the girl," he said, "but I think it would reassure both of them and aid Melissa in her recovery."

I hoped that seeing what Florus had inflicted on a runaway slave would make Chryseis less eager to appear before him. If she waited until we returned to Rome, we could find a more trustworthy magistrate to open her document, one who wasn't Marcellus' puppet.

"All right, go ahead," I said. "But, doctor, would you and Carolus please stay with her every step of the way?"

Chryseis drew her shoulders back. "My lord, I'm not going to run away."

"I'm no longer concerned about you running away," I said. "But I believe there is someone around here who wants to harm you. Luke and Carolus will be there for your protection."

"My master told me this will protect me," she said, patting her bag with the sealed document in it.

I hope he's right, I thought. I haven't been able to.

Chryseis and her escorts went on their way. The rest of us passed through the inn and out into the stable. Anyte and two of her women were inspecting their horses' harness. Our arrival did not seem to interest them at all.

"Lady Anyte, I hope your trip is an easy and a safe one," I said in greeting.

She remained unimpressed by my cordiality. "Do you need to see me, Gaius Pliny?"

"Before you leave I'd like to again offer apologies for the profanation of your ritual. Rome tries to respect the religious practices of all its subjects. I'm sure the men responsible regret their impious act." Tacitus nodded his head.

Only now did Anyte look up from the leather straps in her hands. "Not as much as they will by the time I get through with them."

That response caught me completely off my guard. "Oh, I didn't know . . . you had learned who they were. Have you . . . confronted them yet?" I hated to think some other unfortunate innocents had fallen victim to 'justice' wrongly meted out.

"Not yet. But they will be dealt with," she said. "When I return to Ephesus I'm going to consult my books and put an incantation on them. It will be a powerful curse."

Something in her eyes told me that this would be no anonymous curse. She had names in mind – and the correct ones, I was sure – to insert in the appropriate places in the formula. I could feel Tacitus shuddering. I tried to remind myself that such things are shams and could have no real power over me.

"I hope it will mollify you – and the goddess – somewhat if I give you the man who killed your sacred hound and raped Melissa in the precincts of the tri-form goddess' temple."

At first she was dubious. She looked Matthias over, as though I had claimed my horse was Pegasus and she wanted to see where his wings were glued on. "How can I be certain this is the right man?"

"One of his accomplices identified him last night, before this man killed him. And here's the conclusive proof." I turned Matthias around and showed Anyte the bite marks on his arms. I didn't even mind that I had to twist them a bit.

Anyte took the lead rope from Tacitus and jerked Matthias toward her wagons. He began screaming, in Greek no less, "You can't do this! Have mercy!" Two of the women tied him to a wheel.

Timothy took a step after him, then turned to me. "Gaius Pliny, must you? How can you so callously turn that man over to such a horrible fate? What gives you the right?"

"What gives any of us the right to rule over the fate of another? And yet we do it all the time."

"But to put him in the hands of those witches? Couldn't you

turn him over to the proper authorities?"

"Florus wouldn't do anything about him. His crimes weren't against Roman citizens. He'd just be turned over to the boularchs. They would have a hard time proving anything against him, with all his accomplices dead. Remember, he stabbed Simon in the back. He killed at least one man in Antioch. Who knows how much more blood he has on his hands? This way he'll be dealt with in something like the fashion he deserves. Or would you have him go free?"

Timothy shook his head. "I know he's done horrible things. But to set yourself up as the sole arbiter of his life is a weighty matter. In the book that Luke gave you, you can read where Jesus said, 'Do not pass judgment and you will not be judged. Do not condemn and you will not be condemned.' And our teacher, Paul, said in a letter to the church in Rome, 'You who sit in judgment have no defense. By judging other men you condemn yourselves.'"

"You Christians are a strange lot. If no one will pass judgment, then we hand our world over to the criminals. Matthias brought this on himself by his own actions."

Matthias cried out, "I have friends in Ephesus! They'll get – "

One of the acolytes gagged him.

Anyte approached me and, with a gleam in her eye, whispered, "Don't worry. He won't get to Ephesus."

I couldn't meet Timothy's gaze.

* * * *

We went back into the inn and made our way to Melissa's room. As we passed the dining room I heard Marcellus and Florus talking. Carolus and the two guards stood outside the door of Melissa's room. Just as we arrived, the door opened and Luke and Chryseis emerged. I sighed in relief at the sight of her. She was wiping tears from her eyes.

"Why did they do that to her? Was it because she tried to get me away? Am I to blame for what she suffered?"

Luke put an arm around her shoulder. "Don't take it on yourself, child. Everything that happens to us is part of a plan. We just have to find the meaning behind it."

He sounded like a second-rate Stoic philosopher. "Do you still want to see the governor?" I asked Chryseis.

"I have to do what my master told me, don't I?"

It was hard to argue with a slave who was so insistent on obeying her master, even after his death.

"We'll go with you," I said. "And I swear I will not let anyone hurt you. If there is even the first sign of danger, we'll run and not worry about the consequences. Are we all agreed on that?"

Carolus, Tacitus, and Damon nodded. Timothy made no sign.

"I'm too old to do much running," Luke said, "but I could offer myself as an obstacle in the path of anyone who might be pursuing you."

"Damon," I said, "do you have your sling?"

"Yes, my lord. But it's of little use at close range."

"And Carolus, are you armed?"

"Always, my friend."

"Then I guess we're ready. Chryseis, please don't speak until I tell you to."

Shielding Chryseis in the center of our group, we entered the dining room and stood before the table where Marcellus and Florus appeared to be finishing a light meal. Several slaves stood around in attendance. The only one I recognized was the big-eared fellow, Phrixus. I was glad to see that at least one of Cornutus' slaves had survived Florus' inquisition.

"Good morning, Gaius Pliny," Florus said. "I hope you're here to eat, but the size of your *clientela* and the serious expression on your face suggest otherwise."

"Excellency, there is a matter that needs your attention."

Annoyance spread over his face. "Can it not wait? I prefer to begin business at the second hour."

"I think this can be disposed of quickly, sir."

He sighed. "All right, then. Proceed."

I pulled Chryseis up to stand beside me. "Excellency, this is Chryseis, the missing slave of Cornutus."

Florus laughed. "I've seldom seen a slave with such an ill-fitting name. There's nothing 'golden' about her."

Marcellus was by no means amused. He slapped his open hand on the table.

"Are you troubled by something?" Florus asked.

"Forgive me, excellency. I hired a man to search for this girl. I'm just sorry someone else has the satisfaction of bringing her back to face justice."

"Yes," Florus said. "I suppose she'll have to be dealt with." I could see from his face that he was looking forward to inflicting some kind of torment on her. Carolus' arm bumped me as he put his hand on his chest, ready to reach inside his tunic for his knife.

"Excellency," I said, launching into the speech I had been improvising, "this girl is no criminal. Surely you can't – "

Chryseis interrupted me. "My lord, are you a Roman magistrate?"

Florus looked down his nose at her. She did look more like a street urchin than a goddess, with her hair whacked off and clumsily dyed and her white skin showing around the edges of her gown where the dye on her skin hadn't penetrated. "Of course I am, child. I'm the proconsul of this province."

"My master, Lucius Manilius Cornutus, told me if anything ever happened to him, I should give this to a Roman magistrate and have him open it." She reached into her bag and drew out the pouch sealed with Cornutus' seal.

The governor took the object dubiously, a slight sneer on his lips.

"You'll notice, excellency," I said, "that the seal is unbroken."

"True. But how do I know it's genuine?"

"There are still some of Cornutus' slaves around, aren't there?"

"Yes," Florus said. "In fact the fellow with the big ears. I've been keeping him around just because those ears amuse me . . . Where is he?"

Phrixus stepped forward out of the shadows in the corner of the room. "I'm here, my lord."

"Take a look at this." Florus handed him the leather pouch. "Is that Cornutus' seal?"

"Yes, my lord. There's no doubt."

"All right, then. Let's see what's in it." Florus took the pouch back, broke the seal and extracted a sheet of papyrus, also sealed with the same symbol. Breaking the seal on that, he unrolled it and began to read aloud:

> *This is the will of Lucius Manilius Cornutus. It su-*
> *persedes any and all other wills I have made.*

Marcellus let out a yelp. "What? It can't be!"

"Why can't it be?" I asked. I could see that Marcellus and I were going to fight this battle through Florus. I hoped I could provide the governor with enough spine to keep him standing until the end.

"Why would a slave be carrying a Roman nobleman's will in her dress bag?" Marcellus asked.

Florus looked uncertainly at the document in his hand. "That does seem odd."

"It bore Cornutus' seal, excellency," I reminded him. "You authenticated that. It was sealed twice. At least read it and see what it says."

"I don't suppose we've anything to lose," Florus said. He resumed reading:

> *First, and most importantly, I hereby manumit my*
> *slave Chryseis, whom I marked on her left buttock*
> *with my brand of a ram's horn when she was eleven*
> *years old.*

Florus looked at Chryseis in disbelief. "Is this that child?"

"Yes, excellency," Luke said. "I examined her a few days ago when she fell and injured herself. She does bear the brand described in that document."

"This just gets more and more curious," Florus said. "Let's see what's next."

> *I acknowledge her as my daughter by a slave*
> *woman, Helga, and hereby adopt her as my lawful*
> *child. To her I leave all my possessions, whether*
> *money, land, slaves, or livestock, and all my houses*
> *and the furnishings therein.*

"By the gods, no!" Marcellus wailed.

Florus looked at him as though he were going mad. Then he continued reading:

> *Furthermore, I manumit my slave Deborah, also*
> *known as Melissa, whom I love as no other, and*
> *appoint her as guardian and advisor to Chryseis,*
> *if Chryseis shall not have attained the age of twenty*
> *before my death.*
> *I, Lucius Manilius Cornutus, write this with my own*
> *hand and seal it with my own seal.*
> *Given on the Ides of September, in the year when*
> *Vesuvius erupted.*

"That's preposterous!" Marcellus blurted, breaking the silence that followed the reading. "It must be a forgery." He grabbed the will from Florus' hands and read over it himself.

"Why so?" Florus asked.

"Well . . . I mean . . . it just can't be genuine. By the gods, she's a slave!"

Florus shook his head. "No, as of this moment – indeed, since the moment of Cornutus' death – she has been and is his daughter and the heir to all that was his."

Marcus Carolus began to weep openly. Chryseis stood unmoving, uncomprehending. "What do you mean, my lord?"

"Just what I said. Didn't you know, child . . . excuse me, my lady? Didn't you have any idea that you were his daughter?"

Chryseis' breath came in short gasps. "No, my lord. I was never told anything. All I knew was that I was a slave. And he branded me!"

"He did that to protect you," I said. "It was the only way he could guarantee to identify you in the event something happened to him."

Marcellus stormed out of the dining room, stopping at the door to glare back at us. "Don't start spending that money yet. You'll have a difficult time making that flimsy little document stand up when you get back to Rome."

XVII

Chryseis looked at me, then at Florus.
"May I go tell Melissa?" She sounded like a child who wants to show off a birthday present.

"You don't need to ask anyone's permission," I said.

"You're free to come and go as you please," Florus added.

"Do you mean it?"

"It will take some time to get accustomed to your new status," I said. "I was seventeen when my uncle died, and I was adopted in his will. I inherited great wealth, as you've done today. At first it's a heady sensation to know you're absolutely free of any control. Then you realize that *you* have to make all the decisions that were previously made for you. The responsibility becomes very heavy."

"But, my lord . . . I mean, Gaius Pliny, I have no one to help me. I know nothing about all this."

"You'll have more help than you suspect. Phrixus here will help you manage things, as he helped your father. Melissa will be by your side. I will help you in any way that I can. And there is one more person who, I'm sure, will continue to be devoted to you." I put a hand on her shoulder to turn her slightly so she faced Marcus Carolus, who had sunk into a chair and seemed to be having difficulty breathing.

"This is your uncle, your mother's brother."

"Marcus Carolus, my uncle? That's wonderful!" She threw

her arms around his thick neck and he hugged her tightly. When they broke their embrace, Chryseis said, "Will you come with me to tell Melissa?"

"Of course," Carolus said. "I think it would be wise if you did not go out alone just yet. There may still be some danger facing you."

"Sir," Florus said, "if you are her closest relative, perhaps you should keep this will. I suspect it will be quite safe with you."

I was prepared to accompany Chryseis and what was now her entourage, but Luke tugged at my tunic to hold me back as they left the room. He stepped toward Florus' table, pulling me with him.

"Excellency, there is a question I would like to raise with you in private."

"Go ahead," Florus said.

"May I ask that the slaves be sent out of the room?"

"Is that really necessary?"

Luke leaned over and whispered, "This concerns what may be perceived as a serious error in judgment on your part, sir. I thought you, Pliny, and I could discuss it in the utmost privacy, to spare you any embarrassment. We all know how slaves carry tales."

I was just as surprised as Florus was. He motioned for the slaves to leave the room.

"What's on your mind, doctor?" The very question I wanted to ask.

"I'm seeking clarification on a point of law. Is it true that a freed slave receives Roman citizenship along with her emancipation?"

"If the owner was a Roman citizen, yes," I said.

"Does that emancipation and receipt of citizenship take place upon the death of the owner or when the will is read?"

Suddenly I suspected where he was leading us. The old doctor would have made a cagey lawyer. "I think," I said, "one could argue that it is effective upon the owner's death. Isn't that what you suggested, excellency?"

Florus nodded in agreement, like one of Socrates' students in a Platonic dialogue walking into a trap.

"Then Melissa received citizenship while she was locked up during the night when Cornutus died?" Luke asked.

"I would be comfortable arguing that in court," I said.

Florus nodded. "Yes, I suppose so."

"Then, excellency, that means that, technically, she was a Roman citizen when you ordered her whipped. And isn't it against the law to inflict corporal punishment on a Roman citizen without a trial?"

Florus reacted like a man who's walking through the woods when someone in front of him bends a branch back and lets it go unexpectedly. It caught him right across the face.

"What are you saying?" he asked weakly.

"You flogged a Roman citizen without a trial, excellency," I said. "That's not supposed to happen under any circumstances."

Florus began to sweat. "But I didn't know she was a citizen. How could I have known it?"

"My friend Paul, who was a citizen, was beaten in Philippi," Luke said. "The magistrates there didn't know either, simply because they didn't take the trouble to inquire."

"It's a magistrate's duty, isn't it," I said, "to find out such things before he orders punishment? It never hurts to err on the side of caution. You can always order punishment later. You can never undo it. Rome does not look kindly on people who punish her citizens without trial. I'm sure, excellency, you remember what happened to Cicero when he executed Catiline and his fellow-conspirators."

"By the gods! They tore his house down and sent him into exile."

I knew I probably couldn't make this claim stand up in a court in Rome. A clever advocate would have little trouble bolstering Florus' defense that he had no knowledge of Cornutus' will and no reason to suspect that this particular slave woman would be emancipated by it. On the other hand, I could argue that favored slaves in a household are commonly freed in their owner's will. A judicious magistrate might have thought to check on that before laying on the whip.

Florus was getting desperate. "Gaius Pliny, you know my mistake was an honest one. As a magistrate I'm required by law to torture the slaves of a murdered Roman citizen. How could I have known what he said in his will?"

"Oh, excellency, I understand your position entirely. I would vote to acquit you."

His eyes grew large. "Do you really think I'll be brought to trial?"

"That's entirely up to Melissa."

"Could you speak to her on my behalf?"

As long as Melissa could feel the welts on her back — and that would be for the rest of her life — I didn't think she would listen eagerly to anything I had to say. But Florus thought I was her friend. Why not take advantage of that misconception?

"I could urge her not to press a charge against you."

"The magistrates in Philippi," Luke said, "came to Paul's cell and apologized to him in person."

"I'll do that," Florus said. "Yes, I'll do that. Right now. And you will speak to her on my behalf?"

"Yes, I will," I said.

He grabbed my hand and shook it. "Thank you, Gaius Pliny. Thank you. I will be forever in your debt. If I can ever help you in any way, don't hesitate to ask. I'll do anything for you."

I almost wished he hadn't made it so easy. "There is one thing, excellency . . ."

* * * *

I had very little time to spend with Chryseis the rest of the day. There were so many other matters to be dealt with before my fellow-travelers resumed their journeys. Some were easy to clear up. Tacitus reported that Orophernes had brought even more news about Lysimachus' odd comings and goings. Tacitus had gone straight to Lysimachus and learned that the randy old philosopher had been contending for the affections of a local young man. One of his rivals had taken exception to the foreigner's intrusion. The affair had come to blows, most of which landed on Lysimachus' face.

A bigger puzzle was the whereabouts of Tiberius Saturninus. I felt some sympathy for the man. Gambling comes as naturally to most Romans as going to the games. But some people do develop an overwhelming urge to engage in either activity. I've known a few people in my circle to get almost morose on days when there are no games scheduled. The chariot races barely satisfy them; there's not enough bloodshed. But on the days when there are games to attend, these same people become lively and animated, almost frenzied. They're waiting at the amphitheater when the gates open. Saturninus seemed to have that kind of uncontrollable desire to gamble. What caused me greater concern was the way his compulsion had thrown him into Regulus' clutches. His gambling wouldn't hurt anyone but himself. As Regulus' servant, there was no telling how much damage he might do.

Luke and Timothy were more worried about Saturninus than even his brother-in-law, Gaius Sempronius was. He had no intention of delaying his departure if Saturninus did not turn up.

"Good riddance to him, I say," was Sempronius' final comment.

Tacitus and I accompanied the two Christians as they searched for what Luke called their "lost sheep" in several disreputable tabernas along the harbor. Saturninus had been in most of them during our stay – he sold his knife to the owner of one – but no one could recall seeing him since the previous evening.

"Never seen a fella with such bad luck," one man told us. "And such little sense. If he won a bit, actually got ahead, he wouldn't take his winnings and quit. Not like the fella that was with him."

"There was someone with him?"

"Yeah. Marcellus, I think his name was. Now, he was a much smarter man with his money. But your fella, he had no sense at all. He'd keep at it 'til he'd lost whatever he'd won. And yet, he'd go out and come back in a while with a little more money to lose."

"*Now* I'm worried about him" I said as the four of us left the taberna. "If Marcellus was with him, I have a feeling this isn't going to end well."

We ate a surprisingly good lunch at the next taberna. The food reminded me of what I had tasted in some of the peasants' huts on my estates – clean and earthy, not overcooked and slathered with sauces. The owner remembered seeing Saturninus, but he had been alone.

"I wonder," Tacitus said, "if he started the evening alone, then was joined by Marcellus. Or did Marcellus start out with him, then leave him at some point?"

"If he didn't leave Androcles' inn with him," I said, "how could he ever have found him in this neighborhood? Isn't your latter alternative more likely?"

"The only way we'll find out," Timothy said, "is to ask Marcellus."

"You must be joking," I said. "After this morning, do you think Marcellus would help us in any way? He'd as soon – "

I was interrupted by a slave bursting into the taberna. He came right to our table. "My lords! My lords! You was the ones lookin' for that Saturninus?"

"Yes," I said apprehensively.

"We've found him. Come on!"

At a run we followed the slave to a taberna two blocks away. He led us into the small stable attached to it.

"There's no animals here right now," he said, "so nobody come in here until just a bit ago. That's what we found."

'That' was Saturninus' body, hanging from one of the beams in the ceiling. His tongue was sticking out of his mouth and his eyes bulged out. In his death agonies his bowels and bladder had let go. Luke and Timothy ran to him and started to take him down.

"Wait!" I said. "Let me look him over first, please. It's too late to help him."

They stood back. I walked around Saturninus' stinking, suspended corpse, swinging eerily from Luke's and Timothy's touch. One more reason why the name 'Smyrna' would always be synonymous with the stench of death for me. Saturninus appeared to have tied the rope to a vertical post and looped it over a beam. With the noose around his neck, he must have stepped off of an old wagon. His feet hung level with my knees. His hands were tied behind his back with a strip of cloth torn from his tunic. Tightly gripped in one hand was a sheet of papyrus. I pulled it out and signaled for Timothy and Tacitus to get him down.

Luke and I examined the papyrus. It was a short letter to Saturninus' wife. He explained that he had gotten so desperate for money he had prostituted himself to a man that evening, then lost the money. He finally realized how low he'd sunk. *I would have opened my veins,* he wrote, *and died in a more dignified manner, but I sold my knife earlier today.*

"May the Lord have mercy on his soul," Luke said. "It's ironic. He told me he was first attracted to our faith by hearing the story of Jesus' crucifixion and how Roman soldiers gambled for his robe at the foot of the cross."

* * * *

Tacitus was somber as I joined him on the stairs for the walk to the baths.

"I can't wait to get back on the road tomorrow," he said. "I've seen all I care to see of Smyrna. The only consolation is that we'll have a lot to talk about for the rest of the trip."

"I'm not going with you," I said.

"And why not?"

"I've just had a long talk with Melissa and Chryseis. Marcus Carolus and I are going to stay here for a while, until Melissa is well enough to travel. It'll give us time to help them get adjusted to their new position. I've written letters to some people in Rome who need to know what's happened. I'd like you to take them back with you."

"Of course."

"I'm convinced Cornutus' will is unbreakable, but that won't stop his father from contesting it, if he's still alive. And any others, such as Regulus, who may have hoped to profit from Cornutus' death or his father's, will raise trouble for Chryseis as well. We've got to alert our friends."

"Marcellus is sailing tomorrow morning. He'll likely get to Rome before I do. And he may get away with murder."

"So now you're willing to consider what I've suspected all along?"

"At this point, if you said you thought he killed Saturninus, I wouldn't argue with you."

"I think he did kill Saturninus."

"But how − ?"

I raised my hand to silence him. "You said you wouldn't argue."

"All right, I won't. But how are you going to prove anything against him before he leaves tomorrow?"

"He isn't gone yet."

"Pliny, be reasonable! Florus considers the case closed. And everyone will be leaving tomorrow. What can you hope to do in the few hours you have left?"

"I told you. I do my best work under pressure."

* * * *

Florus and I made sure we arrived early for the intimate dinner party he had arranged that evening at my request. He had taken over Androcles' small dining room and had it set up it in good Roman fashion, with three couches around a table. I could hardly remember the last time I had been able to recline at a meal like a civilized human being. It didn't bother me at all that I was on the low couch, the one assigned to less distinguished guests. Florus had the high couch, reserved for the host, and Marcellus would be offered the guest of honor's position on the middle couch.

When Marcellus arrived, accompanied by more slaves than he needed, he didn't seem to think it unfitting that we had left the place of honor for him. He settled himself and his slaves removed his sandals and brought out his plate and cup. That was the signal for me to motion to Damon to bring my new cup.

"That's a lovely piece," Marcellus said, saluting me with his own cup.

"I bought it as a token to remember the extraordinary events of the past few days."

"Where did you find it?"

"At a silversmith's shop, on the north side of the agora."

"I'll have to see about getting one myself," Florus said. "I feel left out with my poor clay cup."

We drank in silence for a moment. Then Florus said, "Quite a remarkable turn of events, eh? The slave girl turns out to be the master's daughter. Tongues will wag in Rome for weeks about this!"

"Chryseis − excuse me, the lady Manilia − is going to have a difficult time fitting in," I said, "where she has been regarded as, and considered herself to be, a slave all her life."

"Her new-found grandfather is going to be outraged," Marcellus said, "if he lives to hear of it. He's been quite ill for several months. A tumor of some kind in his stomach. Very painful. Some of his friends have been urging him to take his own life, but he's determined to hang on until his son arrives."

"I'm sure," I said, "that Chryseis will win him over."

"The old man is strongly opposed to citizenship for children born to slaves." Marcellus poured more wine for all of us.

"He doesn't have any choice in the matter," Florus said. "Cornutus' will is quite explicit."

Marcellus laughed in his slimy way. "There's not a will that can't be broken. That's what the courts are for."

"But Cornutus' father is too old and sick for a lengthy court case," I said.

"He has friends who will assist him, I'm sure."

"Regulus among them?"

"Foremost among them," Marcellus said with a lift of his eyebrows.

Florus lay back on his couch and closed his eyes.

"He doesn't hold his wine very well," Marcellus said.

I nodded and took a sip from my cup. "Cornutus was a man who could hold his wine . . . Why did you kill him, Marcellus?"

Marcellus laughed. If I had never met the man before, I would have thought it a merry, light-hearted sound.

"The wine must be getting to you," he said. "Why do you think I killed Cornutus? Do you think I went into his room and cut his heart out? Florus has already pronounced his verdict. It was the slave Phoebe who did it."

"No, I know who cut his heart out. That wasn't what killed him."

Marcellus shifted on his couch and raised his head, as though he found what I had said extremely interesting. "Then how did he die?"

"He was poisoned."

"What an amazing claim! How was it done? By whom?"

"I think you did it. How, I haven't quite figured out yet."

"Well, while you're thinking about it, why don't we have some real wine?" He sent one of his servants out to get his special wineskin. When the servant returned Marcellus broke the seal on the plug himself. He paused before pouring the wine.

"If you want to really talk about Cornutus, and not just banter back and forth," he said, "why don't we send the slaves out?"

Florus' slaves were reluctant to leave at first, but I assured them that it would be for only a short time. As soon as we were alone Marcellus poured us both a generous cup of wine. It smelled rich.

"The best part," he said, "is that we don't have to share it with this somnolent non-entity."

I swirled the wine around in my cup but didn't drink any.

"Friend Pliny, what are you afraid of? Have you read too many stories about Nero poisoning people right in front of witnesses? I could take that as an insult, you know." He sipped his wine, looking at me, almost flirtatiously, over the rim of the cup. "I'm drinking from the same wineskin. How could it be poisoned?"

I raised my cup to my lips and tipped it slowly. "It's quite good. Falernian, isn't it?"

Marcellus smiled. "A vintage from the last year of Claudius, in fact." He poured me some more. "Now, tell me what makes you think *I* killed Cornutus. I had only just met him a few days before, as we were leaving Ephesus. He was a likeable enough man, if a bit brusque." He propped himself up on an elbow, as though he were about to hear a thoroughly entertaining story or a piece of juicy gossip.

I raised my cup again and saluted Marcellus with it. "I think you were acting as an agent for Marcus Aquilius Regulus."

A soft snore erupted from Florus.

"Yes. I've heard about your enmity for Regulus. It's entirely uncalled for, you know. He bears you no ill will and would be happy to number you among his friends."

I shook my head. "Regulus has done enormous harm to people I care about. We could never be friends."

"You are young, Gaius Pliny. You haven't yet learned that it's dangerous to take strong stands in Rome, especially when you place yourself in opposition to a powerful man like Regulus."

I rubbed my hands together.

"Your hands feeling cold?"

"There seems to be a chill in the room." I shivered.

"That's just the onset of the effects of the hemlock."

I gasped. "What . . . ?"

"It's acting quickly tonight, but then you're a smaller man than Cornutus was, so that's to be expected. I mixed enough in this wineskin to bring down that big ox. It will finish you off in very short order."

I struggled to get up. "My legs feel numb! Excellency! Mestrius Florus!"

The governor snored and stirred slightly on his couch. Marcellus blocked me from getting to the governor and forced me back down on my couch.

"It's pointless to struggle," he said in an unctuous voice, his face close to mine. "It makes it easier if you just lie back and wait. It's a painless death. You'll just fall asleep, as Florus has done. Only you won't wake up."

"Why? Why did you do it?"

He sat back down on the edge of his own couch, ready to tackle me if I tried to get up again. "Which 'it' are you asking about? No matter. I poisoned you because you know that I killed Cornutus. I killed Cornutus because my friend Regulus needed him eliminated so he can inherit a large fortune from Cornutus' father."

"Regulus, that . . . damn legacy-hunter." My speech was labored.

"You have to admire the man. He is the best in a highly competitive game. He has been cultivating Cornutus' father for a long time. Cornutus was the only surviving member of his father's family, literally the last of the line. Or so we thought. Regulus has finagled himself into the father's will and stood to inherit everything if Cornutus died before his father did. When it became clear the old man was quite ill, he sent me to Ephesus with orders to intercept Cornutus when he passed through there on his way to Rome, as he inevitably must."

"How could you be sure he wouldn't . . . return by ship?"

"Regulus knew that Cornutus despised sea travel as much as you do, Pliny. I hired spies in various inns around Ephesus to let me know who was arriving. I had to get rid of Cornutus as quickly as possible, so all of his property would revert to his father and the old man would die without any heirs."

"Chryseis must have come as quite a shock to you, then."

He gave a rueful laugh. "Indeed she did. And the timing was so ironic. I had already poisoned Cornutus. This rich wine must have loosened his tongue a bit. He said he hoped his father did die, so he could finally acknowledge his daughter. He pointed her out to me. I was thunderstruck. If I had known he had a child, I wouldn't have poisoned him until I'd had time to work out a better plan. Once I found out about the daughter, it became imperative that she be killed immediately, before anyone else learned who she was."

I lay back on my couch, as though having difficulty holding up my head. "But you've failed at that. She's been . . . publicly acknowledged . . . as his daughter."

"Yes, the situation has become complicated, with Marcus Carolus and Melissa both to protect her now. I don't know if I'll be able to get rid of them all before we get back to Rome, but I'm going to keep trying. I'm actually not sailing to Rome tomorrow. I'll get off the ship somewhere up the coast and have time to plan something more effective. That's what Regulus pays me for. And with you out of the way my job will be easier."

"Did killing Tiberius Saturninus make your job easier?"

"By the gods, Gaius Pliny! Your youth is deceiving. What made you suspect that?" He picked up a piece of food, as casually as if we were discussing our favorite chariot team.

"The way his hands were tied." I licked my lips as if having trouble speaking. "A man who tied his own hands behind his back could never have done it . . . so well. He could not have held a piece of papyrus while tying them. And he couldn't have gripped the papyrus so securely if he had picked it up after tying his hands."

Marcellus laughed and shook his head. "Well, it was a rush job. Regulus was finding Saturninus too much of a liability. A man who gambles that compulsively can never be fully trusted."

"'No man can serve two masters,' I've heard."

"Who said that?"

"Never mind. But how are you going to explain my death when the governor wakes up?" I was slurring my words now, getting drowsy. "Or are you going to kill him too?"

"No, there's no need for that. I don't like to have to improvise, but I'll appear to be taken ill, as though there's something wrong with the food. That's believable enough in this place. I'll recover, albeit with a good bit of retching. You won't be so fortunate. Nor will Androcles, since I'll shift the blame onto that fool of an innkeeper."

I sat up and smiled at Marcellus. "I think I've heard enough."

Marcellus coughed out whatever he was eating. "But . . . but . . . you drank it! You were . . . poisoned."

"Doctor Luke told me what the symptoms were and about how long it would take."

"But you drank! How . . . ?"

I showed him my cup. "I imagine it works very much like yours. When I have the Socrates side toward me, the wine flows through a slit under the lip and into the cavity created by the embossed figures. When I press a spot on the Crito side, the wine is released through a slot in the base of the cup, just as Crito tried to secure Socrates' release from prison. I rather like the symbolism, don't you?"

"Very clever! Very clever indeed." He clapped his hands as though applauding an adept play in *trigon*. "The only problem is that you have no real proof. And I will deny that this conversation ever took place."

"Governor, that's your cue."

Florus raised his head and propped himself up on his elbow. "I think, Marcellus, that my testimony in support of Pliny's will count for something."

Terror swept over Marcellus' face. For the first time he saw that he'd been caught, like an animal with its foot in a trap. No matter how clever he'd been in the past, this time there was no escape.

"You were only pretending to be asleep," he said stupidly.

"Yes," Florus replied. "I heard everything."

"You had me worried for a moment, Excellency," I said. "The snoring sounded very convincing."

"I've had a lot of practice. If my wife thinks I've fallen asleep during dinner, she'll go away and leave me in peace and quiet."

"We need to get this villain locked up, until he can be sent back to Rome for trial."

"Indeed. I'll get some soldiers in here." Florus bestirred himself and left the room.

"You must be very proud of yourself," Marcellus said. He lay back on his couch, apparently ready to accept the inevitable. Then he grabbed his wineskin and gulped down a long draught of the poisoned wine.

I ran to the door and poked my head out. "Damon! Get in here!" When he appeared, I said, "We've got to make Marcellus vomit. He's swallowed some poisoned wine. It'll take both of us, I'm sure."

"Stay away from me," Marcellus growled. I turned to find that he had grabbed a knife off the table. "I'm not going back to Rome. Regulus will never let me come to trial. I'd rather end it this way than at the hands of his thugs. He doesn't tolerate failure. Just look at Saturninus."

"We can keep you safe, Marcellus. Help me bring Regulus to justice."

Marcellus shook his head slowly. "There's nowhere you could hide me that Regulus couldn't get to. He has spies and agents everywhere. You can't be absolutely certain that none of your own slaves are on his payroll. How much do you know about the man who shaves you every morning?"

I looked at Damon. If I didn't know that some of my slaves were Christians, how could I be sure some of them weren't passing information along to Regulus?

We could hear the clatter of soldiers drawing near. Marcellus put the knife under the bone that runs down the middle of the chest and thrust it upward.

XVIII

It rained the next morning. The caravan members that Tacitus had wanted to travel with decided to delay their departure. Florus, however, was determined to get back to Cyme and resume his other duties. Tacitus decided to travel that far with the governor and his soldiers, then see what arrangements he could make from there. Chryseis, Marcus Carolus, and I stood by his wagons in Androcles' stable as his slaves finished loading his goods. Luke and Timothy had wished him well and gone to make arrangements for Tiberius Saturninus' funeral.

"At least you'll be as safe as you can possibly be on the road," I said to Tacitus, "with Florus' soldiers to escort you."

"That'll be some compensation for setting out in this rain."

"It is very important that you get on the road. That slave Marcellus sent with a message to Regulus has a long start on you. I'm sure Marcellus' letter told Regulus about Chryseis. If he has time to prepare, it will be that much more difficult to make her claim stand up in court."

"Won't Florus' statement help our cause?" Carolus asked. The governor had dictated a statement authenticating Cornutus' will and describing the circumstances under which it had been opened and read. Tacitus and I each had a copy with Florus' seal on it.

"I'm sure it will," I said. "But Florus is not nearly as influential a man as Regulus is. And knowing how Cornutus' father feels about children fathered on slaves, I can't predict the outcome."

"I do hope my grandfather is still alive when we get to Rome," Chryseis said. "I've known him all my life, but now it will be very different to sit down and talk with him."

"If he is still alive," I said, "I'm not sure when would be the best time for you to meet with him. He'll have to be informed of his son's death. I'll take the urn containing Cornutus' ashes to him."

"I think I should go with you when you do that," Chryseis said. "He was my father."

Yesterday, when we both thought she was a slave, I could simply have told her no. Today all I could say was, "We'll have time to decide about that."

A soldier appeared in the stable doorway. Rain ran down his helmet, with drops falling from his nose guard. "My lord Tacitus," he said, "his excellency is ready to leave."

"I'll be right there." Tacitus embraced me and shook hands with Carolus. He hesitated in front of Chryseis until she hugged him.

"Thank you, Cornelius Tacitus," she said. "I know you've taken great risks on my behalf. I'll look forward to seeing you again in Rome and counting you among my friends."

"I would be greatly honored, my lady." He climbed aboard one of his wagons. His slaves piled into the other and they were on their way. I don't think I realized until that moment how much his friendship had come to mean to me.

"And now, friend Pliny," Carolus said, "why don't we have something to eat?"

"I don't feel very hungry."

"You seem sad," Chryseis said. She placed her hand on my arm. Even as disfigured as she looked, I couldn't help but feel some sort of divine radiance passing from her to me.

"I'm disappointed at how things have turned out," I said.

"I don't understand," Chryseis said. "Are you disappointed that I'm free and have discovered my identity?"

"Not at all! But, aside from that, what have I accomplished? Cornutus and Tiberius Saturninus were murdered. Phoebe was put to death, and Melissa was horribly beaten. Both for no reason. Even the Jew, Simon, who did not deserve to die, was killed before my eyes, with my own knife."

"But the people who did those things have been punished," Chryseis said. "You have every reason to feel proud of yourself. You've thwarted Regulus — "

"I wish I could be sure of that. I may have delayed his plans a bit, but his tentacles reach everywhere. That's one thing the last few days have taught me. I don't know if anyone can stop him."

"I believe you can," Chryseis said. She leaned forward and kissed me lightly on the lips.

Author's Note

Authors and literary critics often debate whether novels should have author's notes. "Say what you have to say in the story" is the usual argument. But this novel has presented a few special problems which deserve brief comment. It can be enjoyed by anyone chooses not to read the next couple of pages.

Using Historical Characters in Fiction

Novelists who use historical persons as characters in their fiction must be careful that those characters speak and act in ways consistent with what is known of their historical models.

Pliny is one of the people from ancient Rome whom we can know best. He left a collection of letters in ten books and a speech in honor of the emperor Trajan. The speech is a dreadful example of political boot-licking, but the letters reveal a humane, generous man who feels confined by an increasingly dictatorial regime. He busies himself with public service, though he finds it futile. It is what wealthy Romans of his day must do.

During his thirty-year career Pliny served in various offices and government departments, finally holding a suffect consulship in A.D. 100. He was also a landowner and a lawyer. He is curious about natural phenomena and a thorough-going skeptic when it comes to religion and the afterlife.

I began to study Pliny when I was in graduate school. His most famous letters are those (6.16 and 6.20) describing the eruption of Mt. Vesuvius in A.D. 79 and the one (10.96) explaining to Trajan how he has handled his investigation of the Christians in the province of Bithynia in 112/113. Another one which shows up in most anthologies is his lament over the death of a friend's daughter (5.16). The more I read of his letters, the more I was drawn to the man. I found a certain affinity with him, perhaps because of the longing for time to write which he (and I) could never seem to find.

I've published several scholarly articles on Pliny the Younger, and he appears in an earlier novel of mine, *Daughter of Lazarus*. I also make extensive use of his letters in my non-fiction book, *Explor-*

ing the New Testament World. A friend of mine who believes in rein-
carnation once suggested that I might have been Pliny. I do not in any
way endorse that notion, although it might make good publicity for this
novel if I were to do so.

I have tried to portray Pliny in a manner consistent with the
personality that emerges from reading his letters. He comes across in
his own words as a bit of a prig, but with an undeniable charm. He's a
sensible man who has little use for chariot races, gladiator games, and
loud dinner parties.

Pliny's friendship with the historian Tacitus seems to me genuine. That's why I've chosen to use Tacitus as his "sidekick" in this book
(and in what I plan as others in a series). One might even think of an
analogy: Pliny is to Tacitus as Holmes is to Watson. I have not tried to
make the characters conform to it rigidly, but it is a thread, or an under-
current, that runs through the book.

Using a historical character in a novel imposes certain limita-
tions on an author. You can't put your character in any place at any
time that you choose. You are strictly bound by what is known of your
character's movements. This book is set in April of A.D. 83. We know
that Pliny was returning from government service in Syria at that time.
Whether he sailed or went by land we don't know, but in his letters
Pliny makes clear his dislike of sea travel, so I think it reasonable to
posit an overland journey, which would have taken him through Smyrna.

The precise movements of some of the other historical characters who appear in the book aren't known, but I have not put anyone
somewhere that he could not have been at that time. There is some
debate, for example, about whether the elder Pliny was in Judaea at the
time Jerusalem was destroyed. One inscription seems to suggest that
he was. Nothing says for certain that he was not.

The name of the governor of the province of Asia where Smyrna
is located presents a historical problem. We know the names of two governors, either of whom could have been in office in April of 83. I have chosen
Lucius Mestrius Florus because he is described as a man with some scientific curiosity, a characteristic which might make him sympathetic to Pliny.
If anyone wants to argue that it is not absolutely certain that Florus was
governor of Asia at this precise moment in time, I can only say that it's not
certain that he wasn't. He will do as well as anyone.

To sort out such details I have relied on David Magie's masterful *Roman Rule in Asia Minor* and C. J. Cadoux's old but still useful
Ancient Smyrna.

Names and Anachronisms

Names pose one of the largest problems an author encounters when writing a novel set in ancient Rome. All those *-us* names begin to sound alike after a while. In this case my main character is a man whose name has been anglicized. We are familiar with him as Pliny, not Plinius. But we call his friend Tacitus. I have decided to use those forms, to anglicize names which we customarily anglicize, and leave less familiar names in their original Latin or Greek form. Even when people in the novel address Pliny in a somewhat formal way as "Gaius Pliny," I have decided just to live with the anachronism. To have him suddenly become "Gaius Plinius" would be jarring.

It is also difficult to find a term for the Greco-Roman practice of a midday rest. I was inclined to use "siesta," but my writers' group found it too anachronistic, so I settled on "midday rest." There are a few other terms, such as "towel" and "handkerchief" which create a similar problem. The Romans used such things, even if their words for them are difficult to translate into a single modern word. There is a glossary of some of the most frequently used, and possibly unfamiliar, terms at the end of the book.

Christians and Romans

I find it difficult to write about the first century A.D. without bringing in some references to Christianity. The new faith was growing fast, and the Romans encountered it on a number of levels. Both the book of Acts and Pliny's letter to Trajan document this. They show that people of both genders and all ages and social classes could be Christians.

Whether the Romans understood what Christianity really taught is another question. On the other hand, the tenets of this new faith were not fully formed by the 80s. Christians in different parts of the Roman world, for example, celebrated Easter at different times and used different books as scripture. The Christians who appear in a novel set in this period should not be spouting the articles of the Westminster Confession. Not even of the Nicene Creed. They were not Catholic or Protestant or Orthodox.

Conclusion

With those technical bits out of the way, I hope you enjoy the book.

Albert Bell, Jr
2002

Glossary of Terms

Baiae—a popular resort on the north side of the Bay of Naples, noted for its warm springs.

Board of Ten Judges (*decemviri stlitibus iudicandis*)—a minor court which dealt primarily with cases where an individual's status as slave or free was in question.

Boularch—the term literally means "ruling council." Like many Greek cities, Smyrna had a committee whose members took turns acting as something like the mayor in a modern town. In Smyrna in the late first century A.D. there were twenty-four boularchs, two for each month.

Caestus—a metal "glove" which fit over a boxer's hand and lower arm. It guaranteed that Roman boxing matches were much bloodier than those of the Greeks.

Calendar—the Roman calendar is similar to ours in the names of the months. The Romans, however, had no concept of the week. They contrived a very cumbersome system of dividing each month by marking certain days: the *Kalends*, the *Nones*, and the *Ides*. The Kalends was the first day of any month. The Nones fell on the seventh of March, May, July, and October, but on the fifth day of the other months. The Ides fell on the fifteenth of March, May, July, and October; in the other months, it fell on the thirteenth. Romans gave dates in terms of how many days before the next of these major divisions, e. g., the sixth day before the Ides of February. Any date after the Ides of a month was recorded as so many days before the Kalends of the next month.

Chiasmus—a rhetorical effect achieved by reversing elements in two consecutive phrases. William Jennings Bryan once said, 'It is better to know the Rock of Ages than the age of rocks.' One could hardly find a better example of chiasmus.

Citizenship—Roman citizenship was much cherished. In the late Republic Roman citizens in Italy were reluctant to see their privileges diluted by having citizenship extended too widely. Under the emperors, however, citizenship became a carrot which encouraged good behavior out of provincials. By Pliny's day citizenship was also extended to women. This did not mean that they could vote or hold office, but it did entitle them to have their legal issues heard in a Roman court. In letters 10.5 and 10.6, he specifically asks the emperor Trajan to extend this privilege to particular women.

Client—in the early days of Rome only the upper class (patricians) had access to the legal system. The only way that lower-class persons (plebeians) could get into court was with the help of a patrician. In exchange for that help, of course, the plebeian had to do whatever service the patrician required. This usually consisted of voting for the patrician or his relatives, accompanying him as he walked around town (a show of social status), and applauding for him when he made speeches. The plebeian also received a daily handout. He was called a 'client' from a Latin word meaning to rely on someone.

Clientela—all of a patron's clients collectively make up his *clientela*. They would usually accompany him through the streets, like a modern celebrity with his "posse."

Colonia Agrippina—the modern city of Cologne (or Köln) on the Rhine River in Germany.

Consul—the chief executive officer of the Roman state before Augustus established the rule of the emperors in 27 B. C. Two consuls were chosen each year. They conducted foreign policy and commanded the army. After 27 B. C. the office was ceremonial but still considered a great honor. Families took great pride in having ancestors who had held the consulship, no matter how many generations back.

Family dependent, see client

Ides—see calendar

Kalends—see calendar

Legacy hunter—many aristocratic Romans were childless. The elder Pliny died without any biological children. Pliny the Younger lost a child when his wife had a miscarriage. They had no other children. The reasons for this situation are debated, but it meant that there was intense competition for a piece of the estates of these wealthy childless people. The satirist Juvenal wonders in one of his poems why a man would want to get married and give up all the attention and gifts lavished on him by people who hoped to be written into his will. In his letters Pliny derides Regulus for his blatant legacy hunting.

Litter—a seat or couch which could be carried by slaves or animals by means of poles attached to the sides. Upper-class Romans favored this mode of transportation. The litter could have curtains around it to provide privacy for a traveller.

Lord—this word is used in this novel where a Roman would say *dominus* and a Greek *kyrios*. Both words mean something like 'master' and are used to address one's superior in a way that emphasizes one's own lowliness. Slaves addressed their owners as *dominus*. By the late first century AD it was becoming commonplace to use the term for the emperor. This created problems for Christians, who used the term to address God.

Lupinaria—a brothel. The *lup-* part of the word is from the Latin word for wolf. Disreputable women were commonly called by that name, similar to the way we today call a woman a "bitch," which is a female dog.

Manumission—by the first century A.D. it was commonplace for wealthy Romans to free some or all of their slaves in their wills. In fact, the emperor Augustus had to place limits on how many slaves could be emancipated because the citizenship rolls were becoming enlarged with former slaves. In several of his letters Pliny deals with issues related to manumission of slaves in wills. (see also Citizenship)

Military tribune—men of the equestrian order filled ranks similar to our lower commissioned officers, such as a lieutenant.

Nomen—a Roman man's name typically consisted of three parts: *praenomen*, *nomen*, and *cognomen*. In a name like Gaius Julius Caesar, Julius is the *nomen*, the family name. Gaius is the *praenomen*, the first name. The *praenomen* is usually abbreviated: L(ucius), M(arcus), P(ublius), etc. Because names were commonly repeated in families, a *cognomen* or third name, in this case Caesar, served as a way of distinguishing one Gaius Julius from another. In a case like Pliny's, where a boy has been adopted into another family, part of his biological father's name would be incorporated into his name. The emperor Augustus, who was adopted by his great-uncle Julius Caesar, was technically Gaius Julius Caesar Octavianus. Pliny, whose father was a Caecilius, became Gaius Plinius Caecilius Secundus after his uncle, Gaius Plinius Secundus, adopted him in his will. An individual could be addressed by one name, such as Pliny, or by his *praenomen* and *cognomen*, such as Gaius Pliny. Traditionally, a Roman woman was given a feminine form of her father's *nomen*. Thus any and all daughters of G. Julius Caesar would be Julia. Pliny's mother was Plinia. A woman named Cornelia was the daughter of a man from the Cornelius family. By Pliny's day the nomenclature for Roman women was changing, and we find some women with two names or with a name based on their grandfather's name.

Nones—see calendar

Pater familias—the oldest male member of a branch of a family. As long as a Roman man lived, his children were technically under his control. All of their property belonged to him. In actuality fathers did not often interfere in the affairs of their adult children, but the legal threat always hovered. Problems sometimes arose when a man lived to extreme old age or became senile. When a man died, his sons each became the *pater familias* of their own families.

Praenomen—see *nomen*

Priapus—unburdened by Victorian or Christian moral sensibilities, the Romans celebrated the creative urge in the form of this god with oversized male genitalia. He was considered a guardian of one's property and a statue of him was often placed in the family's garden. The poet Martial complains that someone stole his Priapus, rather like someone stealing a watchdog today.

Quaestor—lowest of the offices in the *cursus honorum*, the series of offices which qualified a man to hold the consulship. Quaestors managed government finances. A man could be appointed quaestor on the staff of a provincial governor, as Cicero was in Sicily.

Strigl—a curved metal instrument used in bathing. Greeks and Romans rubbed olive oil over themselves and scraped it off with a strigl, in theory taking the dirt with the oil. The mixture of sweat and olive oil scraped off by famous athletes was sometimes made into a beauty cream by "gladiator groupies".

Taberna—a shop of any kind. In particular, a food shop.

Tablinum—a room off the atrium of a Roman house where the master kept his papers and did the actual work of managing his affairs.

Tribunician power—beginning with Augustus, the senate granted to the emperors the powers of a tribune, particularly the power to veto any action of another magistrate or assembly. To maintain the facade of the Republic, this power was granted on an annual basis. The emperors used the granting of this power to date the years of their reigns. Coins will show, for example, TR POT XI, meaning that particular emperor had been granted the power for the eleventh time.

Trigon—a game played by three people, standing at points of a triangle. Beyond that, we don't know much about it. It involved passing a ball or balls. Whether the object of the game was to enable another player to catch your pass, or to do something unexpected so that another player couldn't catch the ball, we don't know.